JIM

A WORN-TORN LOVE STORY

A NOVEL

BY
PAUL ARGENTINI

JIM – A WAR-TORN LOVE STORY

FIRST SUNBURY PRESS EDITION
Printed in the United States of America
September 2011

ISBN 978-1-934597-68-2

Published by:
Sunbury Press
Camp Hill, PA
www.sunburypress.com

Camp Hill, Pennsylvania   USA

To baritono Americo Argentini,
my magnificent dad

Love until you break your heart.
--Charly Dunham to Jim

Theme: *Meditation* from the opera "Thais"
by Jules Massenet

ACKNOWLEDGEMENTS

This novel is better than the one I conceived because of the discerning and perspicacious Allyson Gard. I'm grateful to the critiques and editorial assistance of my bride, Dimmi; mental health counselor younger daughter, Mona; Marilyn Hunter; first cousin Mary Viviani Martin; and Brooke Walker. The author accepts total responsibility for anything and everything erroneous in this novel.

INTRODUCTION

Jim Dorchester is the pseudonym for a medical and psychiatric phenomenon.

Wounded early in the Iraqi War 2003, Jim wavered between life and death for almost a year. His face severely disfigured by fire, he was in the forefront of partial face transplantation from donor tissue. A French and German team perfected a technique that not only was highly effective, but in Jim's case turned out to be a masterpiece.

He received skin grafts for more than half of his body. He fought a constant daily battle against infection. On eight different occasions he was considered hopeless to win out against what seemed a massive, totally debilitating illness and infection. Nurses worked double shifts in tandem to get him somewhat stabilized. When the graft held in one place, the fragile skin was lost in another. At one time, when all hope was lost and doctors felt an overdose of pain killer would be best for him, a passing comment saved his life.

"If the Stem Cell Gun were ready, it would save him," a foreign visiting doctor said.

The gun was used under the strictest of information quarantines because the technique was merely in its primitive stages. In essence, useable skin cells from a healthy part of the patient's body are put in a solution of water and prepared then imposed on the wounds. Astoundingly, new skin was formed on Jim's second degree burns in less than a week after the stem cell gun was used.

That is the limit of the information I am able to relate because of a strict confidentiality agreement.

By the time you are reading this novel, there is every reason to believe face transplants and stem cell gun burn therapy will be commonplace.

In addition, Jim required extensive surgery for broken bones in his pelvis, legs, arms, rib cage; internal hemorrhaging; trepanning to relieve pressure from head injuries; and removal of his spleen.

He lost his memory for six years. At first the cause was attributed to his injuries. There was no hope he would ever regain the knowledge of his first twenty years of life. Then, as fate would have it, he went to visit who he thought was the widow of a close friend who had been in his same unit. That soldier was killed in Iraq. Incredibly, because of a switch in identities the "widow" turns out to be his wife who he does not recognize because of his amnesia.

Despite the transformation in his appearance—the face transplant, the white hair, moustache and beard—and a different name, Jim's mannerisms do not escape his wife's attention. Despite his incredulity, she prevails on Jim to work with a psychiatrist.

After a little more than a year of intensive, groundbreaking therapy the result is this novel.

Because of the strict and stringent privacy laws extant, the author was compelled to walk a fine line between the facts and the fictionalization of the story and the people involved.

This is a love story. It is interrupted in Iraq. It is re-established many years later. Through a complicated psychiatric process, Jim was able to recreate in deep retroactive therapy salient experiences in his early years, which are included in the chapters of his early life as a matter of understanding Jim and the characters involved. All have confirmed to a greater or lesser degree the accuracy of his recollections. These representations are related in the first section of the novel called The Diary.

--The author

PROLOGUE
RECORDING OF THE FINAL PSYCHIATRIC SESSION WITH JIM DORCHESTER.

GA-THOONK! A mortar round exploded in the water just up a ways from the bridge.

"They're walking 'em down! Concentrate your fire on those low buildings!" the lieutenant said pointing behind him.

"No! Lieutenant! It's a ploy!" I shouted to him. "I thought I saw the main body on the other side of the bridge! There! There!" I said pointing. "I can see them on the other side moving up!"

"Concentrate your fire on those houses!" the officer ordered, ignoring my information.

I rolled on my side to the man next to me. "Can you handle the fifty?" indicating the machine gun. The man nodded. "The lieutenant doesn't know what the fuck he's doing!" I started to get up.

The officer put his hand on my shoulder, holding me down.

"My buddy's on the other side! I've got to get to him!"

The officer waved his pistol. "Stay put! I can court-martial you with one shot."

GA-THOONK! GA-THOONK! GA-THOONK!

The mortar rounds walked toward the other end of the bridge.

"Lieutenant! Pull the men! Pull the men!" I shouted. "We can give them cover!"

Small arms fire on the other side of the bridge sounded as if an arms factory blew up.

I could see the Al Qaedas surrounding the other end of the bridge.

In a hail of gunfire, I started across the bridge. "Keith! Keith! Hang on!" I unhinged a grenade with each hand. I pulled the pin on one, and then the other. I stood, exposed to a hail of fire. I tossed one grenade with one hand, and then

3

the other grenade with the other hand, just as I did when I delivered newspapers on each side of the street. I crashed to the ground.

GA-THOONK! A mortar landed in the water to my left.

I got up and ran, then skidded to the pavement. I looked across the bridge.

I saw a horde of Al Qaedas closing in on the end of the bridge. I tried to pick out Keith.

GA-THOONK! Another mortar landed on the other side, closer to us.

GA-THOONK!

I turned and ran back toward the HumVees.

I reached the first one, started the engine and headed across the bridge.

GA-BLAM! A rocket propelled grenade exploded in the thick of the men near the lieutenant.

I stomped on the gas just as I started across the bridge.

I didn't hear the rocket propelled grenade hit. I felt the seat rise up. My body slid sideways. I remember my face crashed into the window. I learned later my leg tore the steering wheel off its post. The last thing I felt was the melting heat. The last thing I remembered was thinking, "Gabbie! Help me!"

* * *

Mary the psychiatrist slid behind the wheel of the HumVee. Jim sprawled out in the back.

"Jim?" Mary spoke in her calmest, professional voice.

"Yes?"

"Are you comfortable? You are safe and under hypnosis."

"Yes."

"Jim, you felt you had to take care of Keith. Why? Was he slow? A diminished mental capacity?"

"Keith? No. He could hold his own. He had his own style."

"But you thought he needed some hand-holding?"

"He was a . . . wise guy? You know, apathetic, insouciant. Giving everyone the business. Like he did the Gorilla."

"What was that?"

"Jokester things. If a guy's sleeping and you put his hand in a bucket of warm water, it makes him piss his pants. When he did that to the Gorilla, the guy wanted to cream Keith, and I stood up for him. Keith and I were called the twins, so he thought of swapping our blouses and making the Gorilla think I was him and Keith was me."

"Did it work?"

"Well, yeah! The Gorilla wanted to pound on Franklin, but when I showed up as Franklin, the Gorilla decided he made a mistake. You know, things like that."

"And that's how you took care of Keith?"

"Yes. You know."

"How could he be sure?"

"Oh! Because I . . . "

"Because I what?"

"Because he knew he could count on me."

"And he could count on you?"

"Yes! He made me promise for Christ's sakes!"

Mary paused for long moments. She knew they had just stepped into a potential mine field.

"Jim, from what Gabbie told me about your life in Great Farraday, you didn't have much time to have a close guy friend. A lot of your time was spent earning money. You gave all your free time to your grade-school sweetheart, Gabbie."

"Yes."

"So, when Keith came along, you were both in a new situation, trying to make adjustments; you found the two of you were more or less alike. Compatible. Good buddies. You two against the Army."

"Yes."

"Then it was you two against the Al Qaeda."

"Yes."

"Jim, we can take a break until tomorrow."

"No. S'okay. I'm good."

"Okay. So, as good friends, what did you promise each other?"

"Nothing! Nothing! We'd just look out for each other. That's all!"

"Okay. So, as good friends, what did you promise each other?"

"Nothing! Nothing! We'd just look out for each other. That's all!"

"Jim, who is this mysterious 'Charlie?'Or is it 'Charly?'"

"There is no Charlie."

"You mentioned Charlie and taking care of Charlie as you did Keith and your brother. What happened with Charlie?"

"There is no Charlie."

"Was he in the service with you and Keith?"

"No! There is no Charlie."

"Did you promise to take care of Charlie as you did Keith?"

"Yes, I promised Keith."

"It was more than a promise, wasn't it? It was an oath."

"It was a promise!" Jim said.

"It was more than a promise! It was a vow! A vow is an unbreakable promise!"

"Yes! Yes!"

"What was the vow?"

"I don't remember."

"Keith would remember it, wouldn't he?"

"No! No! He wouldn't remember it! I would remember it!"

"What do you remember?"

"That I wouldn't let the Al Qaeda get him!"

"And he promised he wouldn't let the Al Qaeda get you."

"Yes."

"Jim! How could either one of you make such a promise? How could you be so sure? Hasn't the Al Qaeda captured other American soldiers?"

"Yes."

"So, there is a difference. What made the difference, Jim?"

Jim grabbed the back of his head with both hands, and tried to hold back a loud gasp. Tears began to flow. "Alive! We promised not to let the Al Qaeda get us alive!"

"And did you make the same promise to Charlie?"

"No! There is no Charlie!"

"And the only way to keep the Al Qaeda from getting Keith alive was to . . . ?"

". . . to kill him! To kill my best friend! To shoot him dead!"

Mary let the sound of his sobbing fill the inside of the HumVee.

"And did you shoot Keith dead?"

"No! No! I didn't! I broke my promise! I didn't take care of him as I promised!"

"Jim, how do you know that?"

"When I came back with the water and ammo, I looked across the bridge. I saw Keith hunkered down against a cement cornerstone. Keith looked up and across the bridge. Keith waved to me. I waved back. That's when I knew the officer was wrong; the major part of the Al Qaeda was on the other side of the bridge. I saw them! That's when I looked across the bridge in my scope. I saw Al Qaedas close in behind an American soldier, tear his gun away, and lift him off the ground. They started to drag him away backwards, and I saw his face. I put the scope on the soldier. It was Keith."

"Jim! Jim! Shoot! For Christ's sakes! Shoot!" he seemed to be saying.

I brought my crosshairs across Keith's face, then back onto his nose.

I knew what he was saying. He was mouthing the words: "Jim! Jesus Christ! Jim! Shoot!"

Mary held her breath. The unasked question captured her attention as if a shot resounded in the truck.

Keeping a level voice, Mary asked, "Did you shoot?"

"No! Goddammit! I didn't shoot!"

"Jim. Think. Very hard. Did you shoot?"

"No! I didn't shoot!" Jim started crying. "No! I couldn't shoot! I couldn't shoot my best friend! I couldn't shoot Keith! I promised I'd take care of him! I couldn't let him down like I let my kid brother Tommy and Charly Dunham down! Too much! It was too much! I should have died!"

"But you promised to shoot Keith if he was captured. He was captured, Jim. Did you see him get captured?"

"Yes."

"You saw him captured. Did you shoot? You promised! Did you shoot?"

"No! Keith was the best buddy I ever had in the world! He was the only friend I ever had in all my life! I couldn't shoot him!"

"But you had to shoot him!"

"I know! I know!"

"He expected you to do him that favor. You weren't killing him. You were doing him a favor!"

"I know!"

"He expected you to save him from having his head sawed off!"

"Yes! Yes!"

"So you had to shoot him! You made that vow to each other."

"Yes! I had to shoot him!"

"So you did!"

Jim hesitated. "No! No! No!"

Mary pulled away from Jim. She studied him. She held her forehead. She raddled her eyebrows and glowered. In her mind information, considerations and possible conclusions were categorized.

BOOK ONE

1

FORT BENNING, GEORGIA --SUMMER 2003

Jim Dorchester was about to nod off.

"Hard dying hurts," the video instructor said. "You didn't join the Army to get killed. It can happen. Dying may not last long, but son-of-a-bitch! You'll remember it for as long as you live."

Jim sat upright. *Funny fuck, isn't he?*

Standing before a screen, the instructor scanned the recruits to let the words sink in.

"This is an actual film shown as we received it. Be prepared, the gore is real. It is not for public consumption. It is not being shown to you for no reason. Nothing has been changed. There is no sound, for which you will be eternally grateful."

Jim found the training movies a break in the exhausting basic training routine that took them from reveille to lights out.

"The film will give you an object lesson about your enemy," the instructor went on. "In the Army, you'll be in harm's way, as they say. You are here to learn how to protect and defend yourself while carrying out your mission. The best way you have to survive is to rely on the Army's seven core values, which spell out LDRSHIP."

Keith Franklin, Jim's schoolboy chum, sat beside him. He whispered, "Hey! Kimo Sabe. When's the show?"

Jim shrugged.

The instructor droned on: "These letters stand for loyalty, duty, respect, selfless service, honor, integrity, personal courage. The soldier's code is self-respect. Integrity is a value you develop by adhering to moral principles. It is the truth others place in you. The more choices you make based on integrity, the more this highly-prized value will affect your relationship with family and friends, and, finally, the fundamental acceptance of yourself. You must rely on these seven core values. As a soldier you can rely on nothing else."

Jim shifted in his seat.

"At one time there was such a thing as the Geneva Convention," the speaker went on. "You may have heard that it required a captured soldier to reveal only name, rank, and serial number. As a prisoner of war, you could expect some small modicum of humane treatment. You cannot expect even that anymore. The reason is because your enemy today does not abide by the Geneva Convention. He is a terrorist. A terrorist is a bigot: has only one objective—to kill you, the infidel. An infidel is anyone who does not agree with him. A terrorist is prepared to blow him or herself up for God, country, 74 virgins, or to fill a boring moment. Someone who murders in the name of God is not human, and knows no mercy."

Keith glanced around. He gave Jim the elbow.

The instructor paused. "Why are we showing you this film? One: So you'll know your enemy. And, Two: To put fire in your guts when you face them and make you ripping mad! Be the best soldier you can be to stay alive because no matter how it comes, dying hurts."

2

The film started. Fuzzy and grainy at first, it cleared up.

A young man with a growth of beard sat on the floor with his hands behind his back. He had on an army shirt, open at the collar. The subtitle in white, block letters read: The prisoner.

On the screen appeared a bearded man wearing a turban, carrying an AK 47. He pointed the weapon at the seated man's forehead, then gestured as if the gun had been fired. The prisoner kept shaking his head. His eyes darted about. He hitched about. He was offered a cup from which he could drink. He turned his head away from it. Two potbellied men wearing turbans appeared. They grabbed his arm. A hand appeared holding a syringe. The seated man twisted and turned to shake off the injection. His jaw tightened.

The sub-title read: The infidel refuses to be sedated.

The prisoner clenched and unclenched his jaw. He strained to sit upright.

Keith rapped Jim. "What the hell?"

Jim shook his head. "Watch."

The AK-47 was stuck in the seated man's face again.

A heavy-set man with a turban and thick, black beard shouted at the captive. He remained resolute. Again, he exerted himself to sit up.

There were several more short scenes interspersed with black and blank screens.

The camera stayed on the seated man for a long while. A hand was seen grabbing him by the hair. He was pulled forward onto his knees. Then, the prisoner's head was pulled back, exposing his throat. Into view came a hand

12

holding a short, broad knife. It was put to the man's throat.

The subtitle read: The infidel is told his death is near.

"Oh! Shit! Man!" Keith said half-aloud to Jim. "They're going to cut his throat! Jesus!"

A hand holding a cup offered drink to the captive. He shook it off.

The view of the captive was blocked when the back of a man wearing a turban blocked the camera. The man moved aside to show the captive's Army blouse being cut off.

The man on the floor looked up. His eyes darted from one side to the other. He was taking short, shallow breaths.

The body of a man crossed in front of the camera. The man's hand grabbed the captive's hair, pulling his head to one side, twisting and bending his neck awkwardly. The man then put the wide, short blade to the captor's neck. He began to saw at the flesh.

The captive's mouth and eyes flew wide open, and though the film was silent, it was apparent the man was screaming at the top of his lungs. The man with the blade sawed at the neck back and forth, back and forth in short, hard chops. Blood geysered from the cut artery, then spurtled to an ebbing trickle.

The executioner's hand exerted more and more pressure. The blade cut deeper and deeper into the captive's neck.

Keith grabbed Jim's arm. Jim could feel him shaking and saying, "Jim, God! Jim! God!"

On the screen, the blade had difficulty when it reached bone.

Exerting all the effort he could, the executioner continued to saw until he cut through the cervical bones, and slashed through the other side of the dead man's neck. When the head swung free, the body toppled.

The executioner held up the severed head and shook the bloody blade.

Savage, crazy bastards!

The screen went to black.

Jim whistled softly.

Keith, head between his knees, was blowing out his guts.

3

Jim Dorchester understood the world's right, wrong, and shades of gray. Even more, he knew that moral choices were the essence of life. One made them with no guidance whatsoever. They came from the purple colored springs deep in the inner recesses of one's own soul. They were conjured by thoughts, dreams, wishes, and wants. Their secrets were what truly defined the person. He seemed to have a gyroscope about such things. His mother, wherever she may have gone, said he was special because he was born with a caul, which he kept under alcohol in a jar. He didn't know about being unique. There was one thing he was certain about. He was nothing compared to his inamorata Gabbie. She had to be a saint to be understanding about the sticky moral choice he made after so many years of separation. Unbelievably that choice was to keep them apart for god knew how much longer.

The Jim and Gabbie story began when he went slack-jawed at the anonymous vision their first day in seventh grade at the Catamount School in Great Farraday, Massachusetts. She was the one for him. Absolutely. She was seated two rows away, and two seats down from him. His mouth drooped, his head leaned forward, his eyes opened as big as half-dollars. When he caught himself almost drooling onto the desk, he swallowed. It went down the wrong way and he ended up in a coughing, hacking fit. He knew she turned to look at him as everyone else did. He just wanted to crawl inside the inkhole in his desk and die.

The crux came three weeks later when he had a slip of hope that he was going to actually talk to her. At recess Jim caught a glimpse of her in the girl's section of the schoolyard. An Indian summer day, jackets were thrown in piles on the benches. He was handed the Spaulding Pink ball.

Gee! How he didn't want to do this right now, he said to himself, his mind on her. "Okay, make a circle," Jim ordered. He closed his eyes and turned on his heels several times. He stopped, his index finger pointing straight out. He touched the kid in front of him. "You're number 1, 2, 3," he said numbering the players going clockwise, "4, 5, and I'm number 6."

"What about me?" asked the skinny kid with glasses who stood outside the circle.

"There are only six boxes, you can't play!" the freckle-faced kid said.

"No!" Jim said. "We'll play with a spare. When you get knocked out of your box when you miss the ball that bounces in your box, you take the spare's place. The spare moves up like everyone else, except he just watches for one play. You're number 6, Kid," he told the boy with glasses, "and I'll start as spare. Let's go! Serve it up!" He bounced the Spaulding Pink to the player in the Number 1 box.

Jim liked that. It made him feel good when the guys would crowd around him waiting for direction. In that case, rather than waste time, Jim sized up the situation, and voiced the best way he saw things to be done. In his mind, he was the take-charge Lone Ranger, except he didn't give away silver bullets. With the advent of digital technology he was able to lay on the floor listening enraptured to the 1940's hero's sonorous voice call out, "Heigh-ho, Silver! Away!"

He stopped to look in the direction of the slide. He could tell where she was in the playground by her squealing exuberance. Or, her high-pitched laugh that cut over the usual playground cacophony. He could not ignore her siren call, which caught him like the pain he got in his side when he ran too hard, too long.

"Ay! Jim-my!"

He turned. He was wasting precious playing seconds holding up the game while he just stood, looking off in the distance. He had worked his way up to server in the Number 1 box. Now he was on his third serve and killing the other players. That's when her voice came to him. He looked around. He caught her movement.

"Jesus! Serve! Jimmy! Serve!" box number four yelled at him.

Jim sent the Spalding Pink in a hard bouncing slice that aced the number four box and sent the kid who swore to be the spare. The players shifted up a place.

Jim bounced the ball to the number two box. "You do it!" The kid moved up.

Jim looked around for his adversary, the strict and stone-faced Mrs. Tawney. She was the supervisor of the proctors. Her usual perch was in the center of the schoolyard. She looked over her territory as an owl would. "Mrs. Swivelhead," the kids had named her. Not a thing went on in her domain she didn't know about. Jim had to slip past her.

Jim ambled towards the slide. He could feel the girl's vibrations, a magnetic pull. How close could he make it to her? He was liable to catch hell.

He had seen her every recess since classes started that fall. That was almost three weeks ago. She wore a tight knit cap that hid most of her almost-blondie hair, a long-sleeved shirt, skirt, and knee-high stockings. Usually she pulled her hair back severely into a tight ponytail. It made her nose look tiny, her lips always in a pout, and her dark brown eyes like a baby seal's. There was a compelling charm in the proportions of her face. He saw her showing her classmates, "This is ballet Position One! Position Two!" She would say, "Pretend you have a string attached to your head holding you straight up." He noticed the other girls stopped slouching and stood tall and straight to imitate her motions.

But there was more than that. He couldn't put his finger on it. There was an air about her; the way she carried herself, the way she interacted with others. She listened intently when someone spoke to her. It was a naïve reticence that made him see her as an Alabaster Doll, which he saw in the Boston Museum of Fine Arts on a school field trip. Jim passed her within touching distance dozens of times, but not once did he find the courage to overcome his shyness to address her. They never spoke, not once. So, endless moments passed for Jim in the classroom staring from his seat to hers, watching her listen, write, read, draw, stand to answer a question, get up to leave for the day. He heard Mrs. Tawny say her name a hundred times, but he could not remember it once so addled by her was he. She lived on the snooty side of town. It added to her persona, and detracted from his self-confidence.

He walked in her direction, rolling down the sleeves of his shirt. He watched her reach the top of the ladder. She shouted, "Slide! Slide!" She hoisted herself up on her arms ready to kick her feet under her and down the slide. He drifted her way. So far he wasn't spotted by the tower guards. He ran his fingers through his loose, shaggy hair. He thought he had okay looks for a guy. His friends, especially Keith, confessed they thought themselves handsome when they looked in the mirror. It made him raise his eyebrows. "Wow! Really?" Then he remembered the teacher talking about Narcissus, who looked at his reflection in the brook and fell in love with himself. That was Keith, all right. Jim would never waste his time doing that, not when there was someone like her around! Raising his arms, he could feel the strength in his upper body. It showed especially when he played handball. He could crush the Spalding—always pronounced Spall-ding--with either hand. "I've got it!" he'd shout as he slid towards the wall to save a shot that ricocheted just inches inside the line.

He could feel Swivelhead's eyes on him. If he didn't talk to her today, the sun wouldn't shine on the world forever.

Blinking back the sun, he focused on "her" at the slide. All he knew was that he was moving with one purpose: to get closer to her. Maybe, even, she would look his way and maybe even notice him.

Her skirt went flying. He could see her underpants. He grinned. Her hands went flying up with excitement. "E-e-e-e-e-e-yyyy!" It was a long, curving slide. As she started down, a big girl standing at the bottom moved behind her, and shoved her downwards. She lurched. The bully, eyes wide, covered her mouth with her hands. Gabbie went off the slide feet first and belly-side down. Jim watched her land hard on her knees and hands.

"Yeoww!" she screamed.

Machine pistols be damned! Jim streaked to her side.

He saw her knees were scraped and bleeding. Jim slipped her knee socks down to keep the oozing blood from getting on them.

"Ow!" she said.

He looked into her eyes. The size of them swallowed him even though they were filled with tears. "Coach says you bleed more when you scream. Keep that up, you're gonna need a transfusion."

She stared back into his eyes; hers narrow, wrinkled at the corners, and piercing. Her mouth drawn into a hard cut. "Yeah! Very funny! Go away!" She shook her hands at him.

They held the stare, which was anchored by a penetrating intensity.

Mrs. Tawny bent down, almost face to face with Jim. She pointed to the scrapes. "Oh! She should see the nurse!" She used a tissue to pat at the dripping blood. "I'll have someone walk you to the infirmary," she said.

Jim glared at her. "She can't walk. She's wounded!" He scrunched his eyes staring at her. He wondered why she couldn't see something so simple.

The teacher's eyes narrowed. "Don't you tell me what to do! Get back to the boy's side of the schoolyard! Helen! Helen!" she called to a nearby student.

"You're a teacher. Can't you see she can't walk with her knees like that?" Jim said.

Without thinking, he put one knee on the ground, and scooped blondie up in his arms. "I'll see that she gets to the nurse." He was surprised to find she barely weighed anything. One hand felt her rib cage under her shirt, and the other the smooth softness of her leg by her knee. It all seemed no more to him than if he picked up a football and was walking to the goal line.

"You put her down this instant!" Mrs. Tawney said.

Jim turned to her. "Someone's got to carry her to the nurse."

19

The teacher pushed out her bottom lip and squinted her eyes. "You report to the principal!"

"Duty first!" Jim turned and strode toward the school.

"What do you think you're doing?" blondie asked.

"Rescue squad. Lone Ranger, here, Ma'am."

The other students froze. They cleared a path for them. Jim, chin up, facing straight forward, strode toward the basement door through the honor guard. Even the box ball game stopped.

He became aware her arm was around his neck. Before a half-dozen steps he caught her in his peripheral vision staring at him in a surprised, wondering look.

She pulled him toward her. "Thank you. You know you're in trouble?"

"So?"

"You know what they'll do?"

"I don't care. I'll refuse the blindfold. So? What's your name?"

"Medford."

"I didn't ask where you lived. What's your name?"

"Medford Soldi." She reached around to grab the hand that was around his neck to hold him tighter.

He stopped for a second. "You're kidding, right?"

"You better put me down. Now! You're already in a lot of trouble."

He looked at her hands, "Relax. I'm not going to drop you." He continued his march.

"My name is Medford Soldi."

"Medford? Medford! What kind of a name is that? I can't call you 'Medford'!"

"Why not? That's my name. And that's the town where I was conceived." He looked at her, blinking rapidly. "I don't know what that means either," she said.

"What's your middle name?"

"Gabriella."

"Gabbie it is!"

"Not on your life. Ella, maybe; no Gabbie. I know who you are."

"The Lone Ranger." Jim pictured himself in the saddle as Silver rose on his hind legs.

"I'm glad you're not conceited, Jim Dorchester."

He furrowed his brow. "Your father's a lawyer in town. Right?"

"Yes. You just moved into town with your father."

"How'd you know that?"

"I heard. Where's your mother?"

He felt the veins in his neck pump hard. He wondered if he would feel so vulnerable if he weren't holding such precious baggage in his arms. Any thought of his mother did that to him.

He kicked open the basement door. "I'm taking a short cut to get to the nurse's office."

"I know."

"You're not worried?"

"No. But you should be. The principal's going to make you eat chalk."

It was what would be waiting at home for him that caught Jim's attention. It was a tough go, but he would not shed a tear because of a well-aimed flailing belt. This time, he might even put a smile on his face.

"I'm not worried. I don't want you to bleed to death in my arms or your father will kill me."

"If I fall asleep, then you can waken me with a kiss, Mister Lone Ranger."

"My! How romantic. Why do girls think they look gorgeous sleeping? You're reading too many books. Fall asleep if you want, and the nurse will waken you when she sticks you."

"Mmmmmm!" She nodded. "Me Tonto. You Kimo Sabe."

Oh! Mrs. Tawney! Do I owe you, Jim thought working hard to swallow the bolus of excitement in his throat. The old goat pushed him far enough to free him of his shackles and do what he had to do to meet Gabbie.

The lump was still there when he faced the principal, Ms. Elliot.

"Why are you so angry, Jim?" she asked.

He shook his head. That was as far as the inquisition would go. He was a very, very private person.

"You can be a good student, Jim. I expect you to apologize to Mrs. Tawney for your behavior."

"I wasn't wrong, Ms. Elliot. Mrs. Tawney was. She was just using her position to get at me because she realized how smart she wasn't. Gabbie was badly hurt and couldn't walk."

"Jim, you'll learn soon enough, there will be times you will be in the right, and you still have to back off. It'll happen all your life."

"No, Ms. Elliot. I know better. I will not apologize for being right."

"I see. You're not just being obstinate? You know what that means?"

Jim nodded. "Why would you make me apologize for being in the right?"

"I don't want to do this to you, but I have to transfer you from Mrs. Tawney's class. If I don't, you will be a challenge to her authority. Also, it may prevent any more personality conflicts. You might get along better with Mrs. Johnson. Okay?"

No, not okay, Jim thought. It's bullshit! Why is everyone trying to keep him from Gabbie? "Ms. Elliot? I'd like to stay in Mrs. Tawney's class."

"Simple. Apologize."

As far as he was concerned, she was asking him to stain the Holy Grail. He shook her off. "You don't have to ask my father to come in, do you?"

She stared at him. The question filled in dozens of blank pages. "I will ask your mother to come in, Jim." She saw the color drain from his face.

He shook his head. His eyes clouded over. "No mother."

She cleared her throat. "Jim, you just have to bend a little." He stood mute. "I'll send a note to your dad." She made a little hitch with her head as a form of apology. "I have to do that."

At lunch that same day, Jim saw Gabbie walk into the cafeteria. He turned away. He felt like a convict for denying himself her presence. If he apologized he could be in class with her. Then, he looked into her face as she sat beside him. She bumped his shoulder.

"Hi! The principal transferred me out of your class. I'd rather she made me eat chalk."

"They're trying to keep us apart, you know?"

For Jim, there was a bit less bobble in the world. He smiled at her. "They can try."

"We must be important," she said. "We've only known each other for a couple hours."

"Yeah!" Jim said. "You'd think they'd wait until we planned our honeymoon."

"You are a funny fellow, Kimo Sabe. At least we can meet here in the cafeteria. I'm sorry. It will have to do until we can find another time and place. I like being with you."

"Me with you. I sure am going to miss being in class with you all day."

"Tell me about it."

4

It was Christmas vacation. More than a half a foot of new-fallen snow covered Ice Cube Hill. There wasn't a mark or a track all the way down. It spread like a glazed white frosting over the whole valley.

Jim and Gabbie looked down at the dazzling perfect sheet of snow. A group of sledders slogged up behind them. They seemed to gasp in unison as they looked at the almost perpendicular stretch of sloping hill. Ice crystals blinked back the rising sun.

"I'll beat you to the bottom," Jim said to Gabbie as he cleared snow from the runners of his sled. He looked at her sideways hoping she wouldn't detect his bravado air. So far he seemed to be wearing well with her.

She looked at him and put her mittened hand at his chest. "No! Not fair! You'll let me win!"

Omigod! Jim thought. She is totally unfazed by this suicide run! "No! I wouldn't treat you like that!" he said. "I let you go first then I follow because I'm heavier than you are. It has to be fair! First one to the brook at the bottom! Okay?" *Did she buy that?*

Gabbie saw the other kids were getting ready to go. Anxious to be the first over the snow, Gabbie stepped back, grabbed her sled by the sides, sprinted and took a belly flop, the snow kicking up and showering her face.

Before Jim could follow, Noah Nowarcz, like a predator, had waited. He took off after her. He was Jim's classmate who Jim found little reason to befriend. Now he knew the reason.

Jim was airborne within seconds, the third in line.

Gabbie was screeching and screaming as she looked behind. She thought Noah was Jim.

Just as Gabbie was approaching the bottom where the brook had only a thin coating of ice, Noah caught up to her. He grabbed the rear runner of her sled with his hand and yanked it hard, making it swerve. Gabbie went flying in the air and landed, KA-SPLOSH! breaking through the ice and going into the brook.

Noah was standing and laughing his head off as Jim slid sideways to a stop. He jumped to his feet and headed for Noah. His fists were tight, his teeth clenched.

By this time, Gabbie got up and was taking off her soaked mittens. Her eyes were closed to pencil lines, and she was sputtering.

Gabbie jumped in front of the charging Jim and held him off with her hands upraised. "No, Jim. No!"

"Hold on, Gabbie! I'm going to fix this son-of-a-bitch!"

Jim froze. He saw the lightning bolts shooting from her eyes and her clenched fists. Gabbie turned to Noah.

She swung with all her might. Gabbie clocked Noah smack on his nose.

Noah went flying on his ass. A red shower from his nostrils decorated the snow. His gloved hand reached up to wipe it. He started bawling like a lamb. "I was only having fun!"

She turned to Jim. "Some things you have to do for yourself, Kimo Sabe."

Right, Jim nodded. *An object lesson if ever there was one.* He reached down and scooped up a handful of the powdery snow. Staring all the while into Gabbie's eyes as she waved her hand, he pushed some of the snow into his mouth. With the rest, he showered Gabbie's face. "I pronounce you Queen of the Amazons!"

"And I pronounce you lick my face clean!" She pulled him towards her—wet lips pressed on wet lips.

Meanwhile, Noah blubbered as he dragged his sled up the hill.

A while later, Jim spotted a strange car by his home. Noah sat in the back seat. Immediately Jim knew the ensuing scenario like he knew his father wore a belt.

His father, Glenn, was seated at the kitchen table drumming his fingers. Mr. and Mrs. Nowarcz looked down on him.

"They say their son came home with a bloody nose. Noah told them you picked on him and hit him in the nose just because he beat you down the hill sleigh riding," Glenn said. "They want to see you punished for it. I don't blame them. Speak!"

Jim couldn't believe his ears. If he didn't say anything would he be protecting Gabbie? Or Noah?

"Speak! Speak!" Glenn said.

"Noah is two years older than I am, and you can see for yourself he's fat as a barrel so I couldn't be picking on him. Next, Noah is a liar. I didn't hit him, a girl did. He got a good one on the snout because he deserved it for being a bully. I swear that's the truth on my brother's soul."

"You're the liar!" Mrs. Nowarcz said. "My son never lies. And look at your size! I want your son punished, Mr. Dorchester! He almost broke my son's nose!"

"I'll see that he gets punished," Glenn said getting up, unhitching his belt, a familiar exercise. "You can watch if you want."

"First I want him to apologize to my son," Mr. Nowarcz said.

"Well, let's go do that," Glenn said. He led the way out.

At the front of the house, Mr. Nowarcz waved his son out of the car. "He wants to apologize," he said.

Jim walked up to Noah and stuck his hand out. "I'm sorry you lied," Jim said. Noah stuck his head forward not sure of what he had heard.

They shook hands.

Jim pulled back his fist and swung. He hit Noah smack on his nose, decking him. For the second time that day, Noah screamed out in pain with his nose gushing red.

Jim waved his hand to ease the pain. He turned to the shocked look on the faces of the grownups. "If I can get beaten for a lie, I might just as well have the satisfaction of getting beaten for the truth."

When Jim saw Glenn walk back inside the kitchen, Jim noticed his father had a smirk on his face. Jim started to drop his pants.

Glenn said, "Don't bother; I'd rather have a beer."

Jim broke four eggs in a bowl, added a splash of water, and beat them. He added a handful of cubed ham and Swiss cheese. His father walked into the kitchen, went directly to the fridge without a word, and took out a bottle of beer. Jim wondered if he was in a fouler mood. He kept glancing at his father.

"I'm having eggs for dinner. Can I make you some?" Jim asked. The question he wanted to ask remained anchored in his throat.

"Naw. I had a pulled pork sandwich for lunch." He twisted off the cap. "This will have to do me." He raised the bottle and made it gurgle. "You didn't get to our lawn."

"No." Jim watched the butter melt in the frying pan. He swirled it around, then poured the egg mixture into it, and turned down the heat. "I had to get four others done."

"Did goddamn Sullivan pay you?"

"Yes, Mrs. Sullivan said she had been away. She paid me for the newspaper and the lawn."

"I don't see the money on the table." He dropped the empty bottle in the trash and went back to the fridge.

"It's there, in the envelope with the other money, leaning against the sugar bowl. It's all together." Glenn belched loudly. Jim dug the spatula into the pan as he attacked the eggs. The thought in his mind came out like prisoners breaking free from jail. He held his breath. All he knew was the day his father got the letter from Ms. Elliott, the principal, Jim took a no-sitting-for-a-week beating. "Dad, I'd like to stop delivering the papers."

Less than a month ago his father brought up the idea of Jim paying for his room and board. "You've got too god-damned much time on your hands! You've got a bike; you're going to deliver newspapers!" Glenn declared.

"Dad! I can do a half-dozen papers but I don't know anything about running a whole newspaper route. I don't know how to get them, how to deliver them, how to buy them!"

"Life is tough, see. It's tougher than you will ever dream! You got to learn how to be tough. How to make it in this world! You'll just have to learn how to do all that, right? And just to make sure I'm doing my job right, you get the strap for every dollar you're short! Got it! I'll give you a week to get started."

"Dad . . . "

"Don't you start whining! My father didn't raise me to be a whiner so don't you start!"

"I wouldn't whine just so I don't give you the satisfaction!"

"Just so long as you meet your quota."

"Dad, you know I'm going to do the best I can do, but what if I can't make enough?"

"Maybe you want to think about mowing lawns for a lot more people. That's one way to save your ass!" He guffawed at his own black humor.

Within two weeks Jim developed a newspaper route and built up his lawn-mowing clientele. Although proud of his achievements, he found himself falling asleep doing the dinner dishes.

It was only last week when he went into his bedroom early in the morning.

"Dad? Sorry to wake you so early, but it's really raining a storm. Can you help me run my paper route?"

"It's 5:30 for Christ's sakes! How do you expect me to do my job today?"

"I need a hand, Dad. Just drive me across town to get the papers. I'll do everything else?"

"Crap!" his father said. "I'm not going to lose my sleep for you. Get out of here!"

Jim stood on the porch listening to the torrents of rain. There had to be a smart way to get the job done. There was no way he could deliver the papers without him and the papers getting soaked. By this time he had gotten pretty good pumping the bike while he folded and threw the newspapers onto the porches with either hand. The rain made that impossible. He thought a while. Then put his plan into action.

He didn't even have a learner's permit, much less a driver's license, but he took his father's truck anyway. He went across town to pick up the newspapers from the truck that brought them down from the newspaper. He put them in the bed and covered them with a tarp. He stopped in a gas station under the cover by the gas pumps. There, he folded every newspaper into a square he could fling like a Frisbee onto the porches. At the first house at the head of every street of his route, he stopped the truck and put enough papers for that street on the porch and used it for a base. When that job was done, he drove back home, parked the pick-up and got his bike.

At every home where he had stashed the folded papers, he loaded them into the basket by the handle bars. He used the poncho that came off his shoulders to cover the basket to protect the papers. From there, it was a simple job to reach into the basket, get the newspapers, and send them sailing onto the porches.

"What?" Glenn slammed the bottle on the table. "You want to stop delivering papers? Are you whining? Can't stand the gaff?"

"It's not that. I'm kinda pooped after mowing the lawns, making my dinner, then getting all my homework done. I go to sleep late, and I'm really tired. I have to get up at 5:30 to get the papers and get them all delivered in time to get to school."

"You know the answer. You get it done better and faster, and you'll have some free time! Remember? That's the reason you're doing papers; you had too much free time!"

Jim exhaled long and slowly. His dad just didn't know what was involved. It had to do with the fact that the job just wasn't worth it.

"Dad, I just don't make enough money. They tip me a dime for delivering the papers all month! It takes too much of my time and energy. I'm pooped by the time I get to school."

"Look! Stop being a groaner! It still takes a hundred cents to make a dollar, and every cent counts! You stick to it until you can use the time to make more money!"

"I can't mow lawns at five-thirty in the morning!"

"Don't be a wise-ass. Just do as I say!"

He was implacable. Jim wanted to change the subject. "You musta had a busy day."

"Naw." He threw the bottle cap on the table and reached for the envelope as he took a swig. "Asshole jerk insurance guy been robbing me all these years. I got square. He brought his piece of junk Buick over and said there was oil on the garage floor. I tightened the bolts on the intake manifold so the gasket wasn't leaking. I charged him three-hundred bucks for ten minutes work. I told him too bad he didn't buy a Japanese car with a ten-year warranty. Makes for a nice day."

Jim felt himself cringe inwardly. Using a gun to rob a bank was more honest. He flipped the omelet into the disposal and left the English muffins in the toaster to burn.

"Don't forget to put eggs and muffins on your shopping list," Glenn said, "I'm not paying for them."

6

Jim followed Gabbie down the school bus steps.

He helped put her book bag on her shoulders. "I was going to ask you if you wanted me to carry this, but I've got that little voice inside, you know . . . "

"Yes."

"It's telling me it would be better if you carried your own books."

"Yes, besides, if Mom comes by it's better if I have them. Thanks, anyway. I'm sorry it's an awful long walk to the other side of town. Then, it's even further when you walk me to the flute lesson from there, back to the school to pick up your books, then home. Wow! It's a good thing Mom picks me up after the lesson to bring me home or you'd really have a hike. Really? You don't mind? After doing this a couple times a week for the past month I thought you'd quit."

"Me? Quit? Don't know the meaning of the word. The walk is nothing. I look forward to it. Besides, I understand there are still packs of hyenas in the area. So, you still need an escort, Tonto."

"Another premonition, Kimo Sabe?"

"Hey! This is a lonely stretch from the main road to your house. Who knows what tiger can jump out of the woods from either side! By the way, I still haven't heard you play the flute."

"No. One day I'll have a recital just for you."

"I never knew anyone who was a musician. That makes you special in a special way. Okay, I'll sit hidden right here by the oak tree in case your Mom is going to drive you. Besides, you bring special cookies if we walk to your lesson."

"No, I bring you plain old cookies. I bring the special oatmeal cookies for Silver. My house is just around the turn, as you know. I'll try to hurry."

"I'll watch you."

Jim sat by the base of the oak tree. When he looked up he saw Gabbie was about half way to the turn. He paid particular attention to the little swing she had as she walked, which was emphasized by the book bag. He looked at the ground for acorns.

When he looked up he saw a white van make the far turn. It passed Gabbie. Then, it slowed to a stop. Jim scrunched his eyebrows. He threw down the acorns in his hand and brushed them off. The driver jumped down from the cab. He scanned the road both ways. Jim was seated by the tree and not readily visible. The man walked around to the sliding door and opened it.

Jim heard him call to Gabbie. "Miss!"

Gabbie stopped walking and turned to him. She was a dozen steps or so away from the van.

"My doggie is missing . . ." he said. He continued to walk casually toward her. He was balding, had a growth of beard, and wore a denim shirt and jeans. He positioned his hands in front of him. It seemed to Jim he was indicating the size of his dog.

When he got close to Gabbie, he stopped. Suddenly, he lunged for her.

He grabbed her by the strap of her book bag.

Gabbie screamed. "Leave me alone!" She tried to push him away.

The man began to pull her toward the van.

Gabbie screamed louder.

Jim was on his feet running toward them. "Leave her alone!"

The man looked up at the intruder. He scowled and swore.

Gabbie continued to scream. With her assailant momentarily distracted by Jim, she twisted and pulled her arm out of the book bag holder.

The man turned back to her. He held on to the book bag, and moved to grab her with his other hand.

Gabbie continued to struggle. She managed to twist her other arm out of the book bag loop. She sprinted toward her home. The man's face turned into a gargoyle's. He was left holding the sack.

He dropped the book bag and went into overdrive after Gabbie. After some dozen steps he lunged. He caught her by her jacket collar. She screeched. He wrapped his other arm around her, yanked her off the ground, and turned to carry his prey back to the van.

Jim had reached the van. The man had left the engine running. Jim stopped in his tracks. What could he do? Certainly he was no match for the predator. What did he have to do to free Gabbie? Could he grapple with him? The adrenaline made his heart pound in his throat. He was going to kidnap Gabbie! He was going to steal her away to do bad things to her! Jim wasn't going to let him do that! No! Not if it was up to him! *Do something!* Silently he admonished himself. *Yes! But what?*

The sound of the engine running clued him.

Jim yanked open the passenger door of the van. He reached in, turned the ignition key to shut off the engine. Then, he pulled out the key on a ring full of keys.

He stood beside the van holding the keys high in his hand. "Let her go! Let her go!"

The man glared at him, hauling the screaming Gabbie along.

"Stop! Stop!" Jim shouted. "Let her go or I make your van keys disappear!"

The man continued to move toward the van.

"One more step and they're gone! Stop! Now let her go!"

The man stopped.

Jim shook the keys. "You can't drive away if you don't have the keys!"

"I've got a spare key in my pocket!"

"You're lying!" Jim glanced at the ground. He saw a rock the size of a baseball. He looked back at the man and Gabbie. The creep looked as if he was trying to decide what to do. Jim reached down and picked up the rock. "Let her go! Now! I'll mark your van!"

When the man continued to hold Gabbie, Jim turned. With all his might he threw the rock at the van's windshield. It made a small hole and crazed the rest of it.

"You sonofabitch!" the man shouted holding on even tighter to Gabbie. She continued to scream.

Jim picked up a heavy stick. "Let her go!" He whacked the hood of the van, denting it heavily.

"You fucking bastard!" the man shouted. He pulled Gabbie toward the van.

Jim turned and threw the keys as high and as far into the woods with all his might.

Jim saw black anger contort the man's face, spittle running from his mouth. "You little shit sonofabitch! I know who you are! You watch out! I'm gonna come after you! When I get you, I'm going to eat your balls!" He yanked Gabbie around and threw her on the ground. He charged into the woods.

Jim dashed to Gabbie. "You're okay, Kid! You're okay! Run home as fast as you can and tell your mother! Run! Gabbie!" He helped her up. "Leave your books! Come!" Jim pulled her along toward her home. "Gabbie, don't say I was here! Just say some kid you don't know passing by helped you! Got it? Tonto?"

"Yes, . . . " she gasped for breath, ". . . Kimo Sabe."

In sight of her house, Jim let go of her hand. "There's your house. You'll be safe. I'll watch until you get to the door."

"What if he comes after you?"

"He no can catch The Lone Ranger's Silver! Him too fast Horse!" When Gabbie entered the front door, Jim turned and ran back toward the van but on the other side of the road. He held his breath until he got past the van. He ran full tilt to the main road.

It sure as all dickens puts an end to riding the school bus with Gabbie. Will the cops catch the creep so my balls would be safe? Pain in the ass. How long would he have to keep looking over his shoulder?

Jim met Gabbie in the cafeteria the next day.

"You okay?" Jim asked.

"My mother didn't want me to come to school, but I said I wanted to. The police told my father the van was stolen. They called last night to say they got fingerprints from the van and know who the creep is. There was something about the 'attempted abduction' on the television, and in the newspaper this morning. My father made sure they kept my name out of it. They haven't caught him, but they're sure they will."

"They better!" Jim covered his groin with a book.

Gabbie tilted her head back and laughed.

"Hey! Tonto. I hope he's not from town."

"I said some kid on a bike did what you did. They thought that was very clever. They want to find him to reward him. See, Kimo Sabe, I should have told them it was you."

"And that pervert would know exactly where to find me."

"I'm proud of you. You're true to your hero, not waiting around to be thanked. 'Who was that masked man?'"

"We know; that's all that matters. It makes me feel pretty good!"

"From now on the housekeeper will drive up to meet me at the bus. My parents said when this semester is over they're going to put me in a private school."

Jim shook his head. "Gosh! Gabbie. Never seen anything like it. Everything I try to do gets turned around and works against me."

"Jim?" Gabbie said ducking into her shoulders and whispering to make her words secret. "I've got a great idea!"

"Tell!"

"Tomorrow is Friday!"

"So?"

"So they do all that assembly stuff. No one would know whether or not we're there, so let's cut classes instead of coming to lunch. We can take a walk and be together. We just have to come back in time to get the bus."

7

He had to pedal back three blocks to Mr. MacDonald's house. When the elderly gent came to the door, he greeted Jim with a big smile. "Yes, Jim?"

"Mr. MacDonald, when I counted the money in the envelope you paid me for the newspapers, you gave me too much. A lot too much."

"No, I didn't, Jim. I gave you exactly what I wanted you to have."

"A hundred dollars too much, Mr. MacDonald! You didn't mean to do that."

"Jim, you deliver my paper every single day no matter what the weather—like the post office says, ' . . . through rain and sleet and snow . . .' You know how important the newspaper is for a lonely fellow like me. How dull a day I would have without it, crossword puzzles and all. I want you to know how much I appreciate your caring, and doing the right thing. You are the kind of responsible fellow I want delivering my paper. So, I think I'm getting a bargain."

"I . . . I can't take this, Mr. MacDonald." His hand shook as he held out the fortune.

Mr. MacDonald reached out and took the bill. "Now, Jim, let's say you found this bill in the middle of a street, and you took it to the police station as I know you would, and the captain said it was yours—finders keepers. What would you buy with it?"

Jim's face exploded in a smile. "That's easy, Mr. MacDonald! I'd buy flowers for Gabbie and for my mom if she were home, a football for my brother if he was alive, and for myself, a box of drawing pencils and a tennis racquet! I'd give the rest to my Dad, he needs it."

"Jim, that's exactly what you do. It's your money, and your money alone. You earned it. I really want you to have it. You keep it for yourself."

Jim was only ten years old, but he had begun to understand the ways of the world. Kindness did not beget kindness. There were always people on the other side of the line who were like savages. They would take advantage. He heard the expressions, 'Never give a sucker an even break,' and 'A sucker is born every minute.' To Jim he understood suckers to them meant kind people to him. He felt he was moving in a world where he didn't belong, as if he was living in a room with no exit. He got an itch between his shoulder blades when he sensed something was not right, out of balance. He was plain compelled to do the right thing. Would the world turn for the better for him if he stopped thinking of others first?

Mr. MacDonald said to keep it for himself. That would be easy enough to do. Just fold it up and put it in his secret box. He'd put it right in with his other treasures, like the caul in alcohol. There was the long, edged black ribbon his mother wore in her hair. She gave it to him the last time he saw her, although he didn't know that at the time. Then there was his brother's favorite Yo-Yo. Tommy made it "Walk the Dog" in the sports shop contest and won first prize. He palmed the Spaulding Pink he gave him for Christmas. He also had the smoothest, roundest stone that looked just like an aggie. Gabbie found it when they were at the Old Maid's swimming hole and gave it to him as a token of their love, she said. The next day he took out of the box his proudest doing. It was a peach pit he carved into a monkey eating a banana. He saw one at a carnival and copied it. He blushed when Gabbie went gaga over it. She said she was going to put it on a chain and wear it around her neck.

He didn't think twice about keeping the hundred dollar bill for himself, however. He knew telling his father about the wonderful gift was the right thing to do, but, the itch between his shoulders told him it could not turn out so well for him, no matter what Mr. MacDonald said. He knew his father too well.

"Where did the hundred dollars come from?" his father asked.

"A customer gave it to me . . . as a tip."

"A customer? A tip! What customer would give you this much money? I have to break my ass for days to get this kind of money?"

"Mr. MacDonald."

"Old man MacDonald is a skinflint. Now tell me where you got it?"

"I'm not lying, Dad."

"Course you're lying! You stole it, didn't you? Nobody gives a kid a hundred bucks. I don't want the goddamn cops coming here for my criminal son! I'll keep it in case they find you out. You think giving it to me will make it right? Don't you lie to me!"

"I'm not lying."

"We'll see!" He yanked his belt off. "Drop your pants!"

"Dad. Please don't." At least when Mom cared to be around she'd plead with him, and his brother, Tom, would cry, too, for support. "Dad? Please . . . don't use the buckle . . ."

"My lawn!" Mr. Keegan shouted, breakfast cereal caught at the corners of his mouth, his sharp nose pecking at the air. His white haired, scarecrow of a wife stood behind him to one side, nodding her head to every word he said. "You did a bad job on my lawn! It wasn't done right!"

"It's just the way I do it every time, Mr. Keegan," Jim said.

"No, it isn't. It's not done right. You do it over again."

"Mr. Keegan, I'll do your lawn over again at no cost even though you're wrong."

"I hired you because they said you were so honest you squeaked. Well, you can't cheat me! And you'll do my lawn right every time from now on!"

"I know you're going to tell my father, and he's going to beat the dickens out of me, but you find somebody else after this to do your lawn. You're just a cheap, old fart and I'll probably be the only one who will miss you when you croak."

He turned on his heel, jaw clenched tight, eyes narrow slits. He stopped. He turned. "I'm sorry I said that, Mr. Keegan. That was not a nice thing for me to say. I apologize. Don't ask me to do any more errands for you because I'm never talking to you again."

9

At lunchtime, on cue for the last two Fridays, Jim and Gabbie cut classes. They slipped down to the basement, then out of the building. They never looked back.

Without a word between them, they headed for the Old Maid's swimming hole, which was part of the town's water supply. At this time of the year Jim thought it would be deserted and waiting for them. There was a rumor he heard about the place that made him uneasy. Voyeurs, they called them, that hid in the bushes around the swimming hole who liked to watch the kids swim balliki— the local slang for nude. He thought better about it than mentioning it to Gabbie, especially after her most recent experience. Her parents would flay the skin off him if they knew he was taking her away from school, and that they were alone. He would just be very cautious while they were there.

They weren't bashful around each other at this time. There were only a few high up clouds with not a hint of a breeze, but the cooler fall weather was present.

When they got there the pond was deserted.

"Last one in!" Gabbie screamed.

Jim dropped the books he was carrying. He tugged off first one shoe, and then the other. Then, he looked around into the nearby woods. He glanced over at her. She was tugging her shirt over her head. He pulled his shirt over his head. "I'm going to beat you!" he shouted.

She squealed as she ducked down to slip out of her skirt and panties.

He undid his belt. He hooked his thumbs in his shorts, and then his socks, and pulled everything off with his pants, first one leg, then the other. He sprinted for the water. He saw her diving in, headfirst.

He swam underwater until he saw her legs flailing. He reached over and grabbed her ankles. He let her go quickly and surfaced.

He found her sputtering and spitting water at him. "Sore sport!" She used the heel of her hand to spray him with water. "What if someone else comes?"

He grimaced. "There's plenty of room."

"Ha!" she screamed. She ducked under and swam.

Jim followed and surfaced when she did.

Both took long, easy strokes as they headed out for the middle.

When he caught up to her, she turned on her back and floated. Jim averted his eyes as he went past her. Secretly he wanted to take a peek at her titties, but he wouldn't allow himself . . . at least, not just yet.

"I'll give you a head start and still beat you to shore!"

She yelped, turned, and struck out for shore.

Almost to the shore, she stopped to tread water. "I'm . . . I'm . . . pooped!" she gasped.

"I know . . ." Jim sputtered back.

"Why do you keep looking around like that?"

"Just checking out the day."

"Yes! And Wow! What a day," she said. "Know what? This cold water makes my boobs all nipply."

"I don't want to say what it does to me!"

"Say!"

"No!"

"Yes!"

"It's embarrassing."

"C'mon! We're old friends."

"You go into this water like Arthur and come out like Agnes!"

"Oh! That's funny!"

"You know something else, Gabbie? I will always remember this day. I don't know what makes it special, but I sure feel it. You?"

"Why? Did you get a good look? Hey! Big J. Anytime I'm with you, it's special. You're always so much fun. I can talk to you about anything, and we're always doing fun things."

"That's because you're always ready to explore. To do things."

"Yeah! The only thing we've missed out on is camping out together. I couldn't get that past my mother even if I told her I was going with the Pope." She laughed out loud.

"Know what can make this day special? One we'll never forget? Promise me you'll always be mine. I'll promise I'll always be yours. Okay?"

"Sure. Okay."

"Not good enough. You don't sound sincere."

"I am sincere. Hey! I like you, Tonto."

"And I like you, Kimo Sabe. Now why do you keep looking around?"

"Nothing. Just in case somebody comes."

"Oh! Okay. We'll just have to swear we will only and always belong to each other. I vow my love to you."

"And I vow my love to you."

"For always and always. Until the end of eternity!"

"For always and always. Until the end of eternity!"

"You break that vow, Kimo Sabe, you know what happens?"

"No. What?"

"You rot from the inside out!"

"God Almighty! I would rather die than break that vow. You break the vow,

Tonto, . . . you know what? I couldn't say that. I'd do anything in the world that would make you happy, even if you couldn't stand being with me anymore." *What did it mean to want to be with someone? Was it just habit? And what really caused his stomach to flip and flop when he thought of Gabbie. And what really caused the exciting feeling that bubbled inside him when he was with her?*

He ducked under the water and let it swirl above him. He looked at her hazy, nude figure under the water longer than he realized and came up spluttering and coughing. "Gabbie? I don't know the reason, but I've got to keep these moments right up on top, where I'll always remember them." He reflected on the moment, where he was, the time of day, what he was doing, and mostly, on whom he was with.

"When I tell my girlfriends my feelings for you, they say it's just puppy love, and I'll get over it. Is this puppy love?"

Jim started barking. Gabbie laughed. "Whatever it is," Jim said, "I'm going to feel this way about you until I'm a hundred-and-eleven years old."

"You didn't even have to say that. It's our world and we're going to stay like this for forever."

"We'd better go."

She ducked under, swam a bit. When she came up she said, "Big J. You know, you're right. Just like the poet. If there's something we want to keep, first we must let it go. I'd let you go, Big J, if that's what you wanted. You showed me how much you loved me. I want to show you how much I love you."

He nodded. Now exactly what did she mean by that? He didn't want to seem dumb by asking. He'd wait for another time. "I like when you call me Big J."

"We should go."

As they got dressed he called to her. "We can't do this anymore. You know?"

"Like this, you mean? Skinny dipping? After all these times?"

"Yes."

"Why?"

"Because . . . " he tossed his head. "Because we're older."

"Because I'm getting boobs?"

"Because we're older."

"You never asked to feel them. Do you want to? You'll like it." He looked down and shook his head. "Because I'm getting fuzz?" He looked at her and tossed his head. "And you're getting bigger?" she said. She laughed.

His face flushed. Wow! He certainly thought about what boobs feel like. Somehow he knew it wasn't exactly something he should do. He took a deep breath. "Look! We're older. Don't say anything else that might take this day away from us. It's Jim and Gabbie. Gabbie and Jim. It will always be like that. It will always be this way."

"We're doomed to be together forever!"

He jerked his head. "Doomed?"

43

"Dooooomed!" She nodded her head and grew solemn until he started laughing. She looked up at him. She broke out in a smile. Then, they both deliberately echoed each other's raucous laughter.

"Gabbie!" in a half whisper he called urgently.

"What's the matter?" she whispered back.

"Are you dressed?"

"Yes. Almost."

"I've got the books. Now, do as I say! Run! Run down the path as fast as you can!" he said aloud.

Gabbie ran past him and sped down the path. She made a soft crying noise as she did. Jim followed.

They ran full tilt until they reached the main road.

"Jim!" Gabbie gasped. "Wha . . . What was that about?"

"I'll tell you when we get back to the school."

"Why?"

"Because if I tell you now, you'll freak out."

'Freak out? No, I won't. We're fine. Why should I freak out?"

"Because some weirdo freak was hiding in the woods watching us through binoculars."

"What!" Gabbie screamed. "You're telling me now? You let me walk around with no clothes on while some pervert is watching me? You should have told me! You should have told me! That's why you were looking around!"

"I heard sometimes they do that."

"You know how I am about that! You should have been honest with me! You know how modest and shy I am. You should look out for me! Get away! Go far, far away! I don't want to be with you!"

"Gabbie! Nothing happened!"

"You happened! You probably told them we'd be there! I don't trust you."

"I would never betray you!"

"How can you say that?"

"Because I love you!"

"I don't care! I don't want to see you again!"

"Do you mean that?"

"Yes! Yes, I do!"

"Then, you know what I have to do."

"I don't care what you do!"

Jim walked out into the middle of the road and lay down on his back. "Then, I don't want to live anymore."

"You jerk! Get out of there. A car is coming."

"I don't care. Take it all back."

"Jim!"

"And you're not invited to my funeral!"

"Jim! The car!"

"There's no car."

The police car pulled up alongside Jim. The officer rolled down his window. "Are you all right? What are you doing there?"

Jim sat up. "Officer, I cannot tell a lie. I was making a fool of myself."

"Drinking?"

"No."

"Drugs?"

"No."

"You're Glenn Dorchester's boy. You deliver my newspaper?"

"Yes, sir. And I'm supposed to start cutting your lawn come spring."

"And that's the Soldi girl?"

"Yes, sir."

"You should be in school."

"We thought we'd take a walk."

"I'll drive you both home."

"Do you have to? Can we just walk back to school? I'd rather go to jail than have my father see you bring me home . . ."

Gabbie looked at Jim. "No matter what happens, I'm still not talking to you. Ever again!" She turned to the officer. "Just let us walk back to school, Sir. You musta been a kid once and Kimo Sabe, here, promises to swear off firewater forever."

10

"Dad? Thanks for letting me get my driver's license. That was nice. Can I borrow the pick-up?" Jim asked his father.

"You going to use it to haul fire wood?"

"No. I'd just like to use it."

"For what? To haul a beer keg up in the woods to have a party with your pals?" The beer made a gurgling sound as he polished off the bottle.

"No. A date. I'd like to pick her up to take her to the movie. She's not allowed to walk."

"A date! A date! Really?" He tossed the empty into the wastebasket where it clattered noisily. He took a full one. "I just bet you've got a date!"

"Yes, I've got a date."

"You'd never admit it to me, or you'd better not admit to me you're gay, so it's gotta be a girl date, right?"

"Right."

"Well, let me tell you this, like a father's supposed to do. See? So listen. I'll let you take the truck, but you know what? You better keep it in your pants, see? You get any other notions, and you're in for one of life's tough lessons, like I did when your mother ran away, probably with a drunken sailor!"

"Dad . . . !"

"Think I don't know? You've got your 'date' in the truck, and you're parked in Lover's Lane where it's dark and deserted. Then, before you know it, Bam! she spreads her legs, and it's all over! Well, let me tell you, you get her knocked up don't think twice about bringing her back here! You can hardly pay for your own keep with what you're making, how do you think you're going to pay for two more?" He pulled a chair back from the kitchen table, sat, leaned back and put his foot up on the table. "You make yourself a prize package, Mister, and you make damn sure you go on and live with her family, cause you're not bringing no screeching meemie here! Do you understand?"

"Yes, sir."

"Going to the movies?"

"Yes."

"Movies mean money. You stealing money from me? Why didn't you turn it in?"

"I worked extra to save it up. I run errands. Pick up medicines and groceries. I've been saving up the tips."

"Suppose I asked you for it?"

Jim shrugged, turned, and walked out of the house.

That evening, Jim cut the pick-up's engine in front of Gabbie's home.

He started up the front walk. Gabbie moved quickly out of the house to meet him. "Jim, are you sure you want to do this?"

"Hi! Gabbie." He moved his head back and forth. "We're not doing anything wrong. Your mother and father should know whom you're seeing." He hesitated. "Unless, you're sure I'm holding the short end of the stick."

She stared into his face. "Pissing contest, huh?"

She was partly right. Her father was an arrow in his side, and he had to get to know his enemy. "No," he said. "Just something I read called 'uncompromising integrity.'"

"What does that mean?"

"It means I have to live in my own skin. At one time or another, I have to face myself, and I want to be able to live with what I see. I'm not going to scuttle around your family. I love you too much, and that means I have much respect for them, for, without them, I would not have you. I want them, not to respect me, as much as I want them to know me, and so I can respect myself. Simple. I want them to know I would protect you with my own life. I'm not an enemy. Now, do I come in or is this date postponed?"

"Mom, Dad, this is Jim Dorchester," Gabbie said as she and Jim walked into the family room. The fire was blazing and the television was on. Mr. Soldi, balding, round-faced, vest open, tie askew, was seated in an easy chair reading.

Mrs. Soldi sitting tall, straight, coiffed hair, was sipping coffee.

"Hello," Jim said. He looked at each one directly.

"This is a surprise, Medford," Mrs. Soldi said. "You didn't say anything."

"My fault," Jim said. "I asked Gabbie . . . Medford . . . to go to the movies with me tonight. I thought you should know who she was going to be with." He lit the fuse. Point of no return.

Mr. Soldi blinked rapidly several times, then closed the book. "Dorchester! Your father is the president of the Chamber of Commerce, do I have that right?"

"No, sir."

"I was going to ask if your mother is a volunteer at the hospital," Mrs. Soldi said.

"Oh! Yes! That Dorchester! He has an auto shop right by his house? Over near the fire station?" Mr. Soldi said.

"Yes, that's right." Jim glanced at Gabbie. "No, Mrs. Soldi, my mother is not with us. Just my father and I, we're alone. My mother and father are separated."

"I see," Mrs. Soldi said.

"I want to thank you, young man, for coming here tonight," Mr. Soldi said. "You have me look twice at my perspective on today's youth. I must say I admire your integrity for doing what you think is right. It took some courage and character. I appreciate your consideration. Mrs. Soldi and I would acknowledge that by inviting you to watch television here tonight with Medford for an hour or so."

There it was, Jim thought. The line was drawn with an arc welder like Churchill's descending iron curtain.

"You can do some microwave popcorn, if you like, Medford," Mrs. Soldi said.

"Sure! Jim and I can do it. And, and I'd like to show him my room. I want you to meet Amusee, Jim. Come with me into the kitchen," Gabbie said. She took his hand to lead him out.

Once in the kitchen, Jim put the palm of his hand on his forehead and looked up at the ceiling! *Round One lost! Feel the blood pumping in my throat!* He knew exactly what the scenario portended. *She will not be allowed to go into town with him ever.* They would specifically and deliberately forbid any association with him. That was easy to decode from the charged air in the room.

He avoided her eyes. The sparks would be too visible. He might not be able to hide the contortions on his face. The erupting volcano inside him would render him speechless. Already the feelings in his heart made him unable to swallow. He coughed, pushed his chest out, and took a deep breath. He once read, "To every bad situation, put on a good face." He urged a smile on his face. "And who or what is this 'Amusee'?'"

"Yes! Amusee de Coeur! It's really supposed to be 'amusee de bouche,' French for a little tidbit to awaken the taste buds in your mouth, which is served just before dinner. But Amusee is an Havanese. He is my very own little doggie that will burrow his way into your heart, so it's a good thing I'm there first!"

"Yes! Popcorn sounds great—even without the movie!"

"Yeah! I can fix it gourmet, too!"

"And I must meet this wooffie that you care for so much."

Amusee charged Jim when he came through the door of Gabbie's bedroom. He yipped and bounced on his hind legs, swiping the air with his front paws until Jim picked him up. Jim could not avoid the face licking, and fell on the floor laughing and trying to hide himself. The dog was persistent, until Gabbie picked him up.

"He loves you, too."

Jim stretched out on the floor looking up at Gabbie. "What do we do about your folks?"

The air was thick with frustration. Jim visualized his dreams of a wonderful relationship with Gabbie's dad and especially her mom crumbling like a sandcastle hit with a comber.

There was a knock on the door. Mrs. Soldi opened it and looked at Jim. "Mr. Soldi would like to see you, Jim." When Gabbie started to move, she added, ". . . alone."

Jim turned to Gabbie and mouthed the words: "Do I need a blindfold?" He grinned.

Jim followed Mrs. Soldi into the library. Mr. Soldi had adjusted his tie and buttoned up his vest. He sat behind a desk with a file folder opened before him. "Jim sit if you wish." He shook his head. He'd prefer to get it standing. "We love Medford very much, as you may imagine, and we'll do everything we can in every way for her. Her choice of friends is very important to us. What do you hope to do with your life? What would you like to be?"

"I think I have a gift with art—drawing. I'm not sure yet if I want to be an artist or an architect."

"And school?"

"After I graduate high school? It will have to be Community College for at least two years. I'll have to work my way through."

"I see. Now Jim, from what do you know of a young, grade school girl being molested in the class cloakroom . . .?"

Jim jerked his head rapidly, his brow lined. "Sir, I happened to be a member of that class but I wasn't involved with that nonsense in any way shape or form . . . "

"But you were questioned about the incident?"

Jim immediately knew he was talking about Keith, but what was the reason he was making him a party to it and saying it now? From what he saw on television court room scenes, to Jim he sounded as if he were addressing a jury looking for a conviction. Jim shook his head. "Sir, everyone was questioned about the incident. I had absolutely nothing to do with it. If you don't want to believe me, there's nothing I can do about that."

Mr. Soldi put up his hand. "Don't insult me. I know that. I read the report. I know what it says. But, lay down with a hound dog, one wakes up with fleas. You weren't hanging around with nice friends. Strong family values are important, too. I see your parents have been estranged for a good number of years, and you had a brother who died in a fire, was it? Do you see your mother?"

Jim's stomach muscles tightened, the anger made his eyes turn catatonic, which prevented him from glaring at the man. "Mr. Soldi, I would never let any harm come to Medford. We're better than just good friends. We respect each other. We like to be in each other's company. I want to be with her. I'm not asking her to spend time with my family or my friends. Ask me about me and I will answer you truthfully. I totally respect her in every way. I can assure you there is no need to be concerned about anything inappropriate going on between us now or in the future. There never will be. If you'll allow it, Medford and I will go to the movies in town, stop for a snack and I'll bring her right home. Or, if you wish, I'll come here. Either way is fine with me. She brings meaning into my life. We're special friends."

"Jim, based on what you just said we will recognize you as an honorable person."

"Thank you, sir."

"Good. Then, as an honorable person you will respect our wishes. There are two. Before you come to our home again you are to telephone and speak to either Mrs. Soldi or me. Is that clear? And will you abide by our wish?"

"Yes. As a reasonable request coming from two honorable people, this honorable person can do that."

"Good. Our second wish is that if you do not see Medford here, in our home, then you are not to have any contact with her in any other time, place, or manner. Is that clear?"

"Mr. Soldi, on the television they would say you are ambiguous. Either I'm honorable or I'm not. As an honorable man, I told you I totally respect Medford in every way. I can assure you there is no need to be concerned about anything inappropriate ever going on between us. There never will be. Either you believe this coming from an honorable person or you don't. And, if you don't you are a hypocrite."

"Mrs. Soldi will show you out."

11

As a senior, Jim felt the pressure of time. He had given much thought to timing. "T'was everything!" Shakespeare or someone said. He knew his father would be a raving bear anytime leading up to lunch. He didn't go for the beer until the mid-day break. Usually it was a sandwich, a called-in pizza, a wrap of some kind, or anything that was hot, fast, and filling. Also, it was a wonderful excuse to open an innocent mid-day brew or two. He had to really think of the best approach to his unapproachable father.

Jim eased himself onto the picnic bench. He wondered how his father could eat with the smell of the mechanic's soap on his hands. He slid the loose bottle cap between his hands. "Dad? I'd like to go to the Community College in the fall."

"Hey! You're a big boy! All graduated and educated. Go for it!"

"I was thinking about the tuition. It's more than a thousand dollars. I have to tell you, Dad. The time I had to quit the high school tennis team because you said I couldn't take the time from earning money, you know, mowing lawns? The high school phys ed teacher sent me to see the Williams College tennis director. He said if I spent a little more time on the court, I might have made it for a scholarship. He thought I was that good. It would have been for four years. It would have meant a scholarship at Williams College worth $25-grand a year. For all those hours I spent pushing a lawn mower could you help pay the tuition for community college?"

His father re-set his baseball cap, then stared right into his eyes. "Do you know how many lawns you'd have to do for twenty-five g's?" Jim was very much aware his father

52

missed the object lesson totally. It was deliberate, he knew. The bottle was good for another slug. "Do you have any idea how many generators or transmission jobs I'd have to do for that kind of money?"

"Dad, as usual, you glossed right over the point I was making. So, okay. I can deal with it. I'd pay you back after I graduated, Dad. I don't think I can do enough lawns all summer to pay you room and board and save up enough for tuition and books. Then, if I can't get a truck from you, I'd have to think about bus fare and the rest. It's a one-hour bus ride to Prattsville."

"Didn't school teach you anything? There's no free lunch! Not here, not anywhere! It's about time you got that through your thick skull. What have I been trying to teach you? What are you going to take up? Time and space!" He laughed raucously at his own joke.

"Art. I like to draw. You've never noticed my drawings. I won awards with my work. I think I could be a painter. A fine artist."

"Oh! For Christ's sakes! I'm sure not going to waste any money on you to do some faggy art."

"Illustrators make a good living, Dad. I'm creative that way."

"Look! I've got to get back to work. You're completely responsible for yourself. I tried to be a good father. I made sure you know how tough this life is. Nobody gives you something for nothing. It's a battle every inch of the way. You gotta be tough. I made sure you understood that. You can stand on your own two feet wherever you go. No son of Glenn Dorchester is going to be called a rollover. It's graduation time as far as I'm concerned. You can leave my house and go anyplace and do anything you want. Permission granted. You get yourself into trouble, forget my phone number, you get yourself out of whatever you got yourself into. Now stop breaking my balls. You want to stay here? Pay your way. You want to leave? You wear your own harness and pull your own wagon—just like I've had to do. Good luck!"

Jim knew what the old man was telling him. With only a moment's thought he was grateful for it. The revelation was like staring at the rising sun. Up to now, he was answerable to someone else. As of this moment, his life was his own. He could do with it as he wished. Totally and completely. He understood that fully. It came as a revelation. *I must do for myself.* He would not be dependent on anyone else. As they said, he would be master of his own fate. It was a little scary but exciting as well.

He slid his hand across the table toward the hand holding a mechanic's cloth. The fingernails had black half-moons. He patted the top of it, his voice thick with sarcasm. "You're a good, caring, and generous man, Dad. Thanks."

His father looked at him sideways, nodded. "Fathers and sons should have talks like this. You're right."

Jim watched him swivel off the bench. He belched walking into his cave-like shop.

School. Just another problem to solve.

12

Gabbie saw Jim slip into the dressing room.

She filled her arm with hangers of clothes. "I'm going to see if I like anything," she told her mother. "Would you hold my purse?"

She made her way to the back of the store. She glanced around casually to see if any of the salespeople were around. They all seemed busy. She slipped into the cubicle.

She found herself trembling. She dropped the clothes on the bench.

She turned. Jim caught her in his arms. Breathlessly they kissed, warm, wet, intense.

"I have a surprise for you. Look!" Gabbie pulled back her hair so he could see behind her ear. There was a tattoo.

"Wow! What is it? What does it mean?"

"They are Chinese characters. They say 'Jim Dorchester is my constant and only love for all of my life.' Do you have any idea of the rebellious joy and freedom I feel when I flaunt this before my parents? I feel so sorry for them."

"You do?"

"Yes, that they should deprive themselves of the delight of knowing you and sharing your almost saint-like goodness and good will. What fun the four of us could have together. I don't want to talk about them any more."

It was a while before she spoke. She put her finger to her lips. "I'm a genius. I'm glad I thought of meeting you here."

"I really missed you, prom or no prom. I couldn't go with you, so I wasn't interested."

"You should have gone. You only have one prom. It's okay."

"You? Did you have a good time?"

"You know I didn't, but I went. You know. . . la-di-da girl's school. Beautiful gown. Expensive corsage. Limousine. They must have rented the whole hotel. Nice guy, but I felt badly for him. He tried to feel me up. He showed me a bottle in his pocket and a condom in his wallet. All set. Then, he tried to shove his hand between my legs. You know? And my parents were worried about you."

Jim pulled her closer.

"I've been offered a full scholarship to Julliard."

Jim moved her back a bit. "Julliard! Julliard! The music school? Wow! God Bless you! Congratulations! You're famous already!"

"Ah! Shucks! It's nothing. It just said that I'm a good enough flute player to be trained by them at their expense."

"But that's in New York?"

"I could have chosen any college I wanted. This way, I'll have my own apartment in September. It's my Aunt Mary's, but I'll be alone. I'll be close. Then we can see each other, not like the school in Connecticut where there are no visitors."

"And this summer?"

"Mom was going to take me to Italy as a graduation present."

"Wow!"

"Shhhh! Then, I decided I wanted to attend the summer music school at Tanglewood. My father said he'd pull some strings to get me in. So, without them knowing, I auditioned. They liked what they heard, thought I had a lot of potential so I got in on my own. That's what I'll concentrate on this summer. What about you?"

"I'll use the $1,000 I won for the best painting in the high school art show, plus the $500.00 I was awarded by the Kiwaniis, and $200.00 from the First Great Farraday Saving bank to get started in the Community College as an art major. This summer I have to earn the bucks for the rest. Even with all that help, it seems too impossible now."

"You mean . . . "

"Dad won't pay. It's mowing lawns."

There was a rapping on the door. A voice called out, "Someone in here?"

"Yes! Thank you!" Gabbie said.

Jim pulled her close. "This is horrible. When do I see you?"

"Are you kidding? Mom has me in lockstep. I'm going with some friends—and Mom—to walk around Benedict Pond. The arbutus should be out. I'll call you from my girlfriend's house this afternoon." She kissed him. "Maybe I can slip away for a second."

"We've got to find time so I can do another pencil drawing of you. I love you, Gabbie."

"The poet asks, 'How do you love me?'"

He pulled her tight to his body and then eased her away from him. "And the poet, I read someplace, said, 'How do I love you? I love you like the sail loves the wind, the candle the flame, the flower the sun. And if that is not enough, I love you like the very breath of my being, the very essence of my soul.' Is that enough, Gabbie? There is more."

"Yes. Yes."

"If you do, how do you love me?"

There was a knock on the door. "Can I help with anything?"

"Yes!" Gabbie said. "Give me a sec!" She stripped clothes from hangers, opened the door a crack, and shoved the clothes through. She closed the door and locked it.

"Where were we? Ah! I can tell you how I love thee! I heard a very brilliant lad say, 'How do I love you? I love you like the sail loves the wind, the candle the flame, the flower the sun. And if that is not enough, I love you like the very breath of my being, the very essence of my soul.' Is that enough, Big J?"

She slipped her arms around him, and put her cheek against his chest.

"Oh! Gabbie! It's at times like this I feel like . . . I feel like silk is brushing against my body. It feels like a feather strokes up and down the length of me. The sensation gives me the feeling of floating on warm water, then, it washes over me, and touches me in delicate places. Is this like love?"

"I feel your breath on my cheek, and I want to make it my own. When we hold each other close like this it makes me know I am not complete without you. It tells me what it is to be a woman. There's a tightness in my chest, and I find I must breathe in short, shallow puffs. There is only you and me. Nothing else matters."

"I love you, Gabbie, I love you."

"And I love you, too, Big J. I love you like I've never loved anyone or anything before in my life."

"Oh! Gabbie! I want to feel what it's like to be that close to you. It's like I need you, or I'll ache in my whole body."

"You started to tell me the other day . . . "

Jim could not confess to Gabbie that she brought on almost uncontrollable urges to be close to her that it brought on a horrible aching-aching hurt in his balls. Even a freezing shower brought no relief. "I think I was trying to say I love you." Jim murmured as he put his cheek against her hair. "I like the way you smell. I could stay like this all day."

"Me, too." She looked up at him. He bent down. Their lips touched softly. Their lips parted. The moistness sparked newfound sensations throughout their bodies.

"Wow! That's like dynamite exploding in me!" Jim said.

"It makes bubbles in my brains!"

They found themselves in a hard, long kiss.

Jim squeezed her tightly. "Gabbie, when I kiss you it makes me feel so wonderful! It just fills me with excitement. I can't ever think of my life without you. I will love you forever. I know that as I know I'm holding you. I really believe if I didn't have you, I could will myself to die."

"I get the shivers when you speak like that, Big J. Our souls have already intermixed. They can never be taken apart and separated, no matter what."

There was a knock on the door.

"Oh! shit!" she said. She mouthed the words "my mother!" She put her hand up to her cheek. She whispered, "We're doomed!"

Jim nodded and wondered what would come of it and how soon.

The following afternoon Jim was mowing a client's lawn. A car stopped. A tall, heavy-set man wearing a ten-gallon hat and western boots approached him.

He cupped his mouth. "Hi! Jim Dorchester?"

Jim turned off the mower, and waited for him. "Yes."

"Your dad said I would find you somewhere along this street. What the hell did you do to get Angelo Soldi so mad at you?"

"News to me."

"Well, son, you sure pi-pi-pi-pissed him off. He's come after you with guns ablazin'"

"His daughter and I are friends. That's the only connection I know of."

"Maybe he wants you and his daughter unconnected." He pulled a folded sheet of paper out of his inside jacket pocket. "I'm a process server, and this is for you." He handed the paper to Jim. "Mr. Soldi says you're a stalker and I'm sorry, but I've got to serve you with a restraining order that says you're not to communicate in any way, shape, form, or manner with his daughter; as well as stay the hell away from his daughter, Medford Soldi. At least a hundred feet, anyway, and if you don't, you can go to jail. You got a relative in Timbukto you can stay with? Know a lawyer?"

"You mean besides Soldi!"

"Yup!" He handed him the paper. "Here y'a go! Read all about it. Ain't love grand?"

13

Gabbie and Jim were in St. Peter's Church. They were in the priest's middle section of the confessional. She sat facing Jim, her knees on either side of him on the bench where the priest usually sat. Her arms were around his neck. Their noses were almost touching. Gabbie had discovered its seclusion by accident. When she was home on break, now very protective, her mother escorted her whenever she went to town. If she wanted to see friends at night, they were invited to her home. Then one day, while shopping in town, her mother didn't raise an eyebrow when Gabbie told her she wanted a quiet moment to meditate and have a "deep moment," as her dad said in the serene atmosphere of the church. She was sincere, but while there, she realized it was a perfect place to meet Jim. Jim sent and received his emails at the library.

He clasped her around the waist.

When they broke the kiss, he snuggled against her neck.

"Uh-uh," she whispered. "Don't give me a hickey. We can only stay a minute."

"How I miss you, Gabbie. How I hate to have to see you like this. Christ, even Romeo and Juliet didn't have as much trouble as we have."

"They both died in the end. The worst that can happen is you end up in jail."

"Don't think I don't know that, and don't think you're father won't put me there!"

They heard the church's front door open. Then, leather heels clacked on the floor for a dozen or so steps. They stopped. Jim and Gabbie held their breaths. Gabbie started to snicker. Jim put his finger to his lips. They strained to listen.

"Jim," she buzzed into his ear. "I love you."

"Shhhh!" He whispered very softly, "This is no joke, Gabbie!"

With the anxiety of being caught, they made faces at each other in the dim light.

No more than five minutes later, the leather heels clacked out the door.

In that instant, they searched for each other. Their kisses were warm, wet, and long.

"We shouldn't stay too long," she said.

"Why?"

"They may lock us in!"

"How lucky can we get? I'm going to miss you so much," he said, "especially when I think of holding you like this."

"Me, too. The girls at school keep nothing back! They talk about everything and anything in the plainest of terms. They make me blush. They talk about men and erections, masturbating, and wet dreams. Have you ever had a wet dream?"

"An orgasm while I was sleeping? Yes."

"Well? How was it?"

"A surprise. And very messy. Changing pj's, you know . . . Do girls have wet dreams?"

"Not so far for me. You know, some of the girls say they're not virgins, but I think they're lying just to make themselves think they look 'big.' They say a girl shouldn't be a virgin when she goes to college or she won't be popular. They talk about intercourse, and how they do it and what happens. Just don't get knocked up, they say. Our phys ed teacher talks about sexually transmitted diseases. It makes it sound dirty, unclean. One girl says it hurts when she does it because her boyfriend is too big for her. You know, when we're alone like this, I want us to do it, too."

"Really? Do you think my hormones are retarded? Tell me about it."

"Well?" She scrunched her face.

"Should we do it?" She shrugged. "Gabbie, we're in love. We always will be; sure we should. When I kiss you I get all excited, I mean, really excited."

"I know. Me, too. Sometimes when I press against you, I feel you are hard. How that excites me! My nipples get hard. It makes me get warm. I get wet down there. My toes curl up. I can't help it."

"Me, too. Wow! I would like to. I want to."

"Really? Me, too. God! You know, if you were to touch me there. . . you know. . . I think . . . I think . . ."

"You'd come?"

"Yes."

"God! Hormones! Get thee behind us! I heard something like that in a play. They say once you start, it doesn't end until you do it, and then you've got to do it all the time. Then you get into pregnancy, sexually transmitted diseases, going to Hell, becoming a dope fiend, and you end up raping women! So . . . You know what that means?"

"No. What?"

"One of us has got to say 'no.'"

"But why? For god's sakes!"

"Because you might give me an STD."

"That's a dumb thing to say."

"Just fooling around. We have to say 'no'. . . because they say when that happens you lose your innocence. You know, it's between you and me, Gabbie. We're not going to miss out on anything. We can keep it special between us. Then, when it's okay for us to get that involved, we'll know it. And we'll have fun. No big deal. Okay? That's supposed to be something important. If it's important, it's also got to be special, and what we have between us right now, even without doing it, is special. I don't know if we lose the 'special' if we take that away from each other right now. I want to touch you bad."

"What if I did you?" she asked.

"Gabbie! Not in church! I remember a joke I read on the Internet. A mother was bathing her young son when he points to his genitals and asks, 'Mommie, is these be my brains?' And she answered, 'Not yet, son, not yet.' To me it means you can be a half-wit and have sex. That's not what I want for us."

"From what they say, you can't just do it a little bit. Bang! It just happens. Would you be afraid to do it with someone else?"

"No, I wouldn't be afraid, but I would never do that with anyone else except you, no matter how long we have to wait. And, you know what else? You're a virgin, and I'm a virgin. You and I are going to stop being virgins at the same moment. From all the guy talk that I hear in the locker room, we may have a lot of stumbling around to do to get the sex bit right, but that's going to be our fun. Oh! God! I want to know what it feels like to have you. Okay? That's just how I feel no matter how hard I may get."

"Jim, remember in eighth grade when we sort of broke up? I mean, we just stopped being pals with one another and we'd be with other friends? Well, I went with another boy then. He wasn't like you. He wouldn't ask if he could hold my hand or kiss me. He'd just do it. We'd kiss, but there was nothing to it. It didn't mean a thing. It just didn't do anything for me. So, I know I would never do anything we do with anyone else. Ever."

"I remember that time. I tried making out with Kitty Fischer. She wanted me to feel her boobs and do other stuff. She took my hand and put it right down there between her legs. She unzipped me and wanted to touch me. She really turned me off. But anyhow, it was just a big nothing. I didn't like it at all. I think the next time I saw you after that, I knew what it was all about. So, I can tell you this, Gabbie. The next time I have sex with you, it will be my first time ever."

"There goes my innocence. I'll have to match your qualifications, and I thought a resumé was so important."

The door was pulled open.

Jim saw Father Pasquale over Gabbie's shoulder.

Gabbie squirmed to stand up.

"As if this is the perfect place to commit a sin, my children. What have you to say to me before we talk to your parents?"

"Father, please don't. We're not doing anything wrong except trying to be together."

"What do you expect from me?" The priest stepped aside to let them out.

"Just let us leave," Jim said. "We're here because we can't see each other any place else. We care for each other in the nicest way any two people can. Please, Father. Just let us leave."

"No! I can't do that. I know her parents. I'm obligated."

"Father, we are innocent of anything more than our wish to be with one another. That is all. We will never meet here again. We did so because it was to us a refuge, not to desecrate it in any way. I ask you to be forgiving, and find forgiveness in your heart, as you teach us."

"Enough! Both of you come to the rectory! I will call your parents."

Jim looked at Gabbie. He took her hand and pulled her towards the door. "Father, God will forgive me. You go pray for your sins, including the ones you have yet to commit. Come on, Gabbie. I can't be found with you. I must leave. Your father is itching to send me to jail."

A week later Jim answered the phone.

"Jim? This is Virginia, Medford—Gabbie's friend. I just got a telephone call from her from Kennedy airport. She only had a second, but she wanted me to call you. Her father tried to have you arrested. He couldn't work it out. Anyway, Gabbie was on her way to Switzerland with her mother. She's going to be in school there for at least a year. She'll write when she can. She loves you. Okay?"

"Okay."

"Jim?"

"Yes."

"I'm sorry. It's a real misery. A year will go by fast. I love Gabbie, too. I feel the aches in your hearts. Come by the Garden Center if you want to talk."

14

Jim saw his father park his truck, get out and walk toward him.

Jim waved, shut off the mower, and walked to meet him."Hi! Dad! Sorry, I didn't see you come up."

"Glad to see you're still motivated," Glenn said.

"Are you all right, Dad? You're feeling okay?"

"Sure, I am. Why shouldn't I be?"

"Kind of unusual you coming to see me in the middle of the day. Guess it couldn't wait until I got home tonight. What's up?"

"I thought we should get things squared away before too much time got in between. You seem so busy I don't get to see you much."

"Thank you, Dad. That's nice of you. You don't have anything to square with me. I'm all okay with you. We're fine. I have to stay busy because I'm starting school in September."

"Yes, lately I see you hustling pretty good."

"As you say, it still takes a hundred cents to make a dollar, and I need a lot of dollars to cover everything."

"Matter of fact, that's exactly the reason I come to see you. I can use every cent I can get, too. I've got to replace tools, you know. Now, Jim, you owe me a good bit of money. You still owe me for room and board and for the truck."

"Gosh! Dad! I didn't think . . . "

"I don't care what you didn't think! You owe me and I want to get paid, if you don't mind."

"It's not that I mind, Dad. I'll pay you. I wouldn't cheat my father. I need a lot to pay for tuition, books, transportation. You know. I have to buy my own clothes."

"I'm not Santa Claus. Want to go to school to take up time and space? Then make more and better bucks!"

"There are only nine days in the week, not ten, Dad!"

"You say that to me! You see me breaking my balls till all hours of the night out there!"

"Yes."

"I told you make your paper route bigger!"

"Come on, Dad! I feel kind of stupid riding a bike. The college will put me on the custodial staff in exchange for classes next fall."

"And what are you going to live on? Love?"

"I don't know! McDonald's! I'll work at McDonald's."

"Aren't you ambitious! Some motivation. First, you have to pay me, then you can do what the hell you like with your money and time."

"Dad, it sounds like I can't pay you and school."

"Your school has got nothing to do with me. You owing me has to do with me."

Good Lord! Jim thought. Why is he doing this? "How much do you say I owe you?"

"How much do you have?"

"From the sound of it, whatever it is, I won't have enough."

"Still the same smart ass, I see. About two-thousand should cover it."

"What?"

"That includes room and board."

"I buy my own food!" Glenn glared at him. "I won't have anything for school!"

"Your problem. I expect to be paid."

"It's in a savings account. I can take time to get it tomorrow."

"Suppose you and me go get it right now, so you won't forget?"

"Dad! I wouldn't stiff you!"

"There's always a first time."

"You make it very tough for me, Dad."

"When the going gets tough, the tough get going."

Jim thought it was amazing that his father as well as Gabbie's father were working in a common cause: to send Jim out of town. He had heard the rumor that Angelo Soldi had an arrest warrant all made out in his name just waiting for a judge friend of his to sign it the moment Jim sneezed on Main Street. Jim carried the heartache of losing his kid brother needlessly in a fire, which Glenn could have prevented. Even so, Jim found it very difficult to show the man all his loyalty. Men were supposed to be taskmasters who showed how the world was to be received and returned. For all he knew, Glenn was right. Here he was about to embark on a path that could set him free, truly free.

What kind of a world could it be with no Gabbie? God! It's not like she died, or anything as horrendously horrible as that. He was up against it. He had to find a way to make her his. He used an axe to buck up cords of wood; he ran through the woods for hours; he glared at the night sky unable to go to sleep. His visage grew darker. He scoured every thought to find a way to make Gabbie his.

Then, where one father could not, two succeeded. One was his, the other was Gabbie's. They were the bow and the string that would send him on his mark to share his life with Gabbie. One said find a job, and the other said to get out of town. His father left the classified ads open on the table where he had just finished lunch as if destiny had made its move.

There was a glimmer of hope in the ad his finger pointed to in that newspaper.

The headline in bold letters read: ALASKAN PIPELINE.

The Alaskan pipeline needed contract workers for the new gas line they were putting in. Jim sensed that's where they really made the big bucks. He would work every freezing kickass second and stoke away dead Presidents on the face of U.S. American money. Keith came to mind. He wondered what he was up to? It would be fun to run up there with a buddy. He knew what that was all about.

Somehow he would have to make it all pay for Gabbie and him. It was a forced separation, and he taught himself how to make life's special lemonade.

15

CHARLY

Jim approached the doors of the Albany Office Building. He was about to grab the handle when she stepped toward him.

"You here for Alaska?"

Jim nodded.

"Can we talk over coffee?" She pointed to the café a few doors away.

Jim shrugged. "What's up?"

She didn't answer but led the way. She wore small diamond earrings, had close-cropped blonde hair, parted on the side, and wore a black leather cap. Thin, arched eyebrows sat over light blue eyes. Her nose was straight, her lips full. She had high cheekbones. Jim noticed she was tall with a thin body and a plump ass. She wore jeans, western boots, and a light blue snap-button western shirt. She had to be in her mid-twenties.

She used her hand with manicured nails to point to a booth where Jim sat while she ordered coffee.

At the table, she barely sat when she said, "You came for the ad?" Jim nodded. "I've a friend who works in the office. Number One: Our odds go up getting hired if we apply as a team." She looked Jim directly in the eye. "That's what I'm asking."

"I want the job."

"I mean a team, we're significant others, we're in the same room."

Jim tossed his head. "Okay."

"I need a partner. You need a partner. Will we do for each other?"

"How do we find that out?"

"The last couple of guys I approached thought it would be a great arrangement. They would drive half the time for the pipeline and for the other half they would hump me. It doesn't work that way. I'm serious. No hand jobs. No blow jobs. No nothing. Also, with a partner I don't have to fend off the wannafucks."

"No problem with that. Really. My heart is taken."

"If that's the truth, that's a big hurdle. I'm gay."

"If that's true then you won't come after me if you get a hard-on."

She laughed out loud, big mouthed, toothy. "You couldn't have said anything else to convince me to trust you. I'm cold that way. No libido. Sex is of absolutely no interest."

"Glad we got that out of the way."

"Have you ever driven an 18-wheeler?"

"My father has a garage. I can drive almost anything. You?"

"I have a New York license for a big rig. You?"

"No."

"You don't lie about it. That's what I was told. Your qualifications are the truth and enthusiasm. They need competence and reliability. They'll find you out with a couple questions. When they ask why you are applying, the answer should be something about doing something you really like to do, like driving, and making big bucks. You don't say you need the work. That's the lousiest reason to give you one. Okay?"

"Thanks for the heads up."

So? Why do you want to drive the big dumpers?"

Jim stared at her. "The money. I want to get married and go to school—art. You?"

"To buy a farm near here, Schenectady, and be left alone. If you're not in the crowd you've got to be rich to find tranquility. That's what I want. Not many apply for Alaska, but they gotta feel you're capable. I hope I don't let you down."

"Same here."

"I just met you, but you send a nice message. I trust you. I know I'm not making a mistake putting my trust in you. How do you feel?"

"I never met anyone who was gay. You're not half-bad. I trust you, too."

"Good. We watch each other's back, right? Absolutely, right?"

"Oh! I like your style. Absolutely right. Absolutely. We take care of each other."

"Good. Now we just have to get hired. You need to buy your own airline ticket. There'll be three weeks of training. I have to tell you, there won't be a helluva lot of playthings to do. I'm inclined to work nine days a week because I want to stash away all the bucks I can, but we have to take off one day if we're going to make it through the year. Will you commit for a year? I will." Jim nodded. "This may be our lucky day."

"I scratch your back . . . "

" . . . and we do our own laundry!" She held out her hand. "I can tell quick enough. Shall we do it?" Jim shook his head. "What else do you want to know? Oh! Yeah. They test."

"Drugs? No problem."

"You sure? I've only got one shot with one partner. I can't lose out because of you then show up with someone else. I'm making you my one partner. Be up front with the drugs."

"I do a few beers. You?"

"Drugs? Long gone for me. So? You have a problem?"

"None. I'm Jim Dorchester from Massachusetts."

"I'm   Charly—spelled   C-h-a-r-l-y--Dunham   from Vorhooseville."

"Isn't it spelled C-h-a-r-l-e-y, for a girl?"

"Right. Charlie for a guy, but Charly for me. Is it a go, pardner? What do you think?"

Jim looked hard into her eyes. *I'm supposed to be looking into the valley of my dreams. Charly could be the means to getting my grubstake. It's not what I see in her eyes as much as what I feel looking into them. At first I felt very lucky meeting up with her. The message I'm getting now is that this isn't going to be good.* "I don't know, Charly, I've got a premonition. Maybe we'd better think about it."

"Look, Jim. You're a nice guy. I don't know about you, but I don't have the time to fuck around. I need this job. If I don't hitch up with you, it'll be someone else. But, time's a-wasting."

"I know."

"Jim. We can do it. I'm willing. Give it a shot; that's all we can do."

They shook.

Charly reached into her back pocket. She brought out a folded paper. She opened it and slid it across the table to Jim. "We're heavy equipment operators. This is what we're supposed to do. The pay is almost $40.00 an hour, more if you do mechanic's work. Time and a half is there for the asking. Whatever they charge for expenses, you still bring home a heavy wallet. Here's the job description, but, just remember, they can ask you to do anything. Memorize it. Lie but just a little."

The sheet read: "...operates heavy equipment and other machinery in accordance with all safety regulations and procedures. Maintains and clears roads, airport runway and access roads, landfill areas, vehicle log, inspection forms, maintenance record and daily trip reports. Inspects vehicles and equipment prior to operations; completes shift inspection checklist; inspects and cleans equipment and facility; reports maintenance needs and deficiencies to supervisor. Loads and unloads aircraft with heavy equipment. Must be polite and courteous to the public. May be required to work a non-traditional work schedule to include evening, holidays and weekends and may be subject to 24 hour on-call status. Attend all required scheduled safety meetings. Performs other duties as assigned. Knowledge of traffic laws, ordinances and regulations involved in heavy equipment operation."

"Jim? To clinch it, when they take us on to go to Alaska, we should kiss. You know. Like lovey-dovey happy?"

"Sure. I'll pretend you're my sister."

"Shit no! Like put some emotion in it. It's just for this once. Here, lean over and kiss me."

They half rose and kissed. When Jim broke, Charly grabbed him by the collar. "Once more with feeling like we just got laid." They kissed again. "Son-of-a-bitch! That's almost enough to make me go straight!"

"Charly, just to confirm we really have been together, I caught your perfume. Tell me the name so it establishes us as long-time friends if they ask. I'm sure they'll notice it."

"You're smart. It's called 'Horsemanure'."

"There is one more question," Jim said. She squinted and tilted her head staring into his eyes. "Do you snore?"

Two months later, Jim pulled off his hat with earflaps as he led the way into their room. He hung his jacket on the coat rack then sat on the twin bed. He pulled off his white, air-filled insulated boots. He turned to watch Charly strip down.

"Have you no shame?" She shook her head. "I'm never going to get used to 16-hour days in all this cold," he said.

"I could sleep for a month," she said. "Tomorrow we sleep, eat, and do laundry." She threw her long johns into the basket. Her boobs were small, her patch blond, silky. She slipped into a robe then padded to the tiny kitchen area. She threw Jim a can of beer and opened one for herself.

"You promised me a haircut tomorrow."

"Only thing I can't grouse about is making almost seven hundred bucks today."

"That supervisor, Curtis, is it? He has a thing for you."

"How can you tell?"

"He looks at you and drools."

She laughed. "He's a cheap bastard. He deliberately spoke out loud so I could hear him complain the Indians charge too much for a blow job. I think he expects a sympathy fuck from me for throwing overtime our way."

"Hey! I owe you. How many times have I thanked you?"

"Not enough. That's why I get to shower first. Don't bother with the popcorn. I'll be asleep when you come out. And if they lower the heat in here, I'm getting into bed with you."

"Just snore so I don't get horny. Tell me again. Do you really think we'll come out of this with a hundred-grand?"

"I will for sure. For you, depends on what you leave with the Indian penis fly-traps." She smiled as she tip-toed into the bathroom.

Jim stretched for the pad of paper on which he had written almost a dozen letters to Gabbie. At first they were lengthy. Some nights he could manage only a paragraph. "God! I miss you, Gabbbie," he said aloud when he decided he would skip tonight. His eyes closed. He made himself stand up. He started to strip down. He shook his head as he once again spoke aloud, "God! Those trucks are enormous!"

16

Jim stopped the truck and put on the air brakes when he saw Lem Boswick, the manager, standing by his pickup waving him down.

"Leave the truck and come with me, Jim, we've got a problem," Lem said. He turned to Jim now seated beside him. "The son-of-a-bitch tried to burn the place down."

Who? What? Where? When? the questions skittered across Jim's mind.

Lem looked at Jim then turned away quickly. "It's Charly."

"She okay?"

"No."

"What's wrong? She need a doctor or something?"

"Too late for a doctor."

Jim inhaled deeply.

"Come to the office first, then I'll take you to the dispensary."

Lem pushed a tumbler half filled with whiskey toward him when they got to the office. "Go ahead."

Jim sat up and shook his head.

"Curtis sent you to refuel to get you out of the way. Then, he told Charly she was through for the day. He followed her. She put up a fight. He thought he knocked her out. He . . . you know . . . then realized she was dead. So, he set the place on fire to cover things up. He was seen going in and leaving. The police have him. We're ready to fly you and Charly to town so you know . . . the undertaker and all. Take what time you want, then let us know how we can accommodate you."

Jim blinked rapidly. "I'd like to see Charly."

"Best if you don't, Jim. It's the stuff of nightmares. Remember her as the pretty girl she was. I'll send you a check for both your wages. We'll pay for shipping the casket to your home."

"Mr. Boswick, make the check out for Charly's wages to her next of kin. I believe it's her mother and father. The remains will go to them, too, in Kinderhook, New York. I'll be in town until the undertaker completes all the paperwork for interstate transportation. I will personally see that Charly is taken home."

"Jim? Are you going to be all right?"

"As fine as Charly would want me to be."

Jim rode with Charly from Nome, Alaska, to Mukilteo, Washington. From there he kept her company in the baggage car across the country to Albany, New York; and from there in the hearse to the undertaker in her hometown.

He grabbed a cab to her parents' home. Her father, as rigid as a block of carved ice, spoke to him through the screen door.

"Why are you here?" were his first words when he confronted Jim.

Jim stammered for the first time in his life. "I'm here to pay my respects, Mr. Dunham."

"No need! She was a dyke, worth no more than a shoat!"

"I have a check made out to you for the wages she earned, almost $60,000."

His chin dropped a centimeter in acknowledgement. "Have it here!" he commanded slipping open the screen door almost an inch.

A woman sidled up behind him but remained in the shadows. "Sixty-thousand dollars . . .! "

"The funeral home is waiting to make arrangements . . ." Jim started.

"Pay no never mind to us. Do what you like. Potter's field is fine with us."

"There are expenses . . ."

"Your cab is waiting." The screen door was locked.

"I'm sorry and my condolences . . ."

The inner door was shut firmly.

75

He looked down at his shoe tips. *I've enough in me for you, too, Charly.*

Jim stood alone by the huge bronze casket as a light rain sprinkled his skin. He gulped hard. The cannon ball stayed stuck in his throat. He stared at the single white rose in his hand. He envisioned Charly who was almost in the nude teasing him after they had been together for two months.

"You don't have a hard-on, but I can see you have a hard-on for me."

"I do."

"Thanks, but you wouldn't accommodate me if I begged."

"That's right, and I do love you."

"I know you do. I love you, too. But you won't touch me."

"No."

"Your answer to this miserable world? You love 'em all, the whole fucking world. "

"Yes."

"Way to go, Jim. Love until you break your heart."

Jim brought the flower to his nose. He inhaled deeply every sweet memory he ever had of Charly. He leaned over and placed it on the casket. The earth swallowed it up. He knew it gave Charly the tranquility she yearned. He stopped breathing. In the grotto of his chest he saw spotlighted a bud vase holding a stem that had a perfectly formed leathery leaf and the purest white rose. It radiated and emanated the fragrance of her perfume, which filled his very being. He smiled: Horsemanure.

No one else in the world will know, only you Jim, you sure did a lousy fucking job watching Charly's back. You let her down. You fucking let her down! Just like you let down your kid brother and let him burn to death. You broke your promise. Don't you ever in all your fucking life ever, ever, ever again break your fucking promise! Promise me, if you do, you'll kill yourself first!

17

Six months after Jim left for Alaska, he found himself back living with Glenn at home with as much of a song in his heart as he could have considering what happened to Charly.

He returned from Alaska with more than $55,000.00 in the bank even after the cost of the funeral. It was enough for art school as well as private lessons. There was even enough to marry Gabbie! All he had to do up there was grab a low grade, low responsibility job and take care of himself. He slept the dream of angels, and every one of them was Gabbie. Then, to top it off, less than two weeks later, Virginia from the Garden Center telephoned him. Gabbie was home. Evidently, she had convinced her folks it was vitally important she attend music school at Tanglewood that summer. It caused an excitement he could not contain. He sang at the top of his voice in the shower. He "Whaaaa-hoooe'd!" wherever he was in the empty house. He knew most of the lyrics and constantly sang, "Happy trails to you . . ."

He was so excited by events he couldn't sleep. He was back less than a week. He decided the next morning he would get up with sunrise.

Jim wrinkled his nose when he tasted the cowboy coffee he made for himself. It was brewed just as it was in the black and white cowboy movies he remembered. A handful of fresh coffee went into a pot of water where it met yesterday's grounds, and that was it. Sugar might have made it better if he had some, and cream would have been a bonanza. It was bitter, deep walnut, and rust flavored, but grounds and all he swallowed it anyway. "Until we meet again . . . " he barely sang. "Nope, doesn't make it

77

taste any better," he said out loud. In the old days he would have just returned from delivering the newspapers. Was that ever a crazy, wheel-spinning world. He felt just like the gray-lit dawn that was struggling to become day. It was not a chore to pick up the cup as before. It was a sign. He closed his eyes and took another sip. He had revival in mind.

He looked up when a chair was scraped back from the table. He saw an amorphous figure emanate from grey haze. Straight black hair strung down the sides of her thin face to bulbous tits. She plotzed on the chair. He knew she didn't see him. Eyes agape. Jaw hanging open. He watched her sit sideways across from him at the table, cross her legs, light a cigarette, blow out the match with a stream of smoke, then take another hard, deep drag making a half-inch ash. The end of the butt flashed like a channel marker, limning her face. It was worn, tired, wrinkled like linen. She looked up, and finally took him in. He glanced at his cup.

"Whassa matter? Never seen a bare-assed lady before?"

Jim scraped his chair back signaling a fast escape. He had plenty of practice dashing from Indian whores who charged $200.00 for their ersatz view of Paradise.

"The fuck's going on," his father said pulling on his shorts.

"I think you oughta go watch television," she said, "I just found what could be live action. Seems the more beer you put down, the less you can get it up . . . "

Jim's father grabbed her by the hair and twirled her out of her seat, onto her feet, and propelled her—cigarette waving like a beacon—toward the bedroom. He turned to Jim, his face twisted, making himself look like a knarly tree knot, "Father and son don't fuck the same cunt. Never ever. Law of the universe! Got it?"

Jim nodded. He made himself as small as he could, escape in mind.

"She's not the first! She won't be the last! Okay?" Glenn said to Jim.

"Okay."

"And you never mention this again! Okay?"

"Okay."

"Don't smart ass me! Life's fuckin' tough, see? You're the one that made your mother leave me, and I'll always hold you responsible! You'll always owe me! Get it?"

"Yes." Jim learned that not to answer brought on fury, and worse, when Glenn cussed and was drinking he was borderline volcanic eruptus.

He looked for a brew in the fridge. He tried to slam the door shut.

"I brought you home a six-pack. It's on the bottom shelf."

"You're a smart ass, see? I'd like some privacy in my life, and you're back here haunting me!" He opened the fridge, searched the bottom shelf. He snapped the can open in Jim's face. "Pay me in advance for your rent. I'm not Santa Claus."

Jim stared into his father's fish eyes. The challenge was to foment a little heat in them. No question, he had too much time to think up there. There were a couple of good questions that played and replayed in his mind. He was too young, too deferential, too nice a person to clear them when he was younger. It might give the old man some pain to bring up the subjects. It might hurt his feelings. And then Jim realized he was watching the Aurora Borealis with his eyes closed. He knew it was out there. Whose feelings were really being hurt? To whom was he being kind? Time to put the world in balance.

"You have to pay to get it so why don't I cut the middleman and just give the money right to her?" His head made the slightest nod toward the doorway.

His father stopped in mid-swig. He gulped down what he had in his mouth. In a single move he lifted the can from his mouth and sent it in an arc over Jim's head, beer streaming from it as it floated towards the wastebasket. It missed. Instead it clattered and rattled in the sink. He stood. He leaned over toward Jim and whispered, "You stupid bastard. Bite the hand that feeds you? Tonight? When I come home? You are gone. Moved out."

"Yes. You fed me. You fed me a lot of bullshit. For all the time I was a kid, you should have taken care of me! You were supposed to show me what it was to be a boy, a son. You used me to feed your ignorant, selfish greed. You never gave me a chance to understand if there was anything good in the world. I hated it, and I hated every person in it! I saw everyone else be hard and cruel to everyone else. Just like you. People are mean! They're not nice. They're all hard edges and sharp corners. Life isn't tough! The people in it stink! They don't give a shit about anyone or anything except themselves until they've got everything their fantasy made them think they deserved. Only grandmothers and grandfathers show the pure love because they've got a surplus for not using a drop of it earlier!"

"I see you had to go away to grow stupid! I tried to toughen your skin! And you're the better person for it! Look at you wearing a grown-up diploma so you can cuss your old man!"

"You beat the shit out of me only for one reason. Because you could! Because I was available. You carried such hate in your heart because you couldn't show a drop of kindness to the woman you loved. She told you to go fuck yourself! You made her go to work two crummy jobs a week when all she wanted was to take care of her boys, her family. She took us to church Sunday morning, made a big dinner, and after she cleaned up the kitchen, spent the rest of the day doing laundry, cleaning the rest of the house, and can you believe, *shopping*, while you sat on your ass drinking beer and watching some stupid car race! What kind of sickness drove you to do that to someone you were supposed to love? Did you think you were some great Pasha? When she left your marriage was long over. It was a dead twig dropping from a tree. Now you can tell me why you didn't get someone to take care of us? It wasn't my job to take care of Tommy. I wasn't sure of what the hell to do to take care of myself!"

"You were smart! You were a big boy! It was your job!"

"You were a cheap fuck, Dad! You didn't want to spend a nickel! What would it have cost to have a high school kid stay with us after school? Couldn't you have spared a couple bucks from her salary just to make sure her kids were safe and stayed out of trouble?"

"It was your job to look out for your kid brother! I was working! You knew where to find me!"

"I knew where to find you, but Tommy had no way to find you when the house burned down on his head!"

"He was playing with matches! He was your responsibility! You should have watched out for him! You should have taken better care of your kid brother! He would be alive today if you did!"

"I was in school! Tommy should have been in school. As usual, you were so involved in grubbing for money you forgot to take him that day! He was left home alone! You just plain forgot him! What a stinking reason for a good kid to die!"

"He should have come to the garage and got me!"

"He should have been playing baseball, but you wouldn't buy him a glove! Did you explain that to his mother? Was she understanding and sympathetic to you and your behavior? I guess she wasn't. She told you to go fuck yourself. The trouble is she walked--raced away from you too late. You killed her heart so bad she wouldn't even take me!"

"What are you saying?"

"Don't play innocent! The night you had too much to drink and the first time you tried to slap her around? She broke your wrist with the cast iron frying pan and warned you were never to try that again. Then you both got into a Hallelujah! brawl."

"Jim . . . For God's sakes! Why did you hang around?"

"Glenn, you may not know how to be a father, but I know I am a son. All your beatings couldn't take that way. Your miserliness is an expensive illness."

"Get on out of here! And don't come back! I'll take your rent first!"

"Sorry, Glenn, if it was your dream all these years to be a lonely, bitter old man to stew in your misery, and poison yourself with your own spit, congratulations! You are a winner!"

18

The expanse of lawn sloped from the Tanglewood Shed toward the wide, tall bordering hedge. Jim knew the kids slipped unseen into the grounds by the tunnel it held. Just above that in the far distance was Stockbridge Bowl. Sailboats and powerboats left their wakes to scar the smooth water. Away from the shade of the trees, Gabbie spread the blanket in the sunlight. When she kneeled on it, Jim followed and urged her to lie down beside him.

"Gabbie, do you know when I was in Alaska we were apart a whole lifetime? Did I tell you enough how much I missed you?"

"Shhhhh! Sweetheart! We are one. We touch. We kiss. . . "

". . . we love."

"Yes. Did you notice the man taking photographs up the hill?"

"Of us? Would your father do that?"

"We'll find out soon enough, won't we, when the judge looks at them in the courtroom."

"I've got to find a place to live."

He kissed her urgently, needing her closeness and comfort.

"Sweetheart, what are you thinking?"

Their legs and arms and bodies intertwined motionless for a long moment.

He put his head in the hollow of her shoulder. "How about we stay just like this for the rest of our lives?"

She brushed his forehead, and smoothed his hair. "Did you remember to bring the servants, and the bell to call them to bring our lunch?"

"Gabbie? What do you call it when you talk to yourself and tell yourself things, like a warning?"

"That's called premonition. It's like a telegram you send yourself about something that's going to happen, or that you should do, or a warning. I mean, I think it can be for good and for bad things. I'm not sure. Why?"

"Premonition. I remember. I like that word. Yeah. I send myself telegrams. Sometimes they come true, and sometimes not. Like, I had a premonition about Mr. Smoke. The worst one I had was about Charly. I had one about my father. I see him with a bad sickness."

"Have any about me?"

"You bet. I keep saying to myself to grab onto you and hold on for dear life! Now I wish I knew what to do now that I'm homeless."

"You have no relatives you can stay with?"

"No."

"Friends?"

"I had no time to make friends . . except you. I'm new in town. I'm always working. No friends. Except Keith. Who knows where he is."

Gabbie sat up. "But I have friends! Virginia! I've known her from school almost as long as I've known you! Her father left her the garden center at the south end of town. I bet she comes up with something."

"Yes. I got your telephone messages through her. How could she solve this problem?"

"I don't know. Maybe she'll let you sleep in the barn. At least it won't be under a bridge or in a tent!"

"And you're not concerned I'll fall madly in love with Virginia?"

"Oh! Go ahead, if you want to. She's as sexy a creature you'll ever meet. Her significant other is Ashley. She knows who you are. Give it a shot."

"Isn't it awful to say? I don't have another option."

"I'll come over late this afternoon. Okay? Maybe then you can tell me about riding with my teacher and me to Boston Sunday. I've got a gig—that's what the musicians call it—I've got a gig playing Tango jazz at this club close to Harvard Square. My teacher says I'm ready for it."

"See you then."

"Yes. I've got a class in ten minutes, and I'll be in rehearsal with the orchestra."

Jim rolled over and sat up. He looked at the Bowl, the water now a sun-reflecting blue sheet. He had only known turmoil all his life. It was in his passion for Gabbie, and the moments with her did he understand serenity . . . almost. He was aware of the undercurrent of unease that came because of her parents. It took difficult work to come to an understanding of what that was all about. He did it by pretending Gabbie was his daughter. He would want the very best for her. He would not want her to lower herself to the level of someone who mowed lawns. Of course their love was more important than that, but could her parents, snobs that they were, put that before their own love of her? He knew they would throw themselves in front of a bus for her, and so would he. Draw. He decided it was Gabbie's life. She could speak for herself. She would make her own decision. One thing he could change, he decided, was not to be a mower of lawns. He could be a doctor, lawyer, Indian chief. He would go away and return eminently successful. He would make heads turn. He would get invitations to the homes of the upper echelon. He would try being a snob and see how he liked it from the other side. He didn't know how at the moment. All he knew was, if he didn't, he'd lose everything.

Gabbie sat up and swung around until she was facing him. She put her arms around him. He put his arms around her. Together they remained clamped in their thrall.

A photograph taken at that moment would be entitled "The Kiss." Gabbie wondered what kind of a photographer had just snapped their picture.

Jim looked around. The photographer was gone.

19

Jim finally spotted Virginia in the expanse of the greenhouse. Totally absorbed, she transferred seedlings to pots. He called out to her so she wouldn't be startled. She turned to him, broke out in a wide, toothy grin and waved to her.

"You're Jim Dorchester, Medford's guy. We know each other on the phone. How nice to put that gorgeous body to a radio voice. You have a problem I hear."

"Yes. I need a hiding place."

"Gimme a sec."

Jim watched her work mechanically but carefully. "You're so careful," he said.

"They're living things with a better promise of the future than we have." She was Medford's age. She wore a baseball cap with the visor close-cupped over her eyes. Her auburn hair, held by a rubber band was poked through the hole in the cap, matched her light brown eyes. Her face was oval with high cheek bones and full lips free of lipstick. She wore what seemed to be a perpetual smile. She had on a tight, filled-out tee shirt, jeans, and work boots. She finished filling in the flat, moved it to one side, brushed her hands on her hips, and turned to him. She went up on her toes and kissed him on the cheek.

"Welcome to our refuge. You know enough to stay hidden from Angelo Soldi? Medford called me from her cell phone. If you want, you can sleep in the barn that's just behind this greenhouse. It has a small room with a cot, john, and sink with outside shower. Whenever you want to do your laundry, come over to the house. The same for meals. I live with Ashley, a tall drink of water I love with all my heart. You'll meet her. We're open seven days a week so we can stay afloat. Chip in whatever you are able, and lend a hand if you've got the time and you're not too pooped. Just one rule here: no smoking anything, anyplace, anytime. If you're a boozer or into drugs, find another place. How's that?"

"I have one thing to say."

"What's that?"

"Will you marry me?"

They both burst out into laughter, which trailed them as she led him to his new domicile.

20

That Sunday, Jim was picked up by Gabbie and her music teacher, Hianni Guitar Sanchez.

They were going to the Sounding Board Club in Cambridge, which was a few miles out of Boston, a two hour trip. It was the teacher's car and he was driving. He was stocky, dark-skinned, with long, straight jet-black hair.

Jim and Gabbie rode in the back seat. They sat close to each other and held hands. The three of them made small talk until they reached Springfield. Then, Gabbie talked continuously.

She had become enamored with the new South American musician, Astor Piazzolla. He died only a short time ago. His group focused only on the tango. He had played the bandoneon, an accordian with buttons on both sides. The music was fiery and exciting, and in demand wherever interstellar musicians met. Gabbie studied every moment she was able. Not once did she neglect her classical studies, but the man's music had captivated her soul.

"My teacher, Juan Sanchez, a-k-a Hianni Guitar , introduced me to Piazzolla," she said.

"Ho! She's a natural!" Hianni Guitar said. "I didn't hear her play two bars I knew I had a genius on my hands! Hot chilis! Could she play! She does the classical stuff like she invented it, but does she do something to the tango! I brought her some sheet music and a CD, and she owned it. You'll see at the club. Not lucky to have a flute player there yet, just bandoneon, guitar, and stampado. Gabbie's flute, now makes it hot extreme! You'll hear."

"I'm already excited," Jim said. "How about you, Gabbie?"

"For me, you know, the music really caught me. Jim, you have my soul, but this music! Ah! What can I tell you? I feel so Latin. It came to me so quickly. Hianni Guitar says I must be a witch to capture the essence in so short a time."

"Are you lost to it?"

"As in kidnapped? No. It's music. Music, like you, fills my soul."

"I'm jealous."

"No need. If I had to choose between you and music? You would be my symphony orchestra!"

"What happens," Hianni Guitar started, "it's all very informal. The impresario runs the show. When it's your time to perform, he calls you up to the stage. You play one number. How you do says if you play another or not."

Hianni Guitar led the way into the club and to an open table close to mid-center. It was dimly lit with twenty or so patrons. Most were drinking beer at little square tables. They faced a platform bathed in light that barely had room for two musicians. The bartender was a huge-bosomed, dark-haired. No one sat at the bar. Hianni Guitar brought back Pepsies. He shrugged. "I'm driving."

He continued, "Another guitar, a bass, and me will warm up the place with a couple numbers. The impresario will go up and try to get some money out of the crowd. Because this is your first time, you will play the piece I gave you called 'Oblivion.' It has bandoneon, me on guitar, and bass. He wants you with other pieces to see what you can do, and to cover in case you are . . . not so *marcato*, you know what it means? You are not touched with the gift. If he thinks you are, he will introduce you to stay to play your solo flute pieces, the six tangos-etudes I gave you. Good luck!"

Jim heard the tribal, thumping beat of the tango stir his insides. Gabbie at first played with reticence. With urgings from Hianni Guitar , Jim could see and hear her loosening up and getting with the pumping beat. Then, it seemed all the practice and the feelings inside took over. The audience, in a body, responded with her call. They sat up, became attentive, focused their eyes on her, and took her in. With the final notes of the piece, they responded with a *stampadoes* of both hands and feet. The sound of the flute interwove with that of the bandoneon and the guitars that heated their passions to near boiling. There was no containing their reaction.

It overwhelmed Gabbie. Her mouth was stretched in a toothy grin. She bowed and bowed again. She put her hand to the side of her face. She seemed to mouth the words, "Thank you! Thank you!" Then, the embarrassment began to show when the other musicians stepped off the stage and left her there alone. She covered her face with her hands and flute, and stepped from the stage.

The impresario instantly took her place. Short, mustachioed, open-collared shirt, baggy suit, he held up his hand and nodding all the while said, "It's about time we had such an interpretation of Astore's work!" The audience replied with more stamping and whistles. "How fortunate can we be? Medford Soldi and her God-given gift returns with her solo flute and Six Tangos-Etudes . . . Medford? I didn't ask, but you will play for us?"

When they started the return trip on the Massachusetts Turnpike to Great Farraday, Jim and Hianni Guitar agreed that Gabbie was riding at least eight inches higher than the seat. Jim could not stop gushing with pride and surprise. "The impresario said you have a God-given gift, Gabbie! He said you had a God-given gift! I knew that all the time, I just didn't know what to call it. Every single time we'd go off someplace to be alone, and you would play for me, I knew it was magic. I knew there was something special in you beyond my feelings for you. And to think this gift in you has been in part entrusted to me, too! Remember when you'd play the scales, faster and faster, and I would tell you when the beat changed that fraction of a second? And you would play it over and over until you had it perfect? I had no idea of the wonder of you. A God-given gift, of course that's what you have, Gabbie. A God-given gift. I pray you are able to use it to bring pleasure to the rest of the world forever! Nothing should ever stop you."

No one saw it coming. The car about to pass them crashed sideways into them. It hurtled their car over the breakdown lane, over the mowed strip, rolling them over once into the depression. The airbags deployed. Gabbie screamed. Even though she was held by the seat belt, she slammed into Jim, then fell silent. Jim crashed into the door and struck his head.

In the emergency room, Medford squeezed Jim's hand as she lay on the gurney. "Jim, I don't want my folks to learn of this accident from the police or on the news. Would you call them?"

"Gabbie! How can I do that? The way your folks think of me . . . "

"Jim, you know it's universal. No one is good enough for Daddy's Little Girl. Mr. Sanchez can't call. It falls on you."

"I'll get you a phone. You've got time before they take you to x-rays."

"Jim do you love me? Do I love you? My parents love me, too. They must be told and I want them told as soon as possible. What else must I say?"

"Mr. Soldi, this is Jim Dorchester. Medford is all right. We were in an accident coming back from Boston. A car passing us blew a tire. We are in the Springfield hospital. They're sure Medford is all fine, but they want to do some X-rays and make double sure she's okay to leave. Mr. Sanchez the teacher also is fine. They need transportation home. Either send someone to pick them up, or come yourself. Gabbie asked me to call you. I'm doing so against my better judgment. I'm very sorry this happened."

"Sorry! You son-of-a-bitch! I warned you to stay away from my daughter! I'm going to see that you're put in the slammer where you belong!"

"Mr. Soldi, with all due respect, is that really important now? Do you want the telephone number and name of the doctor treating Medford?"

"I want you to stay the hell away from Medford!"

"I'm sorry you feel that way, Mr. Soldi. Medford has reached her majority, and she can decide for herself who she does and does not want to see."

Mr. Soldi hung up.

When Jim was once again assured Gabbie was fine, he waited a while then left early enough to make sure he didn't run into his nemesis and hitch-hiked home.

21

A week later, Jim strolled down the center aisle of the Music Shed at Tanglewood. He spotted a seat on the left about fifteen rows from the front. Gabbie told him it would be about the best area to sit if he wanted to get a good view of her, as the soloist. He cared so hard that she perform brilliantly he shivered with anxiety. It was what she wanted. It was what he wanted.

He hunkered down. He tried to make himself invisible. Gabbie told him she knew her mother would be there. She wasn't sure about her father. Jim wondered what he would say if he encountered them. He knew it was a real possibility. They could be sitting somewhere close.

The Shed was about a third full then, with seats filling rapidly. From what Gabbie told him, the audience would be made up of parents, relatives and friends of the members of the student orchestra. This was a mid-summer performance. Gabbie could hardly speak, she was so filled with excitement when she tried to give him the news. She had so impressed her teachers and everyone at Tanglewood that she was given a solo with the full student orchestra.

Members of the orchestra were drifting in, checking their music, stands and seats, and chatting with one another.

Jim checked the program, a single photocopied sheet. He nodded and blinked at the third selection: Mozart: Rondeau (from Flute Concerto No. 2 in D. K314). Soloist – Medford Soldi.

"Hey!" Jim exclaimed. He whistled softly. He looked all around. "Now ain't that something! That's my Medford!" he said to no one in particular. He filled with pride. She was going to knock them all into Kinarsi, he thought.

Seats around him filled, and the orchestra started tuning up. He moved over a seat so he could see Gabbie clearly. All the musicians were dressed in white blouses or shirts. The women wore long, black skirts. To Jim, it was amazing how sixty or seventy people—and amateurs at that—were able to start, play, and stop so perfectly in unison. Not a too long held note or an off-key sound, and the piece so beautifully sounding. Amazing, just amazing, he thought.

Jim felt nervous. Did he dare look around to see if he had been spotted by Gabbie's mother or father?

He went back to the first time he had heard Gabbie play this piece. It was a warm summer's day and they decided to walk up Monument Mountain. They cut off the trail and headed for a clearing they had gone to earlier on picnics. The grass was high and smelled sweet. He threw down his jacket for Gabbie to sit on. He flopped flat on his back, his arms under his head, his eyes blinking back the sun dappling through the leaves. With her first notes, he closed his eyes and felt an engaging serenity with a unity to Gabbie, her music, the sunshine, the day, the universe. This must be the magic that Man has sought through the centuries, he thought. There had to be syncopation in the harmony between two human beings that transcended time and space, he reasoned, and this was it. He could feel the vibrations of the music fluttering through his chest, his viscera, his emotional coffers. It would not surprise him, he thought, if he were to open his eyes at this very moment, that he would find Gabbie and he surrounded by every variety of Nature's beings that had been captivated by the magic of her flute. It mesmerized him.

This was the essence of life's experience. He nearly burst into tears knowing how fleeting the moment would be. He merely clamped his eyes tighter shut and listened to her music with all the intensity he could muster. He prayed he could gather enough power to forestall forever the end of the piece. He could not. The composer, in his genius, had already written in the closing coda.

Jim had the same feeling every time Gabbie played just for him no matter where they where: in the forest, on a park bench, on the benches at the football field, in front of the library, at the Old Maid's Swimming Hole when everyone around gathered close by to listen.

Jim felt a tap at his shoulder. When he turned, the woman next to him pointed to the heavy-set man in the aisle. Jim looked up at him. He motioned for him to come out. Jim looked around and wondered the reason. The moment he stepped into the aisle, a second massive man moved up behind him.

"You're wanted in the office," the first man said. "Would you come with us?"

"What's this about?" Jim asked.

The man shrugged.

He led Jim out of the shed, then around to the back of the offices. He was brought into an office and told to sit.

"I'd like to know why I'm here?" Jim asked.

"The police department told us there was a restraining order against you as a stalker and that it was possible you would disrupt proceeding at this performance. When it's over and everyone has left, we'll let you leave, or we may have to call the police. Up to you."

"Okay. Look. My friend is going to perform solo. Just let me watch her. It's such an important event. God! Don't keep me from seeing her! Put me in a straight jacket if you want, but let me watch her performance! Please!"

"Orders are we can't let you leave the office."

"Look! I just want to hear her!"

The man nodded sympathetically. He turned on a switch. Through a speaker, applause came through. He pointed to the program in Jim's hand at the first number and nodded. Jim shook his head. The thought that came to mind was: People! All hard edges and sharp corners.

The number ended, and the applause died down.

Jim pictured Gabbie with her flute getting up from her section and walking to stage center to stand next to the podium. He knew her mannerism was to brush back her ponytail then take a deep breath. He wondered if she would look out over the audience searching for him.

With her first notes Jim inhaled deeply. He swelled with pride. *That's my girl playing.*

At the end of Gabbie's solo performance, Jim was not prepared for the explosive approval of the audience. The

94

applause and whistles were drowned out by the "Bravos!" and "Encores!" that filled the auditorium. He knew Gabbie was taking her bows, shaking hands with the conductor, then the first violinist. She would take more bows. Then, she would walk off the stage.

No matter how hard he tried, Jim could not hold back the disappointment. How could anyone hate someone so much they would deprive anyone of such a beautiful moment? This world was terribly, terribly wrong, first because it and its hard edged and sharp-cornered people undoubtedly were made by some rank amateur god.

He buried his face in his hands, determined to keep the sobs from his jailers.

Hate was so foreign to him. What troubled him more-- right to his core--was how such acrimonious, morbid, rummage could be directed precisely and exactly against him?

22

Jim held Gabbie's hand tightly as they crossed Fifth Avenue with the light.

"Gosh! Your folks couldn't get you out of Great Farraday and away from me fast enough could they."

"Don't be that way, Jim. In a way it's a good thing. I'm in for early enrollment in Julliard, and I've already started with a private instructor. Sometimes it's the other side of the coin that's the operative side."

"I suppose. You know?" Jim said, "This is exciting! I mean walking in New York. The people, the traffic, the honking, the buildings, the showing, the doings, the wonder of everything. The intensity! It's in the air. It's in everything we do. Everything we see. We're constantly in a crowd of people and I find it amazing there is so little contact! It's not like Great Farraday where we could run into your parents. Where we going?"

"Where did you park?"

"Virginia let me borrow the pick-up. I'm near the bridge. What is it? The Williamsburg? Took a long bus ride to get to your building. I have to get back in time to do the papers. Will you be home for Thanksgiving?"

"Yes. My folks have hired an armored truck to drive me around."

"I believe it."

"Can we talk about something else?"

"How's school?"

She pursed her lips, squinted at him. "Take my word for it. It's a toot." They both laughed. "Here we go."

Jim stopped. He followed the expanse of steps. His eyes went up and up and up. "It's magnificent! This is St. Patrick's Cathedral?"

She nodded. "Let's go in."

He followed her like she was his seeing-eye dog. He took in every line and curve of the vaulting expanse. He focused on the alter. "Omigosh! That's the real McCoy? History has been made here? If I become an architect, I'd like to design buildings like this."

She eased into a pew, crossed herself, and bowed her head in prayer.

When she looked up, Jim motioned for her to move over. He sat. "Even an atheist sitting in here would have to believe in God."

"I prayed for you, Jim. Only for you. I prayed and asked the Virgin Mary to keep you safe always."

"How'd you like to get married in here?"

"I just like the idea of getting married."

Gabbie bumped him to make him get up. He followed her out. They continued up Fifth. Gabbie stopped, tossed her head toward the doorway before them. Gabbie looped her hand in a big "follow me" wave, and walked through the doors of Cartier's.

Jim couldn't believe the amount of diamond jewelry in the display cases. The sheer volume made him think of the weekend glassware special at the local supermarket. He acknowledged to himself that he was in as much awe as he would be looking at a cageful of three-headed snakes. He had the uneasy feeling of being closely watched. He'd have to be real stupid to think of stealing anything.

Gabbie, with a nod of her head, and a hand signal, called him over to her. Once by her side, she pointed to diamond rings on display.

Their actions were already registered by the salesperson standing nearby. He was used to women unzipping their hearts before his entablature, and he could read them all. "Which one?"

Gabbie stared up into his eyes. He was actually talking to her. She looked down. She tapped her French polished fingernail on the glass.

"Excellent choice," the salesperson said. Without further direction he took out a pear-shaped diamond ring. He put it before her on a black velvet pad.

She caught her breath. "It's . . . it's gorgeous," Gabbie finally said.

"It's magnificent," Jim said. "Truly, truly something that could make someone stop breathing."

Gabbie looked at him. "What do you mean?"

"I mean, I'd have a heart attack trying to do enough lawns to buy that," Jim said.

The salesperson worked hard to be professional, but a wry smile barely crossed his face at the familiar scenario. "Why don't you try it on?"

Jim glanced up at him. He was having fun, he decided.

Gabbie locked into his eyes. Her eyebrows went up.

"Your left hand would be more appropriate for an engagement ring," the salesperson said.

Gabbie looked down to see her right hand partially raised. She gave him her left hand. He held it lightly with one hand, and with the other, easily slipped the ring onto her third finger.

"Omigod! I'm going to die!" Gabbie said.

"I will if you say we'll buy it!" Jim said. He mouthed the words "How much?"

The salesperson looked from the ring to Gabbie, back to the ring, and then to Jim. "It's a perfect two carat solitaire pear-shaped diamond. It comes with the Cartier appraisal, of course. I can let you have it today at a special price of thirty-seven-thousand dollars. You have exquisite taste, Ma'am."

Jim nodded. "She does. She really does. Ah? Does that include tax?"

The salesman nodded.

Gabbie held her hand so she could stare and stare at the ring. "It is so precious, and . . . and you . . ."

"Wish I had a camera," Jim said.

The salesman said: ". . . and I let you try it on? Why not? I happen to have a daughter. And what woman would ever forget Cartier's after such an unexpected and wonderful experience?"

Jim took Gabbie's hand. "It's exactly what you deserve, Gabbie. Sweetheart. Listen to me very closely. I am going to buy you that ring right now, today."

Gabbie stared at him. "Jim. We are so straight honest with each other. Don't do this."

"Gabbie, this is Jim. I'm not teasing. I saved a lot of money in Alaska. It's enough money for us to get married and for me to start a landscaping business, or something like that. You and I have nothing better to spend it on than something like this."

"You mean? Honest? You would do this?"

"Absolutely. I shouldn't ask you; I should just buy it."

"You are so absolutely adorable and impetuous Jim! I love you." She looked at the salesperson. "You know what?" she said. She put the ring on the velvet square, "We're going to sleep on it." She snickered and twitched her head into her shoulders signaling her embarrassment at the thought as the red flowed up her cheeks.

Gabbie pulled Jim along. "You see? You bring such riches to me, my love. Now, we can do some more 'tomorrow' shopping at Steuben's for some beautiful leaded glass, or we can go have lunch with Auntie Mary."

"Even with monopoly money I'd be broke!" What a tease was this New York! he thought. "Aunt Mary? Lunch? Do we have to?"

"You'll love her. After we'll go to the Bowery, and the stock exchange. We'll stop to see it just so you can say you've been there. I told Auntie I wanted her to meet you, but I wanted all the time alone with you I could get. She got it. She always does. We can grab a bus to meet her at Grand Central Station."

"Really?"

"Really. We're supposed to meet her at the Oyster Bar. It's just great there."

The moment they walked into the restaurant Aunt Mary waved at them from a table.

"Aunt Mary, this is my Jim Dorchester," Gabbie said.

Jim started to put out his hand to take hers, but she grabbed his, and pulled him down to her. She pushed up her cheek. He kissed her softly, and inhaled a heady perfume. "How nice . . . "

" . . . I'm Medford's Aunt Mary. I'm Mary Chicco. To you I'm Mary."

"Thank you, Mary. All the women in this family are beautiful . . . "

"Here for one day and already you can schmooze like a New Yorker! Sit! Please sit! I prefer to sit at the counter, but I like to be more cozy with special people" Mary said. She had what was known as "big hair," blonde, bouffant, stylishly held. Her face was oval, large brown eyes, and full lips. She was barely on the heavy side. "He's a flatterer, Gabriella."

"No, not an idle flatterer. It just happens to be true," Jim said, "and your perfume is a knockout."

"I love your man, Gabriella," Mary said. "It's a good thing I'm going to Italy. Hold on to this specimen very tightly. He and I, we resonate. I want you both to come to be with me at my home in Southampton when classes end . . . "

"Aunt Mary . . . my folks . . . " Gabbie started.

Mary held up a hand. "Remember, even though I don't practice anymore, I'm still a psychiatrist. You needn't say a word . . ."

When Jim and Gabbie left Mary, Jim asked, "Gabbie? Your Aunt Mary isn't going to rat us out to your parents?"

"Aunt Mary thinks they belong in the Dark Ages!"

They hopped a ferry to the Statue of Liberty. They held each other all the way over.

"You can climb up to the arm," Gabbie said. "At one time visitors could climb in the arm, but not anymore. In any case, you can count the steps yourself, or they will tell you how many there are. I will say about four-thousand, but that's as far as I go."

"Gabbie, your Aunt Mary is all woman. Wow, does she transmit! But, there seems to be a sadness. Do you know what I mean?"

"Yes. With good reason. Her husband, Nedo, was a psychiatrist, too. They practiced separately. I don't understand it all, but in psychiatry there is a thing called transference and counter-transference, and stuff like that. From what I understand, Uncle Nedo didn't read the signals right with one of his patients. A woman fell madly in love with him, in every sense of the word. When Uncle Nedo put her off, there, in his office, she shot and killed him. He was forty-two years old. Aunt Mary closed her office and hasn't practiced since."

"Okay! We're here to have fun. Let's shift gears. I'll race you up the Statue!"

They were locked in each other's arms on the ferry for the entire return trip.

They walked around Chinatown. Jim found himself gawking at one thing after another. In a Chinese grocery store, he pointed to a strange vegetable. "What is that?"

The grocer nodded and smiled. "Bakchoi."

"Ah! Bakchoi," Jim said. "How do you say it in English? What is the translation for Bakchoi?"

The grocer, surrounded with several other Chinese clients, all laughed when he said, "Bakchoi, Chinese cabbage; no translation Bakchoi!"

Jim and Gabbie roared with laughter, bending over at the waist, as each took turns repeating, "Bakchoi, Chinese cabbage; no translation Bakchoi!"

Jim and Gabbie found themselves in a darkened doorway just down from her building. They had been kissing passionately for quite a while.

"This is going to drive me absolutely berserk," Jim said.

"I know. I can feel you hard against me."

"I want to make love to you, Gabbie. I can't help it. I just want to know what it's like for us to be together. To burst the universe, you know?"

"Oh! Sweetheart! I am so wet for wanting you. I've got a bad ache below my belly. You can't come up to the apartment. The doorman would rat us out. We shouldn't even if we could sneak in without my aunt knowing. You know what? I don't think she'd say a word! But, we can't put her in that position. If you really feel that way, we can go to a hotel."

"As much as I'd like to, I have to stay cool. We mean too much to each other to cheat on our caring."

"Love, can I do something . . . for you?"

"You mean . . .? Wow! Just saying it makes the urge so strong. I could ask you the same thing. It would be the beginning and we both know we wouldn't stop there."

"Oh! Jim it's going to be a long, long drive . . ."

"No problem. I'll just groan all the way!"

23

Jim was framing the new greenhouse when Ashley called to him. "Visitors!" She jerked her thumb toward the parking area.

Jim walked into the parking area and found an expensive, black car with New York plates.

Two leather jacketed men got out of the front. They approached Jim.

"You Jim Dorchester?"

Jim held his ground and nodded.

The tallest man waved at the windshield. The back door opened. A jean-jacketed fellow wearing a baseball cap crooked to his face got out beaming. "Jim! It's me! Keith! Keith Franklin! Am I glad to see you!"

Jim blinked and nodded his head rapidly. "Keith! For God's sakes!"

They threw their arms around each other, whacking each other's back soundly.

"Oh! Jim! You look so good I could cry!"

For Jim the memories of Keith flooded back:

* * *

Jim hadn't known Keith for more than a week when Keith pushed him into the candy store on the way home from fifth grade. Keith looked at Jim and shook his head signaling him not to say a word. Jim rarely had money to spend on candy. With anticipation he assumed Keith wanted to buy something. Once in, Jim found the sights too tempting and delicious not to savor them mentally. He focused on the black and red licorice squares, which made his mouth water. The chocolate covered raisins were next best to the sugar covered gummy bears. Holy macaroni! Jim hated to come into the store because he dreamt of sampling every single, blooming goody he put his eyes on. So? What was the reason Keith bulldogged him into the store as if some secret clandestine operation was in the works? As much as he would like to, Jim couldn't buy anything if he wanted to.

Keith walked up behind Jim, and whispered, "Follow me out." He charged ahead of Jim leading him to the counter. Keith put down a Mounds bar and a dime. The shopkeeper nodded, picked up the coin, and stared at Jim. Keith just made it to the door when the apron-garbed clerk grabbed Jim by the collar.

Keith disappeared.

"Empty your pockets," the chunky giant said.

"I don't have anything in them," Jim said. He hadn't touched a thing.

"Do it!"

Jim's eyes flew open when he felt the candy bars. "I didn't . . . "

"You're a thief. You don't steal from hard-working people!"

"No, sir!"

"I call your folks, or you take a couple hot ones. That's how I do it."

"Please! Don't call my folks. Mister, I didn't . . . "

"Walk to the back room."

The man used Jim's collar to guide him to the storage room. He put on the light and faced the boy. "You have to do three good things for one bad thing or we lose the balance in God's world, right?" Jim didn't really understand but nodded in agreement. "You have to learn to do good, or you let bad win! This is one good thing I do for today!" He stripped the belt from his pants. "You agreed to this?"

"Yes, sir."

"Good! Now take your medicine like a man! No more stealing. Drop your pants, and bend over!"

Jim quickly slipped his pants down, his legs shaking. "Sir? Please don't use the buckle?"

"Buckle?" The storekeeper's eyes popped open to their widest. "Next time, maybe."

Jim saw him raise the belt and juked for the blow. He remained tense for a few more seconds. Then, Jim felt the man raise the side of his shorts. Jim felt his finger press the purple-colored flesh on the side of his leg. The man groaned deep in his throat, then exhaled as if he had a silencer on his mouth.

"Hey! You!" he said. His voice was hoarse. "Pull up your pants, and get your black and blue ass out of here."

An hour later, Jim saw Keith waiting for him at the corner of his block. Jim stomped right past him. Keith caught up to him and pulled at his sleeve. Jim marched on. He stopped when Keith jumped in front of him and stood in his way.

"Jim, I'm sorry. I didn't think you'd get . . ."

"Keith? You ever hear me swear?"

"Never."

"Then listen good. Get the fuck away from me! You're just plain bad news."

"I'm sorry if he walloped you. He's a Jesus freak and blabs about good and evil."

"He didn't hit me."

"Then what the fuck are you mad about? Because I didn't wait? I deserted you? I ran like hell. I was scared. C'mon'."

"Because you hung me out to dry! You didn't even warn me you were going to try such a stupid thing! You didn't give me a choice! Let me know what you plan to do and I'll tell you if I do or don't want to do it!"

"Okay. You're right. I shoulda told you. I'll tell you next time."

"There's not going to be a next time! Understand? The guy in the store said to tell you he saw you put the candy bars in my jacket pocket."

"Is that why he didn't hit you?"

"No."

"Right. I forgot. You're the Lone Ranger!" Keith said.

"Yeah? Well, asshole. You bought a candy bar. Where's my half?"

* * *

When Keith showed up with candy bars a few days later, Jim asked how he got them.

Keith said, "Stolen goods are sweeter!"

Jim shook off the candy bar. "Keith, I'm not a goody-goody, and I like candy as much as you do . . ." Then with words he would recall many years later, ". . .but you're not bullet proof."

The following week, Keith was walking with smaller steps, wearing a darker face, and his pockets were not loaded with candy bars. He got caught and got the hot ones.

When the subject of girls came up, Jim found Keith near oratorical. He talked about them in ways and manners Jim marveled at, and didn't always understand, which made Jim more than a little curious but not yet willing to experiment. Jim came to the conclusion that Keith was getting private tutoring lessons in arcanum sexualis from a neighbor girl.

Then one day, Jim walked into a classroom to get his books. The room was dark. He didn't see Keith and the girl at first. Then, Jim recognized Keith who was pushing Barbara Buckingham up against the wall while he was kissing her. He could also see her skirt was up and Keith's hand was buried in her pants. Jim reached over, grabbed Keith by the shoulder and pulled him away from the girl. "Stop that, Keith! Leave her alone! You get out of here, Barbara!"

She sped right out of the classroom.

"Whyn't 'cha mind your own business, Jim! What's it to you? Ruin a guy's fun!"

"Fun for you, not for her. It's wrong."

"Does that make it your business?"

"Spot on, it does! It's wrong to do that to a kid. It's called molesting, and you could go to jail for it, in case you didn't know."

"What? She asked for it!"

"I don't care if she shoved her pussy in your face. She doesn't know any better. You don't do that. And you just be ready if she goes home and tells her mother."

"Why would she do that?"

"Look at your hand. You hurt her. She's afraid and she'll tell her mother. Don't be a moron, Keith! Because it's wrong, and she knows that, too!"

The plainclothes policeman knew it as well when he interviewed Jim in front of his father. "The mother filed a complaint," the officer said.

"I wasn't involved," Jim said.

"You damn well better not be!" Glenn said.

"You were involved, Jim, when you broke it up," the detective said. "That's what the girl said. What did you see?"

"Is Keith in trouble?"

"Maybe."

"They were kissing," Jim said.

"Anything else?" the cop asked.

"Not that I saw," Jim said. The lie sent the world off kilter.

"The girl said he put his hand in a very private place and went in there. She said he was doing that when you came into the cloakroom. Did you see that?"

"I thought his arms were around her and she was kissing him back. That's all I know," Jim said. *That's a lie! Boiinnng! He really went off balance. Fucking loyalty.*

"Tell your friend to watch himself. From what you say he's off the hook, but let him know this incident will be on record at the station," the detective said.

"Keith!" Jim said making a thumping noise as he tapped him on his breastbone, "That means if you get caught doing a stupid thing like that again they're going to tie it in a knot!"

"Okay! Jim! Okay!"

"No! Not okay! I'll take care and look out for you, but don't you ever dare count on me to lie for you again!"

"Why should it bother you? You did it for a friend. I'd do it for you anytime! Like it's the first time you've ever told a lie, for Christ's sakes!"

"Yes! Yes! It is! It's the first and last time I've ever lied. Don't disrespect me and count on me to do that for you ever again because, I swear, I won't do it!"

* * *

Jim awoke at the sound of tapping on his window.

Focusing one eye, he saw Keith's face pressed against the pane. The moment Jim opened the window, Keith crawled into the room and slipped under the bed covers.

"I'm c-c-c-old!" Keith said.

Jim looked at him. "It's too late to rob a bank, so you got caught doing a rape?"

"Talk to your father. Tell him he's got to let me stay here."

"You don't know what you're saying. What's up?"

"Jim, I don't want to be away from you. You're my best friend. You take care of me. I don't want to go away."

"What makes you think I take care of you? I couldn't take care of my kid brother. Look at what happened to him."

"What happened to your brother happened, but I want to be with you."

"Are you in trouble?"

"No. My parents are moving. Tennessee! That's no man's land! My father found work there. I don't want to go with him, Jim! He's drunk all the time. You know."

"You can't stay here, Keith. Really. Just don't think about it."

"Okay. Then lend me some money. I'll hide out until my father goes away then I'll find a place to live!"

"That's crazy! You're just a kid. You know you can't support yourself. The best thing you can do for yourself is to go with your dad. We'll stay in touch, okay? Tennessee isn't so far!"

"Jim! We're friends! We have to live close to each other!"

"We'll be fine. Moving away happens to friends all the time. It's not the end of the world. A car just pulled up. I'll go out and see."

"Jim! If it's my father, I'm not here! I'm just not here!"

The revelation to Jim was like a dunk in a spring fed brook on a summer's day. He wondered about the idea of Keith moving away. He was his best friend, no question. He would do anything Jim asked him to do, but it was the burden Jim felt. There was a definite, heavy responsibility in a friendship. It had to be tended, and nurtured, usually more on his side than Keith's, but that was okay. And that's what it was with Keith. He was so darn dependent on him, not for getting into trouble, but getting out of trouble. He had what his father called cockamamie ideas. Keith did things on the spur of the moment, like jumping into a pond with his clothes on. He just didn't plan ahead. When he thought of doing something, he just did it. That was nowhere close to the way Jim worked. Jim liked to think he was clear-headed and rational when he did things. He was deliberate and precise. He closed a door so no one would hear it. Keith let the door slam. He emptied a dishwasher soundlessly. Keith clattered and banged and slammed the dishes, anxious to get the job over with. He was the proverbial bull in a roomful of crystal. Worse was the fact that Jim wanted to succeed. He wanted to match the efforts in the universe and contribute to the well being of the entire civilization. Keith was self-absorbed. He was interested in his own pleasures. When he discovered his penis, he would masturbate every chance he had. It was a sickness, Jim thought. There was no normalcy in what he did because he did most things to excess. And now, he had the news Keith would be out of his life. Unhampered, Jim could pursue his own interests and follow his own dreams. He didn't like losing a friend but it would be a relief. He was ashamed to admit to himself that he was very sympathetic to the new person on whom Keith would now depend. On the hand, it meant not having a buddy to pretend they were big league ball players. They tossed the ball around, hit high flies, and made finger signs between bent knees for curve balls, floaters, and brush backs. They camped in the woods overnight where Keith spent most of the time smoking roll-your-owns. It would take some work to get used to him not being around. Finally, Jim admitted to himself without Keith there would be a vacancy in his life.

With Keith's father waiting at the door, Keith turned to Jim. "Okay. Maybe you're right. But we're friends, always?" Jim nodded. "Promise if I need you, you'll be there! Promise or I'll jump out of the car when it's going ninety miles an hour!"

"Yes." If Keith were privy to his just recent thoughts he could have blackmailed him, Jim thought, into doing anything in the world he wanted. As it was, he put his soul on the line for some undefined, indiscriminate doing somewhere down the road. Bargain, Keith, bargain.

"No! Say 'I promise'."

"I promise."

"If you don't keep your promise may your face and body melt!" The words hung in the air like giant, dripping icicles ready to fall on him. And Jim would remember these omniscient words years and years later if only long enough to damn himself.

Jim felt the shivers flash through him. Damn intuition! Why did his mother, brother, and now Keith expect him to make their world perfect? Automatically, they added what? baggage? to his world. What about someone making his world perfect, or at least restoring his family to some semblance of order? What about someone else seeing that the world was in balance for him? Jim had to depend on Jim.

* * *

Here it was ten years later, and Keith barged back into his life in the parking lot of the Garden Center on a sun-filled day with the bird's singing.

Keith held Jim at arm's length staring at him. He hugged him again, and rapped him soundly. He ushered him away from the two men. "You look so darn great! You have no idea what this means to me!"

"God! Keith! You must be doing very well to have a chauffeur and a beautiful car like that! I had no idea you were in New York! Hell! We could have seen each other earlier!" He was genuinely delighted to see his old-time buddy.

"Well, yeah! Jim! Great! In fact, I was on my way up here from Tennessee to see you, you know, for old times' sake and sort of got side-tracked in New York."

The two men shuffled towards them. The tall one said, "Yo! Keith! Enough with the violin music! We gotta go with or without you, Man! We made the delivery. You make the delivery."

Jim looked at Keith, and then at the men. He got a message in Keith's face he didn't like. He got one from their faces that was even more ominous. "What's going on, Keith? What does he mean about 'delivery'?"

"Look, Jim. You know. Every now and then you run into some situations, and I got into a situation."

"You never change. I'm beginning to get the message, Keith. What's the situation?"

"Remember when you promised you'd always help out when I needed you? You promised? I got no place to turn, Jim. My mother died. My father's liquor-embalmed; he just has to die. Doesn't have two nickels. You're my only friend on this whole earth."

"What do you need, Keith?

"A couple bucks. That's all. Just enough to pay these gentlemen."

Jim looked at them and shook his head. He put his hand on the framing hammer stuck in the loop on his belt. "I have a feeling they don't sell Bibles."

The tall man said, "Happy stuff, Man. We sell happy stuff. We kept your friend and his friends happy for a long time. Like Paradise, you know? When he got more than he could pay for, we suggested a swim in the East River face down with holes to make him sink. He suggested you. Let's do it."

"How much do you owe them?"

"A couple of bucks," Keith said.

The man with the two carat diamonds in his ears, a gold tooth, and a newly shaved dome spoke. "He owes us for us letting him stay here standing. He doesn't have to pay up."

"Yeah? What happens then?" Jim asked.

"If he doesn't pay, we will stop at the first overlook on the Taconic Parkway."

"That so?" Jim said.

"Yeah, Man. We leave him in a kneeling position with a little 9 millimeter hole in the back of his head."

"How much?" Jim asked.

"Not a lot," Keith said.

The tall man pulled his jacket back and put his hands on his hips to show the handle of an automatic pistol in his belt, "It's $11,500.00 U.S. American dollars," he hesitated a moment, " . . .each. If it's handed to us in the next five minutes it's $22,000.00 even."

"Isn't that kind of steep for a little bit of Paradise?" Jim asked.

"We're not like bean counters, Man. Ask your friend there, the crackhead. He throws them there parties," tall man said.

"What if he gave you the slip?" Jim asked. It would be like Keith to try to do that, in delaying the moment with the hope something would come up, and he'd get away.

"Shit! Man! He can walk away any time he want, he know that." The tall one said. "He also know you both can't run that fast. Would he do that to you? We don't get him, we get you. No mind to us."

"That figure negotiable?" Jim asked.

"It was when he buy the crack cocaine. We negotiated down for him. Stupid business to do it twice for the same transaction. Now, let's like move on it, Mr. Deep Pockets."

Jim turned to Keith. "What made you think I had that kind of money, Keith?"

"I didn't. I thought of you, and what the hell did I have to lose? It kept me alive for a nice drive up to the Berkshires . . ." he said, ". . . and part-way back down. Maybe the Lone Ranger got lucky and won the lottery, you know."

"Hey! Jackson!" The tall man said, "Don't think we do this all for you. We have a delivery to make right up the road Prattsville way, and we can't be late. Now? Do we do the discount? Or, do the tour bus keep moving?"

No matter how much he considered and conjured he could not turn his framing hammer into an AK47.

Jim borrowed Virginia's pick-up to drive Keith to his father's house. "Keith? You are pushing the perpendicular to the grave. Do you understand? I need you. I've got a place you can be useful. I'm going to depend on you so you open your hole to do right by me. From right now you don't so much as smoke cigarettes, Keith, or you're out of here I need you to take care of my father.

Two weeks ago Jim was surprised not to find Glenn in the garage when he arrived. He walked out back, then decided he may have gone into the house. He called out his name in the kitchen.

"Yeah!" Glenn answered from his bedroom.

Jim walked in to find him on the bed fully dressed. "What's up? Why are you on the bed?"

"Oh! Jim. I'm glad you're here. I feel like hell. I've been puking my guts all night and morning."

"Something you ate? Drank?"

"Naw! Haven't been able to eat for a couple days."

"How long you been throwing up?"

"Started about a month ago."

Jim got his father into the truck, and took him to the hospital.

Ten days later Glenn was back in his bedroom recuperating from colon cancer surgery. He wouldn't have Jim move back into the house to take care of him. Between Jim and the Visiting Nurse they got him through the first day. Jim decided he would have to run over four or five times a day to tend to his needs. It was a problem.

"Jim . . ."

"Not a word, Keith! Not a word. Get yourself straightened out, and make a life for yourself."

"Jim, you know I'm going to pay you back if it takes the rest of my life!"

Jim shook his head. He knew Keith could not repay him if he had several lifetimes. Then, he bit his tongue to hold it. Wishes, even rotten ones, had a way of finding a home.

"Listen, Glenn. Keith is going to stay here with you and be your care giver until you get back on your feet. Okay? He'll take care of you. He'll bring you a tray, help you get cleaned up, do the laundry. Everything. When you're on your feet and back to work, he'll pay you twice the rent I did to stay here. Okay?" Glenn nodded.

When Jim walked outside Keith was still sitting in the truck. When he saw the dark look on Keith's face, he knew there was more.

"Jim, I didn't tell you all. I got into some bad things in Tennessee. I couldn't help it, you know. One thing after another. So . . ."

"Now, no bullshit, Keith! The whole story!"

Keith looked up at the sky. He crossed his arms over his chest. "I swear to God, Jim, it wasn't my fault! I was into drugs and there was a party at this kid's house, and before you know it a girl was available in one of the bedrooms. She was rotten slammed with bad stuff. It was plain snarky. I did her and that's all she remembered, not the eight or nine other guys that did her. If she wasn't a known hooker I wouldn't be here now."

"Then why are you here now aside from the money you needed?"

"I told the judge I had to come up here to see my dying grandfather. If I fax back Army enlistment papers the judge tears up all the paperwork. I've got a month. If not, I'm a wanted man."

Jim looked aside and rocked his body back and forth. "You know, Keith? The Army, that's not a half bad idea for you. I can see you would be a whiz-bang soldier."

"Jim, I can't do that."

"It's not whether you can or can't. You have no choice!"

"I know. You join up with me!"

"Are you crazy? Not on your life!"

"That's what it is. My life! You gotta come in with me. They have the buddy system. We stay together through basic training and all that. The recruiting officer told me. That's really the reason I came all the way up here. Jim! It would be great together! Remember your promise!"

"Keith? Do I usually swear?"

"No. I know, fuck off."

"Yes, fuck off!"

"Jim. I owe you. Your world is going pretty good. I don't blame you for saying you won't. It's okay, really. I'll stay here until your Dad is all-better. When he goes back to work, I'm going back to New York, and there won't be no next ride to the Berkshires. The sight seeing boats will bump into my floating body."

Two weeks later, Jim found Glenn tinkering in his shop. "Glad to see you've come along the last few days, Glenn."

"Oh! Yeah. Maybe another week, and I can start working on alternators and such."

"You wanted to see me. Where's Keith?"

"Took your old bike and went to town, I guess."

"Things working out okay with him?"

"I guess. He was fine in the beginning; he's slowed down a bit now. Gotta be pushed."

"I want to pay you for his room and board."

"You can start that next week. He has been helping me. But, on that subject, I have to ask for your help. I don't like to, but I've got no place else to go. You worked a long time in Alaska. I need to pay my doctors and hospitals bills."

"What happened to your insurance?"

"Never had any. Didn't believe in it."

"Your savings then."

"I used that all up, too."

"Are you serious? After thirty-years of work?"

"I don't care if you believe me or not. I didn't have any insurance on the house in Springfield. What I got for the lot and a burned down house I needed to use as a down payment to buy this house and garage. The medical bills? I paid them a good chunk. They just need a little more. About the equity on the house and garage. They said they'd take them and put my ass on the street."

"Glenn? A little more?"

"$34,000.00."

"Glenn, I'll need two things from you. First, I want you to know there was more than one time I thought you deserved a good bop on the snout. The only way I put up with you being such a rotten apple was to pretend I was adopted. Then, I used to think if I didn't have such a foul ball as a father, I might be on my road to being president, or I could have been in jail. One thing you taught me, play the cards you're dealt. You probably don't know yourself the reason you were such a miserable father, but you've got to know the reason you treated me the way you did. That's the first thing I want from you."

"The world stinks. Past is past. What do I know about anything? I can't change an inch. I took everything out on you because I always felt you should have died in the fire, not your brother. Then I couldn't get back at your mother for what she did to me, so she left me you to take it out on. I got so mad at times I wanted to beat you with a chain. I know you got the money. You don't pay my medical bills I'll wish the hell I did take a chain to your backside."

"You're sick, Glenn. You won't ever lay so much as bad breath on me ever again. If you want me to pay for your medical bills, you sign over all your property to me. I don't want you to get in the last lick at me when they're lowering you into the hole because your Will left everything to the last whore you were with."

"Are you going to enlist with Keith? Send me half your Army pay!"

"No."

"Buy insurance in my name!"

"No. Nothing, Glenn. Take it or leave it."

24

"I never knew about your father," Gabbie said as they sat in the propagation greenhouse at the Garden Center.

"He was as he was because he could."

"Are you okay with what you did?"

"It was the only way I knew to get control over him."

"You know he was wrong."

"Don't say anything else, Gabbie. I don't want to be angry with you! I want to be mad at the world! At this fucking life! . . . No! I didn't mean that, Gabbie. You are my world, and if I have you, I have everything. You know that."

There was only the sound of the wall clock. Jim looked away from Gabbie. He could feel himself well up inside. He hated to show his misery because his father was who he was. He hated it because he was the one person he should have loved. It was demeaning. The conflict ripped into his guts. It seemed to take the very life from him. He exhaled loudly. "I'm not going to hang around here. Isn't that crazy? Your father, my father. They are the people who are supposed to look out the most for us and boost our happiness. How many times do you remember the old man saying, 'Your happiness is my happiness.' Or, 'I am the only person on earth who would throw himself in front of a speeding bus for you.' Fucking hypocrites. Now they're the only ones causing us the most pain in our lives."

"So? Come on, Jim, Holy Moley, out with it!" Gabbie said.

"My question is what are we going to do?"

"We? What do you mean 'we'?"

"My answer is tied up with you. I don't want to live without you anymore. I want to be with you. I want us to be married, so I can love you as I need and want to love

116

you. Under these circumstances, I can't marry you. All the Alaska money is gone. I have no way to support you, to make sure you continue studying the flute, so I have no right to ask you to marry me. Chastity may be a saintly state but I'm ready to chew through iron bars to make love to you. We could be running smack into a boatload of different and difficult problems."

"Big J, listen to me. I love the flute. I've played it since I was four or five years old. It has been as much a part of me as my arms. Maria Margeritta Regina, who as you know is the first flutist for the Boston Symphony Orchestra, heard me play with the student orchestra. She spoke with me and said she would give me lessons whenever she was here in the Berkshires. She said that I have the potential to become a soloist, such as Jean Pierre Rampal. Oh! How I would love to do that. It's one of my dreams. But, you know what, Big J? It doesn't compare with my dreams of being with you. I would pack up my flute and put it away forever if it means we could be together. Yes, I would. I would put the flute away forever."

What if I did something that inadvertently made her give up the flute? How would you feel then? Jesus! Could it happen? "As if I'd let you do that. When I'd go to Tanglewood and watch you play, I could tell just by the way you performed, the way you held your flute, the total way you were immersed in what you were doing, that the flute is part of your soul, Gabbie. I would never do anything to interfere with that part of your life. Never."

"Perhaps I'll never have to make that choice. So? As you were saying?"

"From the way I saw it, there was only one way things might possibly work out. It may not be the best way, but it is a way. You might not go along with it."

"You know I will. I'll do anything you say!"

"Let me know after I tell you. I want you to marry me right away. Three weeks ago Keith and I enlisted in the Army."

"No! For God's sake, Big J! That's a stupid war we're fighting in Iraq and Afghanistan! You could be killed! How did Keith get you to enlist?" Jim looked away. He scratched the back of his hand. "Big J, I know you. You never

117

mentioned a word about the Army until Keith came along. And I know Keith. I know he used some pressure on you. How could you let him?"

Jim took a deep breath. "I owed him."

"More than you owed me?"

"This had to do with something long before you came along. Gabbie. Please. You have to trust me on this."

"It's just the way you're made, right?"

"Nothing else. It's done. I can't change it. Will you marry me?"

"My father . . ."

"Your father has nothing to say about this, Gabbie! It's just you and me. I just found out we have to report in three days. We have two days in which to marry, that is, if you say 'yes.' There is no alternative to that. I must leave you after that. I don't want to die without you being my bride. Your only decision will be whether or not you will marry me."

"I'll call Virginia and Ashley and announce my decision over lemon meringue pie. Is that soon enough for an answer?"

The following day, as soon as Virginia put the pot of green tea on the table, Gabbie said, "Jim and I have decided to get married."

Ashley looked around the table. "First things first. Cut the pie."

Everyone broke out in laughter.

"We have to get married tomorrow or the day after," Jim said. "I don't know if we'll be able to do it or not. Keith and I report for duty in Albany the day after."

"Okay. I vote for tomorrow," Virginia said pouring.

"Can't!" Gabbie said. "Tomorrow is out. I'm going to Springfield with my mom."

Holding out her plate for the pie, Ashley said, "That's easy. The day after tomorrow then. But? What about a license, and waiting periods, and do they do blood tests anymore? At least you're both over 18."

"I checked the Internet," Jim said. "Massachusetts is out. From what I understand, Vermont is in. No waiting period, no blood tests. It's a matter of getting a license at the town clerk's office--I'm not sure if there's a one-day waiting period--then finding someone in the same county to perform the ceremony. It looks like the best place is Burlington. I'm kinda familiar with it."

"So? What's the problem?" Virginia said. She served pie to Gabbie, then to Jim.

Gabbie looked around the table. "Me. I'm the problem. Not me personally. I have to be seated for the concert at 1:30 in the afternoon. I can't sneak in once it starts, and if I'm not there, my parents will know it."

Virginia waved the server like a baton. "So?"

"The 'so' involves three hours, about, to get up to Vermont, and three hours, about, to get back. That's six hours. If we left here at six in the morning, and got there at nine, it gives us ninety minutes to get a license, and find a preacher, and three hours to get back here. Too close to call," Jim said.

"Easy-breezy," Virginia said. "Just leave here like at three in the morning, and you'll have plenty of time!"

"Yes, okay, but who's going to rap on my parents' bedroom door when I usually leave at 6:30 to be at Tanglewood breakfast before 7:30?" Gabbie said.

"Me!" Virginia said. "Easy-breezy. I'll be over to watch TV with you tomorrow night. Then, when it's time for me to go, you'll go instead, Medford. I'll sleep in your room, and I'll knock on your parents' door when I leave!"

"Oh! So much could go wrong!" Gabbie said. "Can Keith help?"

Jim waved his hand. "No, let's please keep Keith out of this."

"By the way," Virginia said, "when are we going to meet this mysterious Keith?"

Jim shrugged. "He's taking care of my dad. He does his own thing."

The four of them sat quietly. They made faces, pursed their lips, picked at the pie. "Look! What's the worse that can happen with that plan?" Ashley said. "By 1:30 Medford's sitting in the orchestra a married woman, Virginia may or may not have her ass filled with buckshot, and Jim will face three months of boot camp horny as hell!"

Jim shook his head. "Won't work. No matter how early we got there, we'd have to wait until nine o'clock for the office to open. So, we still could leave here at six in the morning with the do-si-do. Add three hours to get back home, that puts us at noon, and still leaves us only ninety minutes to get married."

"So? What's the worse that can happen?" Ashley asked. "If you're in Vermont, and for one reason or another you're still not married by ten-thirty, you head home, and wait until you come home on leave to get married! That would be the worst of the worse."

"Sounds like a plan," Gabbie said.

"I'm up for it," Jim said.

"I bet you are," Ashley said.

Everyone roared.

25

Early the next morning, Jim walked into the kitchen to find Virginia waiting for him.

"You nervous?"

"You bet I am. Shaking," Jim said.

She pointed to the kitchen table. "There's a thermos of coffee and a couple muffins to get you on your way."

"You are something else, Virginia. Thank you."

"And there's also a bridal bouquet of Gerbera daisies, and a tiara made of stephanotis for the bride, and you take one of the daisies for a boutonnière."

"Too much, Virginia. Too much. Thank you, from both of us. When I come back I hope to be a married man!"

When Jim got into Gabbie's car, he leaned over to kiss her. "Good Luck! Sweetheart, I hope we make it."

"No hoping, Big J. We gotta do it. Pray luck is on our side." She put the car in gear and headed north.

Gabbie drove until they got some distance out of town. "I can take over, Gabbie."

"No, I'm fine. Did you sleep last night?"

"Are you kidding? I watched the clock tick off second by second!"

"Me, too."

"Pull over. Let's switch. Have a muffin."

"I'm so wired I'd get frazzled just sitting there staring at the countryside. Oh-oh!"

"What's up?"

"Guess what I've got behind me?"

Jim checked the rear view mirror on his side. He saw the flashing lights on the roof of a State Police car. "How fast are you going, Cookie? Only five miles over. He shouldn't stop you for that!"

Gabbie opened her window, and watched the imposing uniformed state trooper approach.

"Do you know why I stopped you?" the trooper asked.

"I haven't the slightest idea, officer," Gabbie answered as her father instructed her to do.

"License and registration," he said.

"The registration is in the glove compartment, Jim," she said. She riffled through her wallet for her driver's license.

"Gabbie, I don't find the registration in here," Jim said.

"You sure? Dad said that's where it was."

"Nope, not here," Jim said.

"The radar had you over the speed limit," the trooper said.

"Officer, we can't seem to find the registration. My dad just bought me the car. He said it was in the glove compartment, but it's not." She held out her driver's license.

The trooper looked off in the distance, ignoring her license. When he turned back to her, he said, "I may have to ask you to follow me to the station if you don't have your registration."

"Here's my license! And Jim has his. I wish you wouldn't make us do that, officer," she said. She looked at Jim. "What are we going to do? We didn't count on anything like this."

"Hold on," Jim said, "let's see how this plays out first."

"Where are you going?" the trooper asked. He took her driver's license.

Gabbie looked at Jim. "Burlington," Jim mouthed. "Burlington, Vermont," she said.

He studied the license. "Are you Medford Soldi?"

"Yes," she said.

"That so? What's your father's name?" the trooper asked.

"Angelo Soldi," she answered.

"Angelo Soldi is your father? The lawyer?" he asked.

The trooper stared at her for a long while. He tapped her license against his fingertips. "You know I could pull you in for speeding and not having a registration?"

"Yes, officer," Gabbie said.

"Oh, shit!" Jim whispered under his breath.

The officer looked back at his cruiser for a long time. He turned back to Gabbie. "Here," he said, "Let's say this is your lucky day. I'm not even going to call this in. Drive carefully, okay?"

"Officer Bradshaw, Tom Bradshaw?" she said.   He looked at her and nodded, a thin smile at the acknowledgment of his name. "Thank you." He nodded and turned away. She looked at Jim. "What happened?"

Jim watched the trooper walk back to his patrol car, turn off the emergency lights, and make a "U" turn.

"Just the legal community taking care of itself," he said.

"Would you like to drive?" she asked.

"Sure," Jim said, "but if I get stopped, can I hand the cop your driver's license?"

Jim ran around to the driver's side. When they were seated in the car, Gabbie grabbed his arm and leaned her head against his shoulder as they continued northwards. "Hey! Big J, for gosh sakes we didn't factor in going to jail, going directly to jail, so stay alert for the law!"

"Yes, Ma'am. While you were driving, Gabbie, I really tried to be as smart as I could be. I wondered about this passion we have for each other. I wondered if anyone else on Earth ever had the same feelings we have. I remember reading the letters of Abelard and Heloise. Talk about a love story. Do you think you can stay awake while I tell you this absolutely fascinating story?"

"If it's anything like our love story, I bet you a million bucks I'll stay awake."

"That's a bet! Now listen, Heloise was studying in an abbey when she met Abelard, who eschewed the military to become a scholar. As the story goes, he was smitten by her. What are the natural course of events when a guy is just zonked by this beauty? He pursues her! And that he did, and in the most genteel fashion as they say 'He seduced her.' Of that there is no doubt because she became pregnant and bore their son. Just to keep things in order before they became parents they married. Heloise returned to the abbey. On seeing this her uncle decided they had broken up and were no longer an item and could now seek his revenge. The uncle hires a couple of boffo's who attack Abelard in his sleep and castrate him. Heloise is beside herself—as you may imagine—for more than one reason. She continues on to become Abess and he continues his work in scholastical studies. In the meantime, they're still in love with each other and there's one way they can express it—letters. After they have passed on a huge store of their letters is discovered and they are published in a book. Because of these letters and the sentiment expressed in them Heloise and Abelard are known as the greatest lovers of our time. Ah! You ask for an example of their words? Allow me declaim one short paragraph of her words:

I love you more than ever; and so revenge myself on him my uncle. I will still love you with all the tenderness of my soul till the last moment of my life. If, formerly, my affection for you was not so pure, if in those days both mind and body loved you, I often told you even then that I was more pleased with possessing your heart than with any other happiness, and the man was the thing I least valued in you.

Their letters gave me an understanding of this world I could get no other way. I'm not saying I understand it philosophically because I can barely spell the word, but it enables me to see the world in a way that puts me outside the world. It's like not understanding a piece of poetry until you draw from it its own theme. Do you know what I mean? How can I say it? Everyone has to earn a living, that's fundamental. But, I'm saying everyone should find something that makes life worth living. It's something that's bigger than material things, bigger than fame or fortune or power. These are all fake things, meaningless when it comes to considering the theme of one's life. You see, for me, it's got to be more than just to be born, to grow up, to procreate, to grow old, and to die. What an absolutely wasted life that would be. Wouldn't you say, Gabbie?" He looked down at her. She was sleeping. He smiled. There was excitement, and there was that special million dollar excitement What he was feeling was extra million dollar excitement.

He looked at the road to see it run off in the far distance through the Vermont countryside. Mountainous vistas were interspersed with curves into valleys and white clapboard country homes with acres of lawn gathered in villages.

"Oh-oh!" Jim said.

Gabbie immediately sat up rubbing her eyes. "What's up?"

"Can you believe a cop sneaked up behind me when I wasn't looking! He's got his lights on. Shit!"

"Wow! Did we pick the wrong day to do this!" Gabbie said. "Were you over the limit?"

Jim pulled over to the side, put on his emergency flashers, rolled down his window, and watched the officer get out of his patrol car and walk up to him. Jim put both hands on the steering wheel. "Yes, sir, officer?"

"Driver's license and registration," the cop said.

"Officer, my driver's license is in my wallet in my left rear pocket. May I reach for it?" Jim said.

"You do that," the officer said.

Keeping his right hand on the wheel, Jim brought out his wallet. He used both hands to pull out his driver's license. He handed it to the officer. "What's the problem, officer?"

The cop ignored the question and said, "Registration."

Jim glanced at Gabbie. "Would you see if you can find it in the glove compartment?"

Gabbie grimaced, lifted her shoulders. She opened the compartment, and started digging in it.

"Are you James Dorchester?" the policeman asked.

"Yes, I am, officer. Would you mind telling me why you stopped me?" Jim asked.

"We have an APB, an all points bulletin, to be on the lookout for a car just like this. I need to see the registration," he said.

"We can't find it" Jim said.

"In that case, I have to take you in. Would you mind stepping out of the car? Do you have any weapons or drugs with you?" he asked.

"No, sir!" Jim answered.

"Do you mind if I check your car and look in the trunk?" he asked.

Jim looked at Gabbie. She held up a finger, indicating he should wait.

Gabbie leaned over Jim until she could see the officer's face. "Officer, my father is Angelo Soldi, an attorney in Berkshire County. He said if I was ever taken in because my car was on an APB, then we have a right to see the APB the moment we're brought into the station. If the police do not have the APB, then it's an illegal fishing expedition."

"That so?" the cop said. "If you have a driver's license, I'd like to see it."

Gabbie handed it to him.

"Medford Soldi, and James Dorchester, where are you going in such a hurry?" he asked.

"We weren't speeding, officer. . ." Gabbie started.

". . . and we're going to get a marriage license," Jim said.

The officer nodded as he handed back the licenses, and said, "Sorry, wrong people, wrong car." He pointed down the road. "Five blocks, take a left and you'll be at the county courthouse. Priscilla Downherse is the clerk. Tell her Cousin Leonard sent you, and if you need to get married today without waiting, she'll send you to our Uncle Bemis. Congratulations and best wishes!"

Priscilla Downherse charged them twenty dollars for a wedding license and gave them specific directions on how to get to Uncle Bemis. He was already notified they were on the way. He was ready and waiting for them, complete with neighbors as witnesses. The ceremony was perfunctory until Uncle Bemis got to the part where he asked about wedding rings.

Jim and Gabbie looked at each other. They burst out into laughter.

"What a stupid thing to forget!" Jim said.

"What do we do?" Gabbie asked.

Jim blinked rapidly, then pulled a white Gerbera daisy from Gabbie's bouquet. He looked at Uncle Bemis. "We'd like to plight our troth, or whatever, with this flower. Is that okay?"

"A-yeah! As nice a symbol of love as I've ever seen!" the justice of the peace said.

"I pronounce you man and wife."

Jim and Gabbie clung to each other as they kissed.

It was after Uncle Bemis coughed politely that they broke apart. "I'll need signatures," he said.

"I love you, Mrs. Dorchester," Jim said.

"I love you, Mr. Dorchester," Gabbie said.

They were headed south with Jim driving after they parked at a deli. Jim came out with for roast beef sandwiches and iced teas. "This is some wedding breakfast," Jim said, "we'll have to eat on the run. By the way . . . ! I was just wondering . . ."

"Wonder all you want, but don't even think about it!" Gabbie said.

"What? How do you know?"

"You think I didn't think about it, too?"

"We'll pull off at a rest stop!"

"No, my sweet. My honeymoon is not taking a back seat to a back seat."

"Very humorous!"

"Let's go. And don't for God's sake get stopped again!"

"Think positive. We'll make it! Tonight then? Can you come to the garden center?" Jim started his sandwich. "Man! Is this good!"

"You forgot. Right after the concert I'll go to the Cape with my parents. We'll just have to wait until you get leave. We'll meet in New York."

He took a long look at Gabbie. "You know what, Sweetheart? You're right. What matters is that we have each other. What can I say? This is a good beginning for a slow death!"

"Oh! Jesus!" Gabbie said. "Honey! Do you remember what address I gave them to send the copy of the wedding license? They will send it with the Bennington Town Hall as the return address. Did I give the clerk the Garden Center address? Or did I give my mother and father's address? Suppose I did, and they open our wedding license!"

"That," he emphasized, "will be a slower death!"

There was a rap on the window.

Jim saw the same officer that stopped them earlier. He put down the window. "Yes, sir?"

"You're James Dorchester?" the officer said.

"Yes, sir."

"Would you step out of the automobile?" the officer said.

"Yes, sir." Jim got out of the car.

"Turn around, sir, put your hands behind you," the officer said. He put handcuffs on Jim. "I'm sorry to do this, but there is a Massachusetts warrant out for you I found out about after I let you go. I knew you were getting married, so I waited and followed you here. Congratulations, sir, and best wishes to you ma'am!" He patted Jim down.

Jim looked at him. "You're making a mistake I'm sure I can clear up at the station, but I have to tell you officer, you are the one, first decent human being I've met in a long time. Thank you for giving us some slack and allowing us to get married.

"Thank you," Gabbie said, "maybe even we'll name our firstborn after you."

"Heck! That's okay. I always wanted to feel like the Lone Ranger."

"Mrs. Dorchester," Jim said proud of the hard-won accomplishment, "you head right for Tanglewood. I should get this straightened out pretty quickly, and then I'll take a bus home. Okay?"

"Okay," she said. She got out of the car, put her arms around him, and kissed him. "Sweetheart, when am I going to see you?"

"It looks like not until forever!"

Gabbie was on her way south when an hour later it was confirmed that Jim was about to report to the Army and that the warrant was outdated so the judge released him.

By the time he returned to the Garden Center he knew he was too late to catch up to his brand new bride until he came home on leave, which was some three months away. That was 7,862,400 seconds. Exactly.

BOOK TWO

26

THE LECTURE

Dying hurts.

Jim Dorchester had his sweet Gabbie on his mind.

When he heard the words his head snapped up. The Drill Instructor was barking to the lecture hall filled with some seventy other recruits.

Was it a premonition that made him sit up and listen? The recruiting officer back home had already quoted the refrain about not joining the Army to die but to serve. It sounded so grandiose. Now he was getting the uncensored stanza.

"You didn't join to get killed, though it can happen. Dying hurts, But it may not last long," the Drill Instructor said. "But son-of-a-bitch! You'll remember it for as long as you live."

Jim sat upright. *Funny fuck, isn't he?*

The DI's words ran like helicopter blades through Jim's brain. Fuck! He was only twenty, had yet to get laid, and here this fellow was making funny about growing a marble cross on his chest.

The lecture went on, ". . . and the second time you die you're going to feel the same pain all over again. That means you'll feel it twice as much."

How the hell did he know that? Jim caught the DI's eye. Was he talking about me? Jim asked himself. He was yet to be issued Army clothes but they already put a shroud on him.

"Hey!" the DI said, "We're going to teach you how to kill. You're going to blow a man's brains out as easy as swatting a fly. The faster you learn to do that, the longer you stay alive. Well, if that's the way it's going to be, you might as well take the Medal of Honor or Silver Star with you. It'll give your relatives solace, and you know what? It'll prove you were a helluva good soldier."

Really?

27

INSIDE JOB

Late that afternoon, Jim stood a quarter of the way down in the Army barracks. Rows of double bunks with foot lockers at the front lined both sides.

Keith Franklin tried to get by him with his arms filled with an assortment of personal items.

"I told you to stay away from me, Keith. You're nothing but trouble since forever."

Keith dumped everything on the cot next to Jim's. "I tried! I tried! Son of a bitch! I can't stand it! If that rotten recruiting bastard told me there was no smoking in this man's army, the fuck I woulda never joined!"

"You're a chronic griper," Jim said.

"I've got a god-damned nicotine fit! I could smoke horseshit."

"Do you know Gabbie and I won't see each other until after Basic? I almost went AWOL even before I got into the Army! Then, somehow we managed to sneak in between the barbed wire and get married, and then we couldn't find time for a honeymoon."

Keith froze. He scrunched his forehead and made wolf's eyes. "I didn't know that!"

"How could you know that? You're always so involved with yourself."

"You mean . . . ?"

"Yes. You were out of it for the last week, Keith. You were on a crack float sailing like a dirigible."

"Lemme finish," Keith said. "Are you telling me, you and Gabbie . . . You know. After all the time you two were going together you didn't even once . . . ? No hanky-humpy?"

"No. Never. We didn't even fool around, you know? We weren't being goody-goodies. We had something special between us, and we wanted to keep it that way. It was even more special because we never brought that into our world as much as we would have liked to do so. We sure came close."

"Guess you know all about blue-balls!" Keith laughed. "I have to tell you about my Cindy Jo I left back in Tennessee. First time we were in the sack, she said I didn't have to bite her ear before I took her cherry, because she didn't have one!"

"Bite her ear?"

"You know, like the nurse slaps your ass before she rams home the needle? Sort of to distract your attention from the impending poke?"

"Oh."

Keith pulled out his wallet. "Did I ever show you this?" He held out a photo. "Cindy Jo. God! I get a hard-on just looking at her. No one makes it like we do." He put his wallet away.

Jim shook his head. "I don't think of Gabbie that way. I told you it was special between us. I think of her as the fragrance of a flower, the warmth of the sun, the hint of a breeze, the sweetness of clover, the babble of a brook, the rustle of a leaf, the echo of a note . . ."

"Now you are a poet? I get the idea."

"I adored her from the moment I set eyes on her in grade school. I have no reason to live except for her." He sighed.

"Wow! That must be tough when you're that crazy about each other. I thought I knew what hooking up was about until I met Cindy Jo. Man! Talk about dying and going to heaven. Somebody showed her how to fuck and she showed me! I'll tell you about it sometime. Look. I tried to get a bunk up front."

Jim nodded. He pointed toward the latrine. "I hear you. Had a bit of a problem up there?"

Keith opened his footlocker to store the items he had dumped onto the cot. "That miserable bastard up there threw my stuff onto someone else's cot so his queenie could have mine and be close to him. Fucking gorilla.

Gorilla, that's what I call him. Don't get mad. Get even. Right?"

"Leave me out of it, Keith."

"The Gorilla is so tired from all the running and walking, he fell asleep. Come on. You watch while I fix him up. He's in exactly the right position. He's in the lower bunk with his hand hanging over the side."

Jim hesitated, then followed Keith to the entrance of the latrine.

Keith slipped out then came back in after only a few moments with a bucket partially filled with water with some slight steam coming from it. "They used to do this on the farm all the time!" he said. He moved to the bunk with the sleeping recruit. Keith carefully immersed the man's hand in the water.

Other nearby soldiers saw what was going on. They stopped what they were doing to watch.

When Keith noticed the sleeping man's crotch started getting wet, he took the bucket away, and ran to put it in the latrine. He walked back to stand beside Jim.

"Fucking son-of-a-bitch!" Gorilla said sitting bolt upright.

"Ha-ha-ha!" Keith laughed. He pointed to the gorilla, and said, "Look at Mamma's boy! He pissed his pants!"

The soldier's lips curled down, his eyes narrowed, and he clenched his hands. He jumped out of the bunk to look down at the spreading wet at the front of his pants. "Who the fuck did this?"

"Looks like it's an inside job to me," Keith said.

The Gorilla's hands were shaking in front of him, his eyes opened wide. He grimaced as he looked around. "I know about this fucking game!" He swiped at the water on his hand.

He caught Keith's smirk. His arms were crossed.

"You fucker! You die!" He charged toward Keith.

Jim stepped between them. "You don't know who did this. Nobody knows who did this. It's your first day in the Army, and do you know you can get kicked out for pissing in your pants? I wouldn't let the Drill Instructor find you looking like that."

Jim turned and motioned Keith to move. Keith stood his ground. Jim gripped his bicep, swung him around and moved him ahead of him. "Don't be stupid. I can save you one time. Twice, you can give your ass to Jesus."

They stopped by their bunks. Keith swung around to confront Jim. He nodded. Then, he barely touched his shoulder with his fist. "Thanks, Kimo Sabe."

28

INSIDE INFO

Jim heard his name called. He looked up.

"Jim! Hurry!" A soldier near the latrine waved him to come down.

Jim strode quickly to the doorway.

"The big guy is after your friend."

Jim ran into the latrine. Several soldiers were washing up before lights out. The one called "Queenie" was off to one side. Jim was in time to see the Gorilla punch Keith in the belly.

"Ooofff!" Keith blew and doubled over.

The Gorilla pulled his other hand back to do a number on Keith's face. Jim, too far away to stop the blow, shouted, "I wouldn't do that!"

"Yeah?" The Gorilla turned to him. "Wait in line. I got some for you, too, you double asshole!" He turned back to Keith.

"Ten-Hut!" a voice called out.

All the soldiers except Keith jumped to attention as the Drill Instructor entered.

"What's going on?" He spotted Keith in distress. "What's your problem?"

Struggling to subdue the pain and to stand erect, Keith answered, "My stomach, Drill Instructor! I got sick, Drill Instructor!" His voice was shaky, subdued.

"I can't hear you!" the DI said.

Pulling in a deep breath, Keith shouted, "I got sick, Drill Instructor!"

"If you're malingering you'll wish you were near death! Do you need medical attention?" the DI asked.

Exerting himself, Keith said, "No, Drill Instructor!"

The DI looked at each of the men in a stare they had come to know. He was sizing up the situation. "All of you in here! Around the barracks two times!" the DI said. "You've got five minutes before lights out!"

In unison, every man shouted, "Yes, Drill Instructor." Jim led the men out in a fast walk.

After they had come back into the barracks, at lights out in their bunks, Jim whispered to Keith, "Why'd he come after you?"

"I was in the latrine when Bob Foster, known as 'Queenie', came up to me and asked me to make the Gorilla leave him alone. He said he was forcing him to do things he didn't want to do. He was terrified of the guy. When the Gorilla came over, I pushed Queenie behind me and told the Gorilla to leave him alone. That's when he clocked me."

"I like to mind my own business," Jim whispered, "but now you and the Gorilla have made it my business. I've got Fire Watch tomorrow night. When does the Gorilla make Queenie meet him in the latrine?"

"Queenie said about an hour after lights out, when everyone's sleeping," Keith whispered back. "What are you going to do?"

Jim nodded his head rapidly. In low tones, he said, "When the Gorilla follows Queenie into the latrine, I'm going to deck him. Goodnight."

Keith smiled at him, and answered, "Ah! The Lone Ranger rides again!"

The next evening at lights out, Jim, on Fire Watch duty, toured the sleeping barracks. He used his flashlight to check the doorway and went into the dimly lit latrine. He walked past the stalls to the end and shined his light into the showers. He started to turn to leave, then stopped. He took a step backwards, and put the light in the corner. In the shadow he found the Drill Instructor standing with his finger to his lips. Then, he made a circular motion with his hand indicating to Jim that he should continue his rounds. Jim understood immediately the reason the DI was there.

Jim turned, walked out the front door to continue his rounds. There, in the shadows, he found two military policemen. He walked up to them and acknowledged them with a nod. They nodded back and hitched their thumbs toward the barracks. Jim toured the outside of the barracks and returned to the MP's. He was there only short moments, when the front door opened and the DI waved for them to come in.

Jim followed the MPs into the latrine.

The Gorilla was standing in the nude, his hands covering his genitals.

To one side was the soldier known as "Queenie." He was nude from the waist down. He held a towel to his backside. Blood ran down the inside of his legs.

The DI pointed to Jim. Speaking quietly, he said, "You continue your rounds outside." Then, turning to one of the MPs he said, pointing to the Gorilla, "Sergeant, collect that man and his gear and take him to the brig. You, Corporal," he said pointing to the other MP and then to Queenie, "Collect that man's gear and take him to the medical center."

On his rounds, Jim pondered the question that bugged him: Who told the DI about the rendezvous?

29

DYING HURTS

Training movies were a break in the exhausting routine that took them from reveille to lights out. "Dying hurts . . ." the lecturer started this one.

Jim race-walked out of the hall after the beheading lecture. He thought about it as he headed for the gym. He picked up his pace and started to run as hard as he could to get away from the vision and stink of Keith barfing his guts, and the sheer bestialic savagery he and the others were too mesmerized not to watch. When he got to the gym door he was ready to crash into and through it at full force.

"What's open?" Jim asked the phys ed tech.

"Body bag!"

Jim was before it in shorts two minutes later trying to drive his fists through it from one side to the other. He delivered with the same intensity a half-dozen blows when the phys ed sergeant held a pair of workout gloves against the bag at nose level. Jim put them on even though his knuckles already were bleeding.

He had to work the film out of his thoughts, out of his mind, out of his skull!

He realized—as he himself knew it--he had just seen the purest extreme of man's inhumanity to man, the manifestation of humankind with every single bit of love, kindness, goodness, caring, and tenderness removed. And, the perpetrators were so stupid they actually filmed it for the world to see. The film was the theocratic product of an ignorant society built on the sexual satisfaction of the male in all its permutations from cliterodectomy to pedophilia to the approved assassination of a wife for a failing grade in fornication. It approved as humane the burying of a woman

139

up to her shoulders and stoning her to death. It was a society that produced no symphonies, no sculpture, no paintings, no theatre, no scientific advances. Jurisprudence was limited to the grossly harsh, unappealable atavistic Sharia Law. Gabbie told Jim in a letter of attending a United Nations session and becoming aware that such people dressed in Western suits of Italian silk, which cost more than $3,000., yet, because of their lack of hygiene in their fancy suits they smelled worse than rotting garbage. To them a human life was worth about as much as a handful of windblown sand, which meant with unabashed aplomb they could proslytize their own to blow themselves up in the name of their god. To prove they were moving upwards in the civilized world those who stole now only had one hand cut off. It was a peace-loving society unless one did not believe as they did, in which case they sawed off heads. This society was the personification of ultimate, absolute ignorance acquiring only enough knowledge to use modern technology to serve their ignominious purposes—to blow the world back past the Dark Ages to the ninth century.

The workout sergeant pulled the bag away from Jim. "A heart-attack is not the best way to get out of this man's army. Cool down: three laps around the track, two laps in the pool, and you're outta here. That's an order, Private. What? Did you just find out your wife's fucking your cousin?"

Under the scalding shower, Jim pressed the heels of his hands against his eyes as he fought to remember the word his English teach made him look up. It was perfect for what he was trying to understand. It had always been difficult for him to harbor a deep dislike for anything. He was working hard to understand his world as it suddenly changed for him this day. Then, he thought of the word, and understood how he could face the next day.

The cruelty of these peoples to other living human beings was anathema to Jim.

30

A PENNY SHORT

Jim, on his knees, reached far behind the john. He felt the coin move under his rubber gloved finger. He pushed the damp rag into the corner to soak up the water. He pulled everything toward him. He wrung out the cloth, struggled to pick up the penny, and finally took off the glove to pick it up easily.

"That son-of-a-bitch!" Keith said from the next stall, "I'm going to put itching powder in the Gorilla's jockstrap. Tell me he didn't snitch to the DI or we wouldn't be on latrine duty!" When Jim didn't reply, he looked out to see Jim with his mouth pushed to one side with the Drill Instructor standing above him.

The DI was six-feet, three-inches, with shoulders that just made it through the doorway. Except for his eyebrows and eyelashes, he didn't have a hair on his head.

"On your feet, you two!" the DI shouted.

Jim and Keith stood at attention side by side.

"The order was to clean the latrine without a single word and to find all the coins you are able! Maybe as many as thirty-five! Now, drop and give me twenty right here, right now!" the DI ordered.

"Yes, Drill Instructor!" Jim screamed. "Twenty five push ups!"

"Yes, Sir!" Keith said.

"Yes, Sir! Yes, Sir?" the DI screamed. "Do you think I was born with a silver spoon in my mouth? Do you think I was born to royalty and had everything done for me? Do you think I had servants that said 'Sir! Sir?' In the dark of morning I had to go out and cut wood for the stove. I had to earn my living from the time I was thirteen! No one gave me a dime. Don't you ever 'sir' me again and make me feel like a pampered ass! Do you understand me?"

"Yes, Drill Instructor!" Keith shouted.

"I'm hard of hearing!" the DI said.

"Yes, Drill Instructor!" Keith bellowed.

"I said drop and give me thirty, right here, right now!" the DI ordered.

Jim and Keith dropped to the floor to do push-ups. Keith collapsed at twenty-four.

When Jim completed his thirty, he jumped to his feet and stood at attention.

The DI moved beside Keith. "My grandmother could do thirty with one arm behind her back! On your feet!"

Keith got up and stood at attention. "Yes, Drill Instructor!" he screamed.

The DI looked at Jim. "He owes me ten! Drop and give them to me!"

"Yes, Drill Instructor!" Jim shouted. He dropped to the floor, did ten push-ups, and jumped to attention.

"I told you there were thirty-five coins hidden in here. I was wrong! There are thirty! Find them all before lights go out at 2100, that's in forty minutes. This place better be spotless and all the coins neatly stacked on the first sink when I inspect in the morning. Reveille is at oh-five-thirty. I've got a feeling your first day in this man's Army is going to be a long day for you both tomorrow. There's a one-mile run on the menu right before breakfast."

"Yes, Drill Instructor," both screamed.

When the DI left, Jim held up seven fingers, indicating how many coins he had found. Keith held up two fingers and shook his head. He wore a pained expression of dismay.

Jim cupped his hand at Keith's ear. "We find the coins first, and then we clean the latrine. Got it?"

Keith nodded, a smile creasing his face. He mouthed the words, "Yo! Kimo Sabe!"

The next morning, the entire barracks stood at attention in their underwear in front of their bunks. The D.I. stopped in front of Keith. "You owe me ten from last night. Drop down and give me twenty!"

"Yes, Drill Instructor!" Keith screamed. He dropped and started doing push-ups.

The D.I. moved before Jim. "My grandmother could have cleaned that latrine in less time than you two did with one arm tied behind her back! I found only 29 coins in the stack."

"Yes, Drill Instructor!" Jim shouted.

"Well! Where's the last coin!" the D.I. asked. "Shall we send you a-cleaning the latrine once again?"

"No, Drill Instructor," Jim yelled.

"Why not?" the DI asked.

"Because the missing coin is in your pocket, Drill Instructor!" Jim shouted.

"Oh! So you're a Houdini, are you?" The D.I. asked. "A magic man and a mind reader, too?"

"No, Drill Instructor!" Jim shouted. "I saw the outline of the coin in your pocket."

"Because you're so fast, we're going to do a one mile run in under eight minutes before breakfast, so you will do two miles in under fifteen minutes. If you don't, you can either miss breakfast or miss picking up your M16A2 rifle and going to war without it! Do you read me?"

"Yes, Drill Instructor, I do!" Jim screamed.

Less than an hour later, Jim nudged Keith to move over so he could sit to eat breakfast with him.

Keith wrinkled his brow. "You ran almost two miles?" Jim nodded. "In fifteen minutes?" Jim nodded again. "How the fuck j'you do that?"

"You remember my father, Keith? I owe it all to him," Jim said. "I had to deliver my newspaper route on a bike. Peddling and running's all the same."

Jim marched up to the Gorilla who was standing facing his bunk. "Hey! I hear you're looking for me. I hear you're going to pound my ass into Kentucky."

The Gorilla turned around. He stared at Jim. He looked at his name stitched to his blouse over his pocket. It read "Franklin, K." The Gorilla furrowed his brow. "Are you Franklin?"

"You can read. That's what it says."

"No. I'm not looking for you. I'm not looking for no Franklin."

143

"You sure?"

"I'm sure. Not looking for no Franklin."

"Who you looking for then?"

"I don't know, but I'll know when I see him!"

Jim turned on his heel. He headed back to his bunk. He pulled off Keith's blouse. Keith was waiting for him wearing Jim's blouse with his name on it. "Go down and drive him crazy," Jim said.

Keith walked very slowly as he passed the Gorilla bunk. He acted as if he was walking to the latrine.

"Hey! Asshole!" the Gorilla said to Keith.

Keith ignored him. He continued walking.

The Gorilla ran until he was standing before him. "I was calling you, Asshole."

"Oh!" Keith said, "I thought you were talking to yourself."

"Your name Dorchester?"

"You pretending you can read?"

"I got you now, Asshole. Dorchester, huh?"

Keith walked into the latrine, turned around and went directly back to his bunk. Jim was waiting.

"Did he stop you?"

"Like he read the script."

"Good! Give me my blouse back."

Jim and Keith swapped blouses.

Jim strode back to the Gorilla's bunk. "I understand some asshole is looking for me?" The Gorilla turned around.

"Not me!" he looked at Jim. "I'm looking for Dorchester."

Jim pointed to the name on his blouse. "I'm Dorchester. You got a problem with me? I'm going to kick your balls up so high you'll have to swallow to breathe. Now, what the fuck do you want?"

"You're not him! You're not him!"

Keith walked up beside Jim. "Everything okay with you, Dorchester?" He looked into the Gorilla's eyes.

Jim looked at Keith, then at the Gorilla. "Fucking asshole here says he wants to beat up on the DI's grandmother. What do you think of that?"

Keith shrugged. "I think we should ask the DI what he thinks of that."

When Jim turned away to follow Keith, he pulled off the blanket and sheet from the Gorilla's bunk so he'd have to make it all over again. "That's for wasting our time."

"Good job, Kimo Sabe," Keith said.

31

THE VOW

"This man's Army can take night infiltration maneuvers in the fucking Georgia swamps and shove them up their kazoo!" Keith said. He swiped at his camouflaged face that glistened in the dark from bug spray.

"Keith?" Jim said. "You don't hear me use that language. It doesn't impress me. I've asked you not to use it."

"They can take these fucking MRE's and shove them up there, too!"

"Meals ready to eat aren't too bad," Jim answered. "You don't have to cook 'em."

"Yeah! You just love this crap, don't you?"

"The truth is I needed the Army more than it needed me."

"What are you talking about? This platoon wouldn't have gotten to this designated site if you didn't know how to read a fucking map. How'd you do that?"

"Easy. If you look at a map and it shows you're here, and you want to go there, you just cross the intervening distance, and there you are! Like one recruit on one side of the river yelled to the other how he could get to the other side. Rebel on the other side looks up and down the river and shouts back, 'You are on the other side!'"

"Good thing we came into this fucking man's Army as battle buddies or I'd still be trying to identify my left foot from my ass! Tell me again what the fuck is a klick? The sarge says my objective is two klicks north. What the fuck does he mean?"

"A klick is slang for a kilometer. A klick measures just over a half a mile."

"Great. I'm walking. How far is half a mile?"

"A city block? Yeah?" Jim looked at Keith. Keith nodded. "A city block is exactly a half mile. For you, add a couple hundred feet and that's close enough. I'm turning in."

"How can you sleep with all these fucking bugs and up to your ass in alligators?"

"There are no alligators."

"We've got leave in ten days. You anxious?"

"To see Gabbie? It's what makes me do everything right. I don't want to screw up and have them take leave away from me. So listen! Don't you screw up and do anything to change that, or you owe your ass to God!"

"God! Me screw up! I can't wait for the first move into Cindy Jo! I didn't know what making love was like until the first night I spent with her. I told you, I used to sleep over the garage at the Tennessee horse farm. Her mother worked there as a cook. One night I woke up to find Cindy Jo slipping into bed with me. God Almighty! She used to look so young and virginy, that's what I thought. When I told her I didn't want to be the first, she laughed! The first time we fucked she let me have her the way I wanted. Then, she said I was being selfish, I should make love to her so she could have some fun, too. I said, 'Sure! Show me how!' By Golly! did she ever!"

"You mean, a different position?"

"You being a virgin and all it wouldn't make any difference to you what I said. Kimo Sabe, you're such a straight arrow I bet you haven't seen a fuck film?"

"No, I haven't."

"Never?"

"Never."

"Wow! Well . . . The way it's done all over the world is that the guy goes in and takes long, slow strokes and gradually moves faster and faster, in and out, in and out. Before he knows it, he rings the bell. She's left hanging, and he can't catch his breath."

"What do you mean?"

"About what? Oh! Yeah! He's got his jollies and blasted off, but she's barely off the starting line and waiting for her reward."

"You mean . . . "

"Yeah. The girls love sex, too! She needs to come, too. What the hell. And, Cindy Jo has the answer. So, we stoke the fire in her for a bit. She loves to get her tits massaged. Then, I work the clitoris and get things all warmed up and wet. When she's ready, she brings me in all the way a couple times, then she holds me in there, pubic bone to pubic bone. She makes me rock her pubic bone to pubic bone very quickly, about as fast as the regular way when you're coming. She moves me out just a little bit. Then, I catch on. I keep the rocking motion fast, and withdraw my hard-on a tiny bit more each time. There's one time, right in the beginning, I don't think I come out more than a half-inch and pump back in, and it drives me absolutely fucking crazy out of my mind! I could do just that all night, but there is a need to crash through the clouds. So, I keep the same fast in and out, but pull out just a bit more each time. Jesus! Christ! Almighty! You can't believe it when I find myself pulling entirely out of her and crashing back into her full force! By the second time I'm all the way out and pound my hard-on all the way in until our pubes crash. She's got a little finger way inside that snaps the head of my penis and goes inside my pee hole, and I explode into a million tiny pieces! I think she's going to suck me right into her body by pulling me in with my penis! Ba-Boom! Hand grenades go off in my brain! I'm so short of breath I think I'm going to pass out. Just as I think I don't have another sensation in my body, her inside muscles clamp onto the base of my penis, and I think it's going to explode; it is harder than a fire hydrant. Like bands of steel, they tighten and release, tighten and release! I want to die! I can't stand the ecstasy another second. I collapse. She helps me roll off and over, and she moves with me and gets on top. She squeezes out every contraction she can for what seems like five minutes. I'm dead. I'm just dead. I can't move a muscle. I'm in oblivion! And, you know the best part, Jim?"

"I can't wait to hear."

"Ten minutes later, we do it all over again. And that, my battle buddy, is a worthwhile battle. See what you're missing?"

"You can't miss what you don't know about."

"Maybe, but I hope you took notes, because your chance will come . . ."

Jim interrupted him. "Keith . . . Don't move. Not a fraction . . . " Jim slid his hand onto Keith's knee. He continued to slide it down his leg.

"Fuck! Jim! I hope you're not getting horny!"

Jim whispered, "Shhhh! I'm not trying to get funny, just don't fucking move!" His hand was on Keith's hip when he lunged behind him. In one move, he brought out a snake that was twisting and wriggling. Jim held it just below its head. He finally managed to grab its body down lower.

He held it up for Keith to see in the dim moonlight.

Keith's eyes and mouth were opened wide. His head shook from side to side.

"Keith?"

He stared straight ahead but shook violently.

Jim stood, moved away and hurled the snake into the night.

When he turned back to Keith, he was in the same position and still shaking. Jim slapped his face solidly. Keith began to blubber. When he didn't stop, Jim slapped him again.

Keith pulled Jim down beside him. "A garden snake bit me when I was just a kid. I was terrified. It hung onto my hand. I couldn't shake it off. I grabbed a stick and hit it. I cut it in half, but it still held on! I don't know how I did it, but I finally grabbed it behind the head and pulled it off. I can't help it, Jim. I freeze up when things like this happen."

"It was just a snake. Couldn't harm you if it tried."

"Jim. I have to ask you. I hear chances are pretty good we'll end up in Iraq."

"Yeah. I heard that, too. We'll do special tactical field exercises, and then we'll go to OSUT—one station unit training--doing weapons and maintenance training. Then, we'll have a one-week leave. Maybe Afghanistan, maybe not Afghanistan. Maybe Iraq, maybe not Iraq."

"Jim, if we go wherever, you've got to make one promise you can't break."

"And that is?"

"I can't stand pain. When I was a kid, you remember, my grandmother just had to tell me she was going to beat me with a belt and I would fall to the floor and cry! Jim! You can't ever let them get me alive! Do you understand? You can't let them take me prisoner! Never! Ever! Fuck! I have nightmares thinking about those bastards sawing my head off! No matter what you have to do, you must not let them get me!"

"Look! You're never going to be taken prisoner! I swore I was going to take care of you! And I will!"

"But if I am! If I am! Do you understand? Jim, do you know the worst sickness in the world? Loneliness. My father was a son-of-a-bitch drunken bastard. My mother was a drugged up housedress. My father used to beat the shit out of me because he was so fucking mad at the world. I grew up only knowing I was lonely. It's the base shit of the world. If it wasn't for you, I would have run in front of one of those tractor-trailers that passed my house. Jim, you kept me alive. I thought I could shake it in the Army. I'm glad I found you again. Jim, you are like the big brother I never had and needed so badly. If you had an older brother, you know, like your kid brother had you, then you'd know what it was like to have someone look out for you. Like it or not, I need you to be my friend. I don't want to do anything to change that. Okay? So, I count on you. I've got to count on you for this. My father taught me pain before I could walk. What we watched—the head sawing--don't let that happen to me. Okay?"

"I understand, Keith!"

"Are you sure?"

"I understand, Keith! I know what you're saying! I know exactly what you're saying. I won't let them get you." Jim knew he had to turn it around to make him feel like the human being he was. He wanted him to have some of his own spirit to work on. "Now you promise you won't let them get me!"

Keith pulled his head up. His forehead wrinkled. He grabbed Jim's arm. "I never thought of that! Yes! Yes! Of course. I promise, Jim! I promise! Just like buddies should do! We'll take care of each other. This is a pact we cannot break! I promise! I promise!"

Jim said he would do better than that. They would make an irrevocable vow to each other: they would not let the other be captured by the terrorists.

"I won't let you forget," Keith said, "I will remind you of this promise every single day."

"That's fair, Keith," Jim said, "but there's one thing you've got to underline. A prisoner of war is a failure. As a soldier it is your duty to fight your way out of a situation. You don't let yourself get caught! Use every bullet and weapon you've got to battle the enemy, and when you can't uppercut them, or bite them, or kick them in the balls, then you use wile to slip away from them. You get back to your buddies to fight another day. Becoming a prisoner is not acceptable."

"But Jim . . ."

"Yeah! Yeah! I will keep my vow."

32

NO SHOW

Jim could not sleep all night before they were going on a week's leave. Keith was going to see his girl in Tennessee.

With his heart booming in his chest, Jim arrived at the Garden Center expecting to fill his arms with Gabbie.

"Gabbie's in Rome with her mother," Virginia said, "she expects to be there for a couple weeks."

When he realized he would not see his Gabbie, his soul totally deflated.

They were in a greenhouse.

Virginia went on. "I found that out from the housekeeper just yesterday. Whatever happened, she didn't even have time to leave a message on our answering machine."

Jim, in his Army uniform, exhaled loudly. He had a seven-day leave. He had come to the Garden Center to fetch Gabbie to go on their honeymoon. He leaned against the potting bench. He rubbed his short-cropped hair. He looked up at the sad-faced Virginia, and nodded. Gabbie had been kidnapped away from him. "Any idea how long before she comes back?"

"Come on. Time for lunch." Virginia spread mustard on the pumpernickel bread for the ham, Swiss cheese, and lettuce sandwich she was making for him. "She'll be in New York to continue classes in two weeks. That doesn't help. Your leave will be up."

"Yes, it will. I'm due back for special advanced individual training in eight days. After that, if the rumors are correct, Keith and I will be sent to Iraq or Afghanistan."

"Oh! Lord! What a stupid, criminal war. I hope you don't have to go. Can you get leave after this training?" She slipped the sandwich before him and poured iced tea. "This okay?" she said holding up the glass, "We don't have beer."

"Tea is fine. I don't think we'll get anymore leave."

"I'm so sorry. I know you and Gabbie didn't have a honeymoon."

"No. We were going to run up to Lake George. It seems without her I'm taking only half-breaths. I close my eyes and can smell her perfume. It was a big deal for us just to hold hands, you know? The times we were together there was a subtle breeze that washed over us that made us be in the same moment. We didn't dare hold each other too closely because we knew how challenging it would be when we had to leave one another. At times, she would put her hand on my shoulder as we walked. Our steps were always in unison, walking in each other's tracks without even touching the ground. Once she asked me if I'd like to feel her boobs. I'd like it, she said. I told her she didn't have to tell me, but I knew myself and that I wouldn't stop there. Then, I would catch her smiling and know she was smiling at a flower in bloom. Birds, especially hummingbirds, mesmerized her. She could stand in a garden, and they would come by her and chortle for her. If she'd have held out a hand, I know they would have landed on a finger. She was so much a part of the universe. I would tease her, but I really meant it when I told her that when she stood in a flower garden it was impossible to tell her apart from God's work. How can I tell you how marvelous it was to be with this special creature? Do you know she would give her allowance to charity and not say a word to anyone? It was only when I saw her do it that I knew, and I never told her. If she knew I knew, she would be embarrassed. It's one of life's thrills, I suppose, to do something good in secret and have it discovered by accident. Do you know why she's so good with the flute? She plays every single note as if it is the only way she can stop an angel from crying. Every note is buoyed by the pleasure she has in playing it. She is such a special creature, Virginia; I wonder very often how I have been so lucky to have been allowed into her life."

"Not finding her here, I can imagine how disappointed you are."

"Oh! Yes. It'll just make it sweeter next time we meet." He dug into the sandwich. "Ummm! Good!"

"So, what are you going to do?"

"If you'll let me, I'll help out around here until I have to go back. I don't look forward to seeing my father."

"Really?"

"There won't be any joy in him seeing me. He'll just bug the hell out of me as he did in his one letter to make sure I make him the beneficiary of my insurance policy. He says I'm to take out as big a policy as I can because chances are I won't come back. Nice thought, isn't it? My father. I think he's going to be disappointed when he finds out I'm married."

When his father learns that fact, he told Virginia, he didn't wish to sound like an ingrate, but the thought of it gave him a particularly warm feeling.

33

THE SWITCH

Jim reached for his wallet to pay for the drinks when Keith held up his hand.

"Yo! Kimo Sabe! On me. What a fucking disappointment! Holy Christ! How did this happen Gabbie wasn't there? Oops! I left my wallet in my footlocker."

Jim put money on the bar. "Gabbie's parents had to know I was in the service. My feeling? I think Mr. Soldi made it his business to know when I was due home on leave, so Mom and Pop decided to get Gabbie way out of the picture. They had spoken about Italy before, so it didn't seem like anything unusual when she was hoisted abroad this time. What a crazy world. Gabbie didn't even have time to leave a message on Virginia's answering machine."

"But Jim! Gabbie's a big girl. How come she didn't raise a storm, or something?"

"That's not hard to figure out. I understand perfectly. She would never disrespect her parents. She is going to school. I think I come in on a par with that for right now."

"When does she come back to the States?"

"She'll be in New York when we're through with our special training. Hey! I didn't mean it to be all about me; what happened on your leave? Did you see Cindy Jo for more of that super-action?"

The bartender stood in front of them. "Another beer," Jim said.

"I'll switch to Johnny Walker Black and soda," Keith said. "Medicine for the emotionally wounded. You know, I hate to tell you this. I went to the horse farm expecting to find Cindy Jo. Instead . . . Oh! My God! . . . I find her mother still working there as a cook. She told me Cindy Jo found a guy, got married, and moved out. Boy! That hurt."

"That's rough."

"What's rough is just before I got into that mess with that hooker? I was sent away from the farm after Cindy Jo's mother walked in and found me humping her daughter."

"You never told me that!"

"What I'm going to tell you is even better. Mamma told me I could stay in my old quarters while I was on leave."

"Did you?"

"I didn't have a better plan, just feeling horny as hell."

"So? What happened?"

"I went in town cruising for some available young lady, but nothing. I went back to the farm. Two minutes after I'm in bed, Mamma comes in bare as a jay bird looking for nookie. Man! Was I surprised."

"And you accommodated her just so it wouldn't be a total waste?"

"Waste? Now I know where Cindy Jo got her hot little ass. Ready for another?" Keith raised his glass at the bartender.

Jim put another bill on the bar.

Keith shook his head. "Just for starters, in basic combat you were my supply post for stamps, cough drops, chewing gum, foot powder, moleskin, toothpaste, and borrowing your shower sandals. How did you know to bring all that stuff?" Keith asked.

"I asked a fellow who just finished basic. He clued me in. I'm glad you're letting me pay, Keith, because it's makes it easier for me to ask you for a favor. In fact, a couple of them."

"Done! You don't even have to ask."

"Wait. You can get into trouble. I know. You have trouble to find trouble."

"My middle name. What?"

Jim took a swig and hesitated. "We're shipping out right after we finish this training.

No time to get a leave. Emergency leave only if someone is seriously ill, or a death in the family, compassion stuff like that. Sometimes even that doesn't work. But, we can get a twenty-four hour if someone will cover our duty station when we're gone. I want to get to New York to be with Gabbie. One day won't cut it. I need two. Here's the play. We both apply for a one-day leave. Say you get leave for Saturday. I get leave for Sunday. I cover for you, you cover for me."

"How can that work? You still only get a day?"

"Not if you take my place the first day."

"How do I do that?"

"They call us the twins. Remember what we did with the Gorilla? You wear my blouse with my name on it. I'll wear yours."

"Won't work. We're in a shipping-out unit so they'll spot check dogtags on the way out."

"Glad you thought of that. If you will, we swap I.D. tags. Besides, our numbers are successive, one number difference, because we came in together. And the other thing I noticed is we have the same blood type. Crazy, isn't it? It will work."

"No good. That's okay going out when we know they check them, but what about when you come back?"

"No problem. I'll take leave on Saturday as Keith Franklin wearing your dog tags, and come back on Sunday as Jim Dorchester because when I just walk through the gate they don't check anything, including meat tags. I've got the duty Saturday night, which you cover as me, and you've got the duty Sunday night, which you'll cover as yourself. Easy breezy."

"God! Jim. I don't know. You know what happens when you put your ass on the line and then screw up—it's the fucking stockade! I understand those miserable guard bastards jam their batons up the prisoner's asses just for practice. That's the last place I'd want to be."

"What? Are you telling me I should find someone else?"

"That may not be a bad idea, Jim. Let me think about it, okay?"

"Okay, but let me know in enough time to find someone else. Something else you can do right now. I need to borrow all the money you can spare. I've got to take a plane to Kennedy. I don't have time for the train, bus, or hitchhiking. Too chancy, too. And I've got to get a hotel room at the airport. Gabbie and I would waste too much time if I had to get into mid-town Manhattan and then get back out to the airport. This way, she meets me there. It's the only way it can happen."

Ten days later Jim left Battalion Headquarters exuberant over the fact that the one-day leaves worked out as Jim and Keith had planned.

Jim rapped Keith on the shoulder. "Ya-hooo! Buddy! I won't forget this. I just stopped by for my travel bag. Remember you take the duty today for me, and for yourself tomorrow."

"Jim . . . I don't know. I'm not sure . . . I don't want to get caught and go to the stockade."

"Yes or no, Keith. I've got a plane to catch."

"I don't know, Jim . . ."

"Sorry, I've got to go. Just do me a favor, Keith. Just stay on base. Go to the NCO club and drink beer all day, or whatever. I'll take my chance on getting nailed for going AWOL. Okay? Got it? The monkey's off your back! See you!"

"Has Medford Dorchester checked in?" Jim asked the airport hotel clerk.

"Yes. Room 823. We call it the Honeymoon Suite. Shall I call?"

"Don't bother. I'll beat you to it."

Jim rapped on the door. It was opened by a short, beefy man holding a newspaper. "Yeah?"

"I'm looking for . . ."

"Lady in here just checked out. I had to wait while they cleaned." The blood drained from Jim's face. "You okay?" Jim nodded. "What room are you looking for?"

"Eight-two-three."

"Up one flight."

When Jim tapped, Gabbie opened the door and stood there. She was beguiling in a floor length, pink negligee.

Jim sucked in his breath. He held a bouquet of red roses, a gift-wrapped box, and a bottle of champagne. "I've . . . I've been looking . . . I'm looking for Mrs. Dorchester."

"Yes. What kept you?"

34

FAST CONCLUSION

Jim reached for Gabbie. He kicked the door closed.

They both dropped everything to put their arms around each other.

They locked in a long, hard kiss.

"Gabbie! I'm shaking so badly!"

"I'm trembling, too!"

"Lord! You put smoke in my veins!"

"Oh! God! You turn my body into fire."

Ten seconds later, both were nude. Jim crashed down onto the bed, their lips locked.

He felt her breasts against his chest. He felt the smoothness of her waist. "God! Gabbie! You are beautiful! An angel!" His hand slipped over the softness of her belly. His erection was so hard it hurt. He hesitantly reached to touch her mound. He felt her button; her wet, smooth lips.

"Son-of-a-bitch!" Jim exclaimed. He grabbed himself and ran to the bathroom.

Gabbie sat straight up. Her forehead wrinkled. She thought a moment. Then, she tried to subdue her laughter. Unable to control herself, she broke out into her wild, raucous laughter, as only she knew how to do.

Jim appeared in the doorway. "So? You find this funny?"

With tears streaming down her face, Gabbie nodded. "Yes! Yes! Kimo Sabe! How do I love thee? Let me count the ways!"

Jim ran to her, flopped on the bed, and covered her with kisses. "Ah! My dear! I have not yet begun to fight!"

"Yes! How memorable! How memorable!"

During the early part of the evening, Gabbie groaned and rolled over. "I just realized, my dear, sweet lover. You are a liar!"

"I am not! Why do you say that?"

"We swore to each other we'd kiss virginity goodbye together!"

"Far as I'm concerned, I did!"

"Oh! You awful dragon! Where did you learn to make fireworks like that? I came at least three times in a row. I'm not supposed to do that, especially the first time!"

"Secret?" Gabbie nodded. "The instructions came in a box of Popsicles."

When Jim and Gabbie checked out, the clerk noticed they each wore a fresh-washed, scrubbed, rosey look. When Jim paid the bill the clerk understood everything. For the two solid days they were guests, they never left the room, and there was only an additional charge for soft drinks.

35

ONE MONTH LATER - MOSEL, IRAQ

It was at sunrise. He glanced at Keith sitting beside him in a trash-can Hummer. They were in a military convoy on a bumpy, dusty, hazardous road not knowing when they would be blown to smithereens.

They were riding on what felt like iron wheels. Jim tried to hold himself in check while Keith just let his body shake like gelatin, splatting against Jim with every bump. Just moments before, Keith pulled down the bandana from his nose and mouth and shouted, "How the fuck did we get here?"

It was a smart-ass rhetorical question for Jim because Keith pretty much was the defining reason and knew exactly how they got here. Jim noted that in this particular world blame was Teflon coated, it stuck to no one.

He gripped his rifle white knuckle tight. He was aware after nearly a month of action what to expect. Like the first tickle of a sneeze, he waited for the familiar explosion, a dull "WHOOMP" of an improvised explosive device going off. He dreaded the sound. It meant death and carnage. Usually, it came from the head of the convoy of U.S. Army Humvees and armored personnel carriers. They were headed for the center of Mosel, an insurgent stronghold. It was early morning, just about the right time for deadly mischief. They had come about far enough. Jim counted on it. He knew in the usual pattern, the Iraqi terrorists went for the second or third vehicle in the convoy depending on how fast the observer dialed in the correct cell phone number. He was in the fourth APC. Wouldn't it be his luck for them to change their pattern or that some numbskull lost time to re-dial a wrong number, he thought.

The 'WHOOMP!' blasted Jim's reverie and wiped the smile from his face.

From his other three-day patrols, Jim knew a rocket attack would follow.

The skidding truck lurched. Keith sprawled against him, and then was thrown to the floor with another soldier on top of him.

"Dirty fucking bastards! Fight like cowards!" Keith screamed.

The soldier seated directly across from Jim was propelled out of his seat. A bullet had caught him at the base of his neck and blew his face off. The body landed in Jim's arms. Blood soaked down his arm and over his body armor. Jim pulled himself out from under the corpse. "Get out! Get out!" Jim shouted. He kicked open the hatch.

"Let me out! Let me out!" Keith screamed.

There was the sound of metal scrunching, screaming voices and flying bullets.

Keith tumbled out with Jim landing on top of him. Others followed.

VOOMP! A rocket landed in the wadi, the dry river bed beside the road. Jim could see the IED had blown the first and second vehicles over onto their sides. Smoke and fire were billowing from the first one. Men were screaming. Small arms fire pinged! and thunked! against the vehicles.

Keith sprawled down alongside Jim. "Where the fuck are those rotten bastards?"

Jim shouted at the vehicle just behind them. "Get that fifty going! The roof!" He pointed across the way toward the tallest building in the line of houses. Jim emptied a clip in that direction. "Fire! Keith! Fire!"

Keith shook his head like a dog just out of a pond.

"Look at me! Look at me!" Jim ordered. He looked into Keith's eyes. His pupils reacted. "Why aren't you firing?"

"Jim, I don't want to die!"

"What makes you so special? We wait for the third rocket, then we move!" Jim clawed at the dry, pebbly sand beneath him. The dust caught at his throat. He had enough of lawns, but a clump of it here would make this horrible, barren, shitty land a momentary paradise.

VOOMP! VOOMP! Rockets landed short of the second and third vehicles. Another went over Jim's truck. VOOMP!

Their fifty-caliber machine gun set up a staccato response. The last vehicle picked up the cue. The smoke of burning diesel filled his nose and mouth. Men screaming in pain had become a familiar, ear-grating sound over the days.

Keith by rote emptied his clip at the compound.

Jim pulled Keith upright and hauled him into the wadi. "They're walking the rockets toward us! Move!" He shoved Keith ahead of him. Together they ran toward the end of the convoy. They dropped to the ground. Shooting between Humvees, they both emptied two clips toward the buildings.

VOOMP! The Humvee they had been in exploded.

"Jesus Christ Almighty! Jim! Those fucking bastards!" Keith screamed.

"Stay down! Stay down!"

Ga-DOOM! Ga-DOOM! The guns from the half-tracks let go. Ga-DOOM! Ga-DOOM! The top floors of the buildings disappeared or fell to rubble.

The attack lasted for fifteen minutes. "Four killed, six wounded!" the medic shouted. Three Humvees were scrap metal.

"Can we go home now?" Keith asked.

Not everyone wants to go home, Jim thought. This was a piece of cake compared to the barrage he got at home.

VOOMP! VOOMP! Rockets landed short of the second and third vehicles. Another went over Jim's truck. VOOMP!

Keith nodded and emptied his clip at the compound.

Jim shook his head. "We got overtime. See the lieutenant coming this way? Guess what fun he's got in mind for us! We're going to sweep those buildings and look for caches of weapons. Remember what we learned about booby traps. You don't have to smell their armpits to be killed by them. You follow me in, do you understand? Right in my footsteps! Don't touch a thing! Not a thing or you'll kill us both!"

Keith grabbed Jim's arm and held on. "Remember, you promised!"

"Yeah! I remember."

"Jim, I know you remember. Just say it."

"I promise! Okay? I double dare promise!" He shook him off. What a pain.

Rocket propelled grenades, mortars and machine gun bullets created a deadly symphony.

Jim slammed a fresh clip home and nodded. Yes. He promised Keith. He made him a vow. It was a millstone he himself put around his own neck. It wasn't unusual for him to do that, but he was just a tiny bit beginning to resent it. It was his burden, and he readily accepted the responsibility, except it worked both ways. It could be Keith who had to keep his promise to Jim. *Would Keith be able to do it?*

Jim and Keith moved up to the first house.

Shots from inside splintered the door.

"Set?" Jim asked. Keith nodded. "Go!"

Jim stepped in, taking out a figure in the corner. Immediately he swung around and let go at the rear doorway where two men were about to disappear. They crumpled in a heap. Another figure moved in the further corner. Jim fired three times.

Keith fired a blast in the corner where the first figure had been nailed. "Holy shit!"

"Never mind! Stay alert! We blocked their getaway." Jim shouted. He also saw that one of the figures they cut down was a kid, perhaps 13 or 14. "Follow me!"

The next two houses they went through were strewn with bodies. Blood puddled on the floor.

Jim stopped to unwrap bubble gum. He handed a piece to Keith. "The blood! The stink of blood makes me think I'm sucking on brass lifesavers."

"Fucking charnel house!" Keith said.

The sound of an AK47 sent bullets splattering over their heads.

"Across the alley!" Jim said hoarsely. He signaled to other soldiers cutting out of the house ahead. They stepped over two soldiers who were hit and down on the ground. "Go!"

Keith followed him.

"Set?" Jim asked. Keith nodded. Jim broke in. He saw movement going into a hallway. Jim fired and sprinted toward the figure. He kicked open the door. In the room he found two terrified women huddled on a carpet glancing nervously at a rifle on the floor. Snuggled behind them was what looked like an older boy. Jim waved him forward indicating he should raise his arms. He complied. Jim pushed him against a wall. He started to pat him down, then felt an object in his bottom. Jim yanked down his pants. A cell phone dropped to the floor. "Al Qaeda!" Jim shouted. He kicked the phone out of the way. The man broke away and started running. He had just reached the doorway when Jim fired. The man's legs went out from under him. He landed dead.

Jim said, "I hate the son of a bitch for making me shoot him!"

Keith handed Jim water. "Don't be mad. You're liable to get the Silver Star for that. Sure as holy shit he used that phone to set off the roadside bomb." He jerked his thumb towards the women. "You think, so they shouldn't go to waste, we get laid?"

In the alley, Jim knelt down by a soldier who was lying spread-eagled. He was staring at the sky. Jim undid his chin strap. He looked into his eyes. "Where are you hit . . . ?" he started. He held the man's chin.

The soldier turned a bit toward him. "Please don't let me die."

"Help is right here . . ." Jim started. "Stay with me! Stay with me, brother!" He felt the skin lose life beneath his hands. *Whose mother's son are you whose black bottom was so lovingly cleaned and on whose smile higher than a vertical Wall of China were built dreams of generations more of thee? Thy duty done for distant strangers who knew you only as a place holder. An argument now as a model of duty and sacrifice and doing right by assholes who run the other way. Who knows by what magic we traded places, friend. You are permanently out of balance. It can never be made up to you. So what? What difference does it make this dead flesh of yours? Yes, it allows the safe and selfish to mock you with impunity. People are too rotten to the core. You didn't save a one.* There were long moments while Jim's mind raced from the serenity of the lush Berkshire Hills to this caustic, dry, meaningless Arab land. Then, he allowed Keith to help pull him upright.

Two days later Alpha Company was relieved and returned to headquarters.

Jim was stripping off his bloody, dirty blouse. "God! War does not smell like Calvin Klein!" Not so bad. His world, Keith's world, was still in balance. They were alive and in one piece. So what? What did it mean? Nothing. *Whoever you are, fuck you. Would you like to trade places?*

"What can we do? Ours is not to reason why, ours is to take a hot shower."

"Wish that every politician, those inbred lawyers, breathed this shit for twenty years before they decide to shove a crazy war up America's ass!"

"They don't have to live it. What the fuck do they care? I hope history books fuck them over, as they should be." Keith walked past him. "Dirty rotten sons of fucking bitching bastards!"

"Damn! Invent new cuss words, Keith. Yours are all worn out!"

"I guess you haven't heard? The troopers guarding the bridge right outside the city that were taken prisoners? Fucking miserable bastards just sent back just their helmets and meat tags. They can lie about this war. They can deny the truth. We won't find their bodies in one piece because no one says anything, but do you know they express mail their guts to the White House?"

"Maybe they're still prisoners."

Keith glared at Jim. "That doesn't take you off the hook with your promise! See? Besides, are you thinking of a hot shower? Don't even go there! We're going back out right after chow down . . . and that may be MRE!"

"Do you know that meals ready to eat were called 'C' rations in the Second World War? Going right back out? That's a lousy joke."

"I need a pair of dry socks."

"Good luck."

"I know you carry a spare pair with you. You said you may fight hungry, but you're not doing battle without dry socks."

"Yes."

"Can I borrow them? Mine are soaked, and I'm worried about gangrene."

Jim looked at his hound dog eyes. He reached under his vest, and tossed him the socks. "And use powder! Hey! You took my last clean blouse! The one I'm wearing is kind of sticky, red, and stinky. What have you got?"

"No clean anything. You can have this blouse back, or take the one out of my bag. At least it doesn't have any bugs."

Jim dug the blouse out of Keith's bag and held it up. "God! What do you use? Anti-deodorant or camel dung? And I can barely read your name. But, it's better than the one I have on."

"Jim?" Keith said. "You're getting to be a real pain in the ass. I hope you don't wear that fucking bloody body armor into the mess hall. The cooks will fry it and serve it up. And when you get another jacket, remember to get extra water, too." He paused for a long moment. "Jim? Do you still have that bad feeling about going back out?"

"What bad feeling?" He knew what he meant. The bad itch between his shoulder blades.

Two hours later, Jim and Keith were seated side by side in a personnel carrier headed back to Mosel.

Jim broke the silence. "Keith? What's wrong?"

"I got nooky on my mind. I get a headache when I miss it this bad. Imagine, out here in this fucking godforsaken land, bouncing around in this piece of crap they call armored, and all I can think of is getting laid."

"There are worse things to think about."

"You? Do you miss it?"

"I don't think of that. I think of Gabbie. I sure miss her." He took off his helmet and stared at the photo of Gabbie stuck to the inside top of it. "She is the most beautiful creature on earth. When I get home, I'm going to put her in a glass case, just like a doll, to make sure nothing ever happens to her. When I see her, I'm going to go up to her and grab her hand, and I won't ever let it go for the rest of my life. God, Keith! . . ." He held his forehead with his hand, the premonition surging again in his gut. This was not a good thing. He knew when rotten things happened at home he had to deal mainly with just his father. Now, he just had to deal with a war. He shivered. The foreboding struck like the midnight tolls.

". . . Whatever it takes, I've got to see Gabbie again, even if I have to mail my skin home!"

36

THE INCIDENT

"That's the difference between us." Keith took off his helmet, and swapped it with Jim's. "Look. Like you. I keep a photo of Cindy Jo in my helmet even though she's not my girl any more. I keep it as a memory of a world-class fuck." Keith reached over and pulled the photograph of Cindy Jo out of his helmet. He held it up and brought it to his mouth.

"Keith! Is that enough reason to still carry her picture?"

"Yeah! Man! Nature abhors a vacuum, and her picture still gives me a hard on. She'll do until I fill it!" Keith said.

Jim reached into his helmet on Keith's lap, and took out the photo of Gabbie. Keith said, "Love's got nothing to do with it. All I can think of when I look at Cindy Jo is the first time she taught me how to fuck. Man! I've told you how sinful it is to have such ecstasy in this world. I think of my hard-on in her pussy, and all you think about with Gabbie is holding hands."

VOOMP! Rockets and small arms filled the air.

VOOMP! VOOMP! VOOMP! VOOMP!

"Holy shit!" Jim said.

Jim and Keith slapped the photos they held into their own helmets, threw on the helmets in their laps, and grabbed their rifles.

"Out! Out! Out!" ordered the first lieutenant.

"Holy good Christ!" Keith said. "We've got the whole fucking Al Qaeda tribe after us!"

"Out! Keith! Out!" Jim screamed. "There isn't enough armor on this piece of crap to stop a hard-boiled egg!"

Both of them rolled out and took cover behind it.

The small arms fire sounded to Jim like hundreds of marbles landing on an empty metal drum.

VOOMP! VOOMP!

"There's our objective!" the lieutenant screamed. "The bridge! They're after the bridge! We've got a column about four klicks away heading for it. If they can knock out the bridge our column will be a sitting duck for them! They're counting on us! Let's go! Move! Move! Move!"

Jim and Keith, hunching low, followed a half-dozen other soldiers in a line toward the bridge. It was less than twenty yards wide. The banks were steep. The water was deep, rapidly moving.

The troop took up defensive positions at the entrance of the bridge. Small arms fire continued to ping and thunk! around them.

VOOMP! BOOOOOM! A rocket nailed the last Humvee in the column sending up fire and smoke.

The lieutenant pointed to Jim and three other men. "You two bring up extra ammo. You two bring up water! We're going to be here for a while. Move! Move! Move!"

GA-THOONK! A mortar round landed far up from the bridge.

Jim led the way to the line of trucks. He found a supply of water. He gave two cases to the man behind him and put one under each of his arms. "Got the ammo?" he called out. Two soldiers running bent over indicated they had it. Jim led the way back to the bridge.

"Pass 'em out!" the lieutenant said. "Take up positions!"

"Where's Keith?" Jim asked.

"Who?" the lieutenant said.

"Franklin!" Jim screamed.

"I sent six men to the other end of the bridge!" the officer said.

"I'll join them!"

"Stay put! I need you here!"

GA-THOONK! A mortar round exploded in the water just up a way from the bridge.

"They walking 'em down! Concentrate your fire on those low buildings!" the lieutenant said pointing behind him.

"No! Lieutenant! It's a ploy!" Jim shouted to him. "I saw the main body on the other side of the bridge! There!

170

There!" he said pointing. "I can see them on the other side moving up!" He looked across the bridge. He saw Keith hunkered down against a cement cornerstone. He looked up and across the bridge. Keith waved.

Jim waved back.

"Concentrate your fire on those houses!" the officer ordered, ignoring Jim's admonition.

Jim rolled on his side to the man next to him. "Can you handle the fifty?" indicating the machine gun. The man nodded. "This guy doesn't know what the fuck he's doing!" Jim started to get up.

The officer put his hand on Jim's shoulder, holding him down.

"My buddy's on the other side! I've got to get to him!"

The officer waved his pistol. "Stay put! I can court-martial you with one shot."

GA-THOONK! GA-THOONK! GA-THOONK!

The mortar rounds walked toward the other end of the bridge.

"Lieutenant! Pull the men! Pull the men!" Jim shouted. "We can give them cover!"

Small arms fire and AK-47s burped on the other side of the bridge as if a munitions factory blew up.

Jim could see the Al Qaedas surrounding the other end of the bridge.

In a hail of gunfire, Jim started across the bridge. "Keith! Keith! Hang on!" He unhinged a grenade with each hand. He pulled the pin on one and then the other. He stood, exposed to a hail of fire. He tossed one grenade and then the other. He crashed to the ground.

GA-THOONK! A mortar landed in the water to Jim's left.

Jim got up and ran, then skidded to the pavement. He looked across the bridge.

He saw a horde of Al Qaedas closing in on the end of the bridge. He put his rifle to his shoulder. He tried to pick out Keith.

GA-THOONK! Another mortar landed on the other side, closer to the Americans.

Jim looked across the bridge in his scope. He saw Al Qaedas close in behind an American soldier, tear his gun away, and lift him off the ground. They started to drag him away backwards. He faced Jim.

Jim put the scope on the soldier. It was Keith. His face was stretched into a terrified mask.

"Jim! Jim! Shoot! For Christ's sakes! Shoot!" he seemed to be saying.

Jim brought the crosshairs across Keith's face, then back onto his nose.

Jim could see Keith mouth the words: *"Jim! Jesus Christ! Shoot! Don't let them take me!"*

GA-THOONK!

Jim dropped his rifle. He turned and ran back toward the Humvees.

He reached the first one, started the engine and headed across the bridge. "Hold on, Keith! I'm coming! I'll be right there!"

GA-BLAM! A rocket propelled grenade exploded in the thick of the men near the lieutenant.

Jim stomped on the gas. He started across the bridge.

GA-BLAM! but Jim didn't hear it. He felt the seat rise up under him. His body slid sideways. His face crashed into the window. His leg tore the steering wheel off its post. The last thing he heard was the explosion. The last thing he felt was the melting heat on his body, his arms, his legs, his face. The last thing he screamed was, "Gabbie! Help me!" The last thing he thought of was, "Oh! Fuck! Dying hurts!"

37

ARMY MEDICAL UNIT, BAGDAD, IRAQ – OCTOBER 2003

"Keith! Keith!" the voice sounded as if it came through a drain pipe. Then again, "Franklin! Franklin!"

He tried to open his eyes. The effort to do so was too great. He rocked his head from side to side. Fucking headache! "Who? Who?"

"Keith Franklin! Wake up! You've been asleep long enough! Keith! Keith!" It was a male voice.

"Okay! Okay!" He kept his eyes closed. He was swimming through steel wool. He had to remember how to breathe. His head was being squeezed in a vice. There was motion, in his chest. It was his heart beating. He felt the slow boom-boom of a death march drum. Physical sensations were working to come back. God! He hurt. God! He was tired. He felt . . . confined. No, more than just confined. It felt like he had several blankets on him. Through the screen of eyelashes he glimpsed first white, then recognized it as the white of a bandage. Was his entire body bandaged? He tried to identify the faint aroma. What was it? A flower? A perfume? No. It was mediciny. Sort of antiseptic, that was it. The voice was at him again. Go away!

He could hear the babble of voices coming from the end of the bed? "He was in all that bad doing up in Mosel. That's a bad crap of a place. They lost a lot of men in his platoon, including the first lieutenant. This fellow came in on the medivac so burned and banged up they didn't think he'd make it. He's been sedated for more than five weeks. . . Much too long."

"Keith! Wake up! Come on, Trooper, wake up!"

"Who?"

173

"No mumbling! Say your name: Keith Franklin! Keith Franklin!"

"Keith . . . ?"

"That's right! Keith. You were hurt very badly. You've been out of it for the last five weeks. Are you in pain? You shouldn't be feeling any pain."

"Hurt . . . "

"Are you hurting?"

"Where . . ." Oh! Lord! He was too tired to think. Thoughts would not come to him. Where was he hurt? Gunfire. Rockets. Mortars. No. In his brain. Something was making him wince. Something was causing him great pain. A wound was being probed. An aching break was being hammered. He shut it down! Ah! Cover it up. Relief. Smoothed over. Hidden. It was gone. How boring. It was repeated over and over and over. He knew the routine. When the pain increased to where it began to feel good, he knew he would pass out. Masochistic son-of-a-bitch.

"You're in the burn unit with a TBI, a traumatic brain injury. You've been burned up quite a bit, and you've had a concussion. Keith! Keith! Are you with me? Don't shut me out! Keith!" It was a human voice?

He had to know. He tried to fight through the porridge in his brainpan. He blinked, the light shooting live steam into his head. He urged his lips to move. The man put his ear closer to his lips. "Jim Dorchester . . . " he tried to say.

"Yes, Jim Dorchester. We'll find out about him for you." He looked around at the white coats at the foot of the bed. "Jim Dorchester? Was he in Alpha Company?" He turned back to his patient. "Right now you have to think of yourself. You were badly burned and got tumbled around a good bit in the HumVee. Your name was almost burned off your blouse. Also, they brought in your helmet with your girl's picture. Good thing. When you can sit up, we'll put the picture of your girl where you can see it. We've got to get you to Germany. We haven't been able to set any of your broken bones, and you have a lot of them. Your face . . . Some of the best plastic surgeons are there. You can't move. We've got all your burns covered. The rest of you is all bandaged up. Wherever you go, they'll bring your girl out to see you. I'm sure you'll be glad to feast your eyes on Cindy Jo."

"Cindy Jo . . . ?"

38

TRAUMATIC BRAIN INJURY UNIT
ARMY MEDICAL CENTER, GERMANY – SIX WEEKS LATER.

Nothing made any sense. I thought I could think, but I couldn't. I didn't feel anything, and then I felt recurring blasts of pain. I couldn't remember if I remembered. There was a lot of bouncing, and pushing, and being rolled around, here and there, Bang! up against something, then long periods of . . . nothing. I didn't think I owned anything beside my own thoughts. Not an arm, or a leg, or a body, or any part of a human being that I had in total control. There was a lot of fog time. I was in the middle of a cotton ball with light filtering in and out sometimes, and sometimes out and in. There it went again. A carnival ride. I was upside down, and then suddenly I was downside up. Yeow! The pain! The belly-ripping pain hoisted my gut to the sky. Knock it off! I was riding a circle. At times pressure would be on my eyeballs, and the next time my ass was catching hell. What was interesting, though, was that I couldn't remember drinking or eating anything. Yes, I could swallow, but I didn't know what I was swallowing. Spit? Just spit? No, I just went through the motions. I don't ever remember biting into a pumpernickel ham and cheese with mustard sandwich. I would have known that, especially with a huge slug of Bock beer as a chaser. Oh! Shit! The pain. My stomach didn't exist so how could I feel hungry, or anything. I felt alone. Alone in orbit. I was making long, lengthy turns as I was aimed. Do you know what I mean? Not moving in any direction, just being aimed. What I know is that I went through this a good number of times. No noise, no rustling, no whisp o' the wind. Just there, being there, that spot wherever it was. Yes, it was right in between. It was in between going into pain, or just like a starship, going out of pain. The crazy thing, the pain was like a football. It wasn't here, or there. It just was. And it wasn't mine. Then, it was. Or it wasn't. I wouldn't bet the farm on anything, but I would bet it was there. It was like another person. Me, myself, I and it. Then, it would abandon me. Then, it got fancy. The balloon of pain would rise and fall, rise and fall, but always it was tied to me with a long string. I couldn't see it, but I knew it was there, the string, that is. I played a game. I could pull it a bit and the pain would loom. Figuratively I blew it away, and it would sail. Oh! No more! No more! No more!

39

THE BURN VICTIM

Yes, I am a human, thinking brain.

I believe I'm in a body. Lord! It's gotta be a human body.

Thoughts come to me.

I don't know who I am. I have no memory. I have no point of reference with which to understand what has happened to me.

Cognizance comes to me slowly. Very slowly. Over eons of time, I think.

There are moments when I know of excruciating pain. It doesn't last long. It never does because when it does the pain drives me senseless, which I am most of the time. I can't help it; I feel moribund.

Through this black-to-grey filmy haze I understand I am as stationary as a tree. From the little I understand, I have a bark on me, too. Concentrating on my condition I conclude whatever my mind is in is one huge bandage.

There are other unwelcome sensations, messages that flicker here and there in my mind.

I feel cold. I would shiver if I could.

I am thirsty. I would drink if I could.

I am hungry. I would eat if I could.

I cannot hold these thoughts for long—whatever 'long' means—because I only know of time intellectually as a unit of measure--but I have no way of measuring it as I use it up.

A moment dances before me and taunts: Am I past? Present? Future?

If I were to indicate the passage of time with three ellipsis points—like this: . . . –I could fill pages with these dots and each would signify a moment? A minute? An hour? A day? A week? A month? A year? How about a lifetime?

Darn! I can't seem to remember anything. Well, I am having trouble with time. I am developing an excellent memory for pain. No, I don't remember how long ago, but I remember the fishhooks pulling at me, slowly at first then really clawing at me, ripping a banner into many ribbons, which flay me like lead-tipped cat o'nine tails leaving similar strips behind. Yet, see? I feel nothing. Then I do. For a bit.

Pervasive only is the blackness.

Somehow—instinctively I think—a good bit of time has passed. I get the sensation of being unwrapped and wrapped. It seems to go on for an inordinate amount of time, not that I can tell but it just goes on and on.

The coldness has changed. It seems one side of me is warm and the other side is cool.

My thirst is undiminished.

I feel great.

Then, whatever it is that's making me think plays tricks on me.

The next moment I am in the depths of some weird discomfort.

"How are you, Handsome!" Then, "You son-of-a-bitch! Don't you dare quit on me! Listen to me! Listen to me! Breathe, you sonofoabitch! Breathe! You fucking die on me, I'll make you regret it!" And then, "There you go, Sweetie."

"Who am I?" I ask. I have no idea, I answer. But why?

Doesn't everyone have an identification? A name? God! A sex? Hell! Yes! I'm a male. Not a boy, I'm sure. A man. I'm sure of that. Funny how one knows.

I'm beginning to discover. I understand. I am thinking. In what language am I thinking? Interesting, isn't it? How wonderful I have a vocabulary. English it is. I don't think I know any other language. I know about things. How do I know about them? I just do, that's all. What I want to know is what is around me? I would answer, but I don't know what could be around me. For now, the world of sound is around me. That's all. I hear things. I couldn't identify one sound until I thought about it very hard.

179

Whistling, that's what it was, very low, and merry it was, but soft and precise.

Sound. I know sound now. Like I said, I'm not always around but it comes to me as if from far, far away and step by tiny step draws closer and closer. The pain or the darkness finds me before much too long.

I hear voices. Not a lot. Not always. Mostly it's a woman's, feminine, yes. Bits and pieces come to me, sing-songy, bright, cheery. "Good morning!" Something. Then, it comes the under-rumble. Male voices I hear in the distance. Whispering. Serious, academic, not chit chat, but profanities. I don't stick around for whole cadences. I go back to searching nooks and crannies in this brain. I recognize the speech cadences: One for questions, another for orders, another for reflection; another for visiting.

Glory! Glory! Glory! I just found out I can see! I am not blind as I thought. Through this long, thin tube I can tell there is light. It filters in between threads of gauze. Whew! How good is that to know?

Then, I change my mind. Damn! I'm blind! I'm blind! The light is gone.

Jerk! Yes. It's nighttime.

Discoveries. I love 'em! I'm breathing. Yes, I can tell. Exploring further, I do believe I catch a rhythm. Heartbeat, that's it. Do you know what I know now? I've got fingers. Yes, I can move them. More than that, two hands. Can you believe, I can count up to ten!

Soccer time! I should be able to scream, but I can't. I have found I have a body. At these times, it's tumbled across a field. Over, over and around, stop! The other way, stop!

That's about as long as it lasts, too. If I feel that salty, sea breeze cloying stickiness I know I'll soon be on that athletic field and very quickly it's lights out.

The voice--gruff, mean--tells me to move my toes. Toes! I have them? I have them! Let's see, how does one move toes? It's exhausting. I'm too tired to do this. Sleep, I need just sleep.

In this world, I make my own world. In my world there is me. I don't know what my name is so I'll call myself "Fellow," as I am a good Fellow. There is a voice that is a woman's. She speaks to me quite confidentially. I get it now that I am either sick, or hurt, or broken apart. I can't be too wrong if I call the voice "Nurse." The other voices are male. They seem to make pronouncements and issue orders. I can't distinguish one from the other because there are so many. They come and go. All male voices are "Boss."

My world comes to me in different sections at a time. I discern the passage of time by the different events I acknowledge whenever I become cognizant of my being. Usually something untoward is happening to my body, which now I know I have. I can tell when Nurse is frenetic, upset about something. I don't wonder about it when the pain, or the cold, or the heat, or the thirst, or the wrapping that engulfs me. I think she knows about it before I do. I can't tell if she fixes it or not because usually I slip off into the darkness.

Despite everything Nurse must be doing for me, I miss most her touch. That would tell me what's going on with me. Wherever she would touch me, I would know about it wouldn't I? Wherever it was—arm, leg, body, face—I would know about it, and I would be able to identify my body. She touches me now only in my hearing.

I'll bet it's her hands doing the wrapping. I sense it's going on because now she talks to me all the while it's going on.

40

BROOKE ARMY MEDICAL CENTER, TEXAS

There was a cloying sameness to each day. To Keith it seemed he had to sneak awake to find out what he had to face for the day. It was never a question of whether or not he would be in pain. The question was how much pain.

Someone would come with a hypodermic and give him a shot or feed medication into him as a drink. He'd be off to oblivion in a blink. When he rocked and bubbled back to consciousness, like the emergency row boat hauled behind a vessel, he found tailing him some amount of pain. It wasn't always a lot, but there always was some. The strategy was to work it out so he could get another shot sooner than it was supposed to be delivered. When he was strapped in the bed he would suddenly sit upright and shout, "I need a Scotch and soda!" Most of the time, especially with medical personnel newly assigned to him, it would work. They would ease him back onto the bed and shoot him up.

"I need a Scotch and soda!"

"I'm Nurse Louise, and I'm here to please. That's my name, and your ass is my game!" Her hair was red as a pimento and piled high in a bird's nest on her head. Her eyes were a piercing turquoise, her nose no bigger than the end of her thumb. Her mouth opened when she smiled showing a perfect set of ultra-white teeth. Her hands moved rapidly and constantly, checking the chart, setting the gauges, cleaning up the table, adjusting the linens and pillows.

"I need a shot."

"Chart shows you have two hours to go."

"I need a shot!"

"No."

"Louise? Is that your name? Louise? If you're here to please, then give me my shot."

"My name is Louise McBride. And my answer is 'No.' One way I can get your attention: I'm going to hop up on that bed and hump your ass wild and just before you blow your lights I'm going to hop off. Will that get your attention or do you think you'll be distracted enough so you won't need the shot?"

"If not for pain, I will for rabies."

"Now I know how smart and how dumb you are."

"The mentally handicapped always say that."

"Tell me your name, John, I'll consider giving you a shot."

"John."

"Right. I'll give the shot to John."

"I tell you what. You give me an injection, I'll give you back an injection."

"What have you got my last four husbands didn't have?"

"I'll sue you for sexual harassment! Give me a shot! My name is Keith!"

"Keith, I just came off break. You're going to make this an awful long day for me. You have less than two hours to go before you get another."

"Nurse Louise? Can I whisper something in your ear?"

"Sure."

"Nurse Louise? I have never seen lovelier hair than yours. Won't you be my Florence Nightingale?"

"Of all my patients, I admire you most. That's because you're the only one I've got and had for the last couple years. I'm not going to turn you into an addict."

"Please! Please! Louise. Make the pain go away. I'm hurting so bad!"

"So badly, you mean."

"Just half a shot. Just enough to take off the edge."

"How about I give you the whole shot to do it properly when the time comes?"

"Jesus! You're a fucking bitch with a capital 'C'."

"What's your full name?"

"Keith Franklin."

"What's your serial number?"

"I don't know."

"What's your father's name?"

He shook his head. "Don't know."

"And your mother's?"

"No."

"Any brothers or sisters?"

"I don't know."

"What high school did you go to?"

"Don't know."

"Did you go to college?"

"Don't know."

"What's your girl friend's name?"

"Cindy Jo."

"Did Cindy Jo come see you?"

"No. I don't remember."

"What's your hometown?"

"Don't know."

"Keith, do you know how long we've been trying to fix you up?"

"Give me half a century leeway? I don't know."

"You make matters worse when you don't do as you're told. You were spitting out your medications, which made you hallucinate during the night. You tore off scabs with the bloody bandages. That brought your injuries right back to battlefield condition. You yanked out the catheter and left yourself with a bloody penis. How can you impress a lady with that? You caused more trouble when you took out the drains. I don't like to see you in medically induced comas. You're not going to make me come here and hold your hands all night just to keep you from playing with yourself?"

"Nurse? It's okay. You don't have to give me a shot. I think I'm going to pass out anyway. Will you read to me today?"

"What did you want to hear? Charles Dickens? Mark Twain? I've almost gone through the hospital library. I'll have to go to the local bookstore."

"No. Hamlet. I want you to read Hamlet again."

"I don't think you'll stay awake for the first scene. I have something just as nice." She held up the earphones to a Walkman. "Your favorite. Mozart adagios."

"Ahhh . . . Yes. Nice. But, your voice. Louise. Your voice. I will hear your voice in Paradise. I will always hear your voice calling me back from the brink. All the times I felt I was ready to die. And I was so tired, I just want to let go. Then, always, your voice like a magnet drew me back, drew me back. I will hear your voice through eternity." His head rolled to one side. "I feel tired. Mozart, that will be nice."

"Will you remember I came today?"

"Ummmmm!"

"Good, because I jammed the shot in your ass about a minute ago. Now make it last."

41

Keith put his face to the sun. It pushed the daylight down to his toes. There had been too much time in the dark, under the bandages. Now that they were off, he knew he was coming along. One day he would be able to put the scars and plastic surgery face up to the heat and he would be none the worse. Not yet, though. Nurse Louise straightaway pushed him to the shade. It would be some time yet before his hands could grip and pull the wheelchair. Then he could go where he damn well pleased. Being confined was one thing. Being confined and in pain was another. Being confined, in pain and alone was just a rotten animal. Thank you, Louise, for Mozart. He was more alone than anyone else on Earth because he couldn't even keep himself company. He didn't know who he was. There was no memory in which to retreat. All of life he knew came from a hospital bed, tended to by efficient, cold strangers. They appeared then disappeared, never to return again. Them with their starchy white medicine coats and the ever-present stethoscopes--which they never used on him-- were the phantoms in his nightmares. Was there a statute of limitations on questions? From anyone? Even the man mopping the floor under his bed would stop during his devoirs and ask how he was doing and what was going on.

Except Louise Comma The Nurse, as he called her. She was a savvy chick. She would draw a line in concrete and kick you in the balls if you eyed it cross-eyed. She had a duty, and the duty she did. She kept him from being alone, rotten alone.

"Keith? I'm going to leave you alone here in the shade." She set the locks on the wheel chair. Nurse Louise leaned over before him until she was eyeball to eyeball. "There's music if you want." She adjusted the earphones around his leg by his knee.

"The wireless call button is on your knee, too. Just put your hand on it. Okay?"

"No. I don't want you to go."

"Yes. I don't want to leave you. I'll be right back."

"The aliens will get me."

"No such luck for me. Work on it. Give me a break."

"Tell me again? What's my surprise?"

She straightened up. She looked off in the distance and bit her lower lip. She looked at him. "Okay. I'll tell you when I come back."

"A hint?"

"I think a video."

"Tell me more."

"I think it's a video of you humping Marilyn Monroe."

He looked away from her. "I'll be waiting."

When she returned she was noticeably withdrawn. "You were given permission to see the video. The belief is it may help you to regain your memory."

"What's the video about?"

"You went to Iraq with a battle buddy. In your file it reports you asked about him."

His name was Jim Dorchester. Nurse Louise didn't know if they knew each other before the service. They went through basic together, then advanced individual training. They came to Iraq as battle buddies. Together they were assigned to the same platoon, the same company. They went out on the same patrols. On the last one, Keith was nailed in a HumVee by a rocket propelled grenade. In the meantime, the Al Qaeda captured Jim. A squad on patrol found his dog tags, helmet, and blouse in an empty house. His body was never returned or found. The reports were the body was mutilated, burned, and the ashes scattered.

The video was turned on.

There were subtitles.

The screen showed the entrance to Westover Air Force Base, the largest reserve base in the world.

In the distance, a military cargo plane came in for a landing. It taxied up close to a large, empty hangar. Waiting close-by were a hearse and a limousine.

The camera cut to the plane's ramp. It focused on a flag covered casket.

The subtitle read: "Spc. James Dorchester, recipient of the Silver Star, returns home."

On the screen it showed the military pallbearers in short, scuffing steps, march it out of the plane. They took it into the hangar to an area cordoned off by screens.

The subtitle read: "Mrs. Dorchester to inspect the contents."

The camera switched to an officer opening the door of the limousine. Out stepped a young woman followed by two others. The subtitle read: "Mrs. James Dorchester, and friends." Medford took the officer's arm. She did not look quite twenty. Her face was drawn, tired looking. Her blonde hair was pulled back. She wore a loose-fitting black dress covered with a shawl. Two women, subdued, were dressed in black. They stood behind her. They walked together to the casket. Another officer unlatched the casket. With the help of two enlisted men, the top was removed.

Medford reached in and took out a soldier's helmet. She inspected the outside. When she looked inside, she reached in to remove a photograph. She turned to her friends holding up the picture. She clutched the photograph to her chest with one hand, and put the other to her face.

She kept the photograph and replaced the helmet. She took out a rectangular name tag that had been torn from a blouse. She held it up. Stenciled in black ink it read "Dorchester."

The subtitle read: "Dorchester name tag from returned blouse."

She replaced it.

She very slowly, quite deliberately took out two dog tags.

The subtitle read: "James Dorchester's identification tags."

Mrs. Dorchester handed the tags to the officer and spoke to him. The officer removed one of the tags from the chain. He handed her one. He placed the other back into the coffin.

Mrs. Dorchester turned and walked back to the limousine. Her friends and the officer followed.

The film showed the casket being placed in the hearse. It showed the cortege leading the limousine off the base.

Snippets followed that showed the sign for the Massachusetts Turnpike heading west; Exit 2 at Lee; Route 102 leading to Great Farraday; the welcome sign at the Great Farraday line; a Great Farraday police cruiser waiting there took the first position to lead the funeral cortege, and the sign at the front of St. Peter's Church. The distance traveled, it said, was 47 miles.

The camera focused on the honor guard from the local Veterans of Foreign Wars standing at attention, their rifles before them, on the steps leading into the church. Another group of uniformed soldiers acting as pallbearers lined up at the hearse to take out the flag draped casket.

The film showed the casket marched up the steps to a waiting priest. He sprinkled holy water on the casket. Only then did he allow the casket to enter the church.

The film continued when the casket was brought out of the church and placed in the limousine. Mrs. Dorchester, her two companions and the officer got into the limousine. Several additional cars joined the funeral cortege.

A snippet showed the entrance to St. Peter's Cemetery, the burial site in the cemetery with a covering and chairs, and a mound of earth covered with a green tarp.

Passengers from the other cars gathered at the site. Mrs. Dorchester and her companions took seats. The officer stood close by.

The camera caught the pallbearers marching the casket to the site as the honor guard took up positions to one side. Flower arrangements and sprays were placed on the mound and before it.

The camera zoomed in on a man standing far to one side. The caption read: "Mr. Glenn Dorchester, father of James."

There was no caption for a taxi driving up, and older woman getting out, and standing by the cab to watch the proceedings.

The focus shifted to reciting prayers, then sprinkling sand on the casket. The soldiers lined up on both sides of the casket for the flag folding ceremony. They remained at attention as the honor guard meticulously prepared the flag, then folded it according to tradition. The soldiers passed it between the line in the triangular design. The last soldier made sure it was folded and tucked in as required, held it between both hands, turned, and presented it to the officer.

The camera pulled back to show the officer holding the folded flag between his gloved hands marching and standing before Mrs. Dorchester. He bowed presenting the flag to her with his lips saying, ".". . . from a grateful nation."

The film showed the casket lowered into the ground as the honor guard fired their salute.

The film ended.

"Did you recognize anyone or anything?" Louise asked. "Keith? . . ." She looked at his eyes and found them vacant, dull, unseeing. "Keith!" She slapped the back of his hand. "What is it, Keith?" He turned his head to look up at her. "Keith? What happened?"

"I don't know! I just zonked out."

"You certainly went to never-never land. You must have seen or recognized someone? Who did you see? Do you remember where you lost it?"

"I don't remember much of it. Did I fall asleep? Can we see it again?"

Louise had the film run again. She watched him intently. When it was over, she asked, "See anyone you recognize?" He shook his head. "Mrs. Dorchester is pretty."

"She sure is. Very. She had no other relatives?"

"She has a mother and a father living in the same town. They disowned her when she married Jim Dorchester."

"And they didn't go to the funeral?"

"I understand her mother just made a brief appearance at the funeral. It was as much support as she was able to give. It's a sad, long story."

"And the two women?"

"Friends."

"But . . ."

"But what?"

"Why did she have to check out what was in the casket?"

"She made the Army check the DNA from a hair found in the helmet to confirm it was Jim's."

"And was it?"

"Yes."

"So? What's the problem?"

"The same reason they made the film. Mrs. Dorchester refuses to believe her husband is dead. She says she would know it if he was."

42

FOUR YEARS LATER

"Marry me," Keith said. He pushed the scotch and soda aside. He reached across the table and took Louise Comma The Nurse's hand, and nodded. He wore a full beard that was stark white. He had on a short-sleeved Hawaiian shirt.

Her hair was piled on top of her head. She wore a tank top and a skirt. "First if you want to marry me, you have to go to Amarillo," she said.

"That's a helluva long drive. Why should I go there?"

"Because that's where you'll find the end of the line."

"How long have you been taking care of me? Two, three centuries?"

"Thanks. It's been a lot of years. I started with you overseas in a hermetically sealed burn/brain injury unit, and then I transferred with you to a half-dozen rehabilitation units."

"I don't recognize myself."

"Do you know how lucky you were to be sent to Germany? The greatest plastic surgeons in the world worked out their new technique on you. I don't know what you looked like in your earlier life. I understand your surgical team did astounding things for you. I understand you were considered strong enough to get the news about your plastic surgery."

"Whatever it was, I wanted to know."

"The team did a partial face transplant. You received a new lower face from a donor. They gave you new cheeks, a nose, mouth and chin."

"They do that, but I've never heard of it before."

"It's new today, but one day it will be as common as liver, kidney, or heart transplants. It's been over a year, but as you can tell, you're able to eat, drink, smile, talk. The biggest difficulty was adjusting your medication to prevent you from rejecting all of the transplanted tissues you got. You have pretty much conquered this. There's nothing to reveal you had plastic surgery. Yet, you grow a beard. Did you remember wearing a beard . . . you know. . . before?"

"I can't tell you. You're avoiding the question. You keep things about yourself pretty damn private. After all the time we've been together, what are you afraid of? Husband number five?"

"Maybe it's none of your business, and maybe it's number one. I've never married. It seems every guy that proposed, grateful or not, took me for granted as invisible as the air they breathed. They either died or got well and went home never to be seen again. I'm so involved taking care of the patients I fall in love with, I don't take time to put the arm on them. When they graduate from me, they graduate. Then, the next person that needs me comes into my life. I'm always ready for them. I know the difference between true, undying emotional love and the perishable, intellectual, obligatory love. I'm afraid the latter is us."

"That can't happen to us. First, I don't think I'm ready for sex. Then, I have no memory of a life before you. As you know, that makes it very difficult to plan on the future. You have to have something to push against. Until I get my memory back, I'm a very solitary, lonely individual. Tabula rasa."

"'Tabula rasa.' What's that?"

"Psychology, sociology. It means blank page. Every child is born with a blank page for a mind, they say. Some disagree because it seems kids in my day were born knowing how to use a computer. Anyway, my memory is a blank page. Nothing much fills it. I have my language, knowledge. I keep searching for a penchant, something I'm drawn to do to give me a hint of my forgotten life. Was I a baseball player? Pool shark? Ladies man? Alcoholic? For a long while I thought I was a musician. I kept going back to that, like catching a scent on a breeze in the woods. It caused a stirring, deep inside. Nope. No piano, guitar, violin. I don't know cards, or chess. I spend too much time watching television, going to the movies. Haven't you heard enough of this since forever?"

"I'll listen for forever if it helps."

"Okay. So? Shall we order something to eat?"

"I'm good. Another wine, maybe. You know, that's what bothers me. I was supposed to help you get your memory back. For all we know, you may be gay."

He laughed. "Funny! It's like I can be anything I want to be. I can rub the genie bottle, make a wish, and A La Kazam! I am! Gay? I don't think so. Let's go to your apartment and find out."

"Oh! Your apparatus is in working order. I've had to change your sheets."

"I don't want any more hospital or rehabilitation."

"You can be discharged whenever you say. You're on outpatient basis. There's nothing keeping you."

"I know. Nothing except you, and you are my everything."

"Don't start that again."

"Whenever I say I love you, you shush me up. I wish I could say the gold at Fort Knox is behind it, but you must accept my honesty."

"Oh! Keith! I do!"

"Then what? I care for you. I love you deeply. As deeply as I can as a person without a foundation. You are special to me. I want us to have fun from now on. I want to buy a motor home and travel all over this country. We'd make love under the stars, and hike to magnificent overlooks. We'd stop and meet people and take part in festivals, see the sights, meet the mayors, you know? When we're tired of that, we find our jewel of a home. I don't know the reason, but I think near the seashore someplace. We'd do shrimp in beer and do ribs on the barbecue. When we got tired of that, off we go to Europe! I want to see all of Italy, England, France, Germany, Switzerland, Sweden. Then, we'd go to China and Japan; Africa; and maybe even tour South America. Australia might be nice."

"You're painting dreams on a scrim. Foxfire. We'd need another lifetime."

"No. We'll make this one count."

"Keith, I love you. With all my heart. I died with every moan you made, and I sucked wind with every needle I stuck into you. You always found the humor in everything, I think just to make me feel okay. Especially when you were near death. You almost died so many times I could read your signs like a billboard. When I was away from you, not with any others, I would look for a glass of wine. And then I found the best was escapage, and I became a voracious reader. I can see where some caregivers take stronger stuff. I didn't need it. I just needed to be able to hit the relax buttons. After, I was okay and ready for the next to-do. I'll say it again, I love you, Keith. No matter what I say, I feel the resistance. As if you're not totally ready to commit. You're ambivalent. What you mean—you want me but not yet—is not what you say."

"I know. I've got to find out who I am. I can't stand being a cipher. A big zero. If I could get another concussion —you know how that works sometimes?--and get back my life. The real problem with that is one just has a bigger headache."

"You've tried everything psychological. What do you do now?"

"I can start the first day of my new life, right here, right now with you. I can't do it. It would be the cruelest thing I could do. We'll become lovers, inseparable, and then I'll hold you at arm's length and say, 'I remember who I am'."

"Keith . . . I'll take that chance. I know every single inch of your body, renovations and all. Should I tell you what debridement means to a burn patient? I don't have to tell you because that's what I've done to you for years and years! I've had to remove the dead, burned skin—detritus, eschar--from all over your body. I had to be careful my salty tears did not fall on you as I was doing it. You don't remember how painful an ordeal it was because you would be loaded with as much pain medicine as you could endure. It was never enough. Shall I show you how you winced? Shall I show you how you jerked when the pain stabbed you like a hatchet cutting into your flesh? Should I imitate your moans and groans. I can do that because I took them home with me, night after night. I can imitate them perfectly. Even when the doctor would take over because he couldn't stand watching me do that knowing how I felt about you, I could hear you down corridors and hallways. The sound followed me down streets and the television could never be turned up loud enough to drown out your cries as I ripped off your flesh! I've watched your skin grafts take and peel off. I've blown your nose and cut your nails. I know you better than I know myself. Except for one thing. I have a confession to make. I wasn't going to tell you, but it makes no difference how things go. When you feel you're ready to go, to leave the hospital, I'm going to leave the hospital and all, too. I will have to leave the profession. I really don't think I could continue. Well, maybe in a maternity ward . . ."

"You'd quit nursing?"

"Yes. I want to take up basket weaving, or landscape gardening, anything that doesn't have anything to do with human beings. All of my patients, most especially you, all needed something, and expected me to take them back to a perfect world. When I took on a patient I made each one a promise that I would take them back as close as possible to a perfect world. Then, I came to you and broke my promise. I have never left a patient so far from home base. I have never had a patient who was as badly mangled mentally and physically as you. And, I have to say it, I have never encountered any patient who had as much force of power to become whole again. You have astounded everyone who has come into contact with you. More than many times I've heard, 'I'd really like to know how Keith makes out.' Keith, you've got to let us know. Okay?"

"Sure. Why not?"

"So? What happens to you?"

"I'm going to peel myself layer by layer like an onion until I get to me just as you had to do to debride the skin that was no longer of any use to me."

"Bravo! We've all tried to help you do that, to no avail. What are your plans?"

"I have my military record. Period. As you know, the Army did everything to try to locate anyone I went with to Iraq, or who trained with me. I was only one of a half dozen that survived the engagement in Mosel. I've got a name or two I'll have to chase down. I think my only real chance is to go back to the town where I enlisted. My home address was a horse farm in Tennessee. Someone may not recognize me, but they may know about me. If it's also my hometown, I'll try the schools and hang around the neighborhoods. I'll be praying to hear, 'Yo! Keith! Long time no see!' It'll be a start."

"It's a long shot, but something might jar your memory."

"You, first person I'm going to tell. Now, what's the one thing?"

"One thing?"

"You know me all except for one thing."

"If I tell you, I've got to have it."

"There isn't anything in the world I have right now that I wouldn't give to you, Louise Comma The Nurse. I know you have given me everything you have for all these years. How can I possibly have something to duplicate your gift to me? What is it? It shall be yours."

"It really comes in two parts, like two halves of a ball. You are going to leave me to go find yourself, right?

"Yes. We both know the reason."

"You will go away, and I pray you will come back."

"Yes. At this moment, it is my fervent wish, too."

"But you may not come back."

"Yes. I may not come back. That may be for any number of reasons."

"Yes, we both know that. You could . . . die."

"You made me strong enough to ward off any infections, but, yes, I could die."

"Short of death, Keith Franklin, if you don't come back to me, you must promise me you will let me know the rock bottom, unqualified reason, no matter how much you think the truth will hurt me."

"I owe you that, Sweetheart. I owe you that in the least. I think you mean to explain it in a way you can understand, even if you don't agree with it."

"Yes. I have to know what was bigger than this love of ours."

"I hope I can come back here, and say, 'I love you,' and nothing else matters."

"I hope so, too. You know, if you don't come back to me, we will never see each other again. I know the pain would be too great for me. I would die if I saw you again and couldn't have you."

"Oh! Lord! I don't know what's out there, but I would die, too. Unless . . ."

"Unless what?"

"We both know and understand . . . a hypothetical? Okay? It is possible if I come upon my old self, somehow, someway, that when I'm that person, I may not remember I was ever this person. If that happens, you become non-existant. This love we have right now, this earthquake of emotions is not even a ripple in a brook. We will be invisible to each other. We will be total strangers. I can't imagine."

"Neither can I. God! I don't know which way to pray! I love you so much I want you to be who you are, and find yourself. I want that, but I'll always be in denial about it. Talk about ambivalence, seeing both sides of the coin."

"You know what could be worse?"

"Yes. I don't want to think about it."

"Yes, talk about ambivalence. What if I learn who I am, and have to choose between being Keith and coming back to you, and being Mr. Joe Memory and remaking a bed in a lost memory."

"I don't envy you. I don't envy myself."

"So? What's the second half of what you want of me?"

"The day you leave the rehabilitation center? I want to know you all. I want us to make love."

43

BROOKE ARMY MEDICAL CENTER, PRESENT DAY

The young man sat in a straight-backed chair directly in front of the desk. He sat upright as if he had been cast from a mold. His crew cut was dead white. His face had a puffy, steroidal look. Looking beneath, one could see it once was much thinner, a more handsome, orderly face. His cheeks were slightly sunken where his molars would have been. His too straight nose and marked jaw line looked changed. Altogether, it made him look older than his brief years. He moved deliberately. His eyes, a drizzly day gray, were half-closed. They focused on the ink pen held by the man behind the desk. He was using it to write in a notebook. The man wore large horn rimmed glasses and a Van Dyke. He had salt-and-pepper hair. He wore no jacket. He had on wide red, white and blue suspenders; a pastel pink shirt with large onyx cuff links; and an orange and purple paisley tie. He continuously pursed his lips as he wrote.

"The shades? Could you draw them?" the young man said. He asked not because he was sensitive to light, but because he found himself more comfortable when he didn't have to see the other person so clearly. It was the inner distance he sought.

The man shoved himself back from the desk. He scurried from window to window to yank down the shades. He turned to look at the young man, nodded curtly to acknowledge he had done his bidding. He returned to his seat.

When the young man first sat he had the sensation to get up, to turn around and to walk right out. Now, fighting

199

the desire, he lit a cigarette. He opened and shut his lighter several times, working the metallic snap and click.

The man looked up and stared at the lighter. He scraped drawers open and rattled them shut. Finally, he found an ashtray. He put it on the edge of the desk.

"You are?" the man asked.

"Keith Franklin. You know that."

"How long were you in Iraq?'

"I don't know. According to the records about a month."

"Did you go to Iraq with a battle buddy?"

"I was told I did. Yes."

"The report indicates you went on patrol every day without a break for three weeks. What was your buddy's name?"

"I was told it was Jim Dorchester."

"Did you go together on patrols?"

"I don't know. The way it worked, I'm told, buddies stay together. One would not go on patrol without the other."

"Was he with you when you were injured?"

"I don't know."

"Did anything happen to him?"

"Yes."

"Was he injured?"

"Yes."

"How badly?"

"I was told he was captured and killed. Look! You've got all this stuff in that file."

"I can look it up, but it'll go faster if I just ask you. How long have you been in the traumatic brain injury unit?"

"TBI? I don't know. As far as I'm concerned, every day I've been in the hospital. What's it been? Some three years and then a couple three more in rehabilitation?"

"You'd like to be discharged from the rehabilitation center."

"Fuck yes. I need to get back to the rest of my life."

"And despite your memory loss you feel you are capable to be on your own?"

"There's not a fucking thing I've got to be afraid of except someone regulating my life. Look! I practically had to learn to speak to myself all over again. I can make myself understood."

"What is your ASN?"

"My serial number? You don't have it? It's on my meat tag."

"No need. It's a memory thing."

"I don't remember."

"And who are you? I know. I already asked."

"Keith Franklin."

"Keith, the way your memory is, how do you know that that's who you are?"

"You tell me."

"Keith, the best I can tell you is that you may be dealing with a very complicated matter. If I was allowed the time, I believe I could come to the bottom of your situation. It just would take a lot of time. One, your loss of memory could be solely due to your TBI, your traumatic brain injury. Two, your loss of memory could be from a psychologically traumatic event. Three, your loss of memory could be a combination of both. I'm sorry. We can take it no further. My best advice is either learn to live within the limitations imposed on you by your memory loss. You may be lucky to find a clinic that has grant money to take you on, and help you. You may live a more fulfilling life if you just accepted that your memory is permanently lost because of your physical injury."

44

Louise lived in a condo that had a small balcony that overlooked the main drag. It was very early in the morning. Traffic on the road was little to none. Keith sat nude in the dark in a wicker chair, his feet up. He lit a cigarette then tossed the lighter by the deck of cigarettes. He inhaled deeply, and let the smoke whistle out of his lips. It had to have been centuries since the last time he made love, of course before he got banged up. The way he felt at the moment, and as he knew now, he must have been mad, passionately, crazy for it. It was a sharing he sought. He nodded in agreement with his own thoughts that he always got back more than he gave. There wasn't a bit of him that wasn't into it completely. He held nothing back. Every single fraction of a second, from the first to the last thought of making love, was complete absorption. After, it was total collapse. What a magnificent joy it was to love. What a royal ode to life's expression.

Louise came out in a thin wrap. She held a cup of tea. She ran her hand through Keith's hair and down his arm. She sat next to him. She touched his knee, and he looked at her.

"Keith, I feel so complete. I have never, ever been loved and so fulfilled. I was never so totally consumed making love as I have been this evening making love with you. I could whack myself with a lightning bolt for not doing this with you sooner. It's not just because I love you, but also no one ever has made love to me as you have tonight. Where in the name of heaven did this come from? I have never read, or had a friend, male or female, describe such lovemaking before. I have never been so excoriated from my emotional and physical foundation as I found myself tonight. I never knew such a thing could exist. How? Why? Can you tell me?"

Keith reached over to take her hand. "Perhaps, after all these years of dealing with me, a person that needed you so badly to cling to life, your love and caring is answered. You have done a magnificent job. I wasn't taken away from you in a body bag, incinerated, and buried in Potter's Field. Maybe, like the Pied Piper, God gave me a special gift."

She squeezed his hand. "No, my love. You don't understand. It's not just the emotional heights you brought me to; it was how you took me there—physically. You don't make love like anyone else. Your technique is different. It's wham-bam-thank you, Ma'am, for most fellows. Once you're in me all the way, you fill me to overflowing. I don't mean to be clinical, but I must. I must express it to myself. You make us both move together rapidly. You hold me in complete syncopation, in complete thrall. I explode!"

"Yes, I yearned that you respond! I wasn't aware that was what I was doing. I didn't know that was how I made love."

"What do you mean?"

"I have this deep hunger for love. I have this lake that fills to overflowing from an underground river. I must respond to that."

"Underground river. I know I don't want to explore that. The result when you do that is that I pass out. Did you know that? That I passed out? I fainted."

"I didn't know you would pass out, but I knew you did. I had to fight to keep my own self conscious. It is an electrical discharge that fulgurates through my brainpan."

"When I came to, I was still coming. It seems it wouldn't stop. The spasms came and came. It was an exquisite, almost unbearable, performance. I would say there aren't too many men that have your strength that enables you to sustain that technique. All that because I love you so."

"It couldn't have happened if I didn't love you. Are you aware such love-making brings out your angel's hand when I'm far inside . . ."

". . . angel's hand?"

"I can only explain it as an irresistible command that makes me come whether I want to or not, no matter how hard I fight it, that feels like a tiny hand that touches me when I am deep inside you that burrows into the opening of my penis that fills my veins with molten juice. I really believe what one of my psychiatrists told me. Perhaps it answers both of our questions about my love making. He said our memory worked on two levels, intellectual and emotional. Intellectual memories may be blanked out for any of several reasons, such as aging, physical trauma, or in some cases emotional trauma, such as rape or torture. He believed emotional memory always remains, for the life of the person. The way I physically make love is based on my emotional memory. I had to have had a special love in my life that endures in my emotional memory, as we have spoken about before. The term used with animals is 'imprinted,' such as a crow acquiring a human imprint. In my heart I can say I love you, but deep in my heart I know it is a different love . . ."

". . . they call it obligatory love. You feel obligated because of what a person has done for you . . ."

"If you accept that, I do, too. I don't believe I love you any less, just differently. On that basis I ask you to understand the reason I'm compelled to search . . ."

"You're still leaving in the morning?"

"Yes."

"Would you consider postponing for a week? Keith? I can't get enough of your lovemaking. I can't get enough of your being with me. I can't get enough of being with you. You can't leave me after giving me this, this majesty of love. Stay."

He shook his head. He lit another cigarette. "Can't do that."

"Take me with you?"

He shook his head. "I'd love being with you. But, your presence will influence my judgment. I wouldn't be able to find my true self. I might quit before I completed my search. I would have to be anesthetized not to want you every moment. I can't do that to myself. I must know who I am. Louise, I must know who she is."

The silence brought the noise of distant traffic between them.

"No, no you don't."

"What do you mean?"

"We talked about it before. I don't even allow myself to think about this aspect of your . . . 'amnesia.'"

"What do you mean?"

"To do this kind of work, I studied very hard. I have a list of degrees, but all they mean is that I was trained to be a counselor. Once a counselor, always a counselor. You just can't take it out of me. It's how I think. I live in denial with one aspect of what's happened to you. Keith, if you were just in a fugue state, where you lost your memory for some psychological trauma, it would not endure for very long, certainly not for your six years or so. The problem is, there is no way we can ascertain that definitely. Every psychiatrist that's examined you has had to cross the fact that you had a traumatic brain injury. That overrides almost every other consideration about your memory loss."

"That's what I've been told. I'm not really ready to accept it. There is something—like a B-B in a bottle rattling around—inside me that won't let me just abandon a life that belongs to me. I'm determined to find it again, a reprise if you like."

"I pray for you that it's just been a detour. You've mentioned that perhaps another whack or two might bring your memory back. The fact is all that would do is possibly give you another concussion. If it was TBI then your memory could have been totally erased, and you'll never get it back. Or, it could start coming back to you in increments, either spontaneously, or with cognitive animation. Something may spark a long-hidden memory— a sight, a sound, a smell, a touch, anything to do with your senses. Such an event, a stressor, say, no matter how big or small, could be just that minute memory, or it could open the floodgates and bring your past life back to you."

"I see."

"No, my love, you don't see. You don't see what I see, or you would be terror-stricken, too."

'What could that be?"

"That I could lose you."

"Louise, we've talked about all this before. We agreed we would just have to take that chance. It's a roll of the dice: We win all or lose all! Well, yes. I could learn I'm a murderer, or have a wife and nine or ten kids that are counting on me to support them, or . . ."

"Not anything like that. I don't trust anything that has anything to do with the human mind. Psychiatry is an imprecise science. It's got a lot of theory and even more by guess and by gosh. They've described a fugue state as a pathological amnesiac condition that may persist for several months. That's bullshit! They report a fugue patient in that state for almost two years!"

"Maybe he or she was malingering."

"Shit! I wish it were proven he was. Here's the fucking problem. When he returned to the quote/unquote normal state, he had no recollection of his actions during the fugue state!"

"Oh!"

"Oh! Just 'Oh!' I just got that on the Internet!"

"Look! I haven't been in a quote/unquote normal state for over six years! Why are you worried about a fugue state?" Jim flipped his cigarette over the balcony.

"Because that cigarette starting a forest fire and you coming out of a fugue state and not remembering me is a possibility!"

"Holy shit! That could never happen, Sweetheart! How could such a thing happen? We love each other too much! Where else could the world find such a love that it could just up and disappear into the air? No! No! I don't even want to think about it! I will get my memory back. I'm still wearing a dog tag that says I'm Keith, but I may not be Keith. The very worst is that I will have to make a choice between one life and another! You shouldn't worry about my coming back to you with such a strong, deep love between us? How could that happen?"

"It could happen!"

"It couldn't happen!" He lit up.

"I can give you instances all over the place of things like that happening!"

"Crazy! How could someone remember it happening if they never remembered what had happened to them! How can one remember they forgot something if they have no memory?"

"Ahhhhhhh!" Louise screeched and breaking into laughter. "You're crazy! What can I do with you?"

"I'm crazy in love with you, Sweetheart. If I had to live one day without you I would die. Why should you worry about what kind of love it is? A, B, C, or D. Love is love. It's all the same, but different. You shouldn't worry. I will be back. I don't see how I cannot come back to you."

"Okay. A hypothetical. Your memory returns. You don't forget the last six years, you remember them. Now, your memory has returned and the person or persons that you forgot for all these years are just as compelling to you as I am. What do you do?"

He reached over and put his hand in her lap. He let it slide downwards. She guided his hand. Beneath the silk he could feel the opening, and then pressed the bump of her clitoris. "What are my choices?"

"You have only one choice."

"Yes. Suicide."

"If I came along with you, I could argue my own case in person. I wouldn't have to ride with you. I'd get my own motorcycle."

"I can't have you under false pretenses! For God's sakes, Louise, do you think it's easy for me? That I'd rather just stay with you, and the hell with the world as what it was? Do you think I don't love you? I do, and that's the reason I must come back to you as a complete human being, not as a shadow of a shadow. Besides, if you came with me, we'd be stuck in motel rooms for days on end."

"When you leave, I won't follow you."

"I know," Keith said.

"When I think of it I catch my breath: We may never see each other again."

"I know." He took in a long, deep breath. "What then?"

"What then? That's what I ask." She took his cigarette, made the end glow, and crushed it out. The smoke whistled out of her like an angry arrow shooting for its mark. "Keith, if Fate says we're not to see each other, I suppose like an old fire horse, I'll get a whiff of smoke. Before I know it, I find another patient near death and cuss him to life to get my mind off of you. In that case, I don't want to hear your violin music. I don't want to hear your voice."

"Send a dozen roses?" He lit up again.

"Don't you fucking dare! Just don't leave me in fucking limbo. Send me something--something substantial. Send me a sign."

"Like what?"

She took another drag from his cigarette. She handed it back to him. "If not an engagement ring, then a tennis bracelet. Yes, an expensive tennis bracelet. A very expensive tennis bracelet. That would be a very nice double edged sword."

"That would be the least I could do, I would think."

"Oh! Shut up! Keith!" she said as she stood, reached for his hand and moved to go inside, "For God's sakes, take us to see what is beyond Jupiter."

BOOK THREE

45

Keith left Louise with high anticipation and started on his journey to find his memory. The electricity of excitement was offset by the trepidation generated by the unknown. He approached the search philosophically. He may not ever discover a word about his life before Louise. At least she would be his anchor. He could return to her and her loving arms. Or, would this long detour return him to his main road of life, and what would it bring? He smiled at the hospital ceiling bromide: He wasn't a quitter. He'd play the cards he was dealt.

The horse farm kitchen looked like a banquet hall. A broad, long table with chairs rimming it ran down the center. The stove and sinks, serving tables, and gathering tops for dirty dishes went out both ways along the wall from a corner. There were clothes hooks, some with abandoned sweaters, scarves, and jackets along the entrance door wall. Underneath were trays for boots with bootjacks here and there. A spit can for wads of chewing tobacco guarded the entrance near the door. Two ceiling fans were over the table. Black peppered fly strips cut the air in random patterns around the room.

Keith cuddled the coffee cup. He sat with his back at the stove.

"Keith Franklin, you're a sight for sore eyes. Oh! I remember the last time you were here, but I don't remember how long ago," Joyce said. She was round-faced, gray-blonde, and heavy. She wore a chef's jacket, striped pants and clogs.

"But you remember me?"

She poured coffee. "What do you mean, course I remember you. You didn't have a beard then, your hair wasn't white. I can't recollect your face exactly. Must be some ten years. Listen! I'm married now, so bygones are bygones. You know?"

"I'm not looking for anything except information about myself, Joyce. I was injured in the war. I was burned, but worse, I lost my memory. TBI, they call it. Traumatic brain injury. Some sort of a fugue, something. So, I lost a lot of my life. I'm trying to reconstruct it; that's the reason I'm here."

"You don't remember me?"

"No, not at all. Sorry. My service record says I gave this horse farm here in Sheffield, Tennessee, as my address when I enlisted."

"That's right. You were living here. The owners said it would be all right if I let you have the room over the garage. You used to help with the horses."

"Horses?"

"The farm used to raise Tennessee Walking Horses. Not anymore. Things took a turn. The bank foreclosed about four months ago. I used to feed twenty-two hands give or take here every morning, noon, and night, 365 days a year. You don't remember?"

"No."

"Oh! I'm sorry. War doesn't have pretty leavings."

"Can you tell me anything about me? Anything at all? How long did I live here? Did I go to school in town? Did I have friends? You know, anything."

"Keith . . . You seem hurt in a lot of ways. Add to that I don't want to do, but I understand what you're looking for, so I won't lie to you. You used to live in town with your father. An alcoholic, he was. No, that's not exactly right. He was a fucking, drunkard, son-of-a-bitch. Just for exercise he used to beat the shit out of you. Three, four years ago, frozen to death they found him on the railroad tracks about four miles out of town with a bottle in his hand. Does that bring anything to mind?"

Keith stared into the coffee. He shook his head. "Where's he buried?"

"At the town hall there might be records. To be brutally honest? The indigent section of the cemetery."

"When did I come here?"

"Maybe a year and a half before . . . before you went into the service."

"You hesitated?"

"Well, I sure am surprised to see you riding a motorcycle. Takes some daring. The horses. You weren't meant to be around horses. You were . . . timid with them. The animals, they could tell. The doggers didn't like to have you around. You were shaking every time you had to put on a bridle or a saddle. All they'd let you do is walk them around, curry comb them, and help muck out the stables. Once when they told you to give them their ration of oats, you dropped the whole bucket when the horses put the razzle-dazzle on you. You remember that?"

"No."

"You would remember that if I did."

"What else was there?"

"Keith, I always liked you. I didn't know why you came back here, but I was going to tell you right up front I'm married now. I married one of the hands. They kept us on to look after the place. So, if you were stopping by with something else in mind, I'd have to ask you not to stay."

"Joyce, I appreciate your honesty. I'm not here for anything but to remember who I am. I have no idea why I'd be here for anything else."

'Really?"

"God's honest truth."

She drummed her fingertips against the tabletop as she pursed her lips, and looked Keith in the eye. "Let's walk over to the garage where you used to stay."

As they walked side by side, she said, "Do you remember Cindy Jo?"

"Cindy Jo? Wait." Keith reached into his pocket and took out the photograph he was given in the hospital. "This Cindy Jo? I was told I used to keep this picture of her in my helmet in Iraq."

Joyce took the photograph and stopped walking. "Yes. That's my Cindy Jo. That's my daughter. I'm surprised you still carry her picture."

"So?"

They continued walking. "So? It's not a nice story. You came back on leave maybe some four, five, six months after you enlisted into the Army. You came looking for Cindy Jo. You told me then that you were both planning to get married. Do you remember what happened?"

"No."

Joyce took a deep breath. "I told you Cindy Jo had gone away. While you were away, she met a fellow and married him, and left. You were like a leaf in a gale of wind. Like a horse with his tail on fire. You had a lot of time left on your leave, and you didn't know what you were going to do. I said you could stay up there in the garage."

"And I did?"

"Yes. I offered with some selfish thinking on my part. I was alone at the time. In the afternoon, after I cleaned up the kitchen, and had supper pretty much taken care of, I went riding. I loved to ride those beautiful, ballet-dancing Tennessee Walkers. After a couple hours of rubbing against that saddle and getting my snatch massaged and bumped, you know what I mean, I had the flaming hots. So, after supper, when the farm really quieted down, I waited for you to go up to the room, and I followed you. Keith, you may not have been any good around horses, but you were fantastic in the saddle. I was with you all night, and was with you whenever I could slip away. I was so curious, too."

"Curious? About what?"

"Well, let's see what I can do about getting your memory back. I'll do a re-play." She opened the door to the room. "You go lay on the bed for a bit." Keith shrugged, and relaxed on the bed. "Now I'll picture like it was when I busted into the room and found you and Cindy Jo together. I'll give you a flashback of exactly what happened after I opened the door on you two and walked in:

"Cindy Jo!" she called. In her mind she saw the nude couple entangled on the bed. Despite her appearance, Cindy Jo continued a pattern of loud screaming as she kicked her legs in the air. Keith bellowed with each lunge. Both were oblivious of the intruder.

Joyce could not believe the performance, and walked up to the side of the bed.

Cindy Jo, eyes closed, arms clamped around Keith's neck, feet now crossed at his buttocks, screamed, "Oh! Lover! Do you know how to fuck!"

Keith rolled out of her embrace onto his back, and looked up into Joyce's face.

Cindy Jo looked up. "Ma! What are you doing here!"

"I was in the next county, heard you baying like a banshee, and thought you were being butchered! Get dressed and get home, and you, Keith, get your ass out of here, off this property!"

"Do you remember that, Keith?"

"I don't remember that," Keith said. "I don't."

"Too bad," Joyce said. "When you came back on leave I had some selfish, horny thoughts. I wanted to know the reason Cindy Jo screamed like that. I found out. Yessiree, Bob! You sure was special." She shook her head, and looked off blankly for long moments. "But, like I said, now that I'm married I don't ride very often."

46

It was late morning when Keith pulled up before the Robbie Hair Salon in Chadwick, West Virginia, Pop. 21,000. He sat on the stilled motorcycle, feet splayed, and took off his helmet. He stared at the window. He got off the bike, a cigarette lit before he took a step. To settle his equilibrium after the long ride, he walked up the street. He checked out the stores and the activity on both sides. He turned, walked in the other direction. He found nothing different. He hitched his pants and walked into the salon.

"Robert Foster," he said to the receptionist. He took off his baseball cap.

"Oh! Yes! Robbie!" she squealed. She pointed to the first station.

Keith hoped he was the one he was told about that in basic training was known as "Queenie." He was working a client with razor and comb. His hair was bleached blonde in a tight butch. He bent his body at odd angles as he moved around the chair. The baby face made him look like a kid. Keith tried to think of what he may have been like, and guessed he may have grown an inch or so taller. The tight pants, loose silk shirt, and designer shoes may have added to the illusion. He barely glanced at Keith. He continued working. He stopped moving. He was lost in thought. He put down the comb and razor and motioned to a young woman standing in the back. He turned and walked directly up to Keith.

"I'm guessing we were in basic together."

"I know that only because of my military record."

"The fuck do you want? I don't remember your name, and I don't recognize your face."

"I'm Keith Franklin."

215

"Keith Franklin? Oh! Yeah! I recall the name! Let's do coffee." He grabbed his hand to shake it, and held on to it as he led the way out. On the sidewalk, he stopped and pointed to the motorcycle. "Yours?" Keith nodded. "Macho," he said.

Robbie slid into a booth in the restaurant. He didn't wait for Keith to sit before he told him, "You're the first soldier from basic I've seen. Wouldn't give a fuck for the rest of them. Why are you here? It's not reunion time?"

"I've lost my memory. I'm trying to learn about my past."

"Maybe I can help. I remember your buddy, the one they called your twin? What's his name?"

"I think you mean Jim Dorchester?"

"Right! I owe you both for my life." The waitress appeared. "My usual Bloody Mary, Sweetie," Robbie said, then to Keith, "Whatever you'd like. Breakfast, lunch, dinner . . . ?"

"Double Chivas would be fine."

Robbie looked at the waitress and nodded. She left. "Jim? A real warrior. He was my guy. He looked out for me. What happened to him?"

"He got nailed in Iraq the first month. They never did send his body back."

"Oh! Shit! Sorry! I liked him. He was all right. I don't remember which of the two of you it was, but I would have been hamburger in that fucking place. I cursed that brute son of a bitch that kept after me. Do you know the power of a curse? Last I heard someone in the stockade kicked his balls for a field goal that killed him. Does that help?"

"Everything about the service is a blank. Everything I know I got from a file they gave me. So? Tell me."

Robert looked at him strangely. In staccato sentences, he told his story of Army life. "It was you or Jim that saved my ass, pardon the pun."

"I don't remember. I'm sure no one liked what was going on with you."

"You and Jim were the only ones that did something about it. Yeah! He was solid. Tough. A proper citizen. As I remember, neither of you was married."

"From the service record I was shown, and what I was told, Jim married his grade school sweetheart. They went on their honeymoon right after basic. You had to be a pretty good soldier yourself, Robert. Too bad that ignorant, red-necked bastard was in the same platoon. What he did kept you out of Iraq. He must have hurt you real bad to have you discharged. I'd say he saved your life. It would have been a privilege to go to war with you."

He stared at Keith. "You are some guy. Thank you. I don't know how to pay you back."

"I don't expect you to give me back my life."

The waitress made another trip.

"You mean, you don't remember what happened to me in basic? You don't remember basic? Nothing? The last six years or so is just hospital, nothing before?"

"Nothing. No childhood, no parents, no prom, no growing up. Just being a sick soldier, and a fantastic woman who devoted every moment of her life to me kept me alive."

"Keith, I'm not the smartest man in the world. I don't want to give you unwanted advice, but you must believe me. Life is a wound. You're not going to find gold stars and medals in your past. If you found someone who loves you, and you love her, don't be stupid and lose her for foxfire. Go right back to where you came from, grab life with both hands, and marry her."

"How'd you get so smart?"

"Life is wretched. Joy is measured in needle points; pain by the pailfuls. Today is here, snatch it; fuck! Tomorrow may never come. You won't know the true misery until you've had an enema of loneliness gush into your guts. That's when you learn the language of suicide and unhappiness. I counsel other gays. I find a lot of that. I can't help you in any other way, Keith. In thinking about it, gay suited me. I found a partner, and here it is? What? Six years later? We still hold hands and kiss goodnight. No children yet, but hope springs eternal!"

Keith rapped the table. "You're a riot, Mr. Robert. I'm sorry you can't contribute to my autobiography other than those minutes in Basic. Do you remember anything you think might help me remember?"

Robert chewed the celery stalk. "As honest as I can be? Taking everything into account, as I remember the two of you—Jim and you—you weren't the one who would be riding a motorcycle. Do you know what I mean?" Keith shook his head. "We couldn't smoke in Basic, but you would be the smoker. As I remember you and the other fellow, not you would be the beard guy. And, another thing, thinking about it, your walk. I remember the way a guy walks better than his face. I don't remember you walking the way you do. Maybe getting your legs the fuck roasted had something to do with the way you walk now. Something else, I do remember you had a dirty mouth. I don't remember your voice. It's raspier now." Keith pulled down his collar to show a tracheotomy scar. Robbie nodded. "There was another Keith in the barracks, so they referred to you as 'Tennessee.' Are you from Tennessee?" Keith shrugged. "Everyone talked about their girlfriends. You were supposed to get married when you went home on leave. Did you?"

"I didn't know until I went back to Tennessee. That's where I came from. I didn't marry her. If I did, it would have made my search short."

"So now what? I didn't help you very much."

"I have no other place to search. This is the end of it for me. I'll have to live without a memory, without a past. There would be no sense to going back to Mosel in Iraq. What the fuck would I do there? Take pictures of a burned up Army truck? Or sit in it and try to visualize what happened? This ends my search. How depressing can it get?"

"Now what?"

"I wish I could just crawl in a hole. I can't because my conscience won't let me. I've got to see Jim's widow. I was at the firefight. That's all I can tell her. First, I don't know if she'll want to see me."

"Yeah! Follow your instinct. I'll bet she's remarried. Life is for the living. She may not want to re-open that scene. She may resent you for it. I'd think very hard before I made that trip."

"I've thought of that. But, I have to do it for myself. Maybe something she knows will give me back a piece of my life. If Jim and I were as close buddies as you say, I owe it to him to see her. Did I tell you I saw a video of her at Jim's funeral? I guess they all say the same thing. She doesn't believe Jim is dead."

"They never got his body. She could be right."

"No. I went over and over it with Army personnel. There are no more savage, uncivilized, brutal bastards in the world than the fucking ignorant Al Qaeda. If they got Jim and never gave him up, they fried and ate his liver for breakfast, like the mad beasts they are. Got to give it to them, though. They are superior, tough fighters. That's all they know. That's their life . . . and death."

"Keith, go home. Go back to the nurse. You're only going to find trouble with Jim's widow."

"Like what?"

"Like you and Jim were so much alike, almost mirror images. You two used to talk to each other for hours. Everyone in the barracks sort of envied you two. It's like the two of you became shadows of each other. With you so much like Jim, and Jim so much like you, like suppose with so much empathy with one another love blooms. Yea, suppose you meet his widow and through compassion, sympathy, identification, you both fall in love with each other? It could happen."

"That's a fascinating conceit, but it could never happen."

"'Never' and 'always' are used by the arrogant ignorant, and married couples who should never use those words. Would you like to make a sucker bet?"

47

Heading for Massachusetts on the motorcycle, Keith had gone over everything in his mind. The trip would keep him away from Louise for two or three days at the most. He had to see Jim's widow out of respect. He knew she would have questions about Jim's last hours, which he couldn't answer. One of these days he would remember everything. When he did, he would go back to fill in the blanks. He had the same giddy, niggling feeling he had when he went to the farm in Tennessee, and when he went to see Robbie, too.

The tease was he might come across something that would unlock the floodgates of his past and he would become Keith Franklin, Person With A Past.

Keith rode into Great Farraday. It was located in the heart of the Berkshire Hills of Western Massachusetts. It had a population of 8,497 in the winter, and 16,221 in the summer. He cruised southward to the main section of town. He passed gas stations, Domaney's Liquors, and went over the Green Bridge. Very soon he was into storefronts on both sides of the street. He first went by the Methodist, Catholic, and Protestant churches. Then came the post office, banks, library. Next was the main drag with its side streets, restaurants, store windows, and Town Hall. Within the next two miles he passed more churches, gas stations, a cemetery, a large shopping center. Then, finally, he came to The Garden Center.

He pulled into a parking place. He killed the engine, put down the kickstand, and leaned the motorcycle against it. He removed his helmet as he got off, and reached for a cigarette. He lit it. He ambled around the machine inspecting it. It served as an excuse to consider the moment. He kicked the back tire. He walked some more. He kicked the front tire. The cigarette glowed as he sucked in. The smoke blew out of him like a jet. Two more drags and he ground the butt under his heel. It was time to make the move.

He looked up and saw a customer just yards away grappling with a monstrous flower basket hanging from a suspended pipe. The more she pulled at it, the more it got caught on the cross pipe holding a long line of other plants. He saw the pipe was losing its perch. In a half dozen strides, Keith reached up for the falling pipe. A blondie woman was underneath wearing a triangular handkerchief over her head, and jeans and sneaks. She was bent over, deadheading a plant. Her back was to him. She was oblivious to the danger. From behind, Keith put his arm around her middle, lifted and swirled her around. She grunted. He grabbed the pipe with his other hand to hold it up to keep it from klonking her.

"What are you doing?" blondie shouted. "Put me down!"

"Son of a bitch!" the customer said. "Why do they put these so high up?" Carrying the basket, she turned and moved toward the check out, oblivious to the catastrophe she nearly caused.

Blondie made a pirouette out of Keith's arm. "The hell are you up to?"

"Not playing Statue of Liberty, as you can see?" Keith said holding up the runaway pipe.

"You're not playing anything!" she said. "Just get out."

"You want me to let go and leave? You can't see I'm . . ."

"Yes!"

"I'm holding up this . . . You really just want me to drop everything and walk away?"

"Yes! Yes!"

Keith stepped aside. He let go of the pipe. It collapsed spreading the hanging baskets it held all over the place.

Virginia came running over. "Shit! I knew this was going to happen one day!"

Keith headed for his motorcycle.

"Anyone get hurt?" Virginia asked.

When Keith got to his bike, he looked back to see the knot of women looking in his direction. One of them pointed to him. He lit a cigarette. He decided he'd let things cool down, then go back and look for Mrs. Medford Dorchester.

"Hi! I'm a poophead," he heard behind him. "Sorry."

He turned to see blondie. He looked at her. She looked at him. Their visions locked. Long moments passed. She blinked. He responded with a blink. He shook his head. "Oh! Hi! You're no poophead! Anything but. You're just not used to being manhandled."

She stared. "Jim? Is that you? Jim?"

"Jim? No, I'm not Jim, my name is Keith Franklin."

"Oh! My god!" She covered her face with both hands. She bent far over. When she straightened out she let out a loud gasp, almost a cry. She wobbled, unsteadily. He held out his hand to steady her. It took several seconds before she looked up at him. "You're not! Oh! God! Oh! God!"

"Jim and I were in the same unit."

"Give me a second. Let me catch my breath. Lord! I can't tell you how hard I prayed that someone that knew Jim would come to see me! And Keith! Keith? Yes? You were his dearest friend! He loved and cared for you so much. He wrote about you in every single one of his letters to me. So you're Keith! You used to live here long ago? You came up from Tennessee with two other men when Jim was living here. We never met when you were here, too. Oh! Let me hug you!"

They clung to each other for many long moments.

"You're Medford Dorchester? Jim's . . ."

"Yes."

"What a nice reception."

"Come, Jim! I've got to tell Virginia and Ashley! Then, we can go talk! And call me Gabbie. Jim called me Gabbie. Everyone calls me Gabbie."

"Gabbie it is. But, I'm still Keith."

"Oh! Did I call you Jim?"

"S'okay. Should I fix the cross pipe first?"

"Later! I want to listen to you talk until after dinner! Oh! Keith! Keith! You are a ray of sunshine in a world that turned so gloomy since Jim went away. I want to ask you so many things! So much I want to know! Thank you for coming to see me."

"It's been a long time . . ."

"That matters not at all. You're here now!" She led him to Virginia. She had lined up all the fallen hanging pots, and had moved the pipe to one side out of the way. "Virginia! You're not going to believe! This is Keith Franklin! Jim's friend from the army!"

Virginia's eyes went wide and sparkled as her stare tried to penetrate Keith's sunglasses. "Hi! Keith! God Bless you for coming to see Gabbie. Welcome."

Gabbie led Keith past greenhouses, into the house that was part of the property, then through the back door and into the kitchen. "We can sit on the deck. It's beautiful outside. I came in to grab you a beer. You must be dehyrated riding your Harley. Jim said he always wanted one."

"Beer's perfect."

Gabbie sat opposite Keith at the picnic table, which was in full sun. She put down a beer for him and an iced tea for herself.

"Hmmmm! What is that? The fragrance? Are you wearing perfume?"

"The girls and I went out for dinner last night. Yes."

"Tres Jolie."

"Yes! How do you know?"

"I think someone I know wears it."

"Jim spoke and wrote about you so often you seem so familiar. He really cared about you."

"Thanks. From what I've been told, I must have liked him a lot, too. They say he couldn't have been closer if he were my brother. They said if they fought one of us they'd have to fight the other."

"Jim wrote they used to call the both of you The Twins. I can see a lot of similarities, the same height, build. Course, Jim had a mop of brown hair last time I saw him. I want to know . . ."

Keith put up a hand. "Mrs. Dorchester . . . Gabbie. I must tell you something. I don't want to disappoint you, nor do I want you to be disappointed. I didn't know what to expect when I saw you, whether you'd like the idea or not. I do know you may want a lot of information from me. I'd walk through fire to give it to you. I haven't come sooner because I've been disabled and in a hospital since Iraq."

"Keith! That's more than six years ago!"

"Yes. Not good Karma. The point is I have no memory of a single thing beyond being in the hospital. You will want to know about Jim. You and I might just as well ask this bottle of beer for answers. I have no memory. I can tell you I've fallen in love with a nurse that has devoted her life to making me whole again. For her sake I'm searching for answers for who I am. I have no place else to look. So, when I leave here, I'm going back to her. Louise McBride. A redhead with blue eyes, can you imagine? I have only her to go back to. Let the chips fall where they may."

"I'm happy for you for that Keith, but you're saying you can't give me a single detail about the time you and Jim spent in Iraq?"

"That's right, not Iraq or Basic training. Not a single minute. I can tell you, everything I know came second and third hand."

"Were you with Jim when . . ."

"Yes, I think so."

"You can't tell me about Jim's last minutes?"

"No. Not a second. I'm sorry. I got pretty banged up. I spent a lot of time in a hospital, and the rehabilitation centers are sick of me. I have no memory of that other time."

Gabbie's face darkened. "Oh!" She turned away to look off at the horizon. "In my heart of hearts, I cannot believe or accept the fact that Jim is dead. That's all it is, a feeling burrowed in the warmest part of my soul. My hope was whoever was right alongside Jim when he was fighting would be able to tell me exactly what happened. Did he get shot? Did he die right there? Was he evacuated? Was he captured and made prisoner? Did someone actually see what happened? The problem is many of the soldiers he was fighting with, like you, were killed or wounded. There weren't too many others to question. And, those that were there either didn't know Jim or just didn't remember what happened in the madness of the moment. They told me Jim was captured, and those that were with him were all killed.

They said you weren't with Jim. The report said you were in a truck all by yourself when you were wounded."

"Yes. Everything you say is the same information I got."

"Tell me what you can. I know after Basic you made it possible for Jim to get a 48-hour pass so he could meet me in New York where I was studying the flute. Am I blushing?"

"Yes, kind of."

"It was our honeymoon."

"I don't remember that."

"Oh!"

"The history I got is that we were in Iraq for three-four weeks give or take. We were out on patrols for two or three days at a time. Usually it was house-to-house searches, looking for caches of explosives and arms. We had to put up with the improvised explosive devices, which we could never anticipate. I understand I was pulled out of a burning armored vehicle that had been hit by a rocket propelled grenade. There was flaming gas, phosphorus, and incendiary stuff. Parts of me were ablaze, too. Jim was not with me. The lieutenant in charge was killed, and a lot of other good men, so no one could tell me about Jim or what happened to him."

"I see. Keith, they never sent his body back to me."

"I know that. To try to snap my memory back, with not too much hope, they showed me a video of his funeral. I saw you."

"I assume it didn't create a recall, but why 'with not too much hope'?"

"If my memory loss was a fugue, a temporary psychological thing, perhaps. They say a fugue would have to be extraordinary to last, say, three years. The fact is, they really don't know the exact cause, but because of that reason they have to say it's a physical loss, not psychological. I had what they called a traumatic brain injury, a TBI, as they say in the military. When they brought me in, they took out a three-inch-square section of my skull. As is generally known, such injuries cause the brain to swell. With no place else to go, the brain starts building up pressure, which would cause portions of it to die off unless relieved. That three inch window saved me, but perhaps too late to preserve all of my memory."

"And that kept you laid up for more than six years?"

"Yes. That--the memory loss--and almost half of my body—face, neck, back, hands, legs--with third-degree and worse burns; a broken leg, fractured arms, and hairline fracture of my pelvis. They removed my spleen. What you see before you is a miracle of plastic surgery, skin grafts, bone re-sets, and Louise Comma The Nurse. I wouldn't be here without her. I would joke with her and say for more than six years she was my second skin. She gave me a second life."

"You love her, you said."

"The other part of the joke is that she grew on me."

"So? Now what?"

"For me? When I was supposedly all better? First, just recently I went to Tennessee, to the address listed on my service record. It was fast in, fast out. My father was dead, and no one else remembered me. I went to see the only other fellow that was in basic with us. His name is Robert Foster. He remembered Jim and me. He wasn't in the Army more than a month. With no one else either from Basic or Iraq, I have to end my search and make the most of what life I have left. I'm sorry. I wish I could have made things easier for you. I can't get back to Louise fast enough."

"Keith, I'm so grateful you came. There's nothing that could make things easier for me except Jim coming home, or at least getting his body back. Just so you'll know, Jim and I were grade school sweethearts. It doesn't always seem that way. The God of Love kept us apart right from the beginning by putting detours in our road to romance. The other side won, it seems. We made connections but only very briefly. Finally, as if to prove the point that Jim and I were never to be together, he went to war. That really did it. If he's really dead, then as Jim would say, his world and the whole world would be out of balance because we aren't together. With a love such as Jim and I had, it is incredible that we were denied. It's hard to go to the cemetery and talk to a dog tag, a helmet, a name tag from his blouse, and a headstone with his name on it. So? That's it?"

Keith ground out the cigarette. He looked at his fingernails. He folded his hands on his lap. "That's it. Yes. I'm afraid so. In my mind I thought there would be more. I didn't have as much to say to you as I thought I would. Life sucks. I'm sorry. I'm very sorry, Gabbie. My heart goes out to you. I'm afraid I need a hug as much as anyone." He got up and threw out his arms. She was drawn magnetically into them. They embraced, sensing the needed attraction. The compression relieved the frustration. They eased away from each other.

"Keith, it's fine. It's fine. You're too sensitive, so much like Jim. Stay for dinner at least. I see you're anxious to go."

"Upset. Anxious. Disappointed in not really pleasing you. I'm sorry. No. I'll head for home. If I think of anything I'll call you." He started to get up. He sat down. "I have to ask. In the tape they identified Jim's father at the funeral. He was in the background. Do you know where he lives? Perhaps I should go see him."

"I know where he lives. He's in town. You'd be wasting your time, especially if you have nothing to tell him. I was surprised he came to the funeral. He didn't participate or come around. He didn't send flowers or even a condolence card to me. He sat in the back in church. He just watched from off at a distance at the cemetery. He didn't speak to me before or during the funeral, and has made no effort to speak to me since."

"There had to be a reason."

"Yes, for him there was. He was more than upset when he learned he was not getting Jim's insurance money. He threatened to hire a lawyer."

"Ouch! Why did he presume he was entitled?"

"When he learned Jim had enlisted, he hammered him to make sure Jim took out life insurance. He kept saying he'd never make it back, and he should be sure to make things easy for his old man."

"Venal."

"I'll say. He wasn't just greedy--he was a dick, a nasty person. He came to see me the day before Jim's funeral. I was here."

* * *

His pickup truck skidded to a stop, skewed across two parking places. Glenn Dorchester, a baseball cap crammed onto his head, popped out leaving the door open. He threw down a cigarette and scrambled toward the large, arbor area where he spotted Virginia. His face was flush; his hands shook. "Where's Medford Soldi?"

Virginia turned slowly to face him. "There's no Medford Soldi here."

"You bitches hang together, I see that! You're covering for her! I know she lives here on my money! You tell her I want to see her!"

Gabbie turned off the watering hose. She walked toward Glenn until she was in front of him. "I'm so sorry you lost your son, Glenn. When I found out about Jim I went to your house to tell you. You wouldn't answer the door. I'm Medford Soldi Dorchester ."

"I know who the fuck you are!"

"I'm Jim's widow, your daughter-in-law."

"Don't get smart with me!"

"The funeral will be tomorrow."

He mimicked her. "The funeral will be tomorrow! You fucking hypocrite! All crocodile tears and sorrow! That insurance money is mine! It belongs to me! I'm his father! I should get it!"

"That isn't what Jim wanted."

"It's my money! I raised him! I spent a lifetime taking care of him and spending my hard-earned money to raise him! It's mine!"

"Jim said you took every penny he made since he was eleven years old!"

"I kept every cent he gave me in his own bank account! I gave him all that money when he went into the service!"

"There's no way to prove that, I'm sure. I'm his wife, and he didn't tell me about it. Do you want to know what he told me about you? He said, 'It's some heavy rent I pay for the few moments it took for him to inseminate my mother!'"

"You fucking cunt, I could smash your face in!"

Virginia picked up a garden spade, and moved up to stand beside Gabbie.

"Don't waste your energy, Glenn. Instead, come to your son's funeral tomorrow. You can ride with me, or you can have your own limousine."

He spit at her. "Go fuck yourself."

* * *

Gabbie tapped Keith on the back of his hand. "I'd give the money back if they'd return my Jim. I used the money to buy a share into this place with my friends, Virginia and Ashley."

"May I ask? The flute? At the hospital they said there was a flute in the picture of his wife. You said you were in New York and studying the flute. Jim must have talked about it to me, I would think. For a while there I was hoping if I heard familiar topics of conversation it would be like pulling the end of a thread that led to a long ball of memories." He lit another cigarette. Gabbie got him another beer. "Thanks."

"I could use a cigarette myself. The flute? Yes. I was really into music right up to the time I married Jim. I gave up the flute when they took Jim from me. It took the light of music right out of me. My parents helped darken the world for me, and I'm sure for themselves."

"Sorry to hear that. What brought this on?"

"I was thinking of the illusions of life. The hypocrisy we engender when the people who profess to love you, or like the people who should love us—like Jim's father—turn that love into something else. Right after Jim and I had our honeymoon, I got a telephone call from my mother."

* * *

"Medford! Your father and I want you to come home tonight. We'll pick you up at the train station."

"Mother! Is Dad all right? You're scaring me."

"We're both fine. Something has come up that needs for you to be here."

229

"Mother! What are you doing to me? You can't leave me hanging like this! I'm not coming home until you tell me what this is about. Is it my dog? I'm an adult. I can handle my affairs like an adult. There's no need for you to treat me as a child."

"You'll do as I say. We'll pick you up from the six o'clock train."

Gabbie hopped into the back seat of their car. Gabbie tried to solicit information from her father and mother. They would offer no explanation. "We'll discuss it after we're home," her mother said. As a result, the one-hour trip from the train station to home was made with the three of them in dead silence.

Mr. Soldi led them into the house, and into the library. "Sit if you like," he told Gabbie.

"I'm starving. Could we do this over dinner?" Gabbie said. "On the way home from the station we usually stop at a restaurant for dinner, but we didn't tonight. What is going on?"

"You married the Dorchester boy," Mr. Soldi said.

"Is that what this is about! You made it into a federal case! You make it sound ominous and like an inquisition, Father. I was going to tell you both when I came home this weekend. Yes, Jim and I are married. We had to do it in a hurry because he had to report in."

"You married that boy against our wishes!" her father said.

"I didn't know that! You never said a word to me. Even if you did it wouldn't have made any difference. You knew we were dating. And 'that boy' is now your son-in-law, and he is a man serving his country! Jim didn't have time to go through the formality of asking Dad's permission," Gabbie said.

"If he had made the time, then you both would have known it was the last thing on Earth I would have allowed!" Mr. Soldi said. "Thank God the legal community in Vermont and a state trooper thought enough of me to inform me of what you were up to! You marrying that piece of trash!"

"Father! You always told me: 'My happiness is your happiness.' Well, my happiness is being married to Jim! Now why isn't it your happiness!"

"Because you went against my wishes!" Mr. Soldi said.

"So then my happiness is only when it complies with what you want for me, not for what I want for myself! That's being a hypocrite, and you're prejudiced!"

"I'll have the marriage annulled," Mr. Soldi said.

"You'll do no such thing of the kind. I love Jim. I've loved him ever since I was born and God knows, before that! I'm not going to stop loving him now because of your twelfth century ideals about familial obligations!"

"That's the right word," Mr. Soldi said, "obligations! You have an obligation to those who pay all your bills! You have the security, comfort, and benefit of our home. We raised you, provided you with an education to support yourself, and with skills you may enjoy all your life. We have a right to protect our love and investment in you. Like a pedigree dog that has been humped by a mongrel is no longer a pedigree, you have lost your stature. You may try to redeem yourself by cutting it short right now!"

"I appreciate every single thing you and Mom have done for me. You must know: one can control the head, but not the heart. Jim is mine. I love him. Just accept him. Accept us. Not you, nor anyone else will annul my marriage unless I say so. You can forget about that, totally!" Gabbie said.

Mr. Soldi folded his hands in front of him. He squared his shoulders. He planted his feet firmly on the floor. He reached up to scratch his neck. His eyes blank, he said, "Your final word?"

"I'm sorry, Mom and Dad. I love you both very much. I didn't mean to bring you any unhappiness. I thought you'd be overjoyed at my happiness. Yes, that is my final word."

"So be it!" Mr. Soldi said. He waved his left hand, palm wide toward the front door, "Your mother will show you out."

Gabbie jerked her head forward. "What? I can't believe this! What are you saying?"

"Angelo!" Mrs. Soldi jumped up from her chair. "I think we should all sleep on this. We're not thinking clearly at

231

all. Medford, come in the kitchen. I'll make you some eggs . . ."

"She'd had long enough to think about this! I'll not tolerate disrespect in the slightest. You've had plenty of time to approach me. You chose not to. If you feel you are responsible enough to flaunt your willfulness, then you must be prepared to carry your decision entirely on your shoulders."

"It's youthful impetuousness, Angelo! Let it rest and we'll . . ." Mrs. Soldi said.

"Ask her if she would change her position in eight hours, in eighty hours!"

"You can't ask me to arbitrarily follow your wishes. It's my life!"

"Indeed it is. You claim the freedom to be able to do as you wish. I am not going to support anything with which I don't agree. That's being a hypocrite."

"And I have my principles."

"Then as painful as it may be to your mother and me, you must bear the burden of your action. In case it is not clear, I am saying your mother and I are disowning you. You are no longer our daughter, or part of our family. I will cut you out of our Wills. You don't even own the clothes on your back, but because we are generous people you can have them—the clothes you are wearing. Everything else belongs to us and will remain with us," Mr. Soldi said.

"Please, Angelo! Stop this! It is ridiculous that you do this!" Mrs. Soldi said.

"What? You mean you're taking back every single thing you gave me? You're taking back all the love you were supposed to have for me? I can't believe this!" Gabbie said.

"Don't let the heat of your disappointment do this, Angelo!" Mrs. Soldi said.

"I don't compromise in my life, in my work, or in my home. You knew exactly what you were doing, Medford. If you hoped you would get away with it, you're wrong."

"What about my flute?"

"No longer yours. We'll sell it to pay your debts," Mr. Soldi said.

"No! You can't have it! It's part of me! That was a birthday present from Aunt Mary! You know what that flute means to me. You can't mean to cause me that much pain!"

"And the pain you are causing us counts for nothing?"

"I would like to have the paintings and drawings that Jim did of me! What about my clothes! My car?" Gabbie said.

"Angelo . . ."

"Nothing belongs to you. Nothing. You are closed out of your New York apartment and everything in it. I will withdraw your tuition from school. You made your choice. Your mother will give you a hundred dollars to complete the disenfranchisement," Mr. Soldi said.

"Mom! Dad! I find this archaic! No one does this! To add to it, you've taken my flute, the one way I could earn some money!"

"The trust fund left to you by your Uncle Nedo, Aunt Mary's late husband, won't be available to you for another two years, but perhaps you can make a loan on it. That is the last word I'm saying about money," Mr. Soldi said.

"I'll come back for Amusee!"

"The dog stays," Mr. Soldi said. "And leave your cell phone. We paid for that, too."

"Would it change your mind to know that it was Jim Dorchester that saved me from that sexual predator?"

"We knew that," Mr. Soldi said.

Mrs. Soldi's eyes filled with tears.

"You what? You what? Spare me! Do you have any idea what that demented sexual pervert would have done to me if he took me? I do not want to know that you have always known that it was Jim that kept me from a certain tortured death and that you said or did nothing!"

"Yes," Mr. Soldi said, "we knew it was Jim Dorchester. The police found his perfect hand print on the passenger seat on which he leaned when he reached in to get the keys."

Unable to muffle her sobs, Mrs. Soldi ran from the room.

"You knew that for all these years, and you wouldn't acknowledge what he did? You are not just common snobs, you are capital perverted ingrates protecting what? If you had to barter with that crazed pedophile I know you would have given him everything he wanted. What rankled your ego to make you hate another living person so? You're not a loving father, no matter what you think of yourself. You are a morbid control freak. To whom do you two think you gave birth? The Virgin Mary?"

Her father waved her away.

* * *

Gabbie smiled broadly when she looked at Keith. "Can you believe? He didn't even give me five bucks? I walked to a phone, called Virginia, and I've been here ever since. If I see either of my parents in town, they ignore me, although I can tell my mother would like to wave, but she's terrified of my father. I sent them cards on their birthdays, Christmas, and holidays. They sent them back marked: Return to Sender. Finally, I just stopped."

"You didn't hear from them even when you lost Jim?"

"Even when I lost Jim. I left a message on their answering machine saying the same thing I told Jim's dad. They can ride with me to the funeral, or they can have their own limousine. I didn't get a response. I couldn't imagine anyone could be so cruel. And then, during the funeral, I saw my mother come in a cab. She stayed for a bit. Even though I was in near shock over losing Jim, do you know, I felt very sad for my mother."

"Gabbie? You sure you weren't adopted? I can see where selective loss of memory can make for a serene life."

"You're a philosopher, yet! Keith Franklin!"

"Really? They wouldn't let you have the flute?"

"My parents went to Aunt Mary's apartment and took all my stuff, except the flute," Gabbie said. "Interesting, isn't it?"

"Yes, very. I can't wait to hear. Why didn't they take it? It seemed after the dog they thought it was the worst possible way to hurt you."

"Yes, that's true. Because I treasured it so much, when I went to school I carried it in a backpack that I turned around and put up against my stomach. New York, you know? So, whenever I'd leave it in the apartment I hid it, just in case. I used to open the bag to the vacuum cleaner and stick it inside there. With the shock of my parents' actions, I never gave it a thought. It was gone as far as I was concerned. Then, when Aunt Mary returned from Europe she called me. . ."

* * *

"Medford? This is your Aunt Mary. I just got through talking to my sister and told her she and her husband are a first-class pair of assholes. She was trying to make like the two of them were put-upon by an ungrateful daughter. I told them it was such a horrible thing for them to endure that they should think of a double suicide. You come down to see your auntie anytime you please. I had the doorman fired when he said he was ordered by your parents to keep you out. It's my apartment, and I will let you use it unconditionally!"

"Thank you, Auntie, I'd love to see you. Not right away. Jim was killed in Iraq two months ago."

"Your paretic-conceived parents didn't tell me."

"There was a delay bringing what was left back from Iraq. We just had the funeral."

"Medford! My dear! How awful! How just terrible! I'm so, so sorry! I can come be with you. It must be a very difficult time. Hold on. I'll come, sweetheart, I'll come! Just hang on!"

"Thank you, Auntie. I'm okay. I'm with two very dear friends. They are constantly by my side. They do not let me falter. Perhaps some Aunt Mary medicine will do me some good. Oh! Auntie! I loved him so! My heart is broken! And Mother is so terrified she won't even return my calls."

"I'm embarrassed to be related to that ignorant bitch! I can fix a broken brain, but I don't know how to mend a broken heart, my dear Medford. I didn't know how to do it for myself when I lost my precious Nedo. I cried myself to sleep for a long time. I can tell you this: The pain diminishes, the emptiness never goes away. I'll come. Just say."

"Yes, I will."

"Now, what can I do for you? Do you need money? I'll wire some up to you in the morning. Then, come back here to school, we'll be roommates! I'll take care of the tuition. Or we can go to Italia! To our villa in Tuscany! I love it there! Let's go and have fun!"

"Thank you, no, Aunt Mary. I seem to be doing okay, considering. I'm working with the two friends I told you about. There is one thing I'm curious about. The flute you gave me when I was, what, three years old?" Medford laughed. "In your apartment, I always hid it in the bag in the vacuum cleaner. Would you see if it's still there? If it is, would you send it to my folks? They said it belonged to them because I owed them. I don't want to be indebted."

* * *

Gabbie looked off in the distance, then patted Keith's hand. "You know what my Auntie did? She overnighted the flute to me with a note saying she hoped I liked her present for my forthcoming birthday, and that she had sent a check to my idiotic parents in case they were short in meeting this month's bills. I'm sorry she insulted them that way."

"You are? Why?"

"Even if they grew horns out of their heads, they're still my parents. They gave me life. Without my life I could have never known the love Jim and I had."

"They should call you Saint Gabbie."

"They're not that bad, Keith," Gabbie said. "I called Aunt Mary when I knew I was going in to have Ginnie. Do you know what she did?"

* * *

"Hello! Rose! This is your sister, Mary. I'm flying up to Great Farraday right now. Just meet me at the airport. It's urgent and important!"

At the airport, Mary and Anna got into Rose's car. Mary got into the front seat, leaned over and gave Rose a kiss. "Rose, the regrets in life will kill you. I want to save you from chalking up a huge regret, one that could very easily kill you. We're going to the hospital. Your daughter, Medford, is going to have a baby, and you should be there."

"What are you saying?" Rose asked.

"Don't be a jerk, Rose, you had to know this was on the agenda. Nice fellow like Jim and Medford had to ring the bell on the first try. Yes, she's going to make you a grandmamma whether you like it or not. Now, if you want to throw us out of the car before we get to the hospital, that's up to you. Or, we can all go up and sweat out the birth together, like family is supposed to do. I don't know what your caveman husband is going to say or do, but that's your business. Okay?"

Rose waggled her shoulders. She looked over at Mary. She looked straight ahead, then pushed the gas pedal to the floor. "Okay."

In the hospital room, with Gabbie holding the infant, Ginnie, Rose took Gabbie's hand and kissed it. "I'm so very happy for you, Medford. I love you, and I love your child. You and Jim are blessed. I'm sorry your father still lives in the times of the Dolges, but there's little we can do to change that."

"Have you told Daddy?" Gabbie asked.

"Yes. Of course I did. I love the old coot, and I must respect him. He has loved me and has been very good to us. I asked him if he forbade me from visiting you."

"What did he say, Mom?"

"You know your father. Always the attorney. He turned away, shook his head, and waved his hand. He didn't say a word. I'm sorry, Medford. He can't forgive himself for the way he behaved. His ancestors from a thousand years back were speaking. I forgive him. I hope in your heart you do, too."

"Mom, I will always love you both. I'm sorry it pains Dad so much, but I understand because I know him. I think, knowing you can be grandmamma at times will give him some ease, but not much peace. Perhaps one day you can come get Ginnie and bring her home. I really think the sight of her will melt the freeze of his heart."

"Medford, you are so wise. You know what? I wouldn't take that bet. If you will, one day I will come get Ginnie and bring her home with me so she will know from where she comes. Your father may be an antique, but he's not made of stone."

* * *

Gabbie said, "Mom brings or sends Ginnie gifts on her birthday. She stays and plays with her for a while. I think on Ginnie's next birthday? She's going to meet her granpappa."

"I love that kind of ending. Now, what's the rest of the story?"

"What rest?"

"The flute? Do you still play? What did you do with it? It was you. Do you play Mozart's Rondeau?"

"From his Flute Concerto No. 2? No. I haven't touched the flute since I left New York. I put the flute away. I haven't touched it since I lost Jim." She scrunched her face. " . . . Keith? How did you know I played the Rondeau?"

"I thought everyone did!" Keith got up.

"Are you leaving?"

Keith looked out over the horizon. He jammed his hands, palm out, into his back pockets. He paced the length of the deck, and returned to stand in front of Gabbie. "Yes. I'm so sad for everything that has happened to you, most especially losing Jim. Your parents are a tragedy born of ignorance and false stature. Engendering envy from others—putting on a big show--depleted their brains. It made them into shadowless people, pathetic snobs, and made them discard the only worthwhile object in their lives—you. Just a bit of intelligence would make one appreciate the depth of their stupidity. It makes me wonder about a lot of things. Life really stinks, doesn't it? The president of Bowdoin College said he would have the most perfect university in the world if it weren't for the students. You and I? We'd have a perfect world if it weren't for most of the people in it. I'm going to head back home, Gabbie. What I have found here with you and Virginia and Ashley is an oasis of peace and love. I'd like to come back with Louise, if we might."

"If god has a heart, he will see that you do. You're always welcome, Keith. We'd be delighted to see you anytime."

"There's one thing I must do. I'd like to get some flowers and go to Jim's grave. Is it too much to ask if you will come with me?"

On the motorcycle, Gabbie could have held on to the grab bars on the sides of her seat; instead, she chose to put her arms around Keith and put her cheek against his back. It seemed like the natural thing for her to do. The contact seemed familiar.

At the cemetery, Gabbie put her pot of Black-Eyed Susans on one side of the headstone; Keith put his on the other. They stood silently in front of the grave for a long time. Then, Keith stepped up to the headstone, traced Jim's name in the marble. He took off one of the dog tags from around his neck, and placed it with the chain on top of the headstone. Gabbie tried to muffle her cry when Keith turned to grab her. With her face buried in his chest, Gabbie cried uncontrollably until the tears ran dry.

"It's almost seven fucking years, Keith, and it still grabs me like death! Jim didn't deserve this. He was such a good man. He loved me with his whole and entire heart. I loved him so much; it keeps tumbling out of me every single day. Just the thought of him makes me weep. Auntie said the pain diminishes, but the emptiness never does. She was wrong. They're all fucking wrong! Nothing gets easier. Keith, you are an angel for coming here. I will keep you in my prayers every single night."

They returned to the Garden Center. Gabbie turned to Keith still sitting on the bike, "Stay for dinner. You've got to eat someplace. Besides, I like having you here."

"Thanks. I should go. I find and feel so much love around me here I think of Louise. It was a privilege to meet you, Gabbie. It was special to be Jim's friend. I can see you are all of a sweet, loving kind. God love you, you are a marvelous human being. You are one of the loveliest people I will ever meet. I can see why any man would find you precious to love." He took off his sunglasses and stared into her eyes.

"Thank you. Keith?" She looked at him for long moments. Then, she moved closer and stared right into his eyes, first one then the other. She raised her eyebrows. She shook her head.

"What?" He stared at her pulling his eyebrows together.

"Jim. I keep seeing Jim. You remind me so much of him."

"From what I know, we were very good, intense friends for a very short time. We were called twins we looked and did everything so much like each other. He had to have left his mark on me."

"Besides, Keith, I kept you here on purpose. I have a surprise for you I tried not to let out. If you wait ten minutes at the most, there's someone I want you to meet. Someone you have to meet."

"Ah! I had a poking feeling deep inside about it! I don't even need a hint."

"No. I assumed you assumed. I didn't think so. The bus is here."

Camp Watonka was painted on the side of the bus that pulled up before them. The doors opened. A little blondie carrying a backpack bounced down the steps. When she saw Gabbie, she ran towards her, dropped the backpack halfway, and pounced into her arms. "Mommy! I rode the horsie! I rode the horsie all by myself!"

Gabbie crushed her in her arms as the bus went through the gears. "Oh! My little cowgirl made it. You rode the horsie all by yourself! That's wonderful!" She turned towards Keith. "I want you to meet Jim's and my Ginnie. Ginnie, this is Keith."

Ginnie stared into Keith's eyes. "Are you my daddy?"

"Oh! Lord love us! You are so pretty! So adorable! Out of the mouth of babes! I wish I were, Ginnie! I wish I were your daddy! Can I hold you, just to say 'Hello'?" Ginnie reached out for him with both hands. Gabbie transferred her. Keith enveloped her with both hands. "Hello! Ginnie! You are just so beautiful! As pretty as the prettiest flower on earth! Ask your mommy if I can be your Uncle Keith?" He stared at her face for a long time. Ginnie gave him a crushing kiss on the cheek. "Thank you, Ginnie. I'm glad you don't mind my beard, but you know you have to get through the brambles to get to the berries!"

She laughed. "That's funny!"

He kissed her on her cheek, and put her down. He stared at Gabbie. "She's precious. Just precious. God really

240

loved you both. It makes me sadder than ever to understand Jim is not here." He pushed the glasses back onto his face. "You know one thing I wondered about? Where you got your strength? Usually it's a deep faith, religion. I knew you had two stalwart friends, Virginia and Ashley. Now that I've met Ginnie, I know everything." He scraped the ground with his shoe. "I'd better go." He made a move to get on the bike.

"Keith, you can't. Look at Ginnie. You'd break her heart if you didn't stay for dinner."

48

A short time later, Keith drove the bike up to the barn. Gabbie was waiting there holding the door open. He drove it in, killed the engine, and set it on the kickstand. He untied the roll and saddlebags and followed her to the far end.

She held the door open to a smartly decorated room. It had a bed, a television, two recliners, a dresser with a large mirror, floor and table lamps, paintings on the walls, a hardwood floor, a large sink in one corner, and a window that looked out on the garden.

"It's a giant step from Paradise," Gabbie said, "but it's built strictly for creature comforts. I stayed here for a while until we got the bedroom fixed in the main house. You have to turn on the electric water heater if you want to take a shower, which is outside, like on Cape Cod. Come to the main house for a really-oh truly-oh shower and to do laundry. Other wonderful people have stayed here."

"Name one."

"Aunt Mary. She came up for Jim's funeral. She wanted to leave me her Mercedes. I told her I couldn't take it because then she'd have to take her jet to come back up! Do you know? She insisted I have my own transportation. On her own, she decided I could best use a pick-up truck, and that's what she bought for me! I tell you, she is such a special, unusual person. I'm crazy about her. Jim and I had lunch with her when he came to see me in New York. Aunt Mary also came up when Ginnie was born and stayed with me for two weeks. She helped with the bottles and diapers and cuddled and loved Ginnie to pieces. A girl would think her mother wouldn't pass up sharing a new born grand child for anything, but mine almost did—if it wasn't for Aunt Mary she would have missed this part of her life for nothing."

"I apologize for interrupting, but I don't understand. Your mother would have missed sharing her grandchild?"

"I don't want to bore you. It's such a painful part of my life I can barely talk about it."

"You don't have to, of course."

"Let me give you the shorthand version. My parents—my father, really—were so dead set against Jim we became estranged. Awful stuff. When my father heard of the child, his morbid insanity against Jim made him move to Connecticut so my mother couldn't sneak over to see her grandchild."

"Tell me you're not serious?"

"When Aunt Mary was here, she talked to her sister—my mother. She told her to take a private plane up to see her grandchild—and me, I suppose—and fly back. My father would be none the wiser."

"How did that work out?"

"When I saw my Mom, we cried out every bit of juice in our bodies." Her eyes welled. She blew her nose. "Anyway, three years ago my father had a stroke. He's paralyzed. Confined to a wheelchair in a nursing home. Mom comes up every single chance she can. I'm so glad for her to know her grandchild."

"Mark Twain called Annie Sullivan—who's pupil was Helen Keller, as you know--a miracle worker, but it sounds like Aunt Mary is a miracle worker, too."

"She certainly is. Aunt Mary is Ginnie's Godmother. And, she also came up for Ginnie's Confirmation. Something else about Aunt Mary: she paid for and enrolled Ginnie in Columbia University's Class of two-thousand-something-or-other."

"The more I hear about this Aunt Mary, the more I want to meet her."

"I hope you do, too. Maybe you will, who knows? You'll love her, like all of us do. And, Keith, thank you for staying overnight. I've never seen Ginnie so crestfallen as when you said you were leaving. Kindly thank Louise for letting us keep you for a bit. I thought it best to get you settled first. Ginnie has really taken a liking to you. By the way, sheets and towels are in the linen closet. Should we make the bed?"

Keith shook his head. He pointed to his chest. "Some things one must do for oneself, Tonto."

Tonto! Gabbie did a double-take. She stopped in her tracks. She tilted her head, then shook it. Did she hear what she heard? *Tonto!* It was simple to explain. Keith got it from Jim. He copied him in many ways. Possibly it was buried in his subconscious? "Okay. Dinner's almost ready. We'd better hurry back."

Keith closed the barn doors and ran the wooden bolt. They started down the path. "Gabbie, I think you would have had to pry me out of here. Virginia and Ashley seem like just such special people."

"They are."

"And they're gay?"

"Yes. Why?"

"Hard to believe they're gay. When you introduced them, their hugs were not exactly sisterly! Both of them made me feel like a macho man!"

"They're just loving people. They're very open about it. I mean, very open. Don't be surprised about anything they say or do. I for one would never excuse them for a single thing. I'm merely cautioning you not to be judgmental. They are my family. I love them very much."

"I like them very much, too. In fact, Gabbie, I love everything about being here. I have to ask you--although, you don't have to answer, of course--I would be surprised if you're not being pursued. I mean, you can say it's none of my business."

"You mean, am I seeing anyone?" Keith nodded. "Mmmmm. There's an attorney that lives in Prattsville, about twenty miles north. He was doing *pro bono* work for veterans' widows. He's that kind of a guy. He came down to help me with some stuff I had to have done. For a while, I thought it was best for Ginnie and myself to let Jim go. I thought very seriously about marrying him. I just couldn't get over the hurdle. So, I keep pushing him away. Makes no difference to him. Even after all this time, as casual as anything he says he's in no hurry, he'll wait. Imagine! His name is Douglas MacDonald. He takes me anyplace I want to go. He's got his own plane. Even though he knows he can't or doesn't have to try to impress me, we fly out to Martha's Vineyard for lobster. He tries to spend a fortune on me, but I won't let him. I won't take his gifts, even at Christmas. He kisses me on the cheek. That's it. Really, I mean it. No sex. Any other guy would be climbing the walls."

"Really? He must have retarded hormones."

Gabbie wrinkled her eyebrows as she stared through slits at Keith. She shook her head. "Still he waits. He knows me. He knows I don't believe Jim is dead. I don't feel that is so. My heart would tell me. Feeling that way, I couldn't allow myself to be intimate with anyone else. It wouldn't be fair. Is that wishful thinking?"

"Not if you don't miss it."

"I do miss it—with Jim. The fact is we were only together on our honeymoon. As you can see, we hit a home run first try." She laughed.

"God! He was lucky to have had you in his life, Gabbie."

She bit her lower lip. "Dinner must be ready."

49

The dinner table in front of the broad expanse of windows that overlooked the forest of blooming flowers was all set. Large glasses of iced tea were before three of the places, milk before the fourth. A large loaf of Italian garlic bread was in the middle, which was dominated by a huge bowl of salad.

"Keith, you sit at the head of the table where all our guests sit. What would you like to drink? Beer? Wine? Tea is in the pitcher on the table."

"Tea, that's fine, thank you," Keith said. "But, I'm a little uncomfortable at . . ."

"Sit," Virginia said.

Ashley marched in holding before her a huge red pot, which she placed in front of Keith.

Ashley took her seat with them, and automatically Gabbie, Virginia, Ashley, and Ginnie reached out to hold hands. Keith reacted quickly and took Gabbie's and Ashley's hands.

Virginia said, "Keith, would you be kind enough to say Grace."

Everyone bowed their heads as Keith looked around the table. Gabbie glanced up at him. "Problem?"

"Yes," Keith said. "What's Grace? I don't . . . remember what I am!"

The others looked around.

Keith shrugged. "Am I a Christian or a Buddist? I have no idea what to say!" Everyone stared at him. He looked around. "I don't know if I'm a doctor, lawyer, Indian chief! I guess you could say I'm a Universalist!"

Virginia bowed her head. "You'll think of something."

Keith blinked his eyes. "Let me think hard. Okay. Bless us, each and every one of us. Bless these good people who have taken me in and made a home for me. Teach me the ways of their good and great love so I may pass it on. Play ball. Amen."

Gabbie looked at Keith. "That was just wonderful, but what's with the 'Play ball?'"

"Oh! A joke I heard." Keith said. "At baseball games, they'd have someone sing 'The Star Spangled Banner.' At the end of the last stanza it would be, '. . . and the land of the free, and the home of the brave! And immediately the announcer would shout, "Play ball!' So why not end every blessing the same way?"

Everyone at the table looked at their plates, and didn't say a word. Then, Gabbie said, "Keith? That was funny, and I had to hold myself back. I remember hearing that as a kid. Did you happen to remember it from your past?"

Keith wrinkled his eyebrows. "It just came to me."

Virginia glanced at Gabbie, then said, "Keith, be kind enough to serve the Steak Soup."

"Holy Moley! Do you know what a treat this is for me to be part of a family? It's something I don't know if I ever knew," Keith said.

"Uncle Keith?" Ginnie said, "Would you read me a bedtime story?"

"Sweetheart! I would love to read you a story! What a privilege!" Keith said. Ginnie grinned a mile wide.

"It's Gabbie's week cleaning up the kitchen," Ashley said, "so maybe you'll want to pitch in? Virginia and I have some orders to fill."

While filling the soup bowls and passing them, Keith said, "I'm overwhelmed! I feel so necessary."

"That's not the half of it," Ashley said. "May I ask if there is some compelling reason why you must leave tomorrow?" Keith looked at her, shrugged, and tossed his head. "Great! I just assume you can do some carpentry, and it would be nice not to worry about the pipes not collapsing on our customer's heads! Would you mind giving us a hand?"

"I thought you'd never ask!" Keith said. "I offered to fix the one that fell today. I see some of the plastic on the greenhouses could use some attention, too. To be fair, suppose I commit to two weeks. You'll know how best to use me. Who knows? It may be longer, or you may grow sick of me and it will be shorter."

Virginia nodded her head. "Thanks, Keith. We'll take all the help we can get. We'll take the two weeks, but sorry it couldn't be more."

"I know, but there is someone waiting." Keith looked at his soup and nodded his head. He glanced around the table. "I really like being here. It is tempting to stay longer. I have been on a mission. I've given it my best shot. I just have to close the door."

"'Someone waiting' sounds like *cherchez la femme*," Ashley said.

Keith looked directly at Gabbie. "Yes."

"You're in love with this person?" Ashley asked.

"Yes," Keith said. "I love her like the very breath of my being."

"Wow!" Virginia said. "Ashley and I can relate to that!"

"What did you say?" Gabbie asked the spoon halfway to her mouth.

"You mean, the very breath . . ." Keith started.

"No, it's okay. I heard," Gabbie said. "It had a familiar ring to it."

"Wouldn't be above me to plagiarize, from a book, a movie," Keith said. "She was my nurse. Her name is Louise McBride. She's a flaming, beautiful redhead. I call her Louise Comma The Nurse—you know—just to tease. She brought me back from death's door, more than a dozen times, that's how bad I was."

"Mamma said you was hurt, Uncle Keith," Ginnie said.

"Not as bad as your Dad, Ginnie," Keith said. "Is it okay I said that, Gabbie?"

"It's okay. Ginnie knows her daddy was hurt in the war," Gabbie said.

"I can hear your attraction to Louise," Virginia said.

"It would be easy to fall in love because of her devotion to me, but it went far beyond that because she is a lovely, beautiful, wonderful person. Yes, she tended to me in so many ways it is indescribable. Yet, our attraction to each other overrode all that. It seemed to have been generated by the essence of what is called true love even though Louise had another name for it—obligatory love, or something. You know, she took care of me for years and years. I mean, she was a nurse and she tended me in all ways. You know what I mean. Even so, she's embarrassed when I tell her I have X-rated dreams of her."

Gabbie dropped her spoon. It clattered in her dish.

"Mommy?" Ginnie called.

"Mommy has butterfingers," Gabbie said. She looked at Keith. "You may not remember, but I would guess you spent an awful lot of time with Jim."

"What makes you say that?" Keith asked.

"There are an awful lot of similarities. I spent a lot of time with him, and I pretty much know how he thinks, and how he says things. If I were to close my eyes, I would say you were twins. I know you're not Jim because Jim had brown eyes. You have blue eyes."

Keith put down the bread he was holding. He looked up at Gabbie. "I have brown eyes."

"They're blue!" Gabbie said staring at him.

"My contacts are blue," he said. "Louise picked them out for me. She said it made me look like Paul Newman and they matched hers."

50

Early the next morning, without going to the main house for breakfast, Keith waved to Gabbie as he rode out on his bike. He stopped for coffee and croissants at the Dunkin Donuts. After he sat inside and had his breakfast, he ordered the same for a takeout. He got directions to Glenn Dorchester's shop. He had no idea what was waiting for him.

The large, cinder block garage had double bays. It was dimly lit and damp. Keith saw a figure limned by a fluorescent work light that was under a car that was on a lift. He walked towards him. He coughed. "Glenn Dorchester?" he called out. He reached to take off his sunglasses.

The man glanced at him. He finished taking out the bolt to let the oil pour out of the pan and into the funnel. "The fuck do you want around here?"

"I'm Keith Franklin. I was in the service with . . ."

"I know who you are, whatever you call yourself."

"Jim must have written to you about me. I brought you coffee and croissants."

"Least you got that right. Like I said, the fuck do you want?"

Keith shifted from one foot to the other. "I can't tell you an awful lot, but I thought I'd pay my respects . . ."

"Can you tell me why I didn't get the insurance money? His own father. Didn't leave me a dime."

"No."

"You didn't come to bring it to me now?"

"I don't know about the insurance money."

"Whatever monkey-ass scheme you're working, I hope they nail your ass and throw you the hell in jail! I told you

250

once to stay the hell off my property. I'm not going to tell you again. Leave the coffee on the table." He grabbed a mechanics cloth.

"Mr. Dorchester, I don't know who you think I am, but I'd like to know. Can you tell me anything about your son, Jim?"

Glenn wiped his hands. He narrowed his eyes and smirked. "Who the fuck cares?" He turned his back to Keith and walked toward the end of the garage.

When Keith returned to the Garden Center, he parked the bike in the barn and went to find Gabbie in the greenhouse. "Good morning!"

"Good morning!" Gabbie said. "We can do better than Dunkin Donuts for breakfast."

"I'll try to remember that. How did you know?"

She shrugged. "Habits are that way."

"Just point me to the tool shed where I can find hammer and saw, spare parts," Keith said. "I'll start on that pipe you nearly duked it out with yesterday . . ."

"Keith? We're pretty busy here on weekends, so we take a day off in the middle of the week. Ginnie has been after me to go to the Animal Farm close by in New York State."

"You've been there before?"

"Oh! Yes. It's Ginnie's favorite place because she can walk right up and feed the animals. They walk free or poke their heads over the railing. We've usually gone with Douglas—you know, Douglas MacCormack."

"Oh?"

Gabbie nodded. "Yes. As I told you, in my heart of hearts I felt Jim was alive. But, I missed having a man around, and I thought a man's influence would be good for Ginnie. Douglas has been after me to marry him, like really pushing. He talked about financial security, but we're doing okay with the Garden Center. Aunt Mary has let me know Ginnie will be well taken care of when it's time for college. I feel like a traitor. I've been to counseling. What I get there is that life is for the living. Live your life. Play the cards dealt to you. That sort of stuff. Even so, I'm going to call Douglas and say I have other plans. Ginnie really has taken a liking to you like I've never seen before. I'd like you to come, too. Okay with you? We'll take my pick-up. I can pack a lunch . . ."

51

Keith saw the short, heavy man jerk his arms up and down as he walked onto the deck the next morning. Gabbie was pouring Keith a third warm-up.

Douglas MacCormack, a lawyer, parted his hair on one side and had it slicked down. His small, bead-like eyes looked through metal-rimmed glasses that almost touched his cheeks. His nose was large. It went with his puffy lips and broad jaw. He held a large, unlit cigar.

"Thanks, Gabbie. How about some java for you, young lady," Keith said to Ginnie.

"Uh-uh!" Ginnie said, "Cereal for me."

"Douglas!" Gabbie said. "Didn't you get my message?"

"What message?" Douglas said staring at Keith. "Hello, Ginnie!"

Ginnie ignored him.

"Garbage!" Gabbie said. "I left you a voice mail that said I couldn't see you today because I had other plans."

"No. No voice mail. This is your other plan?" he said pointing to Keith. "I mean, we've been keeping Wednesdays for the three of us for quite a while. I just assumed . . ."

"I'm sure your voice mail took the message, Douglas . . ." Gabbie started.

"Since when do I need to take an oath?" Douglas said. "Don't I treat you right?"

"I told you time and again, Douglas, no promises. I returned all your gifts. The flights were fancy and fun, but I was very clear with you. I'm sorry, but I do have plans for today, Douglas," Gabbie said.

Douglas clamped his arms across his chest. "Cancel them! I came all the way down as I usually have. 'Plans,' that's no way to treat me after all this time." His heavy breathing made his arms jerk up and down.

"Mr. MacCormack? Is that your name?" Keith asked. "Would you hold off for one second?" Keith turned to Ginnie. "Ginnie, do Uncle Keith a favor if you're through with breakfast, and get a sweater and your Walkman and anything else you want to take with us. Okay?"

"And don't forget hand wipes to clean up after the dirty little beasts slobber all over you," Douglas mimicked.

"Okay!" Ginnie said. She slid off the chair and left the kitchen.

"Mr. MacCormack, when you made fun of what I said to Ginnie, you made this part of my business. Now, I understand you've been seeing Gabbie for about three years, and in all that time you haven't laid her once," Keith said. Douglas sputtered. "There's only one reason you would put up with that, and it's because you don't need it. You're getting it from your wife. Right?"

"Where do you get off . . ." Douglas started.

"Douglas! You said you were divorced!" Gabbie said.

Keith stepped towards Douglas. "Just say it's not true, and I'll walk out of the kitchen. You don't take Gabbie on a date in this town here because you're concerned you'll be seen, and word will get back to your wife. Gabbie has never been to your home, even on the holidays, because your wife would think three's a crowd. You're a mouth bully, Mr. MacCormack, a cheat and not a very nice person. You want to confirm it? Check it out at Dunkin Donuts. You're a liar because you did get the voice mail from Gabbie because I was with her when she made it," Keith said. "The phone is at your office, not at your home, and we know the reason. Let's just save time. Get your ass out of here, and don't come back."

"Gabbie, when he's gone you will miss my good company!" Douglas started.

Keith moved towards him. "There are times it is better to be alone and lonely than share it with a virus."

Douglas turned and started for the door. He stopped, to look back at Gabbie, then went through the door.

"Wow!" Gabbie said. Her hand was at her mouth. "Keith, I had no idea he was still married. I'm glad it came out. I would have been mortified if . . ."

"Well, I'm surprised, too" Keith said.

"Why?" Gabbie asked.

"Because you didn't whack him in the nose. Some things you have to do for yourself, you know?" Keith answered.

Eyes wide open, shining brightly, Gabbie said, "Yes, yes, I do know." Keith's words had a familiar ring. Again, it made her think very hard about the friendship between Jim and Keith. Whacking someone on the nose was an unusual particularity.

52

The drive to the animal farm took longer than Keith expected because of the frequent stops at the implorations of Ginnie and the need to use the facilities.

Once at the farm it was a matter of feeding quarters into the cracker machines to get the required food for the animals.

Ginnie exploded with laughter every time one of the four-legged animals—deer, goats, sheep, and the like—nibbled away the treat from her hand. Without success she tried to throw crackers through the fencing that held in the monkeys. She had no trouble dropping the food to the bears on the island surrounded with a moat and a high, heavy fence.

When Ginnie started handing the crackers to Gabbie and Keith, they knew she had become tired of the game, and that it was time for lunch. Keith walked back to the truck to get all the gear, and returned to find them at a bench under a large oak tree.

Keith spread the blanket on the ground, and opened the basket. He sat on the blanket, fished out a beer, and told Gabbie, "This is just perfect. It's as good as it gets for me."

Gabbie stretched out beside him. "I'm glad, Keith. You haven't had much to be joyful about in your young life." She called to Ginnie. She was not as much interested in lunch as she was in picking wild flowers. "Do you stay in touch with Louise?"

He shook his head. "No. We agreed. I was on a perilous mission; perilous because it's possible I could never return to her. Perilous, too, because what I could find could kill me."

"How?"

"Psychologically. Discounting the physical injury, if I were hiding something from myself because it was so painful, if it is made known to me, I may not be able to bear it and possibly destroy myself over it."

"Keith, what could be so terrible? You're so young. What could have happened? In Iraq? I suppose I shouldn't ask."

"You can ask anything you want. I've had experts go at me. Whatever—if, whatever—I'm hiding anything from myself, I've done an excellent job. I doubt it would appear by happenstance. You know, something jarring me awake from the nightmare? If this suddenly became known to me, I may not be able to bear the horror of it. In that case I may end up in an irreversible fugue state, or I may find I can live with it."

"That can happen? You're sure?"

"Yes. The happy endings are only in movies. The general conclusion is that I've had a physical memory loss. The other Keith, if there is one, walks the shadows of the nether world."

"Keith, you are a good person. I want for you what is best for you. I like having you around. I don't want either Ginnie or myself to become too attached, if you know what I mean?"

"That's plain, and fair. I promise you this. I'll do what has to be done, and I'll move on, maybe back to Louise. Despite the short time, I can't help the strong affection I have for Ginnie. She's very precious to me."

"As you can see, as you are to us, I mean, to her."

Gabbie drove home. When Keith picked up Ginnie to put her in the pickup, she clasped him tightly, and said she wanted to ride sitting on his lap. She fell asleep immediately with her head resting against Keith's shoulder.

53

Keith used the framing hammer to drive the last of the spikes into the two-by-six that anchored the sill that held the plastic sheet over the roof. He slipped the hammer into the ring on his belt. He pulled out the stapler and set the inner and outer sheets.

"Keith! Hate to stop a good man working," Ashley shouted, "but could you come down for a sec?"

"Sure! Ashley," Keith answered, "would you hit the fan switch so I can see how the air space between the sheets is holding?"

With the sound of the industrial fan, the double plastic sheets of the ceiling filled with air and remained inflated and steady.

Keith slid down the ladder. "What's up?"

"Keith, we're all so amazed at how much you've accomplished in such a short time. Thank you. The new greenhouse for seedlings is dynamite. We've already got plans to fill it with poinsettias for Christmas."

"I'm so glad to help out. It's like a vacation for me. It's fun being with everyone."

"Thanks. I wonder if I can ask you to help with a landscaping job? Gabbie has to take Ginnie for shots and that kind of stuff, and Virginia will take care of the store. I sold a nice job over the weekend. If you would come with me to load up the truck--mulch, some rhododendrons and azaleas we have here, and a quick trip to the wholesaler for the bigger bushes and trees? It may take us until late afternoon . . . or later."

"You betcha! Sounds like fun! Never did landscaping before. You'll have to tell me what to do."

"Great! I'll meet you by where the mulch is stacked. And Keith? We'll work it out: I'll point, you dig." She laughed loudly.

"Of course! You realize the boss buys the lunch. Now, I have a problem. Every place I dig, I find a hole. What do I do with the hole?"

She bent over laughing. "That is where you plant your troubles! We load the truck. You follow me to the site on your motorcycle. I'll show you what has to be done after we unload the truck. I'll go get the stuff from the wholesalers, and return. Got it?"

"Ashley? Can I ask you a question?"

"Yes. Of course."

"Will you marry me?"

Ashley again roared with laughter and rapped him on the shoulder. "You're a Blackbeard! You've already asked Virginia! Keith! I've got to tell you. You have all the essences of Jim. I swear that's who you are!"

It was after nightfall by the time Keith and Ashley returned from the job and sat down to dinner. Ginnie was already tucked into bed. Keith, Gabbie, Virginia, and Ashley sat at the table.

"Keith, I can't tell you what you've done with our gross profit margin in the short time you've been here," Virginia said. "The three of us have been wondering how we're going to square it with you."

"Thanks," Keith said. "Believe me, you already have. I can use all wonderful experiences for my memory bank. I'm keeping this one front and center. That's it. I won't hear anything else. Ashley is done in. Gabbie and I will clean up here."

Keith finished drying the last of the silverware. He put the towel to hang from the counter to dry. He turned and put his back at the sink. Gabbie came in from emptying the wastebasket. She put it down and drifted toward Keith. She stopped in front of him.

"Keith, did I tell you enough times and long and loud enough what a really marvelous time we had the other day at the animal farm? Ginnie is still talking about it. In fact, she took one of the crackers to camp and used it for Show and Tell. You know, that's where . . ."

"I know," Keith said.

"Anyway, you've made an impression on that young lady. For the tranquility you brought her, I owe you, big time."

"I find her too precious myself, Gabbie. It's very easy to love her. I'm glad you said you owe me because I have a favor to ask of you. Gabbie, as I remember you told me you used to play the flute when you and Jim were alone. I'd like to hear you . . ."

"Oh! I couldn't do that!"

"I want you to."

"Please! Don't ask me! I told you I haven't played it since . . ."

"I know all that. First, I want to hear you play, for my own soul."

"No! I won't do it!"

". . . and second, I think you should play for Ginnie."

"What?"

"Why should she be deprived of a heritage that she might have a gift for and might enjoy the thrill of playing? You should stop thinking of yourself and think of Ginnie. Christ, Gabbie! What the hell is it going to cost you to go up and get the flute and let us hear you play? Pay back is a bitch, don't you know?"

"And you know how we love to hang on to our own grand pronouncements."

"No law says you can't change your mind. Tomorrow night, after dinner. We'll all stick around for your performance."

"I bet you can sell ice cubes to Eskimoes."

There was a long pause. They looked at each other.

Keith unfolded his arms to rest his hands against the sink.

Gabbie inched closer to him.

She stared at him, and put the palm of her hand against his chest. She moved up on her toes, pressing against him. Gradually, they moved closer. She hesitated then moved quickly to find his lips with hers. Time was suspended. Their heat welded them together. He put his arms around her, as she encircled him. They kissed with urgent passion. They held each other tighter and tighter.

He moved forward seeking to have more of her body against his. She felt the hardness push into her, and she sought more of it.

It seemed neither one could get enough of the other. "Gabbie! I want you all."

"Keith, you touch places deep inside of me that haven't been touched in ages!"

They kissed again, taking each other in, relishing their sensations. They were two magnets that had connected.

Then, suddenly, Keith broke away. "I can't do this! I knew you were going to kiss me when you walked in the door."

"How?"

"The attraction I felt was just as great as what you felt. Gabbie. I'm Jim's friend, and you belong to Jim. I can't do this. No. I can't betray his memory. I'm sorry."

"Keith, when you hold me like this it brings back memories . . ."

Keith turned out of her grasp. "This isn't right. Don't use me as an excuse just because . . . Any guy would do, but don't use me."

"Keith, tell me you don't feel what I feel."

"What? Explosions? Fourth of July firecrackers? Gabbie, we're creating a problem for which there is no resolution. For me, it makes for a bad, serious problem. I can't do it to myself. I can't do it to you. And I'm thinking of Louise."

Without looking back, he left the kitchen.

54

The following evening after dinner, Keith lined up four chairs in front of the table and had Ginnie, Virginia, and Ashley sit in them. He asked Gabbie if she was ready. She nodded. He jerked his thumb toward the pantry. Gabbie went in and closed the door. Keith turned toward the audience. "Ladies and Gentlemen. It is rare that one sees the emergence of a butterfly, that's true. It is also true that one almost never sees the emergence of a born-again flutist. It will be our pleasure and privilege this evening to hear an outstanding and gifted flutist perform just for your pleasure after a slight detour. Ladies and Gentlemen, playing Sonatina by Beethoven, Medford Gabbie Dorchester." He pointed to the pantry, and Gabbie made her appearance, flute in hand. Keith took his seat. She took stage center, brushed back her pony tail, looked at Ginnie, and put the flute to her lips. She played the first bar and sharped the next note. She grabbed her forhead, then nodded, and put the flute to her lips again. She played the piece flawlessly. When she was through, all four applauded, shouted, and stamped.

"Gabbie! How beautiful!"

"Magnificent!"

"Supreme-Oh!"

"Oh! Mommy! Oh! Mommy!" Ginnie squealed. "I want to play! I want to play!"

Gabbie reached down with one arm to hug Ginnie. "Oh! Yes, sweetheart! You will play! You will play!"

"Show me!" Ginnie said.

Gabbie sat. "Now put your fingers of your right hand right on top of mine on the flute." Ginnie stood slightly to one side of Gabbie. She played Yankee Doodle Dandy with Ginnie's fingers rising and falling with her.

Ginnie screamed with delight and jumped up and down. "More, Mommy! More!"

Gabbie looked at Keith. "Keith? What's wrong? Are you feeling all right?"

Keith put his hand over his stomach. He turned away and grabbed a chair for support. "S'okay."

"No!" Gabbie said. "What is it?"

"The sound of the flute . . . I felt like I ran out of oxygen . . ."

55

The following morning, Keith found Virginia in the greenhouse with the large hanging baskets. "Virginia? I need a second."

"Sure, Keith, what is it? It sounds serious."

"No big deal," Keith said. "By the end of the day I should have almost everything done, including the ventilation system on the nursery greenhouse."

"Say, that's great, Keith! You have been a godsend. We so appreciate what you've done. It gave us a breather."

"I don't want to be an ingrate. Everyone has been so terrific, but I can't stay to the end of the two weeks. I must leave tonight."

"What's wrong, Keith? I sense something is not right. Won't you tell me?"

"I have to get back to Louise. She hasn't heard from me in all this time. She doesn't know where I am. It's not fair to her. I want to be back there with her. I hope you understand."

"Of course I understand, Keith . . . Keith? You've seen for yourself. We're always four-square with each other. What you're telling me, from the vibrations I'm getting, is that what you just said is a good reason, but it's not the real reason. Whatever that reason may be, I hope it's good for you."

"Thanks, Virginia. Don't tell anyone until after dinner. By that time I should be packed and on my way. I hate goodbyes." .

"I understand, Keith. We're all going to miss you. Thank you." She reached up for him, gave him a hug, and kissed him on both cheeks. "You will come back to visit sometime?"

"How could I not?"

Late that afternoon, Keith packed his two saddlebags after stripping down, but left out fresh traveling clothes. He walked outside to the shower.

As he was drying off, he heard Gabbie call. "Hello!"

At the sound of her voice, he hesitated. He shook his head. "Wait a sec!" Keith called out. "Let me get decent! Okay!"

Gabbie walked in to find Keith wrapped in a bath sheet. "Oh! Sorry! Shall I come back?"

"No! S'okay! Come in!"

"Virginia said she wasn't supposed to say until after dinner. She said you were leaving."

"Yes."

"Ginnie would . . . No! Ginnie and I would love it if you stayed just a bit more."

"I have to go. You know that as much as I do."

Gabbie froze. She stared at Keith.

He looked around. "What?"

Gabbie spun around. "Keith! I'm so sorry!"

Keith looked down at himself. "Oh! Me. I've lived with myself so long, and just with Louise who is very familiar with every inch of my body, I just didn't think. I'm sorry, Gabbie."

With her back still to him, she said, "I wondered why you wore long-sleeved shirts in the hot weather."

"I don't wear shorts, either, afraid I'll gross out everyone. They did a great job with my face and neck. The rest was wallpaper with paste and staples. Gabbie? What's the matter?"

"I don't know what to do."

"Come look. See the miracle of modern medicine, and the miraculous work of Louise Comma The Nurse. I don't have a robe to put on . . ."

Gabbie, fists clenched, turned and walked towards Keith.

"Looks like a bad bulletin board, doesn't it?" Keith said. Gabbie looked at Keith's exposed body. "Touch it if you want. It's like leather. My feet were protected by my boots, and it didn't get me where I sat or my lap."

Rivulets ran from Gabbie's eyes to splatter on the floor. "Keith! Keith! I don't care what you say. I don't want you to leave!"

"Gabbie, there's no denying to myself how I feel about you. I feel compelled to take you in my arms, but . . . but Louise. I can't do this to Louise."

"Keith! For God's sakes! I'm on fire! I'm burning up because I want you so badly!"

Looking up at him, she moved closer, put her arms around him, and kissed him.

He let go of the towel and took her to him.

* * *

Keith sat on the edge of the bed and lit a cigarette.

"Keith?"

"Yes."

"I've only made love to one other man on earth with whom I was in love, and the same feelings, the same way, the same action and reaction I had with him, I just had with you. No one else on earth makes love in that special, unique way, except . . . !"

"Jim?"

"Yes."

"You know, as I've come to understand, Jim and I talked a lot. I'm sure we talked about making love to a beautiful woman."

"Just tell me about your feelings."

"What do you want me to say? Yes, ecstasy made in heaven!"

"There! That's what I mean!"

"It was the same for me with Louise!"

"How could that be? That can't be! Jim loved me! He loved only me!"

"I'm sure. I loved only Louise! And she loved only me! Are you confusing me with Jim?"

"No. No, I'm not."

"How can you be so sure?"

"You may have lost your memory, and they may have changed a lot of things about you, all except one."

"Oh?"

"Come back here . . ."

It was past midnight when Keith awoke to find Gabbie dressed pacing the room. "Gabbie?"

"Oh! Good! You're awake! Keith! You've got to do something for me, for us. I went down to put Ginnie to sleep. She'll be okay with Aunts Virginia and Ashley. I want us to go see Aunt Mary."

"Is she okay? What happened?"

"She's fine. While you were sleeping, I talked to her for about a couple hours on the phone. She said we're to come see her. I said we'd leave whenever you got up."

"But why?"

"She's my aunt, and she loves me, and . . . and . . . she's a psychiatrist. She said such cases as yours intrigue her. She just finished a history of a woman with a lost memory for the American Psychiatric Journal. She said she doesn't promise anything. Take it first as just a trip to go see her. She remembers Jim. When we were in New York we had lunch with her. She doesn't promise a thing. I told you the way I feel about Aunt Mary. I want to do this."

"Gabbie! No! Absolutely not!"

"Keith! For me!"

"For nobody, Gabbie! I'm not going to waste another second of my life! Can't you just be satisfied with me the way I am? If you care for me, then take me as I am! Don't you see I'm not sure, but there will be some deliberation on my part in choosing between you and Louise! I don't know. Maybe as Freud said to a fellow psychiatrist who brought him a patient for a second opinion, 'I have studied your client and reviewed his extensive file very closely. My final analysis is the man's a plain, old nutcase.'"

"You're no nutcase, Keith! You need to be made all better! You could be yourself and be all there and be all with me! If there is anyone readily available right now who can help you, it would be Aunt Mary! I see that. You must do yourself, Louise and me a favor and go see her!'"

"I'm sick of talking to doctors and all. I've had my fill. If they didn't do it with listening to me, then I listened to them, and when that didn't work they turned me into a pharmaceutical repository. They've done what they can do. I gave up on finding out anything more about myself. What on Earth do I do about Louise? I find her irresistible. She's expecting me back there unless there are some revelations. And do you know what's happening, Gabbie? I could say I also find you irresistible. Somehow I feel I'm beginning to fall just as madly in love with you!"

"Look, Keith! Whoever you are! We're not going to do this for you! You've got to do this for me! I've got a five-year-old daughter who needs her father! See, my theory is you may be Jim. I could be wrong. I could be right! If you are Jim, why should Ginnie miss out on having a daddy? I've got me, who has been in enough pain for all these years because I lost the one and only love I've ever had or known all my life! Is that good enough? All the promises in the world that love will last until eternity don't mean a thing. What else do you have going on with your life that is worth more than searching out the truth?"

Keith exhaled loudly. He pulled his legs over the bed and lit a cigarette. He inhaled deeply. He blew out the smoke. "Gabbie, right at this moment, there is only one thing that seems sensible and makes sense. Right there on the night table is an envelope. In it is a check. You must take it from Uncle Keith to Ginnie. I want her to have a flute. Get it for her. Now, that takes care of one important thing. The other is the resonance I feel with you."

"'Syncopated vibrations' a musician would put it."

"Yes. Exactly. Just a little while ago I discovered the tattoos behind your ear. I can see they are Chinese or Japanese characters . . ."

". . . Chinese . . ."

". . . I can't read Chinese, but the characters tell me you have only one constant love in your life for all of your life . . . ?"

56

Keith kept his misgivings about "Aunt Mary" to himself. It was his life that was on the line. For everyone else it was a fishing expedition, and he was the bait. Yet, also, he was ambivalent. He looked at it as if it were his only best chance. As with any gamble, there was a price to pay. He had to win. Second best was out of the question.

Aunt Mary's house in Southampton, Long Island reminded Keith of paintings in art galleries he and Louise Comma The Nurse had visited. Each identifiable area was one of several dozen paintings. It was white with blue shutters and trim. There was a pergola covered with wisteria. Under it a wrought iron table and chairs. Roses edged the stylized floor, which was made up of decorative pavers. From the deck one could see a sailboat tied up at the end of the pier. A screened-in summer porch was filled with wicker and hanging baskets. Inside, the country kitchen was filled with antiques, including a large Shaker table and chairs, a six-burner cast iron restaurant gas stove, a pierced metal pie cabinet. The double-door Sub-Zero refrigerator, microwave convection oven, and dishwasher were all faced with stainless steel. In the living room was a large fireplace, two large sofas facing each other covered with dozens of pillows, antique easy chairs, Shaker tables, a piecrust tilt and turn, a butterfly table, and a deeply carved Queen Anne coffee table. There were double and single student oil lamps converted to electric that were either hanging or on tables. There were oil, watercolor, and pastel paintings hanging on the walls with the focus on a Rauchenbach and a Jackson Pollock. The library had floor to ceiling bookshelves all crammed with books. A long, wide Queen Anne table desk was at one end.

He knew the reminders did not bring on indigestion; it was his heart skipping. Louise came to mind.

He patted his chest. Other artists had come to the house to do their paintings of the rooms. The bedrooms upstairs all had antique bedsteads, including the carved four-poster in Aunt Mary's room, and all with Queen Anne Bonnet Top or Flattop highboys or double chests. The lamps and paintings were all antique. Mary's bathroom was done in onyx with a jet soaking tub with candle holders all around, shower, double sinks, mirrors all around, a john, bidet, heat lamps, and drying fans. Two other bathrooms were scaled down versions in royal blue and purple. Now he knew: there really were such things.

Mary strode out of the house to greet Keith and Gabbie when she heard the motorcycle stop in front of the five-bay garage.

"Oh! My precious Gabbie! How wonderful to see you! And Keith I'm delighted to meet you! I hope I can help you both! Come! Come! I have breakfast waiting!" She hugged Gabbie as she went into the kitchen.

"We caught the last ferry from Connecticut to Port Jeff, and then it was a quick run across the Island to get here!" Gabbie said.

"Welcome! Welcome! I have Belgian waffles with fresh cream butter, blueberries, strawberries, raspberries . . . !"

"Your home is lovely . . . may I call you Mary?" Keith asked.

"Nothing else!" Mary said.

"It's been a whirlwind for me, the last ten days or so, Mary. Just being here is a treat, too. Thank you," Keith said.

"Gabbie?" Mary started, "I've got to say it, and I hope you don't mind Keith, but I only met Jim briefly a long time ago, but Keith certainly does remind me of Jim."

"That's the reason we're here, Aunt Mary. After our chat, you insisted you be allowed to do what you can."

"It would be my privilege to do anything for you, Gabbie. Now, I'll pour the first cup of coffee; after that you help yourselves. You two have breakfast while I summarize what I know and the reason you're here. I understand Gabbie has to be back tomorrow night or the next morning.

In this short span of time, let's see if we can't come up with a plan about this situation. Let's not get lost in too much talk, and let's see if we can do this in shorthand."

"Gabbie has given me enough explanations to be absolutely convinced that you, Keith, are really Jim. Let's skip the how's and why's and wherefore's for the moment. Let's accept the fact that you, Keith, have no recollection whatsoever of a life before the tragedy that befell you in Iraq. Let's accept the fact that you have fallen deeply in love with the nurse that saved and preserved you, Louise McBride, and who is waiting for your return. I also understand there may be a serious attraction between you and Gabbie."

"Let's also accept the fact that hospital personnel of every shape and size and discipline have done everything in their power to make Humpty-Dumpty whole again, but with only physical success."

"Jim Dorchester. . . . That name doesn't cause a reaction in you whatsoever?"

"No. None. I've gone all over this a zillion times, Mary. I hate to see you waste your time."

"First, you should know I have not practiced psychiatry for almost ten years, since a patient because of transference killed my husband. My skills may be a little rusty, but you will be the first to know if I believe I may falter. I don't think I will because all this time I've been writing for the American Psychiatric Association and doing a great deal of research. Let me think," Mary said. She looked off to the ocean and drummed her fingers on the table. "This is the way I see it. We are looking at a very difficult proposition primarily because of its complexity. Now, the two of you may stay here for as long as you like, and we needn't talk about Jim again. Okay?" Keith and Gabbie nodded. "Next, if you both go along with this, I must ask for your implicit trust. I share my love for Gabbie and Ginnie with you, Keith. I will look out for all of your best interests, now and always. Okay?" Keith and Gabbie nodded. "Fine. Because my work will take a great deal of time and infinite patience, the first thing, anytime today, Gabbie, we should take you to the private airport nearby to get you a flight to the airport in Great Farraday. That will connect with your obligations up there. I will call you with an assignment, which I ask you to complete as quickly and completely as possible. Keith will remain here with me. If he agrees, I need him to also agree that I may use my treatment with him in a monograph—as an instructional guide to other counselors. After all, I am a teacher and a writer."

Keith pursed his lips. "Sure. Okay. It would be nice to recognize the person you write about."

"Aunt Mary?" Gabbie started. "I don't want any harm to come to Keith, no matter who he is."

"Of course not. My oath as a physician says, 'Do no harm.' I will do my absolute best not to let anything untoward happen."

"And one more thing, Aunt Mary," Gabbie said, "I'm concerned about me putting something on you that I shouldn't. I know you have made up your own mind, but I don't think this will happen, Boom! overnight. How will we ever repay you?"

"Writing the monograph about this case will be fine," Mary said.

"Maybe I should just grab Keith as he is, no matter how much he resembles Jim, and just have us live together this way? What would be so wrong?" Gabbie said. "And how do we know you can do this, and we're not just wasting time when we could be enjoying each other?"

"Keith?" Mary said.

Keith put down his fork. "I could go along with what Gabbie says. The meds at the hospital sure did work a hell of a long time on me in every way. They decided I got a hole in my head, and that's the long and the short of it. In all fairness to Louise, I rejected her same argument. I must make my best effort to get my memory back—if it is available to me. If I don't regain it, then I have the same situation as I had with Louise."

"Let me ask. You both speak very well for yourselves. Who's speaking for Jim Dorchester? In law it could be interpreted as *guardian ad litem*."

Keith and Gabbie turned to each other, their faces were blank, their eyes open wide.

"Aunt Mary. I understand what you're saying. I am chagrined that I didn't think of that. I say you will have to look out for Jim's interests," Gabbie said.

"Jim Dorchester deserves the life given to him if he's alive. If I can't do it, you both will be the first to know as soon as I know. How's that?" Mary said. Keith and Gabbie looked at each other and nodded.

Mary looked at Keith and Gabbie. "We're all agreed to this plan then? Kindly say."

"Yes," Gabbie said, "I'll go back to Great Farraday, and pray every night for all of us."

"There is something I want you to take back with you, Medford, my dear," Mary said. "It's been in process for a while now, but I am transferring my villa in Tuscany to you. It's not as magnanimous as it sounds. It works out to be better for me if it's not on my inventory. Of course, all the maintenance and caretakers are taken care of, including flights to go there and all the sundries . . ."

"Aunt Mary!" Gabbie said. "I can't accept . . ."

"Nonsense! I'm thinking of Ginnie. What a fun place it will be! Imagine her going there on spring break! We'll talk more on this if you wish later."

"Aunt Mary, thank you," Gabbie said.

"I've got to tell you this, Mary," Keith said. "The psychiatrist I saw at the hospital was very smart and knowledgeable. He said he could help me out . . . if he had the time, which he didn't. He said the right kind of intensive therapy was the only answer if it were a psychological problem I was dealing with and not brain damage. Out of thousands of vets that were hurt in the service quite a few had to be left by the wayside. Not enough doctors, time, or money. I could be one of them. If you're willing to devote yourself to me, I most humbly accept your help with gratitude. But, and it's a big but, as the Army psychiatrist warned me, I'm scared as hell the operation will be a success, but the patient will die."

"I know exactly what you mean, Keith, and that could happen. We may find out that it is psychological trauma that caused your memory loss. Then, when we unlock the secret, it may be so abhorrent to you, that you cannot tolerate it. You may even go crazy because of it. Those are the stakes. Understanding that above all, do we go on?"

Keith nodded.

Mary paused. She put her hand to her chin. "Based on our conversation, Gabbie, I'm going to take a giant step. I think it will be fine. To show you how confident I am that I am looking at this with a fresh eye, Keith, allow me to ask you a question. Do you know, or were you ever told they checked your DNA?"

57

"Anna?" Mary said as she reached out and pressed a button on the intercom. It was in the center of the table neatly hidden among the dishes.

"Pronto!" came the reply.

"Anna, we'll need the Mercedes. Our plane is being serviced, so call the Great Farraday airport and ask Ed if he can be down here to pick up a passenger at around two o'clock this afternoon. Then call the Salty Dog and make reservations for luncheon for the four of us. This evening, dinner for two on the terrace. We will have a guest staying for an unlimited period of time in the Degas bedroom. Come fetch us on the deck when it's time to leave."

Gabbie raised her eyebrows. "Aunt Mary, in all this time I never knew you had help!" Mary said. "Anna is responsible for me being me! She is absolutely irreplaceable! She was here when you came down several times, Gabbie. Anna just doesn't like to make herself known. She's a shadow. Yet, she is an . . . everything! She's a chef—she's responsible for this breakfast—is *le major dame* here, my apartment in New York, my villa in Tuscany—no! I gave that to you, Gabbie! And, also Anna is my chauffeur—she also has a pilot's ticket--dresser, shopper, and personal secretary, and personal attendant, like doing my hair and nails. She is my second when I go sailing, and my mechanic for cross-country automobile racing. I pay her a small fortune, which I'm inclined to think she shares with a home for troubled teen-age girls."

"Auntie! I never knew!" Gabbie said.

"Mary," Keith started, "if you don't mind the question, what is the glue that binds?"

Mary raised her chin. "Ah! You are a perspicacious young man, Keith! Of course, there would be 'a glue that binds.' I'm so glad you asked. I must tell you about how I met Anna so you will understand a bit how I work. Perhaps I can induce confidence in you. When I first met Anna she was fifteen years old. Anna comes from a fine, well-to-do Park Avenue WASP home. A family court judge, a close personal friend of ours who knew I had lost my late husband, Nedo, a month or two before, called and asked me to take her on as a patient. He knew I had given up my practice, but thought it might help me get out of my funk. "What's the reason she's locked up in the Bellevue psychiatric ward?" I asked the judge.

"Yes or no? Then find out for yourself," the judge said.

"Intrigued, and needing something, I agreed," Mary said.

* * *

That same morning, Mary went to Bellevue to see Anna.

"Anna! Anna! Look at me! Look at me!" Mary implored.

Under a straight jacket, Anna was nude except for a sanitary pad and belt. She was curled up in a ball on the floor in a corner of the cell. Her long brown hair was full of knots, and dirty. Dried blood ran down her legs. Mary knew instantly Anna was in a fugue state. Mary got a basin with water, washcloths, towels, and a comb. She cleaned up Anna as best she could.

"Anna! I have come here for the last two days! If you do not look at me, they won't let me back to see you!" Mary said. Anna turned away to the wall. "Anna! They are going to hurt me like they hurt you if you don't look at me!"

The words made Anna jerk upwards.

"Look at me! I can make you safe! You will be safe with me. I promise!"

Anna shook her head.

"Yes! Yes! I can hold you safe!"

Anna shook her head.

Mary took off her blouse and her bra. She slid off the cot, and sat on the floor next to Anna. "Anna! Look! Look! I am for you! Look!" Mary turned her head so she could face her bosom. "Look! Anna!"

The abruptness caused Anna to open her eyes. She saw Mary's breasts. Her eyes remained wide open, staring intently. Mary reached over, and gently pulled the traumatized child to her. She cuddled her cheek between her breasts. After more than two hours of gentle rocking, Mary felt the tension slowly ebb from Anna. She knew it was more from fatigue than it was from being at ease.

"Nobody is going to hurt you anymore, Anna. No more hurt. I care for you. I will not let anything happen to you. Never again. You must be brave and strong. I want you to trust me. I will care for you."

The next day Mary just came and sat in the room with Anna while she lay curled on the bed. Mary talked to her all the while reassuring her of her safety. Mary continued to minister to Anna for almost a week. It was late in the day when Anna tried to communicate. She shook her head. She stared at Mary and finally said, "Anna, Anna" with a broad "A."

The next day, Anna was out of the straightjacket and into the pj's Mary had bought for her. They were bright and colorful. She began to speak to Mary briefly in short, sporadic sentences, usually about the day and the flowers Mary would bring, which Mary had to take with her when she left Anna.

By the middle of the following week, Mary's appeal to the judge to have Anna named a ward of the state and be allowed to live with Mary as a foster parent was granted.

Mary brought her to her apartment. She said little to Anna as she showed her around. She told her she was to remain by her side always-always. No matter where Mary went or what she did Anna was to stick to her like a shadow. It made Anna feel secure and comfortable. Mary showed her the bathroom to use. The lock was removed, as were all the medicines and glass bottles—anything someone could use to harm themselves. Mary's bathroom was locked. When Mary went into her bathroom, she kept the door ajar. Anna sat in a nearby chair and hummed tunes.

At first the plan was for both of them to sleep in the guest bedroom, which had twin beds. During the first night, Anna had slipped out of her bed, and crawled into bed with Mary. After that, they changed bedrooms, and both slept in Mary's king size bed.

"I won't send you to any school, Anna, but your education cannot be neglected. I would like to home school you. That means I would be your teacher. I would get school books for your grade level, and you would study and do your work here. It wouldn't be much fun if I had to keep after you to do your work, so, you tell me if you'd like to try it"

"Yes. I think yes," Anna said.

"You would be somewhere in the sophomore class, so that means we may have a problem with chemistry and physics, but I have friends at Columbia that may let us into the labs one or two days a week. I can teach you math when we find out where you stand, so it'll be either algebra, trigonometry or calculus. Music we can do during dinner. Speaking of dinner, whenever you're ready, we can cook together. I can make pastas and sauces of all kinds. I can do Italian, French, German, Oriental, Latino, and Thai! I'll teach you everything, including my dynamite carrot cake, slice o' lemon pie, and blueberry pie, all of which take my magic ingredient of lemon oil. When you're ready to go outside with me, we'll go to my club for tennis, track, swimming, diving, racquet ball—whatever you like. The most strenuous outdoor activity I would like to start as soon as possible is called 'shopping!'"

For the first time in weeks, Anna broke out in a smile and started laughing.

* * *

It was six months later, a lazy Sunday morning, when they were lounging around in their pj's reading the paper. Anna stared at Mary for a long time. "I want to tell you. My stepfather raped me since I was ten years old. His three sons, my step brothers, sexually abused me. They would hold me down and put things in my vagina and my anus."

"Anna, your mother?"

"She would watch her husband ravish me in their own bed. The boys said they would kill my mother if I said anything."

"How did you finally get to Bellevue?"

"My step father was very angry with my mother. He assaulted me very brutally. He tried to sodomize me. I started hemorrhaging. My mother just cried. She said I was going to die. My stepfather took me to the hospital. He said he would harm my mother if I didn't say someone broke into the house and raped me."

Mary held out her hands. "Come, sweetheart, come!" Anna slid onto the couch and into her warm, safe embrace. "You and I are one, Anna, we will always be here for one another. I am very proud of you."

* * *

"Anna has been with me for sixteen years. She is here doing exactly what she wants to do. She passed every one of her high school Regents Exams in the 99th percentile. She passed every single challenge exam for Columbia as a Summa Cum Laude, although she's not interested in a formal degree. One of the first of her educational plans was to become a registered nurse. Do you know the reason? For me! In case I ever needed professional help, she could do it! Anna has a license to fly my Lear jet, which she does with a co-pilot. She could enter the Olympic diving qualification run, and get in, I'm sure. She studied classical piano. When I injured my back sailing, she became a physical therapist. She gives excellent massages. She could be a Formula One driver if she wanted, but would rather have fun in my Lamborghini. She could teach at L'Escoffiere School of Cooking she is so good. She is free to leave, as I told her, and if she did, I would need four others to replace her."

In the doorway appeared a tall, thin woman. Her dark hair was short-cropped. She had large, dark eyes, an almost too-small nose, high cheek bones, and a smile that could beguile. She wore a sleeveless shirt that stopped just above her navel. She wore leather flared jeans and western boots.

"Gabbie, Keith, this is Anna," Mary said.

"Mary? We should leave for lunch," Anna said. "First, I would like to put the Harley in the garage, if I have permission to do so?"

"Thank you, that's very thoughtful," Keith said. "The key is there, but you can just roll it in. Want me to do it?"

Anna shook her head, a hint of a smile on her face.

When Anna was gone, Gabbie said, "Aunt Mary, she's gorgeous! What a precious face! What a body!"

"I think she would be known as a stunner," Keith said.

Suddenly, the motorcycle, with its distinctive roar, came to life. The three of them looked out to see Anna whip the machine around the parking area. She made two donuts where she kept one foot on the ground while the rear wheel raced around in a circle. Anna straightened out, tore to one end, and then came back doing a wheely, riding the bike with the front wheel high in the air. She returned to the far end of the parking area, did a donut to turn around, went immediately into a wheely, and this time brought both feet up onto the seat. She bounced down on the seat, brought the bike down, made a half circle. She brought the front wheel down, headed for the garage as she went up high on the front wheel. She flipped the back end of the bike around right into the garage doorway. She let the front wheel down and let the Harley roll backwards into the garage.

"Oh, my loving god!" Keith said.

"But! Does she do windows?" Gabbie said.

They laughed.

At the front of the house, Anna had opened all the doors of the limousine and waved Keith to sit shotgun with her. "Mesdames should not be crowded," she explained.

58

At the airport after the four of them had lunch, Anna returned to the limo to report Ed was waiting on the tarmac to take Gabbie back to Great Farraday.

Keith and Gabbie walked with their arms around each other past the office. They saw Ed walking around the plane doing his pre-flight inspection. When he saw them, he waved.

"Keith, I have such a premonition about leaving you," Gabbie said.

"Premonition good like Aunt Mary being successful with me, or premonition bad like I'll be stuck forever in the nether world?"

"Nothing like that," Gabbie said. "I'm shaking inside because of the fear I will never see you again. It happened to me once. I'm terrified it will happen again! I wouldn't be able to stand it."

"That's exactly the chance we're taking."

"I know. I just have that bottom-falling-out-of-the-stomach feeling I will never see you again."

"Gabbie, that's not the worst that can happen."

"What could be the worst?"

"That just one of us died."

59

Returning from the airport, Keith and Mary were let out of the limo by Anna under the porte cochere. Mary led the way into the kitchen. She picked a bottle of red wine out of the wine rack, which she gave to Keith wrapped in a kitchen towel. "The official wine cellar is downstairs," Mary said. She grabbed two glasses and an opener. She led the way out onto the deck through sliding glass doors. They sat under an eight-foot-circumference umbrella at a hand-wrought iron table with a glass top. The view was out over the ocean.

"I bring my computer out here some mornings, and I do my best work. The setting is just so compatible with my soul," Mary said. "Would you be kind enough to open the wine, Keith?"

He splashed wine into the glasses. "Salute! You have some lovely lifestyle, Mary, if I may say."

"I owe it all to wealthy parents, and my late husband, Nedo. He had people who couldn't throw money at him fast enough and hard enough. He was an exceptional therapist. He was very ethical and didn't hesitate to work his clients through their problems very quickly. He said it gave them back a lot of their lives to live. I never see a bill, nor do I ever pay one. I have as much cash at my disposal as I wish. It is all taken care of by an off shore corporation set up by Nedo's folks."

Keith looked out over the water to stare at a distant sailboat. When he turned back he saw a dish of h'or d'oeuvres on the table. It's magical appearance made him purse his lips and shake his head asking silently how it got there. "Anna," Mary answered.

The air grew still. "Keith, I need your undivided attention. We are here for a very serious purpose. I am very professional about my work. I am not frivolous about a single part of it. I do not expect or want you to be either. Because I am responsible for everything, I must tell you how it is going to be. If you feel you do not want to put up with a single part of it, then know I appreciate your candor because you will not cause me to waste any of my time. I have reason and purpose for every single thing I do. Therefore, you must consider my request as a command order. You must exert yourself to the extreme to carry out whatever I need or want from you. We start from the truth. If you do not feel like doing something, do not malinger. Tell me the problem. There are more answers than there are problems. Questions?"

"None."

"We will be dealing with something that is very unpleasant—pain. Psychological pain is the worst torture in the world. No one, unless one is aberrant, wants pain. I may request something that you know will be very painful. You must walk through the fire. You must. If you do not, you will live the half-life of a coward. Do you understand what I'm asking? It would be like asking you to twist off your finger."

"Which one?"

"I hope that's not a joke. We will do just fine."

In his room, Keith stripped and let the steaming water from the shower cut into him.

The heat lamps and the fans dried off what the bath sheet didn't absorb. The towel fell away as he dropped onto the bed, his mind racing, dreaming crazily. It wasn't possible someone was taking him into her mouth.

He awoke with a tapping at the sole of his foot.

"Dinner in twenty minutes," he heard.

It had to be Anna, he thought.

60

Keith sat next to Mary as she indicated for dinner.

"I must tell you for your own information," Mary said, "that about three days a week, on no set schedule, you may not find Anna or me available. Should there be an emergency, use the intercom first, but if there is no reply, go to the gym in the basement. It has mirrors on the wall and a bar Anna uses for her ballet practice. It is also where we fence."

"Mary, I'm flabbergasted at the number of things I either didn't know, or forgot and must learn about. Fencing! How popular can that be? In all the time with Louise, I never saw it on television, except for movie stuff, you know. How did you get interested?"

"It's not as weird a story as you may think. My late husband's name was Nedo Chicco. He was named after Nedo Nali. Around 1936 or so, he won six gold medals—a record-making three in foil, sabre, and epee--at one Olympics. My Nedo, of course, couldn't resist following his namesake's passion. He fenced and taught me, and I taught Anna. So? We fence but just the foil!"

"What a charming story."

"I will not be so charming at my next request. Our work will be long and arduous, so we should have started yesterday. But, this week will be fun activities. We're biding time until I get the information I requested from the Army and Gabbie. For instance, tomorrow morning is sailing. When we come back, we'll take a swim, have lunch. Keith? I have to run a few risks if we are going to try to do this *al fresco.* It is rare that therapy can be so concentrated. It is challenging enough under ordinary circumstances for therapist and patient. I must ask, do you play tennis?"

"No. I can't remember ever playing tennis."

"I'm going to ask you to play tennis. We'll go to the club for tennis and cocktails. We'll play mixed doubles."

"You can't ask me to do that? If I've never played, I'll make a fool of myself. I'll look like an idiot on the court!"

"Keith, you must trust me. You know when one digs with a shovel, one shoves the spade down into the earth with the weight of a foot? It makes for a good bite. That's what I'm trying to do with putting you on the tennis court. Gabbie told me Jim was an excellent tennis player. Okay?"

"Okay."

"Good. Let's see what happens tomorrow. Now, after dinner you will need all your resources because you will start writing, by hand, Keith's autobiography, from as far back to as far forward as you remember it." Keith started to speak, but Mary held up her hand. "I will give you particular instructions. Trust me, I know what you are about, meaning what you have been through. Which brings me to the next point. You said you trust me, but I must plant that trust deeper. I want you to be absolutely sure you know who I am and will give me totally everything I need. There will be need for you to do exactly and immediately what I ask you to do. I must count on the fact that you will not hold anything back. You must obey no matter what it is I ask. That's the reason we're going to play for a few days. Okay?"

He looked down and found dinner before him. "Mary, I give you carte blanche."

"You have a right to understand your expectations." Keith started to wave her off, but she shook her head. "I must do this for all the right ethical and professional reasons. I don't think you ever would, but I wouldn't want to hear, 'You never told me.' Or, 'You never warned me.'"

"I think I can tell you the possibilities and the probabilities. I've been living with this for more than six years."

"But this is the first day you have spent with me. I can tell you the score of a baseball game before it begins. You wouldn't want to bet against me. It's nothing to nothing. Let me tell you the score of what we're about. In however long it takes, we may end up nothing to nothing. You will have made no progress whatsoever. Undoubtedly the cause will be because your memory was stolen by the damage to your brain. If that's the case, I will be very sorry because I'm the first not to believe that is the case. I've said so before. Through my work with total cooperation with you, we may bring your memory back. I want you to know, you may regain your memory, but because of what you find there, you may not want it back. In this case, regression, which may be even worse that what you are enduring now. Suicide would not be out of the question. Keith, are you absolutely sure you understand what I have just said?"

"Yes, that what I'm hiding I find so horrible I could not bear to acknowledge it. Not only that, I may find I cannot live with it. With that, I may find putting myself out of this world would be far easier than confronting it. May I tell you? I warned Louise, and I did tell Gabbie the same thing."

Mary nodded. "Yes. Or, you may like what we find. In this case, you have the rest of your life to live. Now, how does this happen? Fugue or fugue state? The clinical definition of a fugue state is: A pathological amnesiac condition that may persist for several months and usually results from severe mental stress, in which one is apparently conscious of one's actions but has no recollection of them after returning to a normal state. Keith, take note I said 'has no recollection of them after returning to a normal state.' In my experience—and I have someone in mind--that may or may not be true. I may create a problem I will get into later. Now, if a person does something they do not like, are ashamed of, or think is bad like a betrayal, let's say, in a particular room in the world in which they live, they shut the door to that room and never wish to enter it again, usually because of the psychological pain reliving it brings them. The memory may be selective and they forget just that room, or they may forget as much of the surrounding time as is necessary to live with it. If it is a morbid situation, sometimes the person feels self-destruction is the only answer, which it never is; it is only one possible answer. If the person can be brought back into the room and be shown all the mitigating factors, and the false illusions concerning the situation, it can be dealt with in a very realistic way. Life will go on. Will the person recollect or not? I don't know. Doing that can be like crossing a desert in search of water. Failure, maybe. Success, maybe. The mind is so intricate, it is beyond intricacy."

Mary went on, "A scenario you should be prepared to face: Once your full memory is back, and let's say for this moment you do recollect, you will have an almost difficult chore of deciding what you will do with the problems your memory presents to you."

"Like what?" Keith asked after eating the last tiny bit of the soufflé.

"You came here with my niece Gabbie. You say you are in love with Gabbie and her daughter Ginnie. You also say you are passionately in love with Louise. Let's say you had the option, you would have to go through some mental gymnastics to choose between the two. But, suppose your memory additionally brings back a wife and a family, or some other impedimenta?"

"Or, Mary, a hypothetical: Suppose because of one thing and another, let's say transference or counter-transference or not, I fall madly, passionately in love with you? That I will forsake the others so that I may remain with you?"

"I like that you are thinking. You understand that is a form of indebtedness. Even simple first aid may bring it on because it is a pure act of caring, and a person who feels very much cared for also feels a depth of gratitude. Some therapists or counselors find they cannot resist the adoration, and their clients fall victim of their own vulnerability. Ethically that should never happen. And Keith, I would not let that happen to you. First and foremost, I am a professional in every sense of the word. My work comes first. Therapists that take advantage of their position and sleep with their patients, or that kind of drek, should be thrown out of the profession. They are not here to make this a better world. They are indescribable, criminal narcissists. Any woman would be flattered to have a man fall in love with her. Who knows? I might fall in love with you, as if I haven't a good deal already just because of the person you are, or I wouldn't be doing this. I'm a professional, but I'm not soul dead. You and I? After this is all over? That would be a magnificent situation. But, to be brutally honest, although professionally I would never let you into my personal life, I do have a significant other. Let's see how it all plays out? Yes? How wonderful to lead an interesting life. More coffee?"

"Mary, whether you know it or not, I'm in love with you already. I understand the ethics involved. I'm never to slip in between your sheets. "

"Absolutely correct. Anything else and I will be forced to refer you to another therapist."

"What about Anna?"

"Anna is a free agent. She is an adult. You already know she is very capable in many, many areas. She speaks and acts for herself. Within the limits of my professional ethics I want you to know I trust her implicitly. Your privacy is absolutely guaranteed by both of us. I need her to help me with my work. I could not do it without her. I have demanded the same ethics and protocol from her as I do of myself. If you have a problem being in therapy with me, and having the possibility that Anna may be privy to what I need to do to have this process move quicker, you must tell me now. I would not allow anything inappropriate. I must emphasize, I have professional boundaries, but when it comes to Anna, they are made of elastic. If I could, I would wish for a couple of lifetimes. It is all so fascinating. I must begin my work."

"Yes, of course. It has been a long day for you."

"Just one or two more items, Keith. You should know I have asked Gabbie as her assignment to give me as detailed a record as she can, her recollections of you from the very first moment she knew or saw you until the very last moment. I want you to know I have been involved with Gabbie ever since her birth, because Nedo and I were Godparents to her. I know you were both grade school sweethearts, a rare, lovely, wonderful joy. She has already sent part of her manuscript to me. Miracle of miracles, I have already received part of your military records."

"I'm sure they will send you more than they gave me."

"Louise McBride has replied to my request and promises a speedy reply."

"It will be her first contact about me since I started this journey."

"I have explained to her that I am a psychiatrist, and that I have your permission to get your private information. As soon as you are able, you can retire to the library, or to the sitting room next to your bedroom, to write in infinite detail every single moment of your life you can recollect. Leave your notes on the desk. Anna will collect, transcribe, and print them out on the computer so I can have them before breakfast."

"I understand. It will be done."

"I want you to understand there is another reason I want you to establish the pattern of writing these notes. I will explain more later."

"Mary? Thank you."

Mary patted his hand. "Wait'll you go through the next couple of weeks!"

When Keith went to his bedroom, he found the bed turned down. Pajamas laid out. There was a time he was sensitive to a breeze on his skin grafts. Ever since then, pj's were forsaken.

61

Keith wore a baseball cap, sunglasses, a white long-sleeved shirt, shorts with a sailor's knife attached to a lanyard, and deck shoes. He found everything laid out for him when he awoke.

He stood at the end of the dock admiring the lines of the sailboat. "Good morning, Mr. Dorchester. May I call you 'Keith'?"

"Oh! Hello! Anna! You just appear! Yes, of course."

"You've sailed?"

"Never."

"Fine. No bad habits to break. Sailing has no master. Everyone learns every moment: a breeze, a wave, an incident, a mis-move. Mary is as close a perfectionist as you will find. Let's go aboard and make ready. We'll take off covers, sleeves, lay out lines, and single up on the mooring lines. Then, I'll take you up front to show you the spinnaker layout. By the way, how are you on shinninying up the mast? You might have to go up if the halyard comes off the reeve."

"I'd have to pass unless it was a dire emergency. If you saw the grafts on my legs . . ."

"I've seen them. Let's all hope it doesn't come to that."

"Keith," Mary said, "there's one major reason we're going sailing. I'm using it as an analogy to putting your trust in me with your life."

Keith noted the transformation in Mary the moment she took the helm. She was wearing a baseball cap, sunglasses, a slicker, shorts and boat shoes. The sails were up and the boat was running smooth and fast. He sensed the daring and the danger. She came about and gave the order to put out the spinnaker. The sail went out without a hitch. Anna indicated an adjustment to Keith to take the pole in about two feet. From then on, the boat flew over the waves.

Keith took in the sensation of pure power from the force of the wind and its control by the sailors, the boat, and sails. He sensed the elation Mary and Anna had to feel at having control over such a dynamic, potentially harmful beast that enabled them to traverse the water so rapidly and exactly as they wished.

Mary ordered in the spinnaker.

Mary had the boat come around and headed back to port.

Mary was the first off the boat at the dock. She headed to the house.

Keith and Anna secured the boat at the dock.

Keith turned to pick up his cap. "Anna, you made it all great . . . fun . . . !"

He turned to see Anna half-way up the dock.

Keith went up the steps two at a time to get to his room. Just as he walked in, the intercom beeped and a light came on.

"Keith." It was Mary. "Luncheon on the deck in ten minutes! Don't shower, we'll go to the club for tennis. Anna! You were superb as always on a magnificent sail. I'll use the Lamborghini. Thank you."

On the deck, Keith poured iced tea for Mary and himself. He looked at the dish before him. "Mmmm! How nice! Lobster crepes."

Mary said, "There's this couple at the club that I've been unable to wipe the smirk off their faces for too long! It's mixed doubles, which you and I know is altogether a different game of something tennis. I'd like to snap their sweat bands. They're just awful! When they win they make raunchy jokes, laugh, and add insult by offering to buy the drinks! I can't tell you how badly I want to beat the holy crap out of them. Let me warn you, if we don't win today, you walk home!"

Keith wore a safari tennis hat, a long-sleeved shirt to cover his burns, shorts which exposed his scars, and tennis socks and shoes. With Mary, he walked onto the

Har-true court hobbling over and shuffling to meet Christopher and Jennifer at the net.

After short introductions, Christopher said, "Oh, why don't you go ahead and serve!"

Keith raised an eyebrow and stared at him. "That's very gracious, sir! But I'll spin my racket and you call whether the "W" is up or down." Keith spun his racket.

Christopher called out, "Up!"

"The letter is "M," as you can see. We'll serve," Keith said. He turned, took Mary by the elbow and headed for the far end of the court. "Mary, would you like to serve first? Or shall I?"

"Keith, you have completely won me over. Now we'll learn about you and tennis."

After a brief warm up, if a radar speed gun were available it would most likely have measured Keith's serves at about 120 miles an hour, faster when he served to Jennifer.

With the final score 6-0, Mary could not run up to the net fast enough to shake Jennifer and Christopher's hands. Mary said, "Oh, what fun! We'll have to do this again! My guest Keith can't remember playing ever before, so I suggested lessons. Do order whatever drinks you'd like and do put them on my bill!"

Mary had the car up to seventy before she took it out of second. "Son of a bitch, Keith! You and I, we're going to succeed with your therapy!"

"Why do you say that?"

"Listen closely. You couldn't remember if you ever played tennis. You don't learn the first time on the court. This was not your first time on the court."

"No, I felt fairly comfortable. What's the point?"

"The point, dear patient, is that you playing tennis has substantiated my belief that your loss of memory is psychological, and, therefore, fixable! You see, like a dancer or a pianist, your muscles have memory. Your tennis muscles remember playing. It's that easy."

"Why?"

"Because Gabbie wrote in your biography that you were one of the top tennis players in high school! Do you know what that means? Locked deep somewhere in your psyche is the ability and knowledge of how to play tennis! I didn't care about those assholes on the court! It was you that was the focus of my interest! Keith! We have something to concentrate on! How do we break the logjam of your memory?"

"I keep thinking, when you do, will I be able to endure what I find out?"

"That's the billion dollar question."

"Mary? I noticed when we got in the car to go play, but it's even more with me now. Perhaps because of the exercise . . . what is the perfume you're wearing? It is so . . . what's the right word? captivating? alluring? Wear it for me . . ."

"Keith, just to set borders, perfume is a very personal thing. Your request is inappropriate. I understand you feel at ease, and that's good, but I will call you on the slightest bit of unprofessionalism between us. We agreed. Yes?"

When Mary and Keith entered the kitchen, Mary turned to him. "Keith, I want you to go to the exercise room. After due consideration, I've decided one of the best therapies for you would be physical therapy. I watched you moving on the boat, and really paid attention to your movements on the tennis court. The scars and skin grafts are causing you some difficulty. You will find Anna is a superb physical therapist, and her work will be a continuation of the meticulous regime you followed after the grafts. May I suggest you get undressed in your room, and wear a bathrobe? We'll schedule it every day for the first week, then every other day, and so on. Just listen to me: Do it with good will? Yes?"

"Yes, of course."

"Anna will be waiting for you."

* * * *

Anna patted the top of the massage table. "Face up," Anna said.

He hitched himself up onto the table.

"If you don't mind, first I must examine you *a capite ad calcem*. That's Latin for from head to foot." A foot pedal raised the table.

He closed his eyes. He felt her hand glide under his neck. She lifted his head and slipped a pillow under it. He could tell a bright light was brought to bear on his face. He sensed the light moved onto his chest. It went over the towel and down his legs. He could tell the light was turned off.

"Keith . . ." Anna's voice was by his right shoulder. "My examination was to be sure I caused you no harm. I'll look at your back later. I know now what I can and cannot do to aid you. You have a right to your privacy. You do not have to inform me of a single thing. You do not have to answer a single question I ask. Do you understand?"

"Yes, I do. I can't hide anything more from anyone else than I am from myself. Ask away."

"I did not know this, but I see you have miraculously come through some pretty severe third-degree—maybe worse--burns. The plastic surgery on your face and neck is just masterful. Some of the work I could see only in the magnifying glass. How good did they reconstruct your old self?"

"I can't say. They have photos when I was medium rare. I have no memory of how I looked."

"That is provocative. Your torso, arms, and legs had similarly majestic work. The recuperative time had to be a long, long time. Some victims with just a quarter of the burns you suffered do not survive past the period of debridement. You must have had a crew of angels."

"Just one. Louise McBride, a red haired beauty who as you know is waiting to hear from me."

"You were a dedicated patient? Only she was your medical attendant?"

"Yes."

"That may be the reason you survived. I noticed trepanning. They removed a portion of your skull no doubt to relieve pressure. You suffered also a traumatic brain injury?"

"Yes. When my truck blew up, I think I whacked my bean pretty good. It is believed to be the cause of my loss of memory."

"That it is due to purely physical reasons?"

"Yes."

"And Mary agrees or disagrees with that?"

"Disagrees."

"She believes the cause after all this time may be a severe, morbid fugue state."

"I would say yes."

"If it is a fugue of any size, shape, or color, then Mary is the expert. If she can't help you, then no one can. Take my word for it."

"Anna, I know to whom I'm talking."

"Thank you. Let's get started. Primarily what I will be doing is to enliven not living skin. By the way you walk and move limitations have come in from contraction, such as leather when it dries. A method of torture with the native Americans was to tie a wet rawhide strip around the victim's head. As it dried, it crushed the skull. To prevent your grafts from causing any difficulty I will apply emollients, such as Vitamin E to you. There are others I have compounded in the laboratory, which I have found worked very well and are beneficial. Also, some autogenerational transgretional techniques may be used. Mary is in total charge. I report to her on your progress after each session. My schedule with you is made to fit her schedule with you. I will post the time you are to come here to meet with me on a stickee in the middle of the mirror above your dresser in your bedroom. Questions?"

"None."

"I'll let you know when I want you to turn over." Keith felt what seemed to be a gentle breeze cross his face. After a few moments he guessed with some degree of certainly that surgery scars were being traced by Anna's fingers no more than a bare sixteenth of an inch. The sensation was so soothing, he fell asleep.

"Keith? I need you to turn over."

She removed the pillow, and Keith stuck his face into the opening cut out in the table.

If she had touched him at all, he couldn't tell. The difficulty was he couldn't be sure he didn't fall dead asleep and missed her touch as she massaged the emollients over his skin. Then, he was aware in a semi-somnambulant mode that her hands were passing over him, but just above his body. When he searched his mind while this was going on, he got the sensation of minimal pressure on his skin. Search as he might, he could only deduce that it was the pressure built up between her hands and his skin. He did feel the tap at his foot. He turned over, sat up and stretched. Anna was gone. He threw on the robe and returned to his room. The hot water from the showerhead stung at first, then became soothing. Keith had the sensation of well being. He dropped the towel and got onto the bed. In his dreams he soared and floated. He spun around then held himself tight to strong pressures. Again, when he awoke he had the feeling a mouth had taken him.

At dinner, Mary said, "Keith, you know I'm very sensitive to people and their vibrations. You seem troubled."

"No, not really troubled. Just wondering if this will work out. You know. Will it be worth all the trouble? Also, what if your premise is wrong that you can get through the fugue—if that's what it is?"

"One goes further with a destination than moving in circles. Based on my training, my experience, being with you, I'm going with a strong instinct."

"Mary? I'm going with you. Dinner, and dinner with you was lovely as always. Thank you." Keith got up.

"Wait one moment, Keith, so you will also know we're going fishing for blues off of Montauk Point tomorrow." Mary pressed a button on the intercom. "Anna, kindly call Geraldo Albano to learn if we may use his boat tomorrow—the big one; perhaps from ten to two? Confirm he will have fresh bait aboard. We'll use the Mercedes. Come fetch us on the deck when you're ready to go. Thank you."

Keith walked into his bedroom. He was not surprised to see the bed turned down, and instead of the pj's, a gold foil wrapped chocolate. He went into the sitting room. Again, he was not surprised to see lined legal writing tablets, sharpened pencils, ball point pens, a glass of pomegranate juice, and the light turned on at the desk.

He sat, wrote the date, day, and time at the top of a tablet. He labeled the page: Keith's recollections, Day One. He took a sip of the juice, thought of Gabbie and Louise, and then tried to bring to mind what the fuck was the first thing he remembered when he regained consciousness after he got blown up in the truck?

62

Keith felt the boat's throbbing engine vibrate through the deck. He watched the water foam and churn behind the barely moving boat. He wore a baseball cap, sunglasses, a windbreaker, shorts and deck shoes. Mary was dressed as he was. She sat in the fighting chair beside him with her feet up on the railing. She was drinking coffee from a stainless steel container.

"You're a good sailor," she said.

"You make it easy to enjoy life. If I'm allowed to say it, you look very pretty."

"'Course you can say it! I may work with the mind but my emotions aren't dead! If you could see the sparkle in my eyes, you'd know how much I approve."

"How many times have you been told you resemble Gina Lollobrigida?"

"Always the counselor, I must ask how you remember her?"

"Watching television with Louise, but you are so much thinner except for . . ."

"I know, my boobs are her size! Ooooops! Anna! Anna!" she called loudly. "You've got a hit!"

Anna slowed the engine even more. Wearing a cap, sunglasses, long tank top and shorts, she walked barefoot quickly on deck. She took the starboard fishing pole out of its holder and handed it to Mary because she was in the starboard chair. "Good Luck!"

Mary shouted, "I hope it's a blue!"

Keith reached for the gaff, a five-foot rod with a handle on one end and a mean-looking hook on the other.

Anna went to Mary's left side and let the line run through her hand.

Keith looked over the fantail. He was beside Anna. He saw the shiny wire leader come up and a large black fish thrashing wildly just under the surface.

"It's a blackfish!" Anna called out. "Careful, Keith! Forget the gaff! Bring this one on deck alive and its teeth could take your hand off!"

Keith pulled the gaff back. He saw the fish attack. It fought fiercely for its freedom. "What can I do to help?" he shouted.

"Relax! I've got it!" Anna said.

He saw Anna reach behind her. Out of the belt in her shorts, she pulled out a Walther PPK. In swift movements, she pulled the fish up out of the water then fired a bullet between the monster's eyes. It stopped fighting.

Keith pointed to the blackfish.

"Anna will have it filleted and packed in ice before you know it. Put that line over again, and Anna will re-bait this one."

Keith nodded. He gazed at the horizon thoughts flashing through his mind. The world was an illusion. It didn't seem to be what one perceived at all. Mary explained to him the fishing was part of her therapy. Whether Keith knew it or not, it was part of the large picture of making him want to regain his memory. The desire was critical. There could be a moment of extreme conflict where Keith would remember the major causal factor of his mental incarceration and be terrified to face it. Mary could be of no help to him there. It was a battle he started in his own mind, and one he had to conquer in his own mind.

It was early afternoon when Keith, Mary, and Anna were in the limousine leaving Montauk.

The salt air and the wine from lunch gave him a feeling of well being. He realized he had eased so smoothly into the life of the leisure class. Only pleasurable activities were allowed and every whim satisfied. He was not so lulled into complacency that he forgot his own hospital ceiling admonition: Life was a toll road. One paid getting on or getting off, but one somehow was made to pay. He smiled to himself. He was an adventurer. He liked the idea of facing the unexpected that lay ahead. Life with a guidebook would be boring.

Mary took his hand. "I'm sorry you can't go riding. My friend has wonderful bridle trails on the property. We go at least once a week. Reading about living on a quarter horse farm in Tennessee I assumed you would enjoy a gallop."

"You'd be right, Mary. I can't remember riding a horse. Anna informed me that when posting—that is, riding with the natural ups and downs a horse makes when walking or trotting—one must grip firmly with the inside of the knees to bounce up at the right time. The fact is the inside of my knees would not be intact for long because of the grafts and the scars. Anna thought if I really wanted to ride, then I'd have to do it at a rapid gallop where I would just stand in the stirrups. I thought that was funny."

"Keith, I'm going to have dinner here which I usually do after riding, so you and Anna go home without me. Your notes from last night were quite thorough. They are just what I need, so continue to do the same. As soon as I get the rest of your history from Gabbie, we'll start to work. The usual therapy calls for a session once a week. It's done for many reasons. Usually it's to frame the event to give it the importance it needs. Also, in pity of the therapist. I'm trying to decide the best technique for you, Keith. If I find it doesn't flow as I think it should and will take a good bit of time—months, you know?—then I will arrange for you to live in town so you may have your own life to live as you wish. Not that I would mind your company—we do have fun, don't we?—but we are doing this to hold your life together and put you back in a world you knew. So, take advantage of whatever leisure time you have now. I believe you have a massage scheduled for later on today."

Anna pulled up close to an intercom that guarded a large iron gate. Centered in large letters above the gate was the name LA ROSE.

She pushed the call button. "Buon giorno, Arturo!"

The gates started to swing open. From the intercom came a man's basso profoundo voice, "Punctuality! The courtesy of queens! Welcome! I shall announce you! Anna! Wait for me until I come out to see you. I want to know when we can do a sail!" It bleeped off.

"Mary," Anna said, "would you be kind enough when Arturo drives you home to bring the riding outfit you leave here. I'll have a fresh one for next time." As the limo's wheels crushed the peastone on the rhododendron-lined driveway, Anna asked, "Mary, would you care for fresh fruit for breakfast?"

"Hmmmm! I think I'll pass, Anna," Mary said.

A light went on in Keith's mind, only because of the tenor of Anna's voice. They had passed a coded message. Of course, Keith decided, Mary would not be back in time for breakfast.

Keith walked into the kitchen, his mind on a cold beer and a smoke out on the deck before he took a quick snooze. When he got to the refrigerator, the door had a note on it. "Haircut! Massage! Ten minutes."

Keith smiled as he opened the door. He thought, it was nice to be cut some slack.

He was in a twilight sleep when the form slipped into his bed.

"Keith, this is Anna. I am to be a shadow in your world. I am a mere placeholder. I shall touch you everywhere except where your emotions repose. I want to be selfless as another has been with me. I am here to meet your needs only. It is the lowest level of relationship. It is a physical, intellectual matter. Do you understand perfectly the reason I am here?"

63

Keith found himself awake at daybreak. Consciousness usually came quite abruptly. It wasn't unusual. It was a left-over from the mad party his life had become. His mind was a whir of thoughts and explorations. This occurred several times in the course of a night or day when he was recuperating. In an instant, Louise would be beside him. She would give him a pain killer with a glass of orange or cranberry juice. She would stroke his forehead. If he didn't go back to sleep right away, she would open a book and read to him. In the course of his treatment she read hundreds of books of all types and descriptions. He noticed his vocabulary improved. Her voice was soothing. If sleep didn't come to him soon, or as in those rare moments when Louise would not be there, he learned to do mental gymnastics to fatigue his brain. What usually worked was to count backwards from 500 by nines. He could not recall getting to the 400's.

Except this morning. There was no Louise. The numbers became too boring. He thought of last evening. It was amazing, he thought, of how quickly he had succumbed to Anna's ministrations. He could not remember turning over. He got a prickly sensation as Anna's hands passed over him. If he allowed his mind to drift down several levels, he felt as if he were in an electrical field. Tiny darts like sparks bounced gingerly off his skin. The sensation seemed medicinal. He thought of the word, but didn't want to say or think it: sexual. He laughed to himself when he thought she gave him blow jobs. Voodoo, he thought. Only vaguely did he remember making a comment about needing a pedicure. It was too painful for him to stretch and reach. Louise took care of it quickly and easily. And now it was Anna's role, if he remembered correctly whether or not she did. Did she? Deftly was it? Like with a tiny laser beam? It was pure magic. He was with her, in her, but she remained totally unobtrusive.

Keith put on his robe. He went into the sitting room to get his cigarettes. He noticed his notes had been taken. There was a fresh tablet and newly sharpened pencils. Keith went to the kitchen. He found the coffee made. He took a cup out to the deck to enjoy with a cigarette.

When he returned to his room, it was cleaned up with fresh bulky towels in the bathroom. Keith went to the intercom. "Anna, thank you for the coffee. I'll be in town for a while this morning. I'll use my wheels."

When Keith got to his bike, he saw a note on the seat. "Legal stuff like breakfast, okay. Caution if you need something illegally stronger."

Keith smiled. *Was Anna reading my mind? Or did she guess?*

64

"Anna!" Keith breathed to himself. He had just returned from town. He walked off the deck into the kitchen. He could feel the essence of her. She must have just left the room, he thought. He stepped quickly to the door leading down to the garage. He opened it and listened. He thought he heard a step.

Keith padded down to the garage. He had left the bay doors open when he took out his bike. It was parked where he left it. It took a moment to adjust his eyes to the dim light at the ends of the garage. He didn't see Anna. He started to walk to the bike.

"Anna? You wanted Anna?"

Keith made her out near the limo. "Yes. I want Anna." He walked towards her. "For heaven's sakes, did you think I was a crack-head?"

"No. I know you're not into crack."

"The note on the bike left little doubt." He stopped by the front bumper. "How would you know I just needed a little high?"

"With the agony you've been through?" She opened the passenger door and reached into the glove compartment. She took out a silver box and held it out to him. "You just had to ask."

"I bet that box has pedigree and even comes with papers?"

"It does."

"Join me?"

"Yes. No fun otherwise."

Keith and Anna closed the garage doors. "Kindly carry this," Anna said. She handed the box to Keith. "It'll fit in your shorts. I couldn't get a pencil in mine."

They walked to the far end of the dock. They sat on one of the benches.

"You do the honors," Keith said. He gave her the box. "I figured out how you knew about this. You read my notes about Louise. There were times nothing could ease the pain. Nothing. She thought of it. When some of the goody-two-shoe doctors would bring it up, Louise would tell them to go fuck themselves. She would have transferred her soul to me if she thought it would help. And here I am, having a good time and her sweating it out every single second. I know it. I know her. God! I'm torn in pieces! And then Gabbie comes along! She's ready to trash her own heart to make mine sound! How does one person deserve all this? And now comes Mary! Jesus Christ Almighty, help us! How does one person deserve this attention?"

"Because you are worth it, Keith. Some people are just like that. They are worth keeping and preserving. You've got to believe that because there are, there really and truly are people in the world that would foul up a septic tank if they fell in."

"Anna, I'm not near as clever as Mary, or you, in fact, but I get the reverberations in your voice of a distant pain. I'm not prying. I know you are a very private person, and I respect that. I admire you for that. There are many things I care about in you. You know, inside me when I realized you had been hurt, I wondered, 'How can I assuage?'"

She waved a hand in front of her face. "Ha! Mary and I agree you are a keeper. And an aphorism for you, self-deprecation needs no endorsement. You certainly are perspicacious and extremely sensitive to catch the nuance in my voice."

There was a long period of silence when they looked out over the water and watched the specters of smoke dissipate. Keith stared at her profile. She turned to look into his eyes.

"Anna, I'm not being nosy. It's because I care that I ask. How is it that a woman as beautiful as you with a gorgeous figure and amazing intellectual capacity does not have a field of pursuers at her door? The emanations, the vibrations I get from you are that you are a man's woman."

"Yes, that's correct. I'm not a lesbian. I am attracted to men, and men are attracted to me."

"I can testify to that."

"You find me attractive?"

"My lord yes! In every sense of the word. But, because of the circumstances, I've contained myself. I did not want to overstep."

"You're not the timid type, not the way you ride your bike."

"I'm not timid, but I do respect boundaries. At first I thought I was just Mary's guest, but I realize now I am Mary's and your guest. I'm here for something I desperately need, and I don't want to get kicked out before we've even started just because I couldn't resist hitting on two beautiful women. I see for Mary there is an attraction for which she stops at Arturo's house, what do you do?"

"Arturo is the major d'omo, the chauffeur at LaRose. For me, I'm with the hoping and yearning crowd."

"I don't see how you will be there for long. Be sure, I'll check in to see how you're doing. You know, Anna? I know what physical pain is. I am just beginning to learn what true psychological pain can be. But, physical pain, isn't it wonderful how the memory of it dissipates so quickly. I guess like childbirth or the whole world would have just one child per woman! And you know what? It's the same for pleasurable sensations. We cannot remember what an orgasm feels like. We only recall it as an event. That's the reason it is pursued by men every other second. "

"May I confess to you something I've never told anyone? I would like to have a child. Not the turkey-baster kind, you know? The child that comes with all the fanfare and window dressing, marching band and hoopla it should have. Of course that means with an ecstasy of love that would be unmatched. The couple—me being one of them, of course—would have a love that would make the gods envious. This theme is dominant in me because of my own childhood. Do you think there could ever be such a thing?"

"Oh, I want that for you, Anna! I think of myself and feel I've been struck by lightning twice! Once with Louise and another time with Gabbie! The strange thing, you see, is that this would never have happened to me if I didn't lose my memory."

"Yes, the circumstances changed, but you remain the same handsome, charming, caring man that you are. You are not narcissistic in the least. You are totally selfless. Yes, it's the narcissists in the world that cause all the trouble. They love only themselves. They think the world revolves totally and completely around them. Run into a man or woman who is like that, who thinks they deserve all the good there is, who allows their egoes to reign supreme, then run the other way! Get away from them. They breed only misery and unhappiness for anyone else because they demand all the attention. They will fart in your face and think you should applaud them for offering their perfume for you to inhale! Oops! Sorry! I have revealed in no uncertain terms my pet peeve. You are special, Keith. You will do for others."

"Anna, why is it with you there are no demands on me? No reaction when I mention Louise or Gabbie?"

"I don't think I can compete with them. You may not like to hear this, but my intention is to help Mary in her quest. If you remember the beauty of love, of love making, it will be like a weapon in your arms cache to fight your memory monster."

"You are that selfless?"

"We'll see if Mary succeeds, won't we? Now, whenever you wish, you saw where I keep the silver box?"

"Yes."

"But Anna!"

"Yes?"

"I like it when we share. I'm afraid I'm beginning to adore you for being my champion."

"Don't get too gracious. I'm crazy about everything I do."

65

That evening, after they sat down for dinner, Mary reached over and took his hand.

"Keith, I am overwhelmed. The epergne—the centerpiece--on the table you had delivered is beautiful. Thank you."

"I'm delighted you didn't say, 'I didn't have to do it.' I found it in a second-hand store. They didn't know what it was. I had the market fill it with fruit and goodies and deliver it. It's not every day one can present a tour de force, and more, have it properly appreciated. It is my pleasure. You have been gracious to a fault, and we have not yet begun to fight. Thank you."

"Anna told me you sent her a huge bouquet of flowers. Do you know those are the first she has ever received from all of the guests we've had here? Keith, you really are something special. There are few people such as you in this world. I'm delighted to try to help you. Now wait until you try the lobster and crab ravioli."

Keith looked down to find the little pasta squares before him. "Mary? How does Anna do it? I mean, not just slipping the plate before me without my even knowing about it, but she was with me until maybe ninety minutes ago, and she has come up with ravioli in that time?"

"Anna is Anna. She is a good witch. She likes being a shadow, and I think she likes you."

"Mary? May I ask? Anna is the true personification and the embodiment of the Renaissance Woman. From where did this gift derive? It has enabled her to cover a spectrum of skills that is boggling to the twenty first century mind. Nothing, nothing threatens or intimidates her. Can you tell me the reason?"

"I may know the possible reason, but I would not say even if I were sure. I would suggest you ask Anna about her early years, and what she has done for herself in the time we have been devoted to each other. I love her very much, Keith. You must know that. She is much more than a daughter to me, more than an alter ego, more like the essence of my breath."

"It was understood from the moment I saw you together. Aren't you both lucky to have each other."

"Thank you, Keith. Anna made a special dinner tonight in honor of our project. She knows we will start work in earnest tomorrow. After dinner, you and I will go into the library where I will, quote/unquote, give it to you straight."

Keith and Mary sat in opposing Queen Anne wing chairs before a cold fireplace. Beside Mary was a 200 year old bottle of Napoleon Cognac.

"Keith, you and I, unlike Columbus who had a destination in mind when he set sail, will start off not having any idea whatsoever where we may end up. May we be so lucky as to land in the comparable East Indies.

"Two: I have received and reviewed written material from Gabbie, Louise, the Army, and you. I have not studied any of it in detail, but I have enough of a perspective to make certain professional determinations at this moment.

"Three: My first decision is that I will proceed on the basis that your memory loss is totally psychological.

"Four: On that basis, after all my work, the result definitively will be: A. That there will be no recollection of any lost memory on your part because the memory loss in fact is due to brain damage. In this case, you will be no better or worse, psychologically or physically, than you are this moment.

"B. There will be a partial recollection of your lost memory.

"C. You may regain your memory loss because of the fugue state with whatever positive or negative ramifications may derive from that.

"In other words, if I regain my memory of the cause, I may bury myself even deeper."

"Yes. We are very protective of ourselves. Our defenses are even more duplicitous than our most conniving mind can conceive.

Keith brushed his cheek as he looked off at the books at the far end of the room. Elbows resting on the arms of the chair, he folded his hands before him. He looked at Mary. "Now, talk to me about success."

Mary pursed his lips and nodded her head. "You may find it worse than failure."

"Then why pursue it?"

"I have enough confidence in my own competence as an analyst to make you well. To make you a substantial, living, breathing person with a life and a love to live! I wouldn't have taken you this far no matter how much I love and care for Gabbie. It's not just your life you're affecting. You are an adult. You have free will. I will allow you all the time you need to think about this and come up with a decision. I would want it no other way. Tomorrow morning should you decide you want to climb on your bike and motor away, come in here, we'll open the 200-year-old Napoleon Cognac and wish you Godspeed. Should you decide to get to work, body, mind, and soul, we'll hold the cognac to toast your success."

Keith pulled his folded hands in tighter to his chest. He crossed his ankles. He dropped his head, and stared at the Oriental rug.

Mary raised her chin and stared at him.

Long seconds passed.

Keith looked up. He threw his hands out wide. "Mary, I am in your hands. I accept full responsibility. I want to show you how much I have thought about this. Mary I want to ask you a question. I am very, very curious about your answer."

Keith stood and began pacing. "Mary, I want to express my gratitude in a meaningful, visible way. This morning, I made a purchase from a very gracious, gentlemanly, and kind jeweler."

Keith reached into his coat pocket and took out a long, thin, gift-wrapped box. "Kindly accept this from the very depths of my heart and soul." He reached into his pocket. "Before you open it there are three others, with one going to Anna, to Louise, and to Gabbie. These are only tokens of an incomparable love. Mary, I pray you are able to take me back to the one that consumes my soul."

Mary carefully took off the ribbon. She unfolded the wrapping to reveal a blue, velvet-covered box. She opened the box.

Mary's jaw dropped.

"Keith! Mary said. "I have received many wonderful favors in my lifetime. I have never seen a more exquisite tennis bracelet in my life! I am too touched! Too touched!" She kissed Keith on the cheek. "Thank you. I will treasure this always."

"Thank you. May I ask my question?"

"Right after you put this bracelet on my wrist, please"

Keith waved his hand in front of his face imitating Anna, which made Mary smile. "Now, what psychological technique are you going to use where everyone else has failed?"

"Keith, I think they failed because they didn't have enough time to devote to resolving your problem. I am going to work on one premise: There was no brain damage loss, but you went through many horrible experiences, so bad you blanked them and your memory of them out of your mind. You coincidentally had a brain injury. If I don't believe that, I have nothing to work on.

"Now, what will my technique be? You have a right to know. It is an eclectic program, a little of this, a bit of that, a touch of those, and some of whatever. I am going to re-establish your memory. I am going to do this by starting at the very beginning. If you will, I will bring you back to your father's orgasm that fertilized your mother's seed. The concept is this: Your memory is like a full basin of water at the seashore. If I were to draw a thin line in the sand up to the water in the basin, the water will trickle down that path. As the water runs from the basin, that little channel gets wider and deeper. Soon water runs into and out of that basin with ease. Think of that line as afferent and efferent nerves taking in and taking out memory. Soon, the memory is yours and becomes a musical fugue where the theme is first given out by one part to go on its way; the theme is repeated by another part at the fifth or fouth interval, and so on, until all the parts have answered one by one, continuing their several melodies and interweaving them in one complex progressive whole, in which the theme is often lost and reappears. Just like a memory that that had been knocked from Scilla to Caribdis and chasing one another because they wish not to get caught and put together to bring to mind a disastrously, unbearable, painful moment. My technique will be unorthodox, but it was one Nedo and I were working with. I will cause you no harm, Keith"

66

Keith sat in his robe on the deck. He lit a cigarette. He wanted to be under the stars; take in the fresh, salt air; and watch the moonlight play on the water. Suddenly he became aware Anna in her robe had slipped into the chair beside him. He turned to her. "I dreamed of you."

"S'okay?" she whispered.

"Sure s'okay."

"I'm glad I slipped into your bed."

"Yes."

"Lover, you didn't hear me. I said I'm glad I did! Man! Am I glad I did. You just taught me there is always something to learn. Arturo was never like this. Your technique is unique and incredible. It is beyond an animal in heat. It is far from brutal lust. It seems it is a natural bursting! Yes, that's it. It's like . . . it's like you're a starving animal wolfing down food. From where comes this?"

"I am compelled to respond. I do it subconsciously. In my search I cannot go down deep enough . . ."

"Deep enough, we know about that don't we? Now I know the reason I want you always."

"Thank you. Someone I loved and proposed to put me off in the nicest way."

"Really?"

"I would say the same thing. You have to go to Kinarsi."

"Why should I go to Kinarsi?"

"Because that's where you'll find the end of the line."

"She must be special."

"Yes."

"She's waiting for you."

"I'm not worthy of her, but sadly, yes."

"I don't want to embarrass either one of us."

"Because guys that ride bikes have dirt for feelings?"

"No. Because you must know how I feel about you."

"Yes."

"And Gabbie feels the same way?"

"Yes."

"And so does Louise Comma The Nurse?"

"Yes."

"Mary has had many guests. Every one has treated me as a servant. You have treated me as royalty. I would like to take advantage of you on the purest level. Then, in thinking about your situation, and knowing you, I knew you couldn't hide your feelings for me. Yes?"

"Something like that. When I was with Gabbie my guilt feelings about Louise were killers. Anna, with so much in a turmoil inside me I cannot help but respond to desire. Hard to believe, but lust is my safe place. On the highest level, it shouldn't happen. But, on the primal level it is beyond instinct. Being together as we have been, doing all the things we have, I couldn't help it, I wanted to know what it would be like to kiss you, I mean really kiss you. In the short time we have been together, I find you irresistible, not because you are here and they are not, but because you have touched a new and different part of the essence of my being . . . Anna, your response tonight . . ."

"Yes."

"Was unique, just as I expected. If I were to characterize you, I find you ethereal. Anna, you are a spirit of the universe, born of the celestial heavens. You are the embodiment, the personification of truth and beauty, the essence of the ideal woman. You are as captivating as the very essence of love. At the same time, it is a given that you are unobtainable. How did I get this close?"

"As remarkably beautiful and haughty are flowers they must be trampled by the bee to remind them of their place in the universe. Despite your kind and generous words, I know my place." She tapped his arm. "Keith?"

"Yes."

"A serious question, if you please. Allow me to include myself. Three women that consume your soul. The day will come you will be forced to make a choice. How will you let the other two know?"

"I asked Louise if I should send a dozen roses."

"And she said?"

"The fuck you will."

"So? Instead?"

"A memento."

"Such as?"

"Have you seen Mary's tennis bracelet?"

"Yes."

"Just like that." Keith shifted to light another cigarette. When he turned back, Anna was gone.

67

After breakfast, Keith walked into the gym and took one of the leather chaises.

When Mary walked in a short while later, she said, "You are in exactly the right place." She pulled a stool behind Keith's head. "Everything will be recorded. First, let me explain the basis for this therapy. I will put you in what may be called a twilight sleep. You will be in a hypnotic state that will make you receptive to my suggestions and promptings. A major difference is that you will remember everything that you do. You must remember everything because the major part of the work falls on you. You must recall and write down in infinite detail everything you recall. The basis for this is that you will retain these experiences as memories. The memories that will come to you will not be fictitious. Even your very early memories may be blurred but they will not be invented. Then, we get to the experiences you shared with someone. That is the reason Gabbie and Louise wrote what they remember. I'm sorry your father would not contribute. He wanted nothing to do with this in any way. He could have been helpful. We have no idea how long it will take, but we will simply forge forward. For example, I will present you with a scenario Gabbie or Louise wrote about. We will see how much of that particular action you recall, and then again when you write about it later. We will do this day by day until we get to the present. Questions?"

"Yes, Mary. I get the picture. I understand the procedure. My fugue state came while I was in action in Iraq."

"Yes."

"How do you get a hint of a scenario of what happened to me in Iraq? There is a brief military history but it is in broad generalities about actions and platoons, but nothing specifically about Jim Dorchester or even Keith Franklin. How do we get that information?"

"Excellent point, Keith. This is all an art and a science. We can label and identify Man's behavior, that's easy. How to restore the pathologically aberrant mind is by guess and by gosh and by luck. Our biggest challenge will be when we finally get you back in Iraq and try to learn what happened. Shall we get started?"

Keith knew it was Mary's voice, but the fingers barely stroking his forehead seemed to be Anna's.

"Keep your eyes closed and pay attention to each note of the soothing music. You have nothing else to do except listen to my voice. Allow yourself to drift, gently, gently. Fine, that is fine. Release yourself to my voice. Good. You will recall everything. When you are awake and I need you to return to the drift I will say, 'Vieni, vieni,' and you will return here. You will do this for no one else and no other voice but mine. When I say 'Awake!' you will awaken.

Session * * *

"Now, you are going to go back to where you received the gift of life in your mother's womb. Go back. Go back. Are you moving there?"

"Yes."

The remainder of that session was spent exploring instances of being an infant.

End Session * * *

When Keith woke up, he told Mary, "I don't mean to be insouciant, but my written report would be: 'I wasn't there!' I would have to guess at what I thought I experienced."

"Do the best you can, Keith," Mary said, "we want to establish a pattern. Then, you will be actually experiencing what we know normally would occur as one gets older."

It was when he was writing about nursing at his mother's breast that he had a weird sensation. What came to him was the warm smell of skin. He closed his eyes and breathed deeply. Yes! Yes! There was a familiarity to the fragrance. Whose? He delved deep into his memory. Then he knew. It was Gabbie's!

There was a bland sameness with mild frustration when it came to reporting what he had experienced over the next few sessions.

Session * * *

Then, the juice was turned on. Keith felt as if he was lying in an electrically charged chaise. Mary mentioned his mother.

"Where are you?" Mary asked.

"Home."

"Who is there?"

"My mother. Glenn, my father."

"What is going on?"

"My mother and Glenn are shouting at each other across the room. Glenn's face is red. He is frightening."

"Does he frighten you?"

"Yes. He makes me cry. He yelled at me to stop. I try, but I can't. He is yelling at my mother."

"Then what happens?"

"He gets mad at me. He grabs my arm and slaps me on my legs. It hurts so much. It makes me cry louder. I twisted and pulled and got away from him."

"Then what happened?"

"I ran to my mother. She picked me up, and was holding me tight in her arms. It made me feel safe. My father yelled some more and got louder."

"That made you more frightened?"

"My mother yelled back at him, and shook her fist at him. When he tried to grab me, my mother turned away so he couldn't get me."

"Did he stop? Did he go away?"

"No! He went to get Tommy out of his crib! My mother dropped me on the bed and took Tommy from the crib and held him tight."

"Then what happened?"

"My father grabbed my ankle and slapped my legs so hard I lost my breath. I think I passed out."

"Was there more?"

"I don't remember."

End Session * * *

Session * * *

"Keith?" Mary spoke softly to Keith on the couch. "You spoke of remembering your mother and father arguing. Then, your father started hurting your mother. What happened, Keith?"

Keith did not utter a word or move.

"Keith, tell me what was going on?"

He made no reply.

"It's all right, Keith. Take a moment. Try to remember the next thing that happened. . . Keith?"

Keith remained silent.

"Keith can you answer me?"

End session * * *

"Anna," Mary said, "if you don't mind, I need you to help clear my logic. Keith was able to respond to questions about his early life. Suddenly, I've run into a stone wall. He will not respond no matter how I state a question. Not a 'yes' or a 'no' in any manner. I would guess he must be about six/seven years old. I have tried different methods of communication. I gave him pencil and paper. I asked him to raise a hand, show fingers, nod his head. Nothing. He has just become incommunicado. After four sessions I know there is a definite problem. I've never run up against anything like this before. I'm stymied. I may have to consult with a colleague. We were doing so well."

In the very early hours the next morning Mary woke up slowly. Then, her eyes snapped open. "Of course!" she said aloud. "How stupid of me!"

Session * * *

"Keith? Can you hear me?"

No response.

"Is your name Keith?"

"No."

"What is your name?"

"Jim Dorchester. My mother calls me James." Mary cupped her eyes with her hand. She let her mouth slip open. *The revelation is significant Keith was Jim. It was the reason he did not respond when she addressed him as 'Keith.'*

"What shall I call you?"

"Jim."

"Jim, you were telling me about your father. What was going on?"

Jim whispered very softly.

"Jim? Just a tiny bit louder, please?"

He barely raised his voice, but Mary understood, "He was hurting my mother."

"Can you tell me about that?"

He shook his head.

"Is there a reason you can't talk about it?"

He nodded his head.

Mary understood immediately that Jim was in the beginning stages of selective mutism. He would speak only in circumstances in which he did not feel threatened.

"Jim, am I your friend?"

He nodded.

"Do you remember sailing with me, and keeping you safe in the strong, blowing wind?"

He nodded.

"And we had fun on the ride, and I brought you back to the dock all safe?"

He nodded.

"I want you to feel safe with me again. I will keep you safe no matter what you say. If I am going to help you, you must tell me what is going on with you. It's okay if you want to whisper. Okay?"

He nodded.

"What happened when your father was threatening your mother?"

He whispered, "I cried. I screamed at him to stop. Not to hit my mother."

"You were a brave boy to do that. What happened?"

"My father took off his belt and chased me around the house beating me because I yelled at him!"

End session * * *

Session * * *

"Jim, you are about eight or nine years old, and you said you saw your parents fighting through the door of their bedroom. Can you tell me what you saw?"

Speaking in a normal tone, he said, "They were yelling at each other. He tore off my mother's clothes. She had nothing on. He pushed her onto the bed and rubbed against her while she kept trying to hit him. When he got up, she ran past me into the kitchen. He chased her. I saw her pick up the skillet and swing it at him. He put up his hand to stop it. There was an awful crack. She was crying and screaming and she told him."

"Jim? What did she tell him?"

He shook his head.

"Jim. It's all right. You can tell me. You must trust me. What did she say?"

There was a long moment of silence. "She said, 'He's not your kid! You can keep the little bastard!'"

"Did she say if she was talking about you or Tommy?"

"Me. James. She said, 'You can keep the little bastard.' She didn't want me. She wanted to give me away."

End Session * * *

Session * * *

"Jim, you indicated in the last session that something else happened between you and your mother. You didn't want to talk about it. Is there a reason?"

"Yes."

"What is the reason?"

"It hurts."

"You're nine years old, and it hurts badly."

"Yes. It hurts more than when my father hits me."

"It hurts a lot because of something your mother said?"

"Yes."

"Jim, it can't make it all right, but it can make you feel a little better if you tell me about it. What did your mother say?"

He squirmed. He shifted his position. "She said I was a bad boy. She said I was a bad boy because I didn't take care of Tommy. I let my father beat him, too. She said I should take Tommy's beatings. She said I didn't do what she asked, and that I lied."

"Did you lie?"

"No, I don't lie."

"What happened?"

"She said because I was a bad boy, and she didn't want to be with me anymore. She said she wasn't going to take Tommy with her because I needed to take care of him."

"Did your mother go away?"

"Yes!"

"Did she take Tommy with her?"

"No!"

"She left him for you to take care of?"

"Yes."

"And did you take care of your brother, Tommy?"

"No!"

"Why not?"

"Because I let him die in the fire!"

End session * * *

Mary was able to move quite rapidly through Jim's teen-age years and his and Gabbie's road to romance that was rife with detours.

From then on, work proceeded on a straight line toward what Mary considered the most relevant area: Jim's time in Iraq. The sessions with Mary and Anna lasted about ninety minutes.

Mary circumscribed Jim's military history. She knew the cause of the fugue was a battle incident. She would have to proceed slowly and carefully. It was a matter similar to unpeeling a pearl to exactly the right depth. Mary hopped from Gabbie's notes to the time Jim went into the service to right over to Louise's notes.

In the main, Keith had no problem recalling the six-and-a-half years he spent recuperating with Louise. He spent hours filling legal pads with his recollections with her. Mary compared Keith's notes with those she received from Louise. She was meticulous in providing an almost diary-like report from the first moment she was assigned to the patient, until the morning he left on his motorcycle to chase down his former life.

Keith continued to recall with ease to recall his trip to Tennessee and his visit in West Virginia, his arrival at the Garden Center, and then the trip with Gabbie to Mary's home in Southampton.

At dinner one evening, Mary asked Keith, "What is the most revealing thing so far in our sessions?"

"Mary, I understand a little bit how you work," Keith said. "You are not asking about a particular event, but rather you are asking about a conclusion."

"I admire how you are always thinking deeper than anyone can imagine. Yes, a valid conclusion that bloats my ego."

"Don't make me guess."

"The conclusion I made was that you did not lose your memory from the injury you suffered. I worked on the premise it was a pathological fugue. Keith, the fact that you needed so little instigation to recall your early years with Gabbie, right up to going into the service; and how well you recall your years with Louise is dead, rock-solid proof that your memory is functioning very well—except for the one area that short-circuited your whole system."

"Fix the blown fuse, you fix me?"

"Not so easy. Fix the broken fuse and you'll be fixed—if you want the fuse to be fixed. If you can't live with what you learn, you may blow the whole fuse box. Or, you may say, 'What was that all about?'"

"I hope you do that."

"To go along with the analogy, I feel like I'm dealing with live, hot wires and I'm standing barefoot in a pool of water as I'm doing it."

"Mary, I don't like living with this hole in my world. I want to tell you now that I can see where I may offer a lot of resistance. Don't let me off too easily. I want you to put the boots to me. I'm asking you to push the outer limits of your professional judgment on just how far you can go. Okay?"

"Nice to get that vote of confidence, but my promise still is to cause no harm."

68

"Anna?"

"Yes. Keith."

"How?"

"I followed your scent through the salt air."

"I had hoped."

"Yes. I brought the box."

"Ummm!"

"You?"

"Uh-uh. No. I want the purity of the moment."

"Me, too. The stars are dazzling."

"Only at this time at the darkest of night."

"Were the boat here, a sail would be more than a transport."

"Yes, the force of unity. Disparate energy shooting off through the nether sphere to coalesce into the point of a piercing climax."

Waves lapping-lapping rhythmically at the poles absorbed the moment.

"Anna."

"Yes."

"Work is progressing."

"Inexorably."

"Damn it," Keith said.

"Yes. Like vital, captivating perfume in a tiny vial. We must have its fragrance. Yet, every day we open the top to make our life complete we are aware that too soon will be only the dissipating memory of it and the pain of the emptiness will remain."

"Unless . . ."

"Yes."

"The attar . . ."

". . . and the vessel . . ."

" . . . were one" was the unsaid given.

"Anna?"

"Ummmm . . ."

"I need the wisdom of the wizened old man sitting Indian fashion before a curl of smoke on top of a mountain in Tibet."

"And what is the knowledge you need of him?"

"The ethereal foundry from which comes that special crucible, you know?"

"Yes. The pot which holds the most molten of the moltens of the Universe."

"Yes."

"In life, if we are very, very blessed and lucky? Our soul becomes a crucible that holds a white hot love the heat of which can only emanate from the majesty of the universe."

"Yes."

"Anna? I have known of such a love."

"Ah! I am so very envious."

"Anna, could there be a second such love?"

"Impossible. The Gods would be envious beyond color, beyond speech. It does not happen. As we are born with just one body, one heart, one life, we can only have one such love. Your wise man would tell you that."

"But! A hypothetical. What if there was a second such love? How would that then be possible?"

"The answer would be found in engineering, chemistry, and emotional metalurgy. You said it. The crucible. The crucible itself is altered, chemically, physically, by the heat of the first love. There is a cause the crucible is altered that allows it to not only be receptive to such a second such love without destroying itself, but in fact yearns for it."

"So? It is possible?"

"I say 'yes.' What do you say?"

69

Then, Mary began again gingerly approaching the subject of Jim's military career under the deepest of hypnosis. Mary seemed to think things were going well, including Jim going to New York to get married. Mary kept meticulous notes of her own and underlined dog tags.

"Jim, I understand how you arranged to make the time to go to New York to marry Gabbie. You and Keith swapped dog tags. Is that right, and why did you do it?"

"Yes. When a unit was about to ship out, they check dog tags when you went off base. They didn't check tags when you returned."

"I understand. Jim, think very hard. Did you and Keith swap back your dog tags?"

Jim wriggled on the chaise. "We must have."

"No guessing. Do you actually recall getting your dog tags back from Keith, and did you give Keith's his?"

Jim clasped and unclasped his hands. "No, I do not actually recall."

"We'll come back to this."

Mary made notes that there were two times Jim changed his demeanor markedly. He was not as glib with the reason Keith had gotten sick watching a training film, and an incident when they were camping out in the deep woods. When the session was over, Mary said to Anna, "Check with the nearby Army reserve unit to find out how we can learn what the typical training films would be in basic training for the first troops going to Iraq."

One of the responses included "Treatment of Captured U.S. Soldiers by the Al Qaeda." It showed a captured soldier having his head sawed off with a knife.

In the very next session, Mary said, "Jim? Let's go back to the training films you saw in basic training. Okay?"

"Yes."

"Do you remember they had one that told of the Geneva Convention, for example?"

"Yes."

"The accompanying film was one about a captured U.S. soldier. Do you remember it?"

"I'm not sure."

"You're not sure about remembering it or seeing it?"

"About seeing it."

"But you remember it?"

Jim hesitated. "Yes, I remember it."

"Tell me what you remember?"

"A soldier was held captive."

"Who held him captive?"

"The enemy."

"Describe the enemy."

"Heavy-set. Black, dirty hair and beard."

"Jim, time is precious. We'll be here until Christmas playing cat and mouse. You know the information I need. What did the Al Qaeda do to the prisoner?"

Jim rocked from one side to the other. He became rigid. He screamed: "He used a knife to saw through his neck until his head came off!"

"Did you throw up when you saw that?"

"No."

"Did Keith get sick?"

There was a pause. Jim answered quietly, "Yes."

"Why did Keith getting sick bother you?"

"Because I have to take care of him!"

That alone told Mary that Keith played a vital role in causing Jim's psychological trauma.

"Jim, tell me about the time you and Keith were on bivouac. What happened?"

"It was just a training exercise."

"Something happened."

"No."

"What was Keith afraid of, and did you take care of him there?"

"Yes! I did! I did!"

"What did you do?"

"I killed a coral snake that was at his back! I told him it was a harmless black snake. Coral snakes are poisonous. He was terrified of snakes!"

"Nothing else?"

"No. Nothing else."

Even though Jim confirmed this, Mary noticed his hands remained clenched.

In the following sessions, Mary began exploring Jim's combat time in Iraq.

Even though almost seven years had passed, Jim's recall was excellent. Without hesitation Jim spoke about arriving in Iraq, making adjustments, including some of the combat action he saw. He spoke about Keith and how they covered for one another through all sorts of action. Jim ended his recall when he was blown up in the truck. He revealed no cause for a fugue.

Time to dig, Mary thought. If the answer to Jim's fugue could be plucked out of a vase, he would have been fixed up a long time ago. His secret was secreted in a deep, deep hidden memory vault.

Mary got an okay from Arturo to borrow their HumVee for a week or so just to have it parked in the driveway. Mary changed the sessions with Jim from the gym to the inside of the truck. It was just at this time Mary received a letter from Louise. The nurse asked Mary not to reveal the contents to Jim until she thought it was the right time.

It took three weeks of Mary's work to get Jim to open up. He said:

It was about two hours after we returned from a fire fight, Keith and I were seated side by side in a personnel carrier headed back to Mosel.

I asked Keith, "What's wrong?"

"I got nooky on my mind," he said. "I get a headache when I miss it this bad. Imagine. Out here in this fucking godforsaken land, bouncing around in this piece of crap they call armored, and all I can think of is getting laid."

"There are worse things to think about."

"You? Do you miss it?"

"I don't think of that. I think of Gabbie. I sure miss her." I took off my helmet and stared at the photo of Gabbie stuck

to the inside top of it. "She is the most beautiful creature on earth. When I get home, I'm going to put her in a glass case, just like a doll, to make sure nothing ever happens to her. When I see her, I'm going to go up to her, and grab her hand, and I won't ever let it go for the rest of my life. God, Keith!. . . I hope I see her again!"

"That's the difference between us." Keith took off his helmet, and swapped it with mine. "Look. Like you, Jim, I keep a photo of my girl in my helmet." Keith reached over and pulled the photograph of Cindy Jo out of his helmet. He held it up and brought it to his mouth. I reached into my helmet on Keith's lap, and took out the photo of Gabbie. Keith said, "Love's got nothing to do with it. All I can think of when I look at Cindy Jo is the first time she taught me how to fuck. Man! I've told you how sinful it is to have such ecstasy in this world. I think of my hard-on in her pussy and all you think about with your girl is holding hands."

VOOMP! Rockets and small arms filled the air.

VOOMP! VOOMP! VOOMP! VOOMP!

Keith and I slapped the photos we had into the helmets, and threw on our helmets and grabbed our rifles.

"Out! Out! Out!" ordered the first lieutenant.

"Holy good Christ!" Keith said. "We've got the whole fucking Al Qaeda tribe after us!"

"Out! Keith! Out!" I screamed. "There isn't enough armor on this piece of crap to stop a hard-boiled egg!"

We both rolled out and took cover behind it.

The small arms fire sounded like hundreds of marbles landing on an empty metal drum.

VOOMP! VOOMP!

"There's our objective!" the lieutenant screamed. "The bridge! They're after the bridge! We've got a column about two klicks away heading for it. If they can knock out the bridge, our column will be a sitting duck for them! Let's go! Move! Move! Move!"

Keith and I, hunching low, followed a half-dozen other soldiers in a line toward the bridge. It was less than twenty yards wide. The banks were steep. The water was deep, rapid moving.

The troop took up defensive positions at the entrance of the bridge. Small arms fire continued to ping and thunk! around us.

VOOMP! Booooooom! A rocket nailed the last HumVee in the column, sending up fire and smoke.

The lieutenant pointed to me and three other men. "You two bring up extra ammo. You two bring up water! We're going to be here for a while. Move! Move! Move!"

GA-THOONK! A mortar round landed far up from the bridge.

I led the way to the line of trucks. I found a supply of water. I gave two cases to the man behind me, and put one under each of my arms. "Got the ammo?" I called out. Two soldiers running bent over indicated they had it. I led the way back to the bridge.

"Pass 'em out!" the lieutenant said. "Take up positions!"

"Where's Keith?" I asked the lieutenant.

"Who?" the lieutenant asked.

"Franklin!" I screamed.

"He's probably one of six men I sent to the other end of the bridge!" the officer said.

"I'll join them!" I screamed to him.

"Stay put! I need you here!"

GA-THOONK! A mortar round exploded in the water just up a ways from the bridge.

"They're walking 'em down! Concentrate your fire on those low buildings!" the lieutenant said pointing behind him.

"No! Lieutenant! It's a ploy!" I shouted to him. "I thought I saw the main body on the other side of the bridge! There! There!" he said pointing. "I can see them on the other side moving up!"

"Concentrate your fire on those houses!" the officer ordered, ignoring my admonition.

I rolled on my side to the man next to me. "Can you handle the fifty?" indicating the machine gun. The man nodded. "The lieutenant doesn't know what the fuck he's doing!" I started to get up.

The officer put his hand on my shoulder, holding me down.

"My buddy's on the other side! I've got to get to him!"

The officer waved his pistol. "Stay put! I can court-martial you with one shot."

GA-THOONK! GA-THOONK! GA-THOONK!

The mortar rounds walked toward the other end of the bridge.

"Lieutenant! Pull the men! Pull the men!" I shouted. "We can give them cover!"

Small arms fire on the other side of the bridge sounded as if an arms factory blew up.

I could see the Al Qaedas surrounding the other end of the bridge.

In a hail of gunfire, I started across the bridge. "Keith! Keith! Hang on!" I unhinged a grenade with each hand. I pulled the pin on one, and then the other. I stood, exposed to a hail of fire. I tossed one grenade with one hand, and then the other grenade with the other hand, just as I did when I delivered the newspapers. I crashed to the ground.

GA-THOONK! A mortar landed in the water to my left.

I got up and ran, then skidded to the pavement. I looked across the bridge.

I saw a horde of Al Qaedas closing in on the end of the bridge. I tried to pick out Keith.

GA-THOONK! Another mortar landed on the other side, closer to us.

GA-THOONK!

I turned and ran back toward the HumVees.

I reached the first one, started the engine and headed across the bridge.

GA-BLAM! A rocket propelled grenade exploded in the thick of the men near the lieutenant.

I stomped on the gas just as I started across the bridge.

I didn't hear the rocket propelled grenade hit. I felt the seat rise up. My body slid sideways. I remember my face crashed into the window. I learned later my leg tore the steering wheel off its post. The last thing I felt was the melting heat. The last thing I remembered was thinking, "Gabbie! Help me!"

* * *

Mary got behind the wheel of the HumVee. Jim sprawled out in the back.

"Jim," Mary said.

"Yes?"

"Vieni. Vieni. Are you comfortable?"

"Yes."

"Jim, you felt you had to take care of Keith. Why? Was he slow? A diminished mental capacity?"

"Keith? No. He could hold his own. He had his own style."

"But you thought he needed some hand-holding?"

"He was a . . . wise guy? You know, insouciant. Giving everyone the business. Like he did the Gorilla."

"What was that?"

"Jokester things. If a guy's sleeping and you put his hand in a bucket of warm water, it makes him piss his pants. He did that to the Gorilla; he wanted to cream Keith, and I stood up for him. Keith and I were called the twins, so he thought of swapping out blouses and making the Gorilla think I was him and Keith was me."

"Did it work?"

"Well, yeah! The Gorilla wanted to pound on Franklin, but when I showed up as Franklin, the Gorilla decided he made a mistake. You know, things like that."

"And that's how you took care of Keith?"

"Yes. You know."

"How could he be sure?"

"Oh! Because I . . ."

"Because I what?"

"Because he knew he could count on me."

"And he could count on you?"

"Yes! He made me promise for Christ's sakes!"

Mary paused for long moments. She knew they had just stepped into a potential mine field.

"Jim, from what Gabbie told me about your life in Great Farraday, you didn't have much time to have a close guy friend. A lot of your time was spent earning money. You gave all your free time to Gabbie."

"Yes."

"So, when Keith came along, you were both in a new situation, trying to make adjustments; you found the two of you were more or less alike. Compatible. Good buddies. You two against the Army."

"Yes."

"Then it was you two against the Al Qaeda."

"Yes."

"Jim, we can take a break until tomorrow."

"No. S'okay. I'm comfortable."

"Okay. So, as good friends, what did you promise each other?"

"Nothing! Nothing! We'd just look out for each other. That's all!"

"It was more than a promise, wasn't it? It was an oath."

"It was a promise!" Jim said.

"It was more than a promise! It was a vow! A vow is an unbreakable promise!"

"Yes! Yes!"

"What was the vow?"

"I don't remember."

"Keith would remember it, wouldn't he?"

"No! No! He wouldn't remember it! I would remember it!"

"What do you remember?"

"That I wouldn't let the Al Qaeda get him!"

"And he promised he wouldn't let the Al Qaeda get you."

"Yes."

"Jim! How could either one of you make such a promise? How could you be so sure? Hasn't the Al Qaeda captured other American soldiers?"

"Yes."

"So, there is a difference. What made the difference, Jim?"

Jim grabbed the back of his head with both hands, and tried to hold back a loud gasp. Tears began to flow. "Alive! We promised not to let the Al Qaeda get us alive!"

"And the only way to keep the Al Qaeda from getting Keith alive was to . . . ?"

". . . to kill him! To kill my best friend! To shoot him dead!"

Mary let the sound of his sobbing fill the inside of the HumVee.

"And did you shoot Keith dead?"

"No! No! I didn't! I broke my promise! I didn't take care of him as I promised!"

"Jim, how do you know that?"

When I came back with the water and ammo, I looked across the bridge. I saw Keith hunkered down against a cement cornerstone. Keith looked up and across the bridge. Keith waved to me. I waved back. That's when I knew the officer was wrong; the major part of the Al Qaeda was on the other side of the bridge. I saw them! That's when I looked across the bridge in my scope. I saw Al Qaedas close in behind an American soldier, tear his gun away, and lift him off the ground. They started to drag him away backwards and I saw his face. I put the scope on the soldier. It was Keith.

"Jim! Jim! Shoot! For Christ's sakes! Shoot!" he seemed to be saying.

I brought my crosshairs across Keith's face, then back onto his nose.

I knew what he was saying. He was mouthing the words: "Jim! Jesus Christ! Jim! Shoot!"

Mary held her breath. The unasked question captured her attention as if a shot would resound in the truck.

Keeping a level voice, Mary asked, "Did you shoot?"

"No! Goddammit! I didn't shoot!"

"Jim. Think. Very hard. Did you shoot?"

"No! I didn't shoot!" Jim started crying. "No! I couldn't shoot! I couldn't shoot my best friend! I couldn't shoot Keith! I promised I'd take care of him! I couldn't let him down like I let Tommy down!"

"But you promised to shoot him if he was captured. He was captured, Jim. You promised! Did you shoot?"

"No! Keith was the best buddy I ever had in the world! He was the only friend I ever had in all my life! I couldn't shoot him!"

"But you had to shoot him!"

"I know! I know!"

"He expected you to do him that favor. You weren't killing him. You were doing him a favor!"

"I know!"

"He expected you to save him from having his head sawed off!"

"Yes! Yes!"

"So you had to shoot him!"

"Yes! I had to shoot him!"

"So you did!"

Jim hesitated. "No! No! No!"

Mary pulled away from Jim. She studied him, her eyebrows scrunched. "Jim. Hold up your right hand. I know you're a rightie. Now, hold your rifle. Put up your left hand and hold your rifle. Look through your telescope." Jim hunched over as if he was peering through a rifle telescope. "You spot Keith in your telescope. He's being dragged away, backwards. The telescope is right on Keith's face. You know you don't want to shoot your buddy, but you know you have to. There is no alternative. Your finger is on the trigger. Jim, show us what you did."

Jim's index finger curled and squeezed the trigger.

"Jim, you squeezed the trigger."

"No! No! I didn't! I didn't keep my promise! I have to get over there and bring him back! I've got to bring him back!"

"Jim, you pulled the trigger."

"No, I couldn't have. I could not have killed Keith. I would not have murdered my friend!"

"Jim. Think of your finger on the trigger. The sight is right on target. What do you do?"

Jim shook his head several times. "I couldn't have! I couldn't have pulled the trigger!"

"But you did. You know you did. You had to do it. You just did!"

Jim squirmed in his seat. "Yes! Yes! I had to do it! I had to shoot!"

"That's what you promised Keith."

"Yes! I pulled the trigger! But I missed! I didn't hit Keith! The bullet went wide! I shot at the Al Qaeda instead! I missed Keith! I missed! That's the reason I got into the fucking truck and tried to get to the other side! I promised I'd take care of him! Like fuck I did! He was so afraid of pain, and I let those bastards saw his head off! Can you just imagine that? How gruesome is that? They strip Keith's shirt off! They make him kneel! This fucking son-of-a-whore takes this blade, puts it against the skin of his neck, and says, 'Rock-a-bye baby!' and starts sawing bit by bit through Keith's neck! Keith is screaming so loud they can hear him in Kinarsi! And that piece of retarded shit isn't trying to get it done in a hurry! He's making it last as long as he can! Keith blows his tonsils out of his throat! And, do you know what else he's doing? He's swearing! In his mind he's swearing! He's swearing at me! 'You rotten son-of-a-bitch, Jim! You promised you would never let this happen to me! You promised! And look at what the fuck these animals are having fun doing? Sawing my fucking head off!' Stop it! Stop it! Stop it! Jesus! Make them fucking stop it!"

"That's enough, Jim. My dear, dear man I do not want you to remember this session. I repeat, I do not want you to remember this session when you awaken. You are not to write about what you remember from this session when you wake up. You will have a chance to do so, but not right away. You will not remember this session. Wake up."

Right after luncheon, Jim said he wanted to take a run on his bike, which he especially enjoyed on brisk fall days.

Mary and Anna remained on the deck.

Anna remained seated while Mary paced with determination from one end to the other. It was a while before she approached Anna, who saw the seriousness in her face and stood to meet her. "Anna, I don't know how I am going to resolve this unsolvable proposition! From what went on in this session, I can tell you this is what I am confronting. Jim and Keith made a vow. In Jim's mind, he saw Keith captured. In the conflict of deciding whether or not he could shoot his dearest friend, his mind goes into a subsidiary pathological fugue and refuses to remember that he perpetrated this horrendous deed! He cannot admit this to himself. It is a ghastly thing to do! Better just not ever to remember he did it! Then, for his own integrity, he has to remember that he did shoot. To assuage this deed, he simply acknowledges that he missed."

Mary went on. "Okay! You and I know this: He did shoot. You and I know this: As an expert marksman, he hit and killed Keith. We know he shot. He said so. Physically his finger went through the motion of pulling the trigger. We accept the fact that he hit his mark. The compounded psychological problem with Jim is: One, to prove to him that he did shoot his best friend, Keith, as an act of mercy, which would absolve him of the tremendous guilt he now feels, and thus kept his promise; and two, also prove that he hit his target to show that his friend was not left up to the savagery of the enemy."

Mary went on. "There is no way because hypnosis will not make the unreality a reality permanently. First, there is the therapist's doubt. Our work is a science and an art. The art is the killer. We rely heavily on interpretation. Despite experience, we could be 180-degrees out of phase with what is real, unlikely as that may be. In this particular matter, I am almost totally certain that Jim fired and killed Keith. But, I wouldn't bet the farm on that. So, how do I prove and convince myself? I do that by proving and convincing Jim that he did do what he promised to do because if he doesn't believe it neither will I. Now, how do we do that? It is a conundrum I cannot resolve at this moment. I don't know how. If I don't come up with a way to do that we have won the battle, but not the war. Everything we have done so far rests on the head of this pin," Mary said. "I've got to take a physical break to get my mind to think, as they say, out of the box. Perhaps the amalgamation of thoughts will enable me to untie this Gordean Knot."

"By 'break' I assume you mean something more than going into the city to see a couple shows?" Anna said. "Are you thinking Bequia?"

"How well you know me! That's the direction. It's been almost a year since we've been there. Yes, let's do it. With this impasse in Jim's therapy, it would be the perfect time. And Phooey! on this art and science stuff. One day St. Anthony is going to whisper in the ear the winning lottery numbers as a reward for all the guesses I had to make in my life."

Over Eggs Benedict at lunch on the deck that afternoon, Jim and Mary sat quietly for a long time. Then, Mary said, "We're stuck, Jim."

"I know. I'm sorry. I wish I could help."

"We're holding on too tightly. I've got to get away from the Hummer, from you—meaning the problem—and I've got to get some air in the system. We're going to

Bequia--in the Grenadines in the Caribbean-- for a week. You are welcome to stay here, or at my apartment in the city . . ."

Jim sat back, nodding his head, staring at her. "As a matter of fact, there is someplace I must go. I have a premonition about Louise. I've told you my feelings for Louise. I would have married her. My instincts say to go see her. My mind asks if it is a wise thing to do especially because we haven't finished our work here yet."

"Do you have reason to see her now? Have you been in touch with her?" Mary asked.

"No. You would have known first. I really don't have a reason as such. I left things as clear and as clean as I could when I left. Nothing has changed. I still don't know who the hell I am . . . Sorry! You know what I mean. As my doctor, what do you say?"

"On the practical side, I've told you we've run up against a stone wall. I don't know how to carry your therapy further. It happens to be at a very critical juncture. I must proceed very, very carefully. I want to do no harm. I need some time to think. Until I come up with a strategy to continue with you, I would say this is an excellent time to take a break. I can't tell you what good or what harm can come from seeing Louise."

"Settled then. I have this irresistible call that I should see Louise. She said she would return to work at Brooke Army Medical Center."

"That's in Fort Sam Houston, San Antonio?"

"Right."

"Excellent! We could drop you off on our way to Bequia, and pick you up on the way back! It was meant to be!"

70

Louise opened the door until the security chain held it. "Keith!"

"Louise! I had to see you!"

"Why are you here?"

"I had a feeling."

"Keith? Thank you for thinking of me. Go away."

"I must speak with you. I want to let you know what's going on."

"I don't care what going on. I don't want to see you."

"Louise, I came all the way . . . What has happened?"

"Keith, I have other interests. Take your shoe out of the door."

"You don't understand, Louise. I must speak with you."

"Keith? Kindly go or I'll call the superintendent."

"I'll call tomorrow. I'm in a motel . . ." On the way, Jim stopped at a bar to try to get over the dead, empty feeling he had inside. With his first drink, he felt puzzled, bewildered. The total rejection clawed at his belly. With the second drink, he had the first inkling of relief. A burden had been removed. He felt like an indentured servant that just had an iron collar removed from his neck. With the third drink, he had to deal with guilt feelings. He was so engulfed they opened the floodgates to mysterious figures and beings. With the welling that surged inside, he realized he had to be alone in case he could not control his feelings. Tears were lapping at the top of the floodgates.

At mid-morning the next day, Jim rang the building superintendent's bell.

"Keith! You've been away!" It was the most emotion the gruff, dwarf-like man had ever shown.

"Yes! Louise doesn't answer her door. I get her answering machine, and she doesn't answer her cell phone. Did you see her go out?"

"No, didn't do that. Most likely at the hospital, that's what. Sure."

"At Brooke?"

"A-yeah."

At the hospital, Jim asked the receptionist, "What department is Nurse Louise McBride working?"

Flipping through the vertical directory pages, the receptionist went first in one direction then another. "No, I don't find a Louise McBride . . . If I remember correctly from a long time ago, Louise worked with the specialty burn unit . . . Let me check."

Jim drummed his fingers as she went through the directory, then turned to another directory. "Here we are! No wonder I couldn't locate her in the staff directory. She's in the Oncology Department. I double checked, and she's there now."

"How do I get there?"

"Here, I'll give you a map. Even I get lost sometimes . . ."

Standing at the Oncology Department desk, Jim heard her behind him. "You were a stubborn, persistent patient, why should you change now?"

Jim moved to embrace her. She stepped away.

"I must speak with you, Louise."

"Can I use the lab?" Louise asked the receptionist. She signaled Jim to follow her.

In the lab, she turned to him, and said, "I wish you had respected my request. You and I have nothing to talk about."

"That's not true, and you know it."

"Your memory? Physically lost, or retrievable?"

"My therapist says we're at an impasse. I may be Jim Dorchester. She called for a break. My instincts made me want to see you."

"Your visit now is like a premature ejaculation. No satisfaction either way. Now get out of here. Who needs you? You've become a real itch. You got the best of me. I have no more to give to you. Don't be a greedy bastard. Just get out of here!"

"Louise, I want to hold you."

"And kiss me?"

"Yes."

"And make the stars twinkle."

"Yes. How about you? What do you want?"

"I want you to take me at my word. I want you to return to New York. I will let you know when I'm able to see you. Come to me then. Can you do that?"

"I don't understand."

"Of course you don't. Do you care enough for me just to do as I ask?"

"I could do as you ask in a heartbeat only if I knew the reason."

"Promise?"

"If you tell me the reason behind your request you want me to leave?"

"Yes. Right away."

"I must know, whatever it is."

"Promise an unbreakable promise?"

"As far as I know, I have never broken an unbreakable promise. I promise."

"I found someone else who excites my soul."

"I don't believe you!"

"I knew you wouldn't. I know you. I know you will have to believe me when I say the person that is so special is just twenty years old and divine. Do me a favor, Keith? Make this as painless as possible. Goodbye, Keith." She put her hand out to shake his.

"Louise! For heaven's sakes!" He grimaced, the corners of his mouth turning down.

Louise walked around him, opened the door and left.

Jim returned to the desk. "How long has Louise McBride been working here?"

The nurse looked up at Keith and shook her head. "Louise doesn't work here."

Jim thought. Louise was thinner, not as robust as she usually was. There was a pallor behind the make-up. A sparkle was missing in her demeanor.

"How long has Louise McBride been a patient!"

The nurse tilted her head, and every so slightly raised her eyebrows.

Jim sprinted for the exit.

He spotted Louise walking, head bowed, between the rows of parked cars.

"Just tell me one thing, Louise Comma The Nurse, what is the name of your best friend in town?" She stared at him. "You don't have one. You don't even know any of your neighbors. You devoted your whole and entire world to me. And you know what? You're not going to get away with it."

Right then and there he gave Louise her gift. He helped her put on the tennis bracelet as the tears streamed down her face.

"I'm taking you home. We'll get your apartment straightened out, and make all the arrangements. I'll come back to pick you up. No arguments. We have hospice up there as well as you have down here."

She fell against him, her head in the hollow of his shoulder. One arm went around him. Her other hand patted his chest rhythmically.

71

Seated at the Tiki Bar with tall Whore's Sorrows before them, Mary and Anna were both lost in deep thought.

Finally, Mary scrunched her face. "You know, when you forget a name, and then it's come on the tip of your tongue and you can't spit it out? That's how close I feel to resolving Jim's problem. The more I squeeze for the answer, the more recessed it becomes. You know what? Look at that beautiful water! I'm going for a swim."

"I'll join you," Anna said. Mary nodded.

Stroke for stroke they went out for more than a half mile. On the way back in, Mary broke from the surface like a whale. "Cè lo! Cè lo!" she screamed in Italian. "I've got it! I've got it!"

As they walked up onto the shore, Mary said, "As a compounded problem, as I see it, it must be proven to Jim that he did in fact shoot Keith dead preventing Keith from being tortured! And the second part of the problem is to convince him that it was absolutely the right thing to do no matter how difficult it was to think about it."

"Yes."

"Anna, I'm wracking my brain. How do we prove to Jim that he did in fact put a bullet into Keith and killed him? The easiest chore is to convince him he saved Keith from torture."

"You know how sometimes the amateur watching a job run into a problem has the answer before the professional doing the job? I'll say it for you. It is easier physically to show him the proof, than psychologically. So! Show him Keith's cadaver."

"Anna! That's would be impossible after all this time? And where is Keith's body? It's been seven years ago! Keep in mind, Jim and Keith switched identities. I know there are goof-ups all over the place, and certainly the Army isn't above a foul-up, but could it be so in this case? Do you realize what this means? Ultimately? One, Jim remains with a lost memory, and we pray he never regains it. Two, his memory is returned and he cannot live with the reality of what he did and goes stark, raving mad. Three, he goes into a catatonic state, which would be worse than the other two. Or, four, he sees Keith's cadaver, sees he died from his bullet, and becomes a free man. I opt for number four."

"Mary, Carissima, to do that you need answers."

"Of course, my dear, but what kind of answers?"

"Military answers!"

"Tell me!"

"Anastasia! Your significant other? That you go horseback riding with at the estate? What was her late husband? Under-secretary of the Navy in Washington? You will need some pull in high places to get a lot of red tape made invisible."

"How perspicacious you are, Anna. I'll get on the telephone right away."

Two days later, Mary sidled up to Anna in a chaise lounge putting on sun tan oil. "Notice the cat-ate-the-canary look on my face?"

"Yes. What is it? Anastasia!"

"Yes. She was just informed a body was recovered by our troops a few days after the action in Mosel. It had no identification on it whatsoever. Through DNA it was identified as the body of Keith Franklin. It took a long while to do that. Somehow the morgue and the hospital didn't compare notes, my guess is because it was too easy to make an assumption that if there is one body, there can't be two of the same people! So, they didn't look for a second Keith Franklin. As a result, the second Keith Franklin was shipped to his father who in the meantime had died. It was a small town where everyone knew everyone else. The local mortician called the VFW who made arrangements for the burial. There is authority for exhumation of the body. Plan on a trip to Tennessee."

"Mary, did you get a copy of the medical report? The cause of Keith's death?"

"That's the reason for the grin. First, I will telephone Jim and alert him that we'll pick him up tomorrow."

72

The next day, when Anna's co-pilot, Fred Brinker, got clearance from the Air Force controller she landed the Leer jet at Arnold Air Force base. It was the closest military field to Keith's hometown in Tennessee.

In the cabin, Mary prepared Jim for the forthcoming scenario. Jim took most of the time to tell Mary about Louise.

Jim, Mary and Anna were escorted to the staff limousine. Within moments they were racing over the rolling Tennessee countryside.

They entered Keith's town. "At least I remember I was here not too long ago," Jim said.

The Army officer directed the driver to the only funeral home in town.

"The proverbial suspense is proverbially killing me," Jim said. "Mary? Can you now tell me the reason we're here?"

"You will see for yourself, Jim," Mary said. "It's a roll of the dice, but I'm convinced it is the only way to go."

The funeral director came out to meet them, and introduced himself. He led them into a room that held a plain, military casket. He started to walk to it.

"Sir!" Mary called. "If you don't mind, we need to do this in privacy." She nodded at the officer and the driver. The three of them left the room.

"Jim," Mary said. "I have a very dear, dear friend, a significant other, you might say, that was able to do us all an enormous favor. She was able to get the Army to exhume the remains of a soldier from Sheffield, Tennessee. Jim, you knew him as Keith Franklin. The fact is the DNA done on the remains shows him to be your friend, Keith. I know this is a lot coming at you all at once. Let me know if at any time you wish me to stop, or if you wish to sit. This body was found totally stripped in a shallow grave far from Mosel by American troops. There were no I.D. tags, no identification whatsoever. There were no dog tags on him because you were wearing his. You could not remember, but you and Keith never did swap back your I.D. tags after your trip for your honeymoon to New York. As a result, you were wearing Keith's tags when you arrived at the hospital. Your injuries were so severe it was assumed you were who the dog tags said you were, and the matter of confirming the identity was inconsequential. From that moment on, you became Keith Franklin. Gabbie was informed she was a widow, which she never believed for a second, even though they sent her your dog tags, which Keith was wearing and which the enemy stripped from his body and returned with your name tag and helmet. But, in the interim she had your child, Ginnie. In the meantime, Louise became your sainted alter-ego. Now, I could have told you all this in Southhampton, but all the pieces didn't fall in place until we were on Bequia. That would not have given us the answer you so desperately need. But, you would not have believed it for a second. Here is the proof you need to believe what we say.

"Before I open the casket and ask you to view the remains, I want you to pay very close attention to what I am about to tell you. Jim, when the body of Keith was found, it had been mutilated, severely mutilated, and I believe I know the reason. Do you understand what I said, and what that means?"

"Yes, Mary. Thank you, I do."

"You believe Keith was dreadfully tortured before they hacked his head off while he was alive because you did not shoot him."

Jim nodded his head rapidly. "Yes. I believe that."

"Even though it was a chore no one in the world would want, you understand you kept your word, and the reason you kept your word? You did shoot him."

"No! No! I don't know that!"

Mary opened the casket. "Look."

Jim took Anna's arm, and stepped before the casket. He looked down. He lost all the color in his face. Anna steadied him.

"Is that Keith?" Mary asked.

Jim turned away and bent far over. With wretching sounds, he said, "Yes! Those fucking bastards sawed his head off! Oh! Keith! I'm so sorry! I don't want to know this!" He turned to run away.

"Jim! Stay with us! Pay attention! You can't see the major part of the mutilation, Jim, because of the uniform, but there is enough for you to have noticed that his head had been severed from the body."

"What the fuck do you want from me? I know that! I just said that! That's what happened because I didn't keep my promise! I didn't take care of him as I should have!"

"Jim, look closely." Mary took his shoulder and turned him toward the body. "I said look closely! What do you see right between his eyes? Jim, that's a bullet hole! That's from a bullet you fired to kill him, and that's what you did and kept your promise. That is exactly the reason the Al Qaeda sought revenge on Keith's corpse, because they could not have the pleasure of sawing his head off when he was alive. The coroner's report, in great detail, shows the mutilation occurred after Keith was dead. I repeat, after Keith was dead! That is proof positive you kept your promise to Keith."

"Yes. I see the moment now. I think my heart stopped when he was in my sights. I died when I pulled the trigger because I saw the bullet kill him. Yes, I did," Jim said. "I remember that clearly. Very clearly. Mary, I need some time alone with Keith."

"I'm so sorry you had that obligation," Mary said. She walked out of the room.

Jim clasped his hands tightly before him as he looked down at his friend. In fast forward he visualized his buddy in the highlights of their time shared together. More than a half-hour passed before Jim was able to express what was in his heart and mind. "Keith, you son-of-a-bitch! You rotten bastard! You gave me such a god-damn lousy job! I hate you for it! I hate you for making me do that to you! But, Keith, you have always been my brother." Jim reached under his shirt and took off Keith's remaining dog tag and placed it on Keith's blouse over his heart. He also tucked the photo of Cindy Jo in his blouse. "Be in peace, Tonto."

When they returned to the jet at Arnold Air Force Base, Jim hugged Mary. "I can never express my indebtedness to you. You made me whole again. You restored our family. Gabbie, Ginnie, and I will never forget you. Thank you."

"Need I say the risk was all yours and well worth it? I am grateful I could be a peripheral part of what you have."

He kissed her on the cheek. "I love you."

"I love you, too, Jim. You're sure you want us to fly back to San Antonio to pick up your passenger before we go to Massachusetts?"

Jim nodded emphatically.

73

Anna brought the jet in low over the private airport in Great Farraday. She taxied up to a hangar, and cut the engines.

Standing in a knot were Gabbie, Ginnie, Virginia, Ashley and Mrs. Soldi. Scattered close by were workers, visitors, fliers, pilots, and office personnel drawn out to see the luxurious jet.

Out of the jet's window, Jim saw Mary hold Louise's arm as they disembarked. Together they hobbled on the tarmac toward the group.

Then Jim motioned to Anna in the cabin. "My dear Nighthawk. I have something for you." He opened the box. She threw both of her hands to her mouth. Jim put the tennis bracelet on her wrist.

She stared into his eyes, first one and then the other.

"Thank you," Jim said.

"We should have made love, you know?"Anna pulled his head down to kiss him warmly. She let it linger. When they broke, she held back a sob and headed for the cockpit.

Mary boarded the plane. Jim turned to her. "Thank you for what you have done for Louise and all of us. We'll be down to see you soon." He took a deep breath. "Words just don't seem to express it all, do they?"

"No need."

"That's why I love you. We're indebted beyond eternity for your gracious love, caring, and work that made it possible for Gabbie and I to go back to living our dream." He kissed her on both cheeks.

Jim hopped off the plane and ran toward Gabbie. He pumped his fist in the air. "Yo! Tonto!"

Gabbie, already sprinting toward him, yelled, "Yo! Kimo Sabe!"

They threw their arms around each other and kissed hungrily.

Jim scooped up Ginnie. The others surrounded them holding each other in a clutch.

"You'll love it here with us, Louise!" Gabbie said.

"You bet," Louise answered. "I'm just going to eat it all up."

The jet roared over the field, waggled its wings, and in a twisting, climbing roll CA-BOOMED the sound barrier as everyone cheered and applauded as Jim's whistle bored a hole in the air before it.

THE END

PAUL ARGENTINI is a Random House best-selling author and prize-winning playwright. He and his bride, Vera, live in Florida. They have two grown daughters, Lisa and Mona.

www.ingramcontent.com/pod-product-compliance
Lightning Source LLC
Chambersburg PA
CBHW020839020726
47497CB00005B/1165